THE GHOST STORY MEGAPACK®

IN THE SAME SERIES

THE GHOST STORY MEGAPACK®

Edited by
JOHN GREGORY BETANCOURT

WILDSIDE PRESS

* * * *

"At Chrighton Abbey," by Mary Elizabeth Braddon, originally appeared in 1871.

"The Haunted Mill," by Jerome K. Jerome, originally appeared in 1891.

"The Lost Ghost," by Mary E. Wilkins Freeman, originally appeared in 1903.

"The Ghost Club," by John Kendrick Bangs, originally appeared in 1894.

"The Shadows of the Dead," by Louis Becke originally appeared in 1897.

"The Room in the Tower," by E. F. Benson, originally appeared in 1912.

"The Haunted and the Haunters," by Lord Edward Bulwer-Lytton, originally appeared in 1959.

"The Drummer Ghost," by John William DeForest originally appeared in 1870.

"Miss Jéromette and the Clergyman," by Wilkie Collins originally appeared in 1875.

"The Spectre Bride," By William Harrison Ainsworth, originally appeared in 1822.

"The Tapestried Chamber; or, The Lady in the Square," by Sir Walter Scott, originally appeared in 1829.

"The Old Nurse's Story," by Elizabeth Gaskell, originally appeared in 1852.

"The Judge's House," by Bram Stoker, originally appeared in 1891.

"At the End of the Passage," by Rudyard Kipling," originally appeared in 1891.

"The Withered Arm," by Thomas Hardy, originally appeared in 1888.

"John Charrington's Wedding," by Edith Nesbit, originally appeared in 1891.

"The Man of Science," by Jerome K. Jerome, originally appeared in 1892.

"What Did Miss Darrington See?" by Emma B. Cobb originally appeared in 1870.

"A Ghost Story," by Mark Twain, originally appeared in 1903.

"The Soul of Rose Dédé," by M.E.M. Davis, originally appeared in 1888.

"The House of the Nightmare," by Edward Lucas White, originally appeared in 1906.

"Reality or Delusion?" by Mrs Henry Wood, originally appeared in 1868.

"Fisher's Ghost," by John Lang, originally appeared in 1859.

"Through the Ivory Gate," by Mary Raymond Shipman Andrews, originally appeared in 1905.

"The Cold Embrace," by Mary Elizabeth Braddon, originally appeared in 1860.

CONTENTS

A NOTE FROM THE PUBLISHER

THE GHOST STORY MEGAPACK®

Welcome to the first of our Ghost Story MEGAPACK®s—we're up to seven now, as I write this, and I have found a way to generate paper book publishing files from our ebooks, so this is very much an experiment to see how well it works. Hopefully, since you're reading this in the paper version, it went well and you are enjoying it!

And, as always, if you like this MEGAPACK®, check out the more than 350 other volumes in the series, covering not just ghost stories, but fantasy, science fiction, westerns, and much more.

Happy reading!

—John Betancourt
Publisher, Wildside Press LLC
www.wildsidepress.com

ABOUT THE MEGAPACK®S

Over the last few years, our MEGAPACK® series of ebook anthologies has proved to be one of our most popular endeavors. (Maybe it helps that we sometimes offer them as premiums to our mailing list!) One question we keep getting asked is, "Who's the editor?"

The Megapacks (except where specifically credited) are a group effort. Everyone at Wildside works on them. This includes John Betancourt, Mary Wickizer Burgess, Sam Cooper, Carla Coupe, Steve Coupe, Bonner Menking, Colin Azariah-Kribbs, Robert Reginald. A. E. Warren, and many of Wildside's authors…who often suggest stories to include (and not just their own!).

AT CHRIGHTON ABBEY,
by Mary Elizabeth Braddon

The Chrightons were very great people in that part of the country where my childhood and youth were spent. To speak of Squire Chrighton was to speak of a power in that remote western region of England. Chrighton Abbey had belonged to the family ever since the reign of Stephen, and there was a curious old wing and a cloistered quadrangle still remaining of the original edifice, and in excellent preservation. The rooms at this end of the house were low, and somewhat darksome and gloomy, it is true; but, though rarely used, they were perfectly habitable, and were of service on great occasions when the Abbey was crowded with guests.

The central portion of the Abbey had been rebuilt in the reign of Elizabeth and was of noble and palatial proportions. The southern wing, and a long music-room with eight tall narrow windows added on to it, were as modern as the time of Anne. Altogether, the Abbey was a very splendid mansion, and one of the chief glories of our county.

All the land in Chrighton parish, and for a long way beyond its boundaries, belonged to the great Squire. The parish church was within the park walls, and the living in the Squire's gift—not a very valuable benefice, but a useful thing to bestow upon a younger son's younger son, once in a way, or sometimes on a tutor or dependent of the wealthy house.

I was a Chrighton, and my father, a distant cousin of the reigning Squire, had been rector of Chrighton parish. His death left me utterly unprovided for, and I was fain to go out into the bleak unknown world, and earn my living in a position of dependence—a dreadful thing for a Chrighton to be obliged to do.

Out of respect for the traditions and prejudices of my race, I made it my business to seek employment abroad, where the degradation of one solitary Chrighton was not so likely to inflict shame upon the ancient house to which I belonged. Happily for myself, I had been carefully educated, and had industriously cultivated the usual modern accomplishments in the calm retirement of the Vicarage. I was so fortunate as to obtain a situation at Vienna, in a German family of high rank; and here I remained seven years, laying aside year by year a considerable portion of my liberal salary. When my pupils had grown up, my kind mistress procured me a still more profitable position at St. Petersburg, where I remained five more years, at the end of which time I yielded to a yearning that had been long growing upon me—an ardent desire to see my dear old country home once more.

I had no very near relations in England. My mother had died some years before my father; my only brother was far away, in the Indian Civil Service; sister I had none. But I was a Chrighton, and I loved the soil from which I had sprung. I was sure, moreover, of a warm welcome from friends who had loved and honoured my father and mother, and I was still further encouraged to treat myself to this holiday by the very cordial letters I had from time to time received from the Squire's wife, a noble warm-hearted woman, who fully approved the independent course I had taken, and who had ever shown herself my friend.

In all her letters for some time past Mrs. Chrighton begged that, whenever I felt myself justified in coming home, I would pay a long visit to the Abbey.

"I wish you could come at Christmas," she wrote, in the autumn of the year of which I am speaking. "We shall be very gay, and I expect all kinds of pleasant people at the Abbey. Edward is to be married early in the spring—much to his father's satisfaction, for the match is a good and appropriate one. His fiancée is to be among our guests. She is a very beautiful girl; perhaps I should say handsome rather than beautiful. Julia Tremaine, one of the Tremaines of Old Court, near Hayswell—a very old family, as I daresay you remember. She has several brothers and sisters, and will have little, perhaps nothing, from her father; but she has a considerable fortune left her by an aunt, and is thought quite an heiress in the county—not, of course, that this latter fact had any influence with Edward. He fell in love with her at a ball in his usual impulsive fashion, and proposed to her in something less than a fortnight. It is, I hope and believe, a thorough love-match on both sides."

After this followed a cordial repetition of the invitation to myself. I was to go straight to the Abbey when I went to England and was to take up my abode there as long as ever I pleased.

This letter decided me. The wish to look on the dear scenes of my happy childhood had grown almost into a pain. I was free to take a holiday, without detriment to my prospects. So, early in December, regardless of the bleak dreary weather, I turned my face homewards and made the long journey from St. Petersburg to London, under the kind escort of Major Manson, a Queen's Messenger, who was a friend of my late employer, the Baron Fruydorff, and whose courtesy had been enlisted for me by that gentleman.

I was three-and-thirty years of age. Youth was quite gone; beauty I had never possessed; and I was content to think of myself as a confirmed old maid, a quiet spectator of life's great drama, disturbed by no feverish desire for an active part in the play. I had a disposition to which this kind of passive existence is easy. There was no wasting fire in my veins. Simple duties, rare and simple pleasures, filled up my sum of life. The dear ones who had given a special charm and brightness to my existence were gone. Nothing could recall them, and without them actual happiness seemed impossible to me. Everything had a subdued and neutral tint; life at its best was calm and colourless, like a grey sunless day in early autumn, serene but joyless.

The old Abbey was in its glory when I arrived there, at about nine o'clock on a clear starlit night. A light frost whitened the broad sweep of grass that stretched away from the long stone terrace in front of the house to a semicircle of grand old oaks and beeches. From the music-room at the end of the southern wing to the heavily framed gothic windows of the old rooms on the north, there shone one blaze of light. The scene reminded me of some weird palace in a German legend; and I half expected to see the lights fade out all in a moment, and the long stone façade wrapped in sudden darkness.

The old butler, whom I remembered from my very infancy, and who did not seem to have grown a day older during my twelve years' exile, came out of the dining-room as the footman opened the hall-door for me, and he gave me cordial welcome, nay insisted upon helping to bring in my portmanteau with his own hands, an act of unusual condescension, the full force of which was felt by his subordinates.

"It's a real treat to see your pleasant face once more, Miss Sarah," said this faithful retainer, as he assisted me to take off my travelling-cloak, and took my dressing-bag from my hand. "You look a trifle older than when you used to live at the Vicarage twelve year ago, but you're looking uncommon well for all that; and, Lord love your heart, miss, how pleased they all will be to see you! Missus told me with her own lips about your coming. You'd like to take off your bonnet before you go to the drawing-room, I daresay. The house is full of company. Call Mrs. Marjorum, James, will you?"

The footman disappeared into the back regions, and presently reappeared with Mrs. Marjorum, a portly dame, who, like Truefold the butler, had been a fixture at the Abbey in the time of the present Squire's father. From her I received the same cordial greeting, and by her I was led off up staircases and along corridor, till I wondered where I was being taken.

We arrived at last at a very comfortable room—a square, tapestried chamber, with a low ceiling supported by a great oaken beam. The room looked cheery enough, with a bright fire roaring in the wide chimney; but it had a somewhat ancient aspect, which the superstitiously inclined might have associated with possible ghosts.

I was fortunately of a matter-of-fact disposition, utterly skeptical upon the ghost subject; and the old-fashioned appearance of the room took my fancy.

"We are in King Stephen's wing, are we not, Mrs. Marjorum?" I asked. "This room seems quite strange to me. I doubt if I have ever been in it before."

"Very likely not, miss. Yes, this is the old wing. Your window looks out into the old stable-yard, where the kennel used to be in the time of our Squire's grandfather, when the Abbey was even a finer place than it is now, I've heard say. We are so full of company this winter, you see, miss, that we are obliged to make use of all these rooms. You'll have no need to feel lonesome. There's Captain and Mrs. Cranwick in the next room to this, and the two Miss Newports in the blue room opposite."

"My dear good Marjorum, I like my quarters excessively; and I quite enjoy the idea of sleeping in a room that was extant in the time of Stephen, when the Abbey really was an abbey. I daresay some grave old monk has worn these boards with his devout knees."

The old woman stared dubiously, with the air of a person who had small sympathy with monkish times, and begged to be excused for leaving me, she had so much on her hands just now. There was coffee to be sent in; and she doubted if the still-room maid would manage matters properly, if she, Mrs. Marjorum, were not at hand to see that things were right.

"You've only to ring your bell, miss, and Susan will attend to you. She's used to help waiting on our young ladies sometimes, and she's very handy. Missus has given particular orders that she should be always at your service."

"Mrs. Chrighton is very kind; but I assure you, Marjorum, I don't require the help of a maid once in a month. I am accustomed to do everything for myself. There, run along, Mrs. Marjorum, and see after your coffee; and I'll be down in the drawing-room in ten minutes. Are there many people there, by the bye?"

"A good many. There's Miss Tremaine, and her mamma and younger sister; of course you've heard all about the marriage—such a handsome young lady—rather too proud for my liking; but the Tremaines always were a proud family, and this one's an heiress. Mr. Edward is so fond of her—thinks the ground is scarcely good enough for her to walk upon, I do believe; and somehow I can't help wishing he'd chosen someone else—someone who would have thought more of him, and who would not take all his attentions in such a cool off hand way. But of course it isn't my business to say such things, and I wouldn't venture upon it to anyone but you, Miss Sarah."

She told me that I would find dinner ready for me in the breakfast-room, and then bustled off, leaving me to my toilet.

This ceremony I performed as rapidly as I could, admiring the perfect comfort of my chamber as I dressed. Every modern appliance had been added to the somber and ponderous furniture of an age gone by, and the combination produced a very pleasant effect. Perfume-bottles of ruby-coloured Bohemian glass, china brush-trays, and ring-stands brightened the massive oak dressing-table; a low luxurious chintz-covered easy-chair of the Victorian era stood before the hearth; a dear little writing-table of polished maple was placed conveniently near it; and in the background the tapestried walls loomed duskily, as they had done hundreds of years before my time.

I had no leisure for dreamy musings on the past, however, provocative though the chamber might be of such thoughts. I arranged my hair in its usual simple fashion and put on a dark-grey silk dress, trimmed with some fine old black lace that had been given to me by the Baroness—an unobtrusive demi-toilette, adapted to any occasion. I tied a massive gold cross, an ornament that had belonged to my dear mother, round my neck with a scarlet ribbon; and my costume was complete. One glance at the looking-glass convinced me that there was nothing dowdy in my appearance; and then I hurried along the corridor and down the staircase to the hall, where Truefold received me and conducted me to the breakfast-room, in which an excellent dinner awaited me.

I did not waste much time over this repast, although I had eaten nothing all day; for I was anxious to make my way to the drawing-room. Just as I had finished, the door opened, and Mrs. Chrighton sailed in, looking superb in a dark-green velvet dress richly trimmed with old point lace. She had been a beauty in her youth and, as a matron, was still remarkably handsome. She had, above all, a charm of expression which to me was rarer and more delightful than her beauty of feature and complexion.

She put her arms round me and kissed me affectionately.

"I have only this moment been told of your arrival, my dear Sarah," she said; "and I find you have been in the house half an hour. What must you have thought of me!"

"What can I think of you, except that you are all goodness, my dear Fanny? I did not expect you to leave your guests to receive me, and am really sorry that you have done so. I need no ceremony to convince me of your kindness."

"But, my dear child, it is not a question of ceremony. I have been looking forward so anxiously to your coming, and I should not have liked to see you for the first time before all those people. Give me another kiss, that's a darling. Welcome to Chrighton. Remember, Sarah, this house is always to be your home, whenever you have need of one."

"My dear kind cousin! And you are not ashamed of me, who have eaten the bread of strangers?"

"Ashamed of you! No, my love; I admire your industry and spirit. And now come to the drawing-room. The girls will be so pleased to see you."

"And I to see them. They were quite little things when I went away, romping in the hay-fields in their short white frocks; and now, I suppose, they are handsome young women."

"They are very nice-looking; not as handsome as their brother. Edward is really a magnificent young man. I do not think my maternal pride is guilty of any gross exaggeration when I say that."

"And Miss Tremaine?" I said. "I am very curious to see her."

I fancied a faint shadow came over my cousin's face as I mentioned this name.

"Miss Tremaine, yes, you cannot fail to admire her," she said, rather thoughtfully.

She drew my hand through her arm and led me to the drawing-room: a very large room, with a fireplace at each end, brilliantly lighted tonight, and containing about twenty people, scattered about in little groups, and all seeming to be talking and laughing merrily. Mrs. Chrighton took me straight to one of the fireplaces, beside which two girls were sitting on a low sofa, while a young man of something more than six feet high stood near them, with his arm resting on the broad marble slab of the mantelpiece. A glance told me that this young man with the dark eyes and crisp waving brown hair was Edward Chrighton. His likeness to his mother was in itself enough to tell me who he was; but I remembered the boyish face and bright eyes which had so often looked up to mine in the days when the heir of the Abbey was one of the most juvenile scholars at Eton.

The lady seated nearest Edward Chrighton attracted my chief attention, for I felt sure that this lady was Miss Tremaine. She was tall and slim and carried her head and neck with a stately air, which struck me more than anything in that first glance. Yes, she was handsome, undeniably handsome; and my cousin had been right when she said I could not fail to admire her; but to me the dazzlingly fair face with its perfect features, the marked aquiline nose, the short upper lip expressive of unmitigated pride, the full cold blue eyes, pencilled brows, and aureole of pale golden hair, were the very reverse of sympathetic. That Miss Tremaine must needs be universally admired, it was impossible to doubt; but I could not understand how any man could fall in love with such a woman.

She was dressed in white muslin, and her only ornament was a superb diamond locket, heart-shaped, tied round her long white throat with a broad black ribbon. Her hair, of which she seemed to have a great quantity, was arranged in a massive coronet of plaits, which surmounted the small head as proudly as an imperial crown.

To this young lady Mrs. Chrighton introduced me.

"I have another cousin to present to you, Julia," she said smiling. "Miss Sarah Chrighton, just arrived from St. Petersburg."

"From St. Petersburg? What an awful journey! How do you do, Miss Chrighton? It was really very courageous of you to come so far. Did you travel alone?"

"No; I had a companion as far as London, and a very kind one. I came on to the Abbey by myself."

The young lady had given me her hand with rather a languid air, I thought. I saw the cold blue eyes surveying me curiously from head to foot, and it seemed to me as if I could read the condemnatory summing-up—"A frump, and a poor relation"—in Miss Tremaine's face.

I had not much time to think about her just now; for Edward Chrighton suddenly seized both my hands and gave me so hearty and loving a welcome that he almost brought the tears "up from my heart into my eyes."

Two pretty girls in blue crape came running forward from different parts of the room and gaily saluted me as "Cousin Sarah"; and the three surrounded me in a little cluster and assailed me with a string of questions—whether I remembered this, and whether I had forgotten that, the battle in the hayfield, the charity-school tea-party in the vicarage orchard, our picnics in Hawsley Combe, our botanical and entomological excursions on Chorwell-common, and all the simple pleasures of their childhood and my youth. While this catechism was going on, Miss Tremaine watched us with a disdainful expression, which she evidently did not care to hide.

"I should not have thought you capable of such Arcadian simplicity, Mr. Chrighton," she said at last. "Pray continue your recollections. These juvenile experiences are most interesting."

"I don't expect you to be interested in them, Julia," Edward answered with a tone that sounded rather too bitter for a lover. "I know what a contempt you have for trifling rustic pleasures. Were you ever a child yourself, I wonder, by the way? I don't believe you ever ran after a butterfly in your life."

Her speech put an end to our talk of the past, somehow. I saw that Edward was vexed and that all the pleasant memories of his boyhood had fled before that cold scornful face. A young lady in pink, who had been sitting next Julia Tremaine, vacated the sofa, and Edward slipped into her place and devoted himself for the rest of the evening to his betrothed. I glanced at his bright expressive face now and then as he talked to her and could not help wondering what charm he could discover in one who seemed to me so unworthy of him.

It was midnight when I went back to my room in the north wing, thoroughly happy in the cordial welcome that had been given me.

* * * *

I rose early next morning—for early rising had long been habitual to me—and, drawing back the damask-curtain that sheltered my window, looked out at the scene below.

I saw a stable-yard, a spacious quadrangle, surrounded by the closed doors of stables and dog-kennels: low massive buildings of grey stone, with the ivy creeping over them here and there, and with an ancient moss-grown look, that gave them a weird kind of interest in my eyes. This range of stabling must have been disused for a long time, I fancied. The stables now in use were a pile of handsome red-brick buildings at the other extremity of the house, to the rear of the music-room, and forming a striking feature in the back view of the Abbey.

I had often heard how the present Squire's grandfather had kept a pack of hounds, which had been sold immediately after his death; and I knew that my cousin, the present Mr. Chrighton, had been more than once requested to follow his ancestor's good example; for there were no hounds now within twenty miles of the Abbey, though it was a fine country for fox-hunting.

George Chrighton, however—the reigning lord of the Abbey—was not a hunting man. He had, indeed, a secret horror of the sport; for more than one scion of the house had perished untimely in the hunting-field. The family had not been altogether a lucky one, in spite of its wealth and prosperity. It was not often that the goodly heritage had descended to the eldest son. Death in some form or other—on too many occasions a violent death—had come between the heir and his inheritance. And when I pondered on the dark pages in the story of the house, I used to wonder whether my cousin Fanny was ever troubled by morbid forebodings about her only and fondly loved son.

Was there a ghost at Chrighton—that spectral visitant without which the state and splendour of a grand old house seem scarcely complete? Yes, I had heard vague hints of some shadowy presence that had been seen on rare occasions within the precincts of the Abbey; but I had never been able to ascertain what shape it bore.

Those whom I questioned were prompt to assure me that they had seen nothing. They had heard stories of the past-foolish legends, most likely, not worth listening to. Once, when I had spoken of the subject to my cousin George, he told me angrily never again to let him hear any allusion to that folly from my lips.

* * * *

That December passed merrily. The old house was full of really pleasant people, and the brief winter days were spent in one unbroken round of amusement and gaiety. To me the old familiar English country-house life was a perpetual delight—to feel myself amongst kindred an unceasing pleasure. I could not have believed myself capable of being so completely happy.

I saw a great deal of my cousin Edward, and I think he contrived to make Miss Tremaine understand that, to please him, she must be gracious to me. She certainly took some pains to make herself agreeable to me; and I discovered that, in spite of that proud disdainful temper, which she so rarely took the trouble to conceal, she was really anxious to gratify her lover.

Their courtship was not altogether a halcyon period. They had frequent quarrels, the details of which Edward's sisters Sophy and Agnes delighted to discuss with me. It was the struggle of two proud spirits for mastery; but my cousin Edward's pride was of the nobler kind—the lofty scorn of all things mean—a pride that does not ill-become a generous nature. To me he seemed all that was admirable, and I was never tired of hearing his mother praise him. I think my cousin Fanny knew this, and that she used to confide in me as fully as if I had been her sister.

"I daresay you can see I am not quite so fond as I should wish to be of Julia Tremaine," she said to me one day; "but I am very glad that my son is going to marry. My husband's has not been a fortunate family, you know, Sarah. The eldest sons have been wild and unlucky for generations past; and when Edward was a boy I used to have many a bitter hour, dreading what the future might bring forth. Thank God he has been, and is, all that I can wish. He has never given me an hour's anxiety by any act of his. Yet I am not the less glad of his marriage. The heirs of Chrighton who have come to an untimely end have all died unmarried. There was Hugh Chrighton, in the reign of George the Second, who was killed in a duel; John, who broke his back in the hunting-field thirty years later; Theodore, shot accidentally by a schoolfellow at Eton; Jasper, whose yacht went down in the Mediterranean forty years ago. An awful list, is it not, Sarah? I shall feel as if my son were safer somehow when he is married. It will seem as if he has escaped the ban that has fallen on so many of our house. He will have greater reason to be careful of his life when he is a married man."

I agreed with Mrs. Chrighton; but could not help wishing that Edward had chosen any other woman than the cold handsome Julia. I could not fancy his future life happy with such a mate.

* * * *

Christmas came by and by—a real old English Christmas—frost and snow without, warmth and revelry within; skating on the great pond in the park, and sledging on the ice-bound high-roads, by day; private theatricals, charades, and amateur concerts, by night. I was surprised to find that Miss Tremaine refused to take any active part in these evening amusements. She preferred to sit among the elders as a spectator, and had the air and bearing of a princess for whose diversion all our entertainments had been planned. She seemed to think that she fulfilled her mission by sitting still and looking handsome. No desire to show-off appeared to enter her mind. Her intense pride left no room for vanity. Yet I knew that she could have distinguished herself as a musician if she had chosen to do so; for I had heard her sing and play in Mrs. Chrighton's morning-room, when only Edward, his sisters, and myself were present; and I knew that both as a vocalist and a pianist she excelled all our guests.

The two girls and I had many a happy morning and afternoon, going from cottage to cottage in a pony-carriage laden with Mrs. Chrighton's gifts to the poor of her parish. There was no public formal distribution of blanketing and coals, but the

14

wants of all were amply provided for in a quiet friendly way. Agnes and Sophy, aided by an indefatigable maid, the Rector's daughter, and one or two other young ladies, had been at work for the last three months making smart warm frocks and useful under-garments for the children of the cottagers; so that on Christmas morning every child in the parish was arrayed in a complete set of new garments. Mrs. Chrighton had an admirable faculty of knowing precisely what was most wanted in every household; and our pony-carriage used to convey a varied collection of goods, every parcel directed in the firm free hand of the chatelaine of the Abbey.

Edward used sometimes to drive us on these expeditions, and I found that he was eminently popular among the poor of Chrighton parish. He had such an airy pleasant way of talking to them, a manner which set them at their ease at once. He never forgot their names or relationships, or wants or ailments; had a packet of exactly the kind of tobacco each man liked best always ready in his coat-pockets; and was full of jokes, which may not have been particularly witty, but which used to make the small low-roofed chambers ring with hearty laughter.

Miss Tremaine coolly declined any share in these pleasant duties.

"I don't like poor people," she said. "I daresay it sounds very dreadful, but it's just as well to confess my iniquity at once. I never can get on with them, or they with me. I am not simpatica, I suppose. And then I cannot endure their stifling rooms. The close faint odour of their houses gives me a fever. And again, what is the use of visiting them? It is only an inducement to them to become hypocrites. Surely it is better to arrange on a sheet of paper what it is just and fair for them to have—blankets, and coals, and groceries, and money, and wine, and so on—and let them receive the things from some trustworthy servant. In that case, there need be no cringing on one side, and no endurance on the other."

"But, you see, Julia, there are some kinds of people to whom that sort of thing is not a question of endurance," Edward answered, his face flushing indignantly. "People who like to share in the pleasure they give—who like to see the poor care-worn faces lighted up with sudden joy—who like to make these sons of the soil feel that there is some friendly link between themselves and their masters—some point of union between the cottage and the great house. There is my mother, for instance: all these duties which you think so tiresome are to her an unfailing delight. There will be a change, I'm afraid, Julia, when you are mistress of the Abbey."

"You have not made me that yet," she answered; "and there is plenty of time for you to change your mind, if you do not think me suited for the position. I do not pretend to be like your mother. It is better that I should not affect any feminine virtues which I do not possess."

After this Edward insisted on driving our pony-carriage almost every day, leaving Miss Tremaine to find her own amusement; and I think this conversation was the beginning of an estrangement between them, which became more serious than any of their previous quarrels had been.

Miss Tremaine did not care for sledging, or skating, or billiard playing. She had none of the "fast" tendencies which have become so common lately. She used to sit in one particular bow-window of the drawing-room all the morning, working a screen in berlin-wool and beads, assisted and attended by her younger sister Laura, who was a kind of slave to her—a very colourless young lady in mind, capable of no such thing as an original opinion, and in person a pale replica of her sister.

Had there been less company in the house, the breach between Edward Chrighton and his betrothed must have become notorious; but with a house so full of people, all bent on enjoying themselves, I doubt if it was noticed. On all public occasions my cousin showed himself attentive and apparently devoted to Miss

Tremaine. It was only I and his sisters who knew the real state of affairs.

I was surprised, after the young lady's total repudiation of all benevolent senti-ments, when she beckoned me aside one morning and slipped a little purse of gold —twenty sovereigns—into my hand.

"I shall be very much obliged if you will distribute that among your cottagers today, Miss Chrighton," she said. "Of course I should like to give them something; it's only the trouble of talking to them that I shrink from; and you are just the per-son for an almoner. Don't mention my little commission to anyone, please."

"Of course I may tell Edward," I said; for I was anxious that he should know his betrothed was not as hard-hearted as she had appeared.

"To him least of all," she answered eagerly. "You know that our ideas vary on that point. He would think I gave the money to please him. Not a word, pray, Miss Chrighton."

I submitted and distributed my sovereigns quietly, with the most careful exercise of my judgement.

* * * *

So Christmas came and passed. It was the day after the great anniversary—a very quiet day for the guests and family at the Abbey, but a grand occasion for the servants, who were to have their annual ball in the evening—a ball to which all the humbler class of tenantry were invited. The frost had broken up suddenly, and it was a thorough wet day—a depressing kind of day for anyone whose spirits are li-able to be affected by the weather, as mine are. I felt out of spirits for the first time since my arrival at the Abbey.

No one else appeared to feel the same influence. The elder ladies sat in a wide semicircle 'round one of the fireplaces in the drawing-room; a group of merry girls and dashing young men chatted gaily before the other. From the billiard-room there came the frequent clash of balls and cheery peals of stentorian laughter. I sat in one of the deep windows, half hidden by the curtains, reading a novel—one of a boxful that came from town every month.

If the picture within was bright and cheerful, the prospect was dreary enough without. The fairy forest of snow-wreathed trees, the white valleys and undulating banks of snow, had vanished, and the rain dripped slowly and sullenly upon a dark-some expanse of sodden grass, and a dismal background of leafless timber. The merry sound of the sledge-bells no longer enlivened the air; all was silence and gloom.

Edward Chrighton was not amongst the billiard-players; he was pacing the drawing-room to and fro from end to end, with an air that was at once moody and restless.

"Thank heaven, the frost has broken up at last!" he exclaimed, stopping in front of the window where I sat.

He had spoken to himself, quite unaware of my close neighbourhood. Unpromis-ing as his aspect was just then, I ventured to accost him.

"What bad taste, to prefer such weather as this to frost and snow!" I answered. "The park looked enchanting yesterday—a real scene from fairyland. And only look at it today!"

"O yes, of course, from an artistic point of view, the snow was better. The place does look something like the great dismal swamp today; but I am thinking of hunt-ing, and that confounded frost made a day's sport impossible. We are in for a spell of mild weather now, I think."

"But you are not going to hunt, are you, Edward?"

"Indeed I am, my gentle cousin, in spite of that frightened look in your amiable countenance."

"I thought there were no hounds hereabouts."

"Nor are there; but there is as fine a pack as any in the country—the Daleborough hounds—five-and-twenty miles away."

"And you are going five-and-twenty miles for the sake of a day's run?"

"I would travel forty, fifty, a hundred miles for that same diversion. But I am not going for a single day this time; I am going over to Sir Francis Wycherly's place—young Frank Wycherly and I were sworn chums at Christchurch—for three or four days. I am due today, but I scarcely cared to travel by cross-country roads in such rain as this. However, if the floodgates of the sky are loosened for a new deluge, I must go tomorrow."

"What a headstrong young man!" I exclaimed. I asked in a lower voice, "And what will Miss Tremaine say to this desertion?"

"Miss Tremaine can say whatever she pleases. She had it in her power to make me forget the pleasures of the chase, if she had chosen, though we had been in the heart of the shires, and the welkin ringing with the baying of hounds."

"O, I begin to understand. This hunting engagement is not of long standing."

"No; I began to find myself bored here a few days ago, and wrote to Frank to offer myself for two or three days at Wycherly. I received a most cordial answer by return, and am booked till the end of this week."

"You have not forgotten the ball on the first?"

"O, no; to do that would be to vex my mother and to offer a slight to our guests. I shall be here for the first, come what may."

Come what may! so lightly spoken. The time came when I had bitter occasion to remember those words.

"I'm afraid you will vex your mother by going at all," I said. "You know what a horror both she and your father have of hunting."

"A most un-country-gentleman-like aversion on my father's part. But he is a dear old book-worm, seldom happy out of his library. Yes, I admit they both have a dislike to hunting in the abstract; but they know I am a pretty good rider, and that it would need a bigger country than I shall find about Wycherly to floor me. You need not feel nervous, my dear Sarah; I am not going to give papa and mamma the smallest ground for uneasiness."

"You will take your own horses, I suppose?"

"That goes without saying. No man who has cattle of his own cares to mount another man's horses. I shall take Pepperbox and the Druid."

"Pepperbox has a queer temper, I have heard your sisters say."

"My sisters expect a horse to be a kind of overgrown baa-lamb. Everything splendid in horseflesh and womankind is prone to that slight defect, an ugly temper. There is Miss Tremaine, for instance."

"I shall take Miss Tremaine's part. I believe it is you who are in the wrong in the matter of this estrangement, Edward."

"Do you? Well, wrong or right, my cousin, until the fair Julia comes to me with sweet looks and gentle words, we can never be what we have been."

"You will return from your hunting expedition in a softer mood," I answered; "that is to say, if you persist in going. But I hope and believe you will change your mind."

"Such a change is not within the limits of possibility, Sarah. I am fixed as Fate."

He strolled away, humming some gay hunting-song as he went. I was alone with Mrs. Chrighton later in the afternoon, and she spoke to me about this intended visit to Wycherly.

17

"Edward has set his heart upon it evidently," she said regretfully, "and his father and I have always made a point of avoiding anything that could seem like domestic tyranny. Our dear boy is such a good son that it would be very hard if we came between him and his pleasures. You know what a morbid horror my husband has of the dangers of the hunting-field, and perhaps I am almost as weak-minded. But in spite of this we have never interfered with Edward's enjoyment of a sport which he is passionately fond of and hitherto, thank God, he has escaped without a scratch. Yet I have had many a bitter hour, I can assure you, my dear, when my son has been away in Leicestershire hunting four days a week."

"He rides well, I suppose."

"Superbly. He has a great reputation among the sportsmen of our neighbourhood. I daresay when he is master of the Abbey he will start a pack of hounds and revive the old days of his great-grandfather, Meredith Chrighton."

"I fancy the hounds were kenneled in the stable-yard below my bedroom window in those days, were they not, Fanny?"

"Yes," Mrs. Chrighton answered gravely; and I wondered at the sudden shadow that fell upon her face.

* * * *

I went up to my room earlier than usual that afternoon, and I had a clear hour to spare before it would be time to dress for the seven o'clock dinner. This leisure hour I intended to devote to letter-writing; but on arriving in my room I found myself in a very idle frame of mind, and instead of opening my desk, I seated myself in the low easy-chair before the fire and fell into a reverie.

How long I had been sitting there I scarcely know; I had been half meditating, half dozing, mixing broken snatches of thought with brief glimpses of dreaming, when I was startled into wakefulness by a sound that was strange to me.

It was a huntsman's horn—a few low plaintive notes on a huntsman's horn—notes which had a strange far-away sound, that was more unearthly than anything my ears had ever heard. I thought of the music in Der Freisckutz; but the weirdest snatch of melody Weber ever wrote had not so ghastly a sound as these few simple notes conveyed to my ear.

I stood transfixed, listening to that awful music. It had grown dusk, my fire was almost out, and the room in shadow. As I listened, a light flashed suddenly on the wall before me. The light was as unearthly as the sound—a light that never shone from earth or sky.

I ran to the window; for this ghastly shimmer flashed through the window upon the opposite wall. The great gates of the stable-yard were open, and men in scarlet coats were riding in, a pack of hounds crowding in before them, obedient to the huntsman's whip. The whole scene was dimly visible by the declining light of the winter evening and the weird gleams of a lantern carried by one of the men. It was this lantern which had shone upon the tapestried wall. I saw the stable doors opened one after another; gentlemen and grooms alighting from their horses; the dogs driven into their kennel; the helpers hurrying to and fro; and that strange wan lantern-light glimmering here and there is the gathering dusk. But there was no sound of horse's hoof or of human voices—not one yelp or cry from the hounds. Since those faint far-away sounds of the horn had died out in the distance, the ghastly silence had been unbroken.

I stood at my window quite calmly and watched while the group of men and animals in the yard below noiselessly dispersed. There was nothing supernatural in the manner of their disappearance. The figures did not vanish or melt into empty air. One by one I saw the horses led into their separate quarters; one by one the redcoats

18

strolled out of the gates, and the grooms departed, some one way, some another. The scene, but for its noiselessness, was natural enough; and had I been a stranger in the house, I might have fancied that those figures were real—those stables in full occupation.

But I knew that stable-yard and all its range of building to have been disused for more than half a century. Could I believe that, without an hour's warning, the long-deserted quadrangle could be filled—the empty stalls tenanted?

Had some hunting-party from the neighbourhood sought shelter here, glad to escape the pitiless rain? That was not impossible, I thought. I was an utter unbeliever in all ghostly things—ready to credit any possibility rather than suppose that I had been looking upon shadows. And yet the noiselessness, the awful sound of that horn—the strange unearthly gleam of that lantern! Little superstitious as I might be, a cold sweat stood out upon my forehead, and I trembled in every limb.

For some minutes I stood by the window, statue-like, staring blankly into the empty quadrangle. Then I roused myself suddenly and ran softly downstairs by a back staircase leading to the servants' quarters, determined to solve the mystery somehow or other. The way to Mrs. Marjorum's room was familiar to me from old experience, and it was thither that I bent my steps, determined to ask the housekeeper the meaning of what I had seen. I had a lurking conviction that it would be well for me not to mention that scene to any member of the family till I had taken counsel with someone who knew the secrets of Chrighton Abbey.

I heard the sound of merry voices and laughter as I passed the kitchen and servants' hall. Men and maids were all busy in the pleasant labour of decorating their rooms for the evening's festival. They were putting the last touches to garlands of holly and laurel, ivy and fir, as I passed the open doors; and in both rooms I saw tables laid for a substantial tea. The housekeeper's room was in a retired nook at the end of a long passage—a charming old room, paneled with dark oak, and full of capacious cupboards, which in my childhood I had looked upon as storehouses of inexhaustible treasures in the way of preserves and other confectionery. It was a shady old room, with a wide old-fashioned fireplace, cool in summer, when the hearth was adorned with a great jar of roses and lavender; and warm in winter, when the logs burnt merrily all day long.

I opened the door softly and went in. Mrs. Marjorum was dozing in a high-backed arm-chair by the glowing hearth, dressed in her state gown of grey watered silk, and with a cap that was a perfect garden of roses. She opened her eyes as I approached her and stared at me with a puzzled look for the first moment or so.

"Why, is that you, Miss Sarah?" she exclaimed; "and looking as pale as a ghost, I can see, even by this firelight! Let me just light a candle, and then I'll get you some sal volatile. Sit down in my armchair, miss; why, I declare you're all of a tremble!"

She put me into her easy-chair before I could resist, and lighted the two candles which stood ready upon her table, while I was trying to speak. My lips were dry, and it seemed at first as if my voice was gone.

"Never mind the sal volatile, Marjorum," I said at last. "I am not ill; I've been startled, that's all; and I've come to ask you for an explanation of the business that frightened me."

"What business, Miss Sarah?"

"You must have heard something of it yourself, surely. Didn't you hear a horn just now, a huntsman's horn?"

"A horn! Lord no, Miss Sarah. What ever could have put such a fancy into your head?"

I saw that Mrs. Marjorum's ruddy cheeks had suddenly lost their colour, that she was now almost as pale as I could have been myself.

"It was no fancy," I said; "I heard the sound, and saw the people. A hunting-party has just taken shelter in the north quadrangle. Dogs and horses, and gentlemen and servants."

"What were they like, Miss Sarah?" the housekeeper asked in a strange voice.

"I can hardly tell you that. I could see that they wore red coats; and I could scarcely see more than that. Yes, I did get a glimpse of one of the gentlemen by the light of the lantern. A tall man, with grey hair and whiskers, and a stoop in his shoulders. I noticed that he wore a short waisted coat with a very high collar—a coat that looked a hundred years old."

"The old Squire!" muttered Mrs. Marjorum under her breath; and then turning to me, she said with a cheery resolute air, "You've been dreaming, Miss Sarah, that's just what it is. You've dropped off in your chair before the fire and had a dream, that's it."

"No, Marjorum, it was no dream. The horn woke me, and I stood at my window and saw the dogs and huntsmen come in."

"Do you know, Miss Sarah, that the gates of the north quadrangle have been locked and barred for the last forty years, and that no one ever goes in there except through the house?"

"The gates may have been opened this evening to give shelter to strangers," I said.

"Not when the only keys that will open them hang yonder in my cupboard, miss," said the housekeeper, pointing to a corner of the room.

"But I tell you, Marjorum, these people came into the quadrangle; the horses and dogs are in the stables and kennels at this moment. I'll go and ask Mr. Chrighton, or my cousin Fanny, or Edward, all about it, since you won't tell me the truth."

I said this with a purpose, and it answered. Mrs. Marjorum caught me eagerly by the wrist.

"No, miss, don't do that; for pity's sake don't do that; don't breathe a word to missus or master."

"But why not?"

"Because you've seen that which always brings misfortune and sorrow to this house, Miss Sarah. You've seen the dead."

"What do you mean?" I gasped, awed in spite of myself.

"I daresay you've heard say that there's been something seen at times at the Abbey—many years apart, thank God; for it never came that trouble didn't come after it."

"Yes," I answered hurriedly; "but I could never get anyone to tell me what it was that haunted this place."

"No, miss. Those that know have kept the secret. But you have seen it all tonight. There's no use in trying to hide it from you any longer. You have seen the old Squire, Meredith Chrighton, whose eldest son was killed by a fall in the hunting-field, brought home dead one December night, an hour after his father and the rest of the party had come safe home to the Abbey. The old gentleman had missed his son in the field, but had thought nothing of that, fancying that master John had had enough of the day's sport and had turned his horse's head homewards. He was found by a labouring-man, poor lad, lying in a ditch with his back broken, and his horse beside him staked. The old Squire never held his head up after that day, and never rode to hounds again, though he was passionately fond of hunting. Dogs and horses were sold, and the north quadrangle has been empty from that day."

"How long is it since this kind of thing has been seen?"

"A long time, miss. I was a slip of a girl when it last happened. It was in the winter-time—this very night—the night Squire Meredith's son was killed; and the house was full of company, just as it is now. There was a wild young Oxford gentleman sleeping in your room at that time, and he saw the hunting-party come into the quadrangle; and what did he do but throw his window wide open, and give them the view-hallo as loud as ever he could. He had only arrived the day before, and knew nothing about the neighbourhood; so at dinner he began to ask where were his friends the sportsmen, and to hope he should be allowed to have a run with the Abbey hounds next day. It was in the time of our master's father; and his lady at the head of the table turned as white as a sheet when she heard this talk. She had good reason, poor soul. Before the week was out her husband was lying dead. He was struck with a fit of apoplexy, and never spoke or knew anyone afterwards."

"An awful coincidence," I said; "but it may have been only a coincidence."

"I've heard other stories, miss—heard them from those that wouldn't deceive—all proving the same thing: that the appearance of the old Squire and his pack is a warning of death to this house."

"I cannot believe these things," I exclaimed; "I cannot believe them. Does Mr. Edward know anything about this?"

"No, miss. His father and mother have been most careful that it should be kept from him."

"I think he is, too strong-minded to be much affected by the fact," I said.

"And you'll not say anything about what you've seen to my master or my mistress, will you, Miss Sarah?" pleaded the faithful old servant. "The knowledge of it would be sure to make them nervous and unhappy. And if evil is to come upon this house, it isn't in human power to prevent its coming."

"God forbid that there is any evil at hand!" I answered. "I am no believer in visions or omens. After all, I would sooner fancy that I was dreaming—dreaming with my eyes open as I stood at the window—than that I beheld the shadows of the dead."

Mrs. Marjorum sighed and said nothing. I could see that she believed firmly in the phantom hunt.

I went back to my room to dress for dinner. However rationally I might try to think of what I had seen, its effect upon my mind and nerves was not the less powerful. I could think of nothing else; and a strange morbid dread of coming misery weighted me down like an actual burden.

There was a very cheerful party in the drawing-room when I went downstairs, and at dinner the talk and laughter were unceasing—but I could see that my cousin Fanny's face was a little graver than usual, and I had no doubt she was thinking of her son's intended visit to Wycherly.

At the thought of this a sudden terror flashed upon me. How if the shadows I had seen that evening were ominous of danger to him—to Edward, the heir and only son of the house? My heart grew cold as I thought of this, and yet in the next moment I despised myself for such weakness.

"It is natural enough for an old servant to believe in such things," I said to myself; "but for me—an educated woman of the world—preposterous folly."

And yet from that moment I began to puzzle myself in the endeavour to devise some means by which Edward's journey might be prevented. Of my own influence I knew that I was powerless to hinder his departure by so much as an hour; but I fancied that Julia Tremaine could persuade him to any sacrifice of his inclination, if she could only humble her pride so far as to entreat it. I determined to appeal to her.

We were very merry all that evening. The servants and their guests danced in the great hall, while we sat in the gallery above, and in little groups upon the staircase, watching their diversions. I think this arrangement afforded excellent opportunities for flirtation, and that the younger members of our party made good use of their chances—with one exception: Edward Chrighton and his affianced contrived to keep far away from each other all the evening.

While all was going on noisily in the hall below, I managed to get Miss Tremaine apart from the others in the embrasure of a painted window on the stairs, where there was a wide oaken bench. Seated here side by side, I described to her, under a promise of secrecy, the scene which I had witnessed that afternoon, and my conversation with Mrs. Marjorum.

"But, good gracious me, Miss Chrighton!" the young lady exclaimed, lifting her pencilled eyebrows with unconcealed disdain, "you don't mean to tell me that you believe in such nonsense—ghosts and omens, and old woman's folly like that!"

"I assure you, Miss Tremaine, it is most difficult for me to believe in the super-natural," I answered earnestly; "but that which I saw this evening was something more than human. The thought of it has made me very unhappy; and I cannot help connecting it somehow with my cousin Edward's visit to Wycherly. If I had the power to prevent his going, I would do it at any cost; but I have not. You alone have influence enough for that. For heaven's sake, use it! Do anything to hinder his hunting with the Daleborough hounds."

"You would have me humiliate myself by asking him to forgo his pleasure, and that after his conduct to me during the last week?"

"I confess that he has done much to offend you. But you love him, Miss Tremaine, though you are too proud to let your love be seen: I am certain that you do love him. For pity's sake, speak to him; do not let him hazard his life, when a few words from you may prevent the danger."

"I don't believe he would give up this visit to please me," she answered; "and I shall certainly not put it in his power to humiliate me by a refusal. Besides, all this fear of yours is such utter nonsense. As if nobody had ever hunted before. My brothers hunt four times a week every winter, and not one of them has ever been the worse for it yet."

I did not give up the attempt lightly. I pleaded with this proud obstinate girl for a long time, as long as I could induce her to listen to me; but it was all in vain. She stuck to her text—no one should persuade her to degrade herself by asking a favour of Edward Chrighton. He had chosen to hold himself aloof from her, and she would show him that she could live without him. When she left Chrighton Abbey, they would part as strangers.

So the night closed, and at breakfast next morning I heard that Edward had started for Wycherly soon after daybreak. His absence made, for me at least, a sad blank in our circle. For one other also, I think; for Miss Tremaine's fair proud face was very pale, though she tried to seem gayer than usual, and exerted herself in quite an unaccustomed manner in her endeavour to be agreeable to everyone.

* * * *

The days passed slowly for me after my cousin's departure. There was a weight upon my mind, a vague anxiety, which I struggled in vain to shake off. The house, full as it was of pleasant people, seemed to me to have become dull and dreary now that Edward was gone. The place where he had sat appeared always vacant to my eyes, though another filled it, and there was no gap on either side of the long din-ner-table. Lighthearted young men still made the billiard-room resonant with their laughter; merry girls flirted as gaily as ever, undisturbed in the smallest degree by the absence of the heir of the house. Yet for me all was changed. A morbid fancy had taken complete possession of me. I found myself continually brooding over the housekeeper's words; those words which had told me that the shadows I had seen boded death and sorrow to the house of Chrighton.

My cousins, Sophy and Agnes, were no more concerned about their brother's welfare than were their guests. They were full of excitement about the New Year's ball, which was to be a very grand affair. Everyone of importance within fifty miles was to be present, every nook and corner of the Abbey would be filled with visitors coming from a great distance, while others were to be billeted upon the better class of tenantry round about. Altogether the organization of this affair was no small business; and Mrs. Chrighton's mornings were broken by discussions with the housekeeper, messages from the cook, interviews with the head-gardener on the subject of floral decorations, and other details, which all alike demanded the attention of the chatelaine herself. With these duties, and with the claims of her numerous guests, my cousin Fanny's time was so fully occupied, that she had little leisure to indulge in anxious feelings about her son, whatever secret uneasiness may have been lurking in her maternal heart. As for the master of the Abbey, he spent so much of his time in the library, where, under the pretext of business with his bailiff, he read Greek, that it was not easy for anyone to discover what he did feel. Once, and once only, I heard him speak of his son, in a tone that betrayed an intense eagerness for his return.

The girls were to have new dresses from a French milliner in Wigmore Street; and as the great event drew near, bulky packages of millinery were continually arriving, and feminine consultations and expositions of finery were being held all day long in bedrooms and dressing-rooms with closed doors. Thus, with a mind always troubled by the same dark shapeless foreboding, I was perpetually being called upon to give an opinion about pink tulle and lilies of the valley, or maize silk and apple-blossoms.

New Year's morning came at last, after an interval of abnormal length, as it seemed to me. It was a bright clear day, an almost spring-like sunshine lighting up the leafless landscape. The great dining-room was noisy with congratulations and good wishes as we assembled for breakfast on this first morning of a new year, after having seen the old one out cheerily the night before; but Edward had not yet returned, and I missed him sadly. Some touch of sympathy drew me to the side of Julia Tremaine on this particular morning. I had watched her very often during the last few days, and I had seen that her cheek grew paler every day. Today her eyes had the dull heavy look that betokens a sleepless night. Yes, I was sure that she was unhappy—that the proud relentless nature suffered bitterly.

"He must be home today," I said to her in a low voice, as she sat in stately silence before an untasted breakfast.

"Who must?" she answered, turning towards me with a cold distant look.

"My cousin Edward. You know he promised to be back in time for the ball."

"I know nothing of Mr. Chrighton's intended movements," she said in her haughtiest tone; "but of course it is only natural that he should be here tonight. He would scarcely care to insult half the county by his absence, however little he may value those now staying in his father's house."

"But you know that there is one here whom he does value better than anyone else in the world, Miss Tremaine," I answered, anxious to soothe this proud girl.

"I know nothing of the kind. But why do you speak so solemnly about his return? He will come, of course. There is no reason he should not come."

She spoke in a rapid manner that was strange to her and looked at me with a sharp enquiring glance that touched me somehow, it was so unlike herself—it revealed to me so keen an anxiety.

"No, there is no reasonable cause for anything like uneasiness," I said; "but you remember what I told you the other night. That has preyed upon my mind, and it will be an unspeakable relief to me when I see my cousin safe at home."

"I am sorry that you should indulge in such weakness, Miss Chrighton." That was all she said; but when I saw her in the drawing-room after breakfast, she had established herself in a window that commanded a view of the long winding drive leading to the front of the Abbey. From this point she could not fail to see anyone approaching the house. She sat there all day; everyone else was more or less busy with arrangements for the evening, or at any rate occupied with an appearance of business; but Julia Tremaine kept her place by the window, pleading a headache as an excuse for sitting still, with a book in her hand, all day, yet obstinately refusing to go to her room and lie down when her mother entreated her to do so.

"You will be fit for nothing tonight, Julia," Mrs. Tremaine said almost angrily. "You have been looking ill for ever so long, and today you are as pale as a ghost."

I knew that she was watching for him; and I pitied her with all my heart, as the day wore itself out and he did not come.

We dined earlier than usual, played a game or two of billiards after dinner, made a tour of inspection through the bright rooms, lit with wax-candles only, and odorous with exotics; and then came a long interregnum devoted to the arts and mysteries of the toilet; while maids flitted to and fro laden with frilled muslin petticoats from the laundry, and a faint smell of singed hair pervaded the corridors. At ten o'clock the band were tuning their violins, and pretty girls and elegant-looking men were coming slowly down the broad oak staircase, as the roll of fast-coming wheels sounded louder without, and stentorian voices announced the best people in the county.

I have no need to dwell long upon the details of that evening's festival. It was very much like other balls—a brilliant success, a night of splendour and enchantment for those whose hearts were light and happy, and who could abandon themselves utterly to the pleasure of the moment; a far-away picture of fair faces and bright-hued dresses, a wearisome kaleidoscopic procession of form and colour for those whose minds were weighed down with the burden of a hidden care.

For me the music had no melody, the dazzling scene no charm. Hour after hour went by; supper was over, and the waltzers were enjoying those latest dances which always seem the most delightful, and yet Edward Chrighton had not appeared amongst us.

There had been innumerable enquiries about him, and Mrs. Chrighton had apologized for his absence as best she might. Poor soul, I well knew that his non-return was now a source of poignant anxiety to her, although she greeted all her guests with the same gracious smile, and was able to talk gaily and well upon every subject. Once, when she was sitting alone for a few minutes, watching the dancers, I saw the smile fade from her face, and a look of anguish come over it. I ventured to approach her at this moment, and never shall I forget the look which she turned towards me.

"My son, Sarah!" she said in a low voice. "Something has happened to my son!"

I did my best to comfort her; but my own heart was growing heavier and heavier, and my attempt was a very poor one.

Julia Tremaine had danced a little at the beginning of the evening, to keep up appearances, I believe, in order that no one might suppose that she was distressed by her lover's absence; but after the first two or three dances she pronounced herself tired, and withdrew to a seat amongst the matrons. She was looking very lovely in spite of her extreme pallor, dressed in white tulle, a perfect cloud of airy puffings, and with a wreath of ivy-leaves and diamonds crowning her pale golden hair.

The night waned, the dancers were revolving in the last waltz, when I happened to look towards the doorway at the end of the room. I was startled by seeing a man standing there, with his hat in his hand, not in evening costume; a man with a pale anxious-looking face, peering cautiously into the room. My first thought was of evil; but in the next moment the man had disappeared, and I saw no more of him.

I lingered by my cousin Fanny's side till the rooms were empty. Even Sophy and Aggy had gone off to their own apartments, their airy dresses sadly dilapidated by a night's vigorous dancing. There were only Mr. and Mrs. Chrighton and myself in the long suite of rooms, where the flowers were drooping and the wax-lights dying out one by one in the silver sconces against the walls.

"I think the evening went off very well," Fanny said, looking rather anxiously at her husband, who was stretching himself and yawning with an air of intense relief.

"Yes, the affair went off well enough. But Edward has committed a terrible breach of manners by not being here. Upon my word, the young men of the present day think of nothing but their own pleasures. I suppose that something especially attractive was going on at Wycherly today, and he couldn't tear himself away."

"It is so unlike him to break his word," Mrs. Chrighton answered. "You are not alarmed, Frederick? You don't think that anything has happened—any accident?"

"What should happen? Ned is one of the best riders in the county. I don't think there's any fear of his coming to grief."

"He might be ill."

"Not he. He's a young Hercules. And if it were possible for him to be ill—which it is not—we should have had a message from Wycherly."

The words were scarcely spoken when Truefold the old butler stood by his master's side, with a solemn anxious face.

"There is a—a person who wishes to see you, sir," he said in a low voice, "alone."

Low as the words were, both Fanny and myself heard them.

"Someone from Wycherly?" she exclaimed. "Let him come here."

"But, madam, the person most particularly wished to see master alone. Shall I show him into the library, sir? The lights are not out there."

"Then it is someone from Wycherly," said my cousin, seizing my wrist with a hand that was icy cold. "Didn't I tell you so, Sarah? Something has happened to my son. Let the person come here, Truefold, here; I insist upon it."

The tone of command was quite strange in a wife who was always deferential to her husband, in a mistress who was ever gentle to her servants.

"Let it be so, Truefold," said Mr. Chrighton. "Whatever ill news has come to us we will hear together."

He put his arm round his wife's waist. Both were pale as marble, both stood in stony stillness waiting for the blow that was to fall upon them.

The stranger, the man I had seen in the doorway, came in. He was curate of Wycherly church, and chaplain to Sir Francis Wycherly; a grave middle-aged man. He told what he had to tell with all kindness, with all the usual forms of consolation which Christianity and an experience of sorrow could suggest. Vain words, wasted trouble. The blow must fall, and earthly consolation was unable to lighten it by a feather's weight.

There had been a steeplechase at Wycherly—an amateur affair with gentlemen riders—on that bright New Year's day, and Edward Chrighton had been persuaded to ride his favourite hunter Pepperbox. There would be plenty of time for him to return to Chrighton after the races. He had consented; and his horse was winning easily, when, at the last fence, a double one, with water beyond, Pepperbox baulked his leap and went over head-foremost, flinging his rider over a hedge into a field close beside the course, where there was a heavy stone roller. Upon this stone roller Edward Chrighton had fallen, his head receiving the full force of the concussion. All was told. It was while the curate was relating the fatal catastrophe that I looked round suddenly, and saw Julia Tremaine standing a little way behind the speaker. She had heard all; she uttered no cry, she showed no signs of fainting, but stood calm and motionless, waiting for the end.

I know not how that night ended: there seemed an awful calm upon us all. A carriage was got ready, and Mr. and Mrs. Chrighton started for Wycherly to look upon their dead son. He had died while they were carrying him from the course to Sir Francis's house. I went with Julia Tremaine to her room and sat with her while the winter morning dawned slowly upon us—a bitter dawning.

* * * *

I have little more to tell. Life goes on, though hearts are broken. Upon Chrighton Abbey there came a dreary time of desolation. The master of the house lived in his library, shut from the outer world, buried almost as completely as a hermit in his cell. I have heard that Julia Tremaine was never known to smile after that day. She is still unmarried and lives entirely at her father's country house; proud and reserved in her conduct to her equals, but a very angel of mercy and compassion amongst the poor of the neighbourhood. Yes; this haughty girl, who once declared herself unable to endure the hovels of the poor, is now a Sister of Charity in all but the robe. So does a great sorrow change the current of a woman's life.

I have seen my cousin Fanny many times since that awful New Year's night; for I have always the same welcome at the Abbey. I have seen her calm and cheerful, doing her duty, smiling upon her daughter's children, the honoured mistress of a great household; but I know that the mainspring of life is broken, that for her there hath passed a glory from the earth, and that upon all the pleasures and joys of this world she looks with the solemn calm of one for whom all things are dark with the shadow of a great sorrow.

THE HAUNTED MILL,
by Jerome K. Jerome

Well, you all know my brother-in-law, Mr. Parkins (began Mr. Coombes, taking the long clay pipe from his mouth, and putting it behind his ear; we did not know his brother-in-law, but we said we did, so as to save time), and you know of course that he once took a lease of an old mill in Surrey, and went to live there.

Now you must know that, years ago, this very mill had been occupied by a wicked old miser, who died there, leaving—so it was rumoured—all his money hidden somewhere about the place.

Naturally enough, everyone who had since come to live at the mill had tried to find the treasure; but none had ever succeeded, and the local wiseacres said that nobody ever would, unless the ghost of the miserly miller should, one day, take a fancy to one of the tenants, and disclose to him the secret of the hiding-place.

My brother-in-law did not attach much importance to the story, regarding it as an old woman's tale, and, unlike his predecessors, made no attempt whatever to discover the hidden gold.

"Unless business was very different then from what it is now," said my brother-in-law, "I don't see how a miller could very well have saved anything, however much a miser he might have been: at all events, not enough to make it worth the trouble of looking for it."

Still, he could not altogether get rid of the idea of that treasure.

One night he went to bed. There was nothing very extraordinary about that, I admit. He often did go to bed of a night. What was remarkable, however, was that exactly as the clock of the village church chimed the last stroke of twelve, my brother-in-law woke up with a start, and felt himself quite unable to go to sleep again.

Joe (his Christian name was Joe) sat up in bed, and looked around.

At the foot of the bed something stood very still, wrapped in shadow.

It moved into the moonlight, and then my brother-in-law saw that it was a figure of a wizened little old man, in knee-breeches and a pig-tail.

In an instant the story of the hidden treasure and the old miser flashed across his mind.

"He's come to show me where it's hid," thought my brother-in-law; and he resolved that he would not spend all this money on himself, but would devote a small percentage of it towards doing good to others.

The apparition moved towards the door: my brother-in-law put on his trousers and followed it.

The ghost went downstairs into the kitchen, glided over and stood in front of the hearth, sighed and disappeared.

Next morning, Joe had a couple of bricklayers in, and made them haul out the stove and pull down the chimney, while he stood behind with a potato-sack in which to put the gold.

They knocked down half the wall, and never found so much as a four-penny bit. My brother-in-law did not know what to think.

27

The next night the old man appeared again, and again led the way into the kitchen. This time, however, instead of going to the fireplace, it stood more in the middle of the room, and sighed there.

"Oh, I see what he means now," said my brother-in-law to himself; "it's under the floor. Why did the old idiot go and stand up against the stove, so as to make me think it was up the chimney?"

They spent the next day in taking up the kitchen floor; but the only thing they found was a three-pronged fork, and the handle of that was broken.

On the third night, the ghost reappeared, quite unabashed, and for a third time made for the kitchen. Arrived there, it looked up at the ceiling and vanished.

"Umph! he don't seem to have learned much sense where he's been to," muttered Joe, as he trotted back to bed; "I should have thought he might have done that first."

Still, there seemed no doubt now where the treasure lay, and the first thing after breakfast they started pulling down the ceiling. They got every inch of the ceiling down, and they took up the boards of the room above.

They discovered about as much treasure as you would expect to find in an empty quart-pot.

On the fourth night, when the ghost appeared, as usual, my brother-in-law was so wild that he threw his boots at it; and the boots passed through the body, and broke a looking-glass.

On the fifth night, when Joe awoke, as he always did now at twelve, the ghost was standing in a dejected attitude, looking very miserable. There was an appealing look in its large sad eyes that quite touched my brother-in-law.

"After all," he thought, "perhaps the silly chap's doing his best. Maybe he has forgotten where he really did put it, and is trying to remember. I'll give him another chance."

The ghost appeared grateful and delighted at seeing Joe prepare to follow him, and led the way into the attic, pointed to the ceiling, and vanished.

"Well, he's hit it this time, I do hope," said my brother-in-law; and next day they set to work to take the roof off the place.

It took them three days to get the roof thoroughly off, and all they found was a bird's nest; after securing which they covered up the house with tarpaulins, to keep it dry.

You might have thought that would have cured the poor fellow of looking for treasure. But it didn't.

He said there must be something in it all, or the ghost would never keep coming as it did; and that, having gone so far, he would go on to the end, and solve the mystery, cost what it might.

Night after night, he would get out of his bed and follow that spectral old fraud about the house. Each night, the old man would indicate a different place; and, on each following day, my brother-in-law would proceed to break up the mill at the point indicated, and look for the treasure. At the end of three weeks, there was not a room in the mill fit to live in. Every wall had been pulled down, every floor had been taken up, every ceiling had had a hole knocked in it. And then, as suddenly as they had begun, the ghost's visits ceased; and my brother-in-law was left in peace, to rebuild the place at his leisure.

What induced the old image to play such a silly trick upon a family man and a ratepayer? Ah! That's just what I cannot tell you.

Some said that the ghost of the wicked old man had done it to punish my brother-in-law for not believing in him at first; while others held that the apparition was probably that of some deceased local plumber and glazier, who would naturally take an interest in seeing a house knocked about and spoilt. But nobody knew anything for certain.

THE LOST GHOST,
by Mary E. Wilkins Freeman

Mrs. John Emerson, sitting with her needlework beside the window, looked out and saw Mrs. Rhoda Meserve coming down the street, and knew at once by the trend of her steps and the cant of her head that she meditated turning in at her gate. She also knew by a certain something about her general carriage—a thrusting forward of the neck, a bustling hitch of the shoulders—that she had important news. Rhoda Meserve always had the news as soon as the news was in being, and generally Mrs. John Emerson was the first to whom she imparted it. The two women had been friends ever since Mrs. Meserve had married Simon Meserve and come to the village to live.

Mrs. Meserve was a pretty woman, moving with graceful flirts of ruffling skirts; her clear-cut, nervous face, as delicately tinted as a shell, looked brightly from the plumy brim of a black hat at Mrs. Emerson in the window. Mrs. Emerson was glad to see her coming. She returned the greeting with enthusiasm, then rose hurriedly, ran into the cold parlour and brought out one of the best rocking-chairs. She was just in time, after drawing it up beside the opposite window, to greet her friend at the door.

"Good-afternoon," said she. "I declare, I'm real glad to see you. I've been alone all day. John went to the city this morning. I thought of coming over to your house this afternoon, but I couldn't bring my sewing very well. I am putting the ruffles on my new black dress skirt."

"Well, I didn't have a thing on hand except my crochet work," responded Mrs. Meserve, "and I thought I'd just run over a few minutes."

"I'm real glad you did," repeated Mrs. Emerson. "Take your things right off. Here, I'll put them on my bed in the bedroom. Take the rocking-chair."

Mrs. Meserve settled herself in the parlour rocking-chair, while Mrs. Emerson carried her shawl and hat into the little adjoining bedroom. When she returned Mrs. Meserve was rocking peacefully and was already at work hooking blue wool in and out.

"That's real pretty," said Mrs. Emerson.

"Yes, I think it's pretty," replied Mrs. Meserve.

"I suppose it's for the church fair?"

"Yes. I don't suppose it'll bring enough to pay for the worsted, let alone the work, but I suppose I've got to make something."

"How much did that one you made for the fair last year bring?"

"Twenty-five cents."

"It's wicked, ain't it?"

"I rather guess it is. It takes me a week every minute I can get to make one. I wish those that bought such things for twenty-five cents had to make them. Guess they'd sing another song. Well, I suppose I oughtn't to complain as long as it is for the Lord, but sometimes it does seem as if the Lord didn't get much out of it."

"Well, it's pretty work," said Mrs. Emerson, sitting down at the opposite window and taking up her dress skirt.

30

"Yes, it is real pretty work. I just LOVE to crochet."

The two women rocked and sewed and crocheted in silence for two or three minutes. They were both waiting. Mrs. Meserve waited for the other's curiosity to develop in order that her news might have, as it were, a befitting stage entrance. Mrs. Emerson waited for the news. Finally she could wait no longer.

"Well, what's the news?" said she.

"Well, I don't know as there's anything very particular," hedged the other woman, prolonging the situation.

"Yes, there is; you can't cheat me," replied Mrs. Emerson.

"Now, how do you know?"

"By the way you look."

Mrs. Meserve laughed consciously and rather vainly.

"Well, Simon says my face is so expressive I can't hide anything more than five minutes no matter how hard I try," said she. "Well, there is some news. Simon came home with it this noon. He heard it in South Dayton. He had some business over there this morning. The old Sargent place is let."

Mrs. Emerson dropped her sewing and stared.

"You don't say so!"

"Yes, it is."

"Who to?"

"Why, some folks from Boston that moved to South Dayton last year. They haven't been satisfied with the house they had there—it wasn't large enough. The man has got considerable property and can afford to live pretty well. He's got a wife and his unmarried sister in the family. The sister's got money, too. He does business in Boston and it's just as easy to get to Boston from here as from South Dayton, and so they're coming here. You know the old Sargent house is a splendid place."

"Yes, it's the handsomest house in town, but—"

"Oh, Simon said they told him about that and he just laughed. Said he wasn't afraid and neither was his wife and sister. Said he'd risk ghosts rather than little tucked-up sleeping-rooms without any sun, like they've had in the Dayton house. Said he'd rather risk *seeing* ghosts, than risk being ghosts themselves. Simon said they said he was a great hand to joke."

"Oh, well," said Mrs. Emerson, "it is a beautiful house, and maybe there isn't anything in those stories. It never seemed to me they came very straight anyway. I never took much stock in them. All I thought was—if his wife was nervous."

"Nothing in creation would hire me to go into a house that I'd ever heard a word against of that kind," declared Mrs. Meserve with emphasis. "I wouldn't go into that house if they would give me the rent. I've seen enough of haunted houses to last me as long as I live."

Mrs. Emerson's face acquired the expression of a hunting hound.

"Have you?" she asked in an intense whisper.

"Yes, I have. I don't want any more of it."

"Before you came here?"

"Yes; before I was married—when I was quite a girl."

Mrs. Meserve had not married young. Mrs. Emerson had mental calculations when she heard that.

"Did you really live in a house that was—" she whispered fearfully.

Mrs. Meserve nodded solemnly.

"Did you really ever—see—anything—"

Mrs. Meserve nodded.

"You didn't see anything that did you any harm?"

"No, I didn't see anything that did me harm looking at it in one way, but it don't do anybody in this world any good to see things that haven't any business to be seen in it. You never get over it."

There was a moment's silence. Mrs. Emerson's features seemed to sharpen.

"Well, of course I don't want to urge you," said she, "if you don't feel like talking about it; but maybe it might do you good to tell it out, if it's on your mind, worrying you."

"I try to put it out of my mind," said Mrs. Meserve.

"Well, it's just as you feel."

"I never told anybody but Simon," said Mrs. Meserve. "I never felt as if it was wise perhaps. I didn't know what folks might think. So many don't believe in anything they can't understand, that they might think my mind wasn't right. Simon advised me not to talk about it. He said he didn't believe it was anything supernatural, but he had to own up that he couldn't give any explanation for it to save his life. He had to own up that he didn't believe anybody could. Then he said he wouldn't talk about it. He said lots of folks would sooner tell folks my head wasn't right than to own up they couldn't see through it."

"I'm sure I wouldn't say so," returned Mrs. Emerson reproachfully. "You know better than that, I hope."

"Yes, I do," replied Mrs. Meserve. "I know you wouldn't say so."

"And I wouldn't tell it to a soul if you didn't want me to."

"Well, I'd rather you wouldn't."

"I won't speak of it even to Mr. Emerson."

"I'd rather you wouldn't even to him."

"I won't."

Mrs. Emerson took up her dress skirt again; Mrs. Meserve hooked up another loop of blue wool. Then she begun:

"Of course," said she, "I ain't going to say positively that I believe or disbelieve in ghosts, but all I tell you is what I saw. I can't explain it. I don't pretend I can, for I can't. If you can, well and good; I shall be glad, for it will stop tormenting me as it has done and always will otherwise. There hasn't been a day nor a night since it happened that I haven't thought of it, and always I have felt the shivers go down my back when I did."

"That's an awful feeling," Mrs. Emerson said.

"Ain't it? Well, it happened before I was married, when I was a girl and lived in East Wilmington. It was the first year I lived there. You know my family all died five years before that. I told you."

Mrs. Emerson nodded.

"Well, I went there to teach school, and I went to board with a Mrs. Amelia Dennison and her sister, Mrs. Bird. Abby, her name was—Abby Bird. She was a widow; she had never had any children. She had a little money—Mrs. Dennison didn't have any—and she had come to East Wilmington and bought the house they lived in. It was a real pretty house, though it was very old and run down. It had cost Mrs. Bird a good deal to put it in order. I guess that was the reason they took me to board. I guess they thought it would help along a little. I guess what I paid for my board about kept us all in victuals. Mrs. Bird had enough to live on if they were careful, but she had spent so much fixing up the old house that they must have been a little pinched for awhile.

"Anyhow, they took me to board, and I thought I was pretty lucky to get in there. I had a nice room, big and sunny and furnished pretty, the paper and paint all new, and everything as neat as wax. Mrs. Dennison was one of the best cooks I ever saw, and I had a little stove in my room, and there was always a nice fire there when I got home from school. I thought I hadn't been in such a nice place since I lost my own home, until I had been there about three weeks.

"I had been there about three weeks before I found it out, though I guess it had been going on ever since they had been in the house, and that was most four months. They hadn't said anything about it, and I didn't wonder, for there they had just bought the house and been to so much expense and trouble fixing it up.

"Well, I went there in September. I begun my school the first Monday. I remember it was a real cold fall, there was a frost the middle of September, and I had to put on my winter coat. I remember when I came home that night (let me see, I began school on a Monday, and that was two weeks from the next Thursday), I took off my coat downstairs and laid it on the table in the front entry. It was a real nice coat—heavy black broadcloth trimmed with fur; I had had it the winter before. Mrs. Bird called after me as I went upstairs that I ought not to leave it in the front entry for fear somebody might come in and take it, but I only laughed and called back to her that I wasn't afraid. I never was much afraid of burglars.

"Well, though it was hardly the middle of September, it was a real cold night. I remember my room faced west, and the sun was getting low, and the sky was a pale yellow and purple, just as you see it sometimes in the winter when there is going to be a cold snap. I rather think that was the night the frost came the first time. I know Mrs. Dennison covered up some flowers she had in the front yard, anyhow. I remember looking out and seeing an old green plaid shawl of hers over the verbena bed. There was a fire in my little wood-stove. Mrs. Bird made it, I know. She was a real motherly sort of woman; she always seemed to be the happiest when she was doing something to make other folks happy and comfortable. Mrs. Dennison told me she had always been so. She said she had coddled her husband within an inch of his life. 'It's lucky Abby never had any children,' she said, 'for she would have spoilt them.'

"Well, that night I sat down beside my nice little fire and ate an apple. There was a plate of nice apples on my table. Mrs. Bird put them there. I was always very fond of apples. Well, I sat down and ate an apple, and was having a beautiful time, and thinking how lucky I was to have got board in such a place with such nice folks, when I heard a queer little sound at my door. It was such a little hesitating sort of sound that it sounded more like a fumble than a knock, as if some one very timid, with very little hands, was feeling along the door, not quite daring to knock. For a minute I thought it was a mouse. But I waited and it came again, and then I made up my mind it was a knock, but a very little scared one, so I said, 'Come in.'

"But nobody came in, and then presently I heard the knock again. Then I got up and opened the door, thinking it was very queer, and I had a frightened feeling without knowing why.

"Well, I opened the door, and the first thing I noticed was a draught of cold air, as if the front door downstairs was open, but there was a strange close smell about the cold draught. It smelled more like a cellar that had been shut up for years, than out-of-doors. Then I saw something. I saw my coat first. The thing that held it was so small that I couldn't see much of anything else. Then I saw a little white face with eyes so scared and wishful that they seemed as if they might eat a hole in anybody's heart. It was a dreadful little face, with something about it which made it different from any other face on earth, but it was so pitiful that somehow it did away a good deal with the dreadfulness. And there were two little hands spotted purple with the cold, holding up my winter coat, and a strange little far-away voice

33

said: 'I can't find my mother.'

"'For Heaven's sake,' I said, 'who are you?'

"Then the little voice said again: 'I can't find my mother.'

"All the time I could smell the cold and I saw that it was about the child; that cold was clinging to her as if she had come out of some deadly cold place. Well, I took my coat, I did not know what else to do, and the cold was clinging to that. It was as cold as if it had come off ice. When I had the coat I could see the child more plainly. She was dressed in one little white garment made very simply. It was a nightgown, only very long, quite covering her feet, and I could see dimly through it her little thin body mottled purple with the cold. Her face did not look so cold; that was a clear waxen white. Her hair was dark, but it looked as if it might be dark only because it was so damp, almost wet, and might really be light hair. It clung very close to her forehead, which was round and white. She would have been very beautiful if she had not been so dreadful.

"'Who are you?' says I again, looking at her.

"She looked at me with her terrible pleading eyes and did not say anything.

"'What are you?' says I. Then she went away. She did not seem to run or walk like other children. She flitted, like one of those little filmy white butterflies, that don't seem like real ones they are so light, and move as if they had no weight. But she looked back from the head of the stairs. 'I can't find my mother,' said she, and I never heard such a voice.

"'Who is your mother?' says I, but she was gone.

"Well, I thought for a moment I should faint away. The room got dark and I heard a singing in my ears. Then I flung my coat onto the bed. My hands were as cold as ice from holding it, and I stood in my door, and called first Mrs. Bird and then Mrs. Dennison. I didn't dare go down over the stairs where that had gone. It seemed to me I should go mad if I didn't see somebody or something like other folks on the face of the earth. I thought I should never make anybody hear, but I could hear them stepping about downstairs, and I could smell biscuits baking for supper. Somehow the smell of those biscuits seemed the only natural thing left to keep me in my right mind. I didn't dare go over those stairs. I just stood there and called, and finally I heard the entry door open and Mrs. Bird called back:

"'What is it? Did you call, Miss Arms?'

"'Come up here; come up here as quick as you can, both of you,' I screamed out; 'quick, quick, quick!'

"I heard Mrs. Bird tell Mrs. Dennison: 'Come quick, Amelia, something is the matter in Miss Arms' room.' It struck me even then that she expressed herself rather queerly, and it struck me as very queer, indeed, when they both got upstairs and I saw that they knew what had happened, or that they knew of what nature the happening was.

"'What is it, dear?' asked Mrs. Bird, and her pretty, loving voice had a strained sound. I saw her look at Mrs. Dennison and I saw Mrs. Dennison look back at her.

"'For God's sake,' says I, and I never spoke so before—'for God's sake, what was it brought my coat upstairs?'

"'What was it like?' asked Mrs. Dennison in a sort of failing voice, and she looked at her sister again and her sister looked back at her.

"'It was a child I have never seen here before. It looked like a child,' says I, 'but I never saw a child so dreadful, and it had on a nightgown, and said she couldn't find her mother. Who was it? What was it?'

"I thought for a minute Mrs. Dennison was going to faint, but Mrs. Bird hung onto her and rubbed her hands, and whispered in her ear (she had the cooingest kind of voice), and I ran and got her a glass of cold water. I tell you it took considerable courage to go downstairs alone, but they had set a lamp on the entry table so I could see. I don't believe I could have spunked up enough to have gone downstairs in the dark, thinking every second that child might be close to me. The lamp and the smell of the biscuits baking seemed to sort of keep my courage up, but I tell you I didn't waste much time going down those stairs and out into the kitchen for a glass of water. I pumped as if the house was afire, and I grabbed the first thing I came across in the shape of a tumbler: it was a painted one that Mrs. Dennison's Sunday school class gave her, and it was meant for a flower vase.

"Well, I filled it and then ran upstairs. I felt every minute as if something would catch my feet, and I held the glass to Mrs. Dennison's lips, while Mrs. Bird held her head up, and she took a good long swallow, then she looked hard at the tumbler.

"'Yes,' says I, 'I know I got this one, but I took the first I came across, and it isn't hurt a mite.'

"'Don't get the painted flowers wet,' says Mrs. Dennison very feebly, 'they'll wash off if you do.'

"'I'll be real careful,' says I. I knew she set a sight by that painted tumbler.

"The water seemed to do Mrs. Dennison good, for presently she pushed Mrs. Bird away and sat up. She had been laying down on my bed.

"'I'm all over it now,' says she, but she was terribly white, and her eyes looked as if they saw something outside things. Mrs. Bird wasn't much better, but she always had a sort of settled sweet, good look that nothing could disturb to any great extent. I knew I looked dreadful, for I caught a glimpse of myself in the glass, and I would hardly have known who it was.

"Mrs. Dennison, she slid off the bed and walked sort of tottery to a chair. 'I was silly to give way so,' says she.

"'No, you wasn't silly, sister,' says Mrs. Bird. 'I don't know what this means any more than you do, but whatever it is, no one ought to be called silly for being overcome by anything so different from other things which we have known all our lives.'

"Mrs. Dennison looked at her sister, then she looked at me, then back at her sister again, and Mrs. Bird spoke as if she had been asked a question.

"'Yes,' says she, 'I do think Miss Arms ought to be told—that is, I think she ought to be told all we know ourselves.'

"'That isn't much,' said Mrs. Dennison with a dying-away sort of sigh. She looked as if she might faint away again any minute. She was a real delicate-looking woman, but it turned out she was a good deal stronger than poor Mrs. Bird.

"'No, there isn't much we do know,' says Mrs. Bird, 'but what little there is she ought to know. I felt as if she ought to when she first came here.'

"'Well, I didn't feel quite right about it,' said Mrs. Dennison, 'but I kept hoping it might stop, and any way, that it might never trouble her, and you had put so much in the house, and we needed the money, and I didn't know but she might be nervous and think she couldn't come, and I didn't want to take a man boarder.'

"'And aside from the money, we were very anxious to have you come, my dear,' says Mrs. Bird.

"'Yes,' says Mrs. Dennison, 'we wanted the young company in the house; we were lonesome, and we both of us took a great liking to you the minute we set eyes on you.'

"And I guess they meant what they said, both of them. They were beautiful women, and nobody could be any kinder to me than they were, and I never blamed them for not telling me before, and, as they said, there wasn't really much to tell.

"They hadn't any sooner fairly bought the house, and moved into it, than they began to see and hear things. Mrs. Bird said they were sitting together in the sitting-room one evening when they heard it the first time. She said her sister was knitting lace (Mrs. Dennison made beautiful knitted lace) and she was reading the Missionary Herald (Mrs. Bird was very much interested in mission work), when all of a sudden they heard something. She heard it first and she laid down her Missionary Herald and listened, and then Mrs. Dennison she saw her listening and she drops her lace. 'What is it you are listening to, Abby?' says she. Then it came again and they both heard, and the cold shivers went down their backs to hear it, though they didn't know why. 'It's the cat, isn't it?' says Mrs. Bird.

"'It isn't any cat,' says Mrs. Dennison.

"'Oh, I guess it *must* be the cat; maybe she's got a mouse,' says Mrs. Bird, real cheerful, to calm down Mrs. Dennison, for she saw she was 'most scared to death, and she was always afraid of her fainting away. Then she opens the door and calls, 'Kitty, kitty, kitty!' They had brought their cat with them in a basket when they came to East Wilmington to live. It was a real handsome tiger cat, a tommy, and he knew a lot.

"Well, she called 'Kitty, kitty, kitty!' and sure enough the kitty came, and when he came in the door he gave a big yawl that didn't sound unlike what they had heard.

"'There, sister, here he is; you see it was the cat,' says Mrs. Bird. 'Poor kitty!'

"But Mrs. Dennison she eyed the cat, and she give a great screech.

"'What's that? What's that?' says she.

"'What's what?' says Mrs. Bird, pretending to herself that she didn't see what her sister meant.

"'Somethin's got hold of that cat's tail,' says Mrs. Dennison. 'Somethin's got hold of his tail. It's pulled straight out, an' he can't get away. Just hear him yawl!'

"'It isn't anything,' says Mrs. Bird, but even as she said that she could see a little hand holding fast to that cat's tail, and then the child seemed to sort of clear out of the dimness behind the hand, and the child was sort of laughing then, instead of looking sad, and she said that was a great deal worse. She said that laugh was the most awful and the saddest thing she ever heard.

"Well, she was so dumfounded that she didn't know what to do, and she couldn't sense at first that it was anything supernatural. She thought it must be one of the neighbour's children who had run away and was making free of their house, and was teasing their cat, and that they must be just nervous to feel so upset by it. So she speaks up sort of sharp.

"'Don't you know that you mustn't pull the kitty's tail?' says she. 'Don't you know you hurt the poor kitty, and she'll scratch you if you don't take care. Poor kitty, you mustn't hurt her.'

"And with that she said the child stopped pulling that cat's tail and went to stroking her just as soft and pitiful, and the cat put his back up and rubbed and purred as if he liked it. The cat never seemed a mite afraid, and that seemed queer, for I had always heard that animals were dreadfully afraid of ghosts; but then, that was a pretty harmless little sort of ghost.

"Well, Mrs. Bird said the child stroked that cat, while she and Mrs. Dennison stood watching it, and holding onto each other, for, no matter how hard they tried to think it was all right, it didn't look right. Finally Mrs. Dennison she spoke.

"'What's your name, little girl?' says she.

"Then the child looks up and stops stroking the cat, and says she can't find her mother, just the way she said it to me. Then Mrs. Dennison she gave such a gasp that Mrs. Bird thought she was going to faint away, but she didn't. 'Well, who is your mother?' says she. But the child just says again 'I can't find my mother—I can't find my mother.'

"'Where do you live, dear?' says Mrs. Bird.

"'I can't find my mother,' says the child.

"Well, that was the way it was. Nothing happened. Those two women stood there hanging onto each other, and the child stood in front of them, and they asked her questions, and everything she would say was: 'I can't find my mother.'

"Then Mrs. Bird tried to catch hold of the child, for she thought in spite of what she saw that perhaps she was nervous and it was a real child, only perhaps not quite right in its head, that had run away in her little nightgown after she had been put to bed.

"She tried to catch the child. She had an idea of putting a shawl around it and going out—she was such a little thing she could have carried her easy enough—and trying to find out to which of the neighbours she belonged. But the minute she moved toward the child there wasn't any child there; there was only that little voice seeming to come from nothing, saying 'I can't find my mother,' and presently that died away.

"Well, that same thing kept happening, or something very much the same. Once in awhile Mrs. Bird would be washing dishes, and all at once the child would be standing beside her with the dish-towel, wiping them. Of course, that was terrible. Mrs. Bird would wash the dishes all over. Sometimes she didn't tell Mrs. Dennison, it made her so nervous. Sometimes when they were making cake they would find the raisins all picked over, and sometimes little sticks of kindling-wood would be found laying beside the kitchen stove. They never knew when they would come across that child, and always she kept saying over and over that she couldn't find her mother. They never tried talking to her, except once in awhile Mrs. Bird would get desperate and ask her something, but the child never seemed to hear it; she always kept right on saying that she couldn't find her mother.

"After they had told me all they had to tell about their experience with the child, they told me about the house and the people that had lived there before they did. It seemed something dreadful had happened in that house. And the land agent had never let on to them. I don't think they would have bought it if he had, no matter how cheap it was, for even if folks aren't really afraid of anything, they don't want to live in houses where such dreadful things have happened that you keep thinking about them. I know after they told me I should never have stayed there another night, if I hadn't thought so much of them, no matter how comfortable I was made; and I never was nervous, either. But I stayed. Of course, it didn't happen in my room. If it had I could not have stayed."

"What was it?" asked Mrs. Emerson in an awed voice.

"It was an awful thing. That child had lived in the house with her father and mother two years before. They had come—or the father had—from a real good family. He had a good situation: he was a drummer for a big leather house in the city, and they lived real pretty, with plenty to do with. But the mother was a real wicked woman. She was as handsome as a picture, and they said she came from good sort of people enough in Boston, but she was bad clean through, though she was real pretty spoken and most everybody liked her. She used to dress out and make a great show, and she never seemed to take much interest in the child, and folks began to say she wasn't treated right.

"The woman had a hard time keeping a girl. For some reason one wouldn't stay. They would leave and then talk about her awfully, telling all kinds of things. People didn't believe it at first; then they began to. They said that the woman made that little thing, though she wasn't much over five years old, and small and babyish for her age, do most of the work, what there was done; they said the house used to look like a pig-sty when she didn't have help. They said the little thing used to stand on a chair and wash dishes, and they'd seen her carrying in sticks of wood most as big as she was many a time, and they'd heard her mother scolding her. The woman was a fine singer, and had a voice like a screech-owl when she scolded.

"The father was away most of the time, and when that happened he had been away out West for some weeks. There had been a married man hanging about the mother for some time, and folks had talked some; but they weren't sure there was anything wrong, and he was a man very high up, with money, so they kept pretty still for fear he would hear of it and make trouble for them, and of course nobody was sure, though folks did say afterward that the father of the child had ought to have been told.

"But that was very easy to say; it wouldn't have been so easy to find anybody who would have been willing to tell him such a thing as that, especially when they weren't any too sure. He set his eyes by his wife, too. They said all he seemed to think of was to earn money to buy things to deck her out in. And he about worshiped the child, too. They said he was a real nice man. The men that are treated so bad mostly are real nice men. I've always noticed that.

"Well, one morning that man that there had been whispers about was missing. He had been gone quite a while, though, before they really knew that he was missing, because he had gone away and told his wife that he had to go to New York on business and might be gone a week, and not to worry if he didn't get home, and not to worry if he didn't write, because he should be thinking from day to day that he might take the next train home and there would be no use in writing. So the wife waited, and she tried not to worry until it was two days over the week, then she run into a neighbour's and fainted dead away on the floor; and then they made inquiries and found out that he had skipped—with some money that didn't belong to him, too.

"Then folks began to ask where was that woman, and they found out by comparing notes that nobody had seen her since the man went away; but three or four women remembered that she had told them that she thought of taking the child and going to Boston to visit her folks, so when they hadn't seen her around, and the house shut, they jumped to the conclusion that was where she was. They were the neighbours that lived right around her, but they didn't have much to do with her, and she'd gone out of her way to tell them about her Boston plan, and they didn't make much reply when she did.

"Well, there was this house shut up, and the man and woman missing and the child. Then all of a sudden one of the women that lived the nearest remembered something. She remembered that she had waked up three nights running, thinking she heard a child crying somewhere, and once she waked up her husband, but he said it must be the Bisbees' little girl, and she thought it must be. The child wasn't well and was always crying. It used to have colic spells, especially at night. So she didn't think any more about it until this came up, then all of a sudden she did think of it. She told what she had heard, and finally folks began to think they had better enter that house and see if there was anything wrong.

"Well, they did enter it, and they found that child dead, locked in one of the rooms. (Mrs. Dennison and Mrs. Bird never used that room; it was a back bedroom on the second floor.)

"Yes, they found that poor child there, starved to death, and frozen, though they weren't sure she had frozen to death, for she was in bed with clothes enough to keep her pretty warm when she was alive. But she had been there a week, and she was nothing but skin and bone. It looked as if the mother had locked her into the house when she went away, and told her not to make any noise for fear the neighbours would hear her and find out that she herself had gone.

"Mrs. Dennison said she couldn't really believe that the woman had meant to have her own child starved to death. Probably she thought the little thing would raise somebody, or folks would try to get in the house and find her. Well, whatever she thought, there the child was, dead.

"But that wasn't all. The father came home, right in the midst of it; the child was just buried, and he was beside himself. And—he went on the track of his wife, and he found her, and he shot her dead; it was in all the papers at the time; then he disappeared. Nothing had been seen of him since. Mrs. Dennison said that she thought he had either made way with himself or got out of the country, nobody knew, but they did know there was something wrong with the house.

"'I knew folks acted queer when they asked me how I liked it when we first came here,' says Mrs. Dennison, 'but I never dreamed why till we saw the child that night.'

"I never heard anything like it in my life," said Mrs. Emerson, staring at the other woman with awestruck eyes.

"I thought you'd say so," said Mrs. Meserve. "You don't wonder that I ain't disposed to speak light when I hear there is anything queer about a house, do you?"

"No, I don't, after that," Mrs. Emerson said.

"But that ain't all," said Mrs. Meserve.

"Did you see it again?" Mrs. Emerson asked.

"Yes, I saw it a number of times before the last time. It was lucky I wasn't nervous, or I never could have stayed there, much as I liked the place and much as I thought of those two women; they were beautiful women, and no mistake. I loved those women. I hope Mrs. Dennison will come and see me sometime.

"Well, I stayed, and I never knew when I'd see that child. I got so I was very careful to bring everything of mine upstairs, and not leave any little thing in my room that needed doing, for fear she would come lugging up my coat or hat or gloves or I'd find things done when there'd been no live being in the room to do them. I can't tell you how I dreaded seeing her; and worse than the seeing her was the hearing her say, 'I can't find my mother.' It was enough to make your blood run cold. I never heard a living child cry for its mother that was anything so pitiful as that dead one. It was enough to break your heart.

"She used to come and say that to Mrs. Bird oftener than to any one else. Once I heard Mrs. Bird say she wondered if it was possible that the poor little thing couldn't really find her mother in the other world, she had been such a wicked woman.

"But Mrs. Dennison told her she didn't think she ought to speak so nor even think so, and Mrs. Bird said she shouldn't wonder if she was right. Mrs. Bird was always very easy to put in the wrong. She was a good woman, and one that couldn't do things enough for other folks. It seemed as if that was what she lived on. I don't think she was ever so scared by that poor little ghost, as much as she pitied it, and she was 'most heartbroken because she couldn't do anything for it, as she could have done for a live child.

"'It seems to me sometimes as if I should die if I can't get that awful little white robe off that child and get her in some clothes and feed her and stop her looking for her mother,' I heard her say once, and she was in earnest. She cried when she said it. That wasn't long before she died.

"Now I am coming to the strangest part of it all. Mrs. Bird died very sudden. One morning—it was Saturday, and there wasn't any school—I went downstairs to breakfast, and Mrs. Bird wasn't there; there was nobody but Mrs. Dennison. She was pouring out the coffee when I came in. 'Why, where's Mrs. Bird?' says I.

"'Abby ain't feeling very well this morning,' says she; 'there isn't much the matter, I guess, but she didn't sleep very well, and her head aches, and she's sort of chilly, and I told her I thought she'd better stay in bed till the house gets warm.' It was a very cold morning.

"'Maybe she's got cold,' says I.

"'Yes, I guess she has,' says Mrs. Dennison. 'I guess she's got cold. She'll be up before long. Abby ain't one to stay in bed a minute longer than she can help.'

"Well, we went on eating our breakfast, and all at once a shadow flickered across one wall of the room and over the ceiling the way a shadow will sometimes when somebody passes the window outside. Mrs. Dennison and I both looked up, then out of the window; then Mrs. Dennison she gives a scream.

"'Why, Abby's crazy!' says she. 'There she is out this bitter cold morning, and —and—' She didn't finish, but she meant the child. For we were both looking out, and we saw, as plain as we ever saw anything in our lives, Mrs. Abby Bird walking off over the white snow-path with that child holding fast to her hand, nestling close to her as if she had found her own mother.

"'She's dead,' says Mrs. Dennison, clutching hold of me hard. 'She's dead; my sister is dead!'

"She was. We hurried upstairs as fast as we could go, and she was dead in her bed, and smiling as if she was dreaming, and one arm and hand was stretched out as if something had hold of it; and it couldn't be straightened even at the last—it lay out over her casket at the funeral."

"Was the child ever seen again?" asked Mrs. Emerson in a shaking voice.

"No," replied Mrs. Meserve; "that child was never seen again after she went out of the yard with Mrs. Bird."

THE GHOST CLUB,
by John Kendrick Bangs

AN UNFORTUNATE EPISODE IN THE LIFE OF NO. 5010

Number 5010 was, at the time when I received the details of this story from his lips, a stalwart man of thirty-eight, swart of hue, of pleasing address, and altogether the last person one would take for a convict serving a term for sneak-thieving. The only outer symptoms of his actual condition were the striped suit he wore, the style and cut of which are still in vogue at Sing Sing prison, and the closely cropped hair, which showed off the distinctly intellectual lines of his head to great advantage. He was engaged in making shoes when I first saw him, and so impressed was I with the contrast between his really refined features and grace of mariner and those of his brutish-looking companions, that I asked my guide who he was, and what were the circumstances which had brought him to Sing Sing.

"He pegs shoes like a gentleman," I said.

"Yes," returned the keeper. "He's werry troublesome that way. He thinks he's too good for his position. We can't never do nothing with the boots he makes."

"Why do you keep him at work in the shoe department?" I queried.

"We haven't got no work to be done in his special line, so we have to put him at whatever we can. He pegs shoes less badly than he does anything else."

"What was his special line?"

"He was a gentleman of leisure travellin' for his health afore he got into the toils o' the law. his real name is Marmaduke Fitztappington De Wolfe, of Pelhamhurst-by-the-Sea, Warwickshire. He landed in this country of a Tuesday, took to collectin' souvenir spoons of a Friday, was jugged the same day, tried, convicted, and there he sets. In for two years more."

"How interesting!" I said. "Was the evidence against him conclusive?"

"Extremely. A half-dozen spoons was found on his person."

"He pleaded guilty, I suppose?"

"Not him. He claimed to be as innocent as a new-born babe. Told a cock-and-bull story about havin' been deluded by spirits, but the judge and jury wasn't to be fooled. They gave him every chance, too. He even cabled himself, the judge did, to Pelhamhurst-by-the-Sea, Warwickshire, at his own expense, to see if the man was an impostor, but he never got no reply. There was them as said there wasn't no such place as Pelhamhurst-by-the-Sea in Warwickshire, but they never proved it."

"I should like very much to interview him," said I.

"It can't be done, sir," said my guide. "The rules is very strict."

"You couldn't—er—arrange an interview for me," I asked, jingling a bunch of keys in my pocket.

He must have recognized the sound, for he colored and gruffly replied, "I has me orders, and I obeys 'em."

"Just—er—add this to the pension fund,"

I put in, handing him a five-dollar bill. "An interview is impossible, eh?'

"I didn't say impossible," he answered, with a grateful smile. "I said against the rules, but we has been known to make exceptions. I think I can fix you up."

* * * *

Suffice it to say that he did "fix me up," and that two hours later 5010 and I sat down together in the cell of the former, a not too commodious stall, and had a pleasant chat, in the course of which he told me the story of his life, which, as I had surmised, was to me, at least, exceedingly interesting, and easily worth twice the amount of my contribution to the pension fund under the management of my guide of the morning.

"My real name," said the unfortunate convict, "as you may already have guessed, is not 5010. That is an alias forced upon me by the State authorities. My name is really Austin Merton Surrennes."

"Ahem!" I said. "Then my guide erred this morning when he told me that in reality you were Marmaduke Fitztappington De Wolfe, of Pelhamhurst-by-the-Sea, Warwickshire?"

Number 5010 laughed long and loud. "Of course he erred. You don't suppose that I would give the authorities my real name, do you? Why, man, I am a nephew! I have an aged uncle—a rich millionaire uncle—whose heart and will it would break were he to hear of my present plight. Both the heart and will are in my favor, hence my tender solicitude for him. I am innocent, of course—convicts always are, you know—but that wouldn't make any difference. He'd die of mortification just the same. It's one of our family traits, that. So I gave a false name to the authorities, and secretly informed my uncle that I was about to set out for a walking trip across the great American desert, requesting him not to worry if he did not hear from me for a number of years. America being in a state of semi-civilization, to which mails outside of certain districts are entirely unknown. My uncle being an Englishman and a conservative gentleman, addicted more to reading than to travel, accepts the information as veracious and suspects nothing, and when I am liberated I shall return to him, and at his death shall become a conservative man of wealth myself. See?"

"But if you are innocent and he rich and influential, why did you not appeal to him to save you?" I asked.

"Because I was afraid that he, like the rest of the world, would decline to believe my defence," sighed 5010. "It was a good defence, if the judge had only known it, and I'm proud of it."

"But ineffectual," I put in. "And so, not good."

"Alas, yes! This is an incredulous age. People, particularly judges, are hardheaded practical men of affairs. My defence was suited more for an age of mystical tendencies. Why, will you believe it, sir, my own lawyer, the man to whom I paid eighteen dollars and seventy-five cents for championing my cause, told me the defence was rubbish, devoid even of literary merit. What chance could a man have if his lawyer even didn't believe in him?"

"None," I answered, sadly. "And you had no chance at all, though innocent?"

"Yes, I had one, and I chose not to take it. I might have proved myself non compos mentis; put that involved my making a fool of myself in public before a jury, and I have too much dignity for that, I can tell you. I told my lawyer that I should prefer a felon's cell to the richly furnished flat of a wealthy lunatic, to which he replied, 'Then all is lost!' And so it was. I read my defence in court. The judge laughed, the jury whispered, and I was convicted instanter of stealing spoons, when murder itself was no further from my thoughts than theft."

"But they tell me you were caught red-handed," said I. "Were not a half-dozen spoons found upon your person?"

"In my hand," returned the prisoner. "The spoons were in my hand when I was arrested, and they were seen there by the owner, by the police, and by the usual crowd of small boys that congregate at such embarrassing moments, springing up out of sidewalks, dropping down from the heavens, swarming in from everywhere. I had no idea there were so many small boys in the world until I was arrested, and found myself the cynosure of a million or more innocent blue eyes."

"Were they all blue-eyed?" I queried, thinking the point interesting from a scientific point of view, hoping to discover that curiosity of a morbid character was always found in connection with eyes of a specified hue.

"Oh no; I fancy not," returned my host.

"But to a man with a load of another fellow's spoons in his possession, and a pair of handcuffs on his wrists, everything looks blue."

"I don't doubt it," I replied. "But—er—just how, now, could you defend yourself when every bit of evidence, and—you will excuse me for saying so—conclusive evidence at that, pointed to your guilt?"

"The spoons were a gift," he answered.

"But the owner denied that."

"I know it; that's where the beastly part of it all came in. They were not given to me by the owner, but by a lot of mean, lowdown, practical-joke-loving ghosts."

Number 5010's anger as he spoke these words was terrible to witness, and as he strode up and down the floor of his cell and dashed his arms right and left, I wished for a moment that I was elsewhere. I should not have flown, however, even had the cell door been open and my way clear, for his suggestion of a super natural agency in connection with his crime whetted my curiosity until it was more keen than ever, and I made up my mind to hear the story to the end, if I had to commit a crime and get myself sentenced to confinement in that prison for life to do so.

Fortunately, extreme measures of this nature were unnecessary, for after a few moments Surrennes calmed down, and seating himself beside me on the cot, drained his water-pitcher to the dregs, and began.

"Excuse me for not offering you a drink," he said, "but the wine they serve here while moist is hardly what a connoisseur would choose except for bathing purposes, and I compliment you by assuming that you do not wish to taste it."

"Thank you," I said. "I do not like to take water straight, exactly. I always dilute it, in fact, with a little of this."

Here I extracted a small flask from my pocket and handed it to him.

"Ah!" he said, smacking his lips as he took a long pull at its contents, "that puts spirit into a man."

"Yes, it does," I replied, ruefully, as I noted that he had left me very little but the flask; "but I don't think it was necessary for you to deprive me of all mine."

"No; that is, you can't appreciate the necessity unless you—er—you have suffered in your life as I am suffering. You were never sent up yourself?"

I gave him a glance which was all indignation. "I guess not," I said. "I have led a life that is above reproach."

"Good!" he replied. "And what a satisfaction that is, eh? I don't believe I'd be able to stand this jail life if it wasn't for my conscience, which is as clear and clean as it would be if I'd never used it."

"Would you mind telling me what your defence was?" I asked.

"Certainly not," said he, cheerfully. "I'd be very glad to give it to you. But you must remember one thing—it is copyrighted."

"Fire ahead!" I said, with a smile. "I'll respect your copyright. I'll give you a royalty on what I get for the story."

43

"Very good," he answered. "It was like this. To begin, I must tell you that when I was a boy preparing for college I had for a chum a brilliant fun-loving fellow named Hawley Hicks, concerning whose future various prophecies had been made. His mother often asserted that he would be a great poet; his father thought he was born to be a great general; our head-master at the Scarberry Institute for Young Gentlemen prophesied the gallows. They were all wrong; though, for myself, I think that if he had lived long enough almost any one of the prophecies might have come true. The trouble was that Hawley died at the age of twenty-three. Fifteen years elapsed. I was graduated with high honors at Brazenose, lived a life of elegant leisure, and at the age of thirty-seven broke down in health. That was about a year ago. My uncle, whose heir and constant companion I was, gave me a liberal allowance, and sent me off to travel. I came to America, landed in New York early in September, and set about winning back the color which had departed from my cheeks by an assiduous devotion to such pleasures as New York affords. Two days after my arrival, I set out for an airing at Coney Island, leaving my hotel at four in the afternoon. On my way down Broadway I was suddenly startled at hearing my name spoken from behind me, and appalled, on turning, to see standing with outstretched hands no less a person than my defunct chum, Hawley Hicks."

"Impossible," said I.

"Exactly my remark," returned Number 5010. "To which I added, 'Hawley Hicks, it can't be you!'

"'But it is me,' he replied.

"And then I was convinced, for Hawley never was good on his grammar. I looked at him a minute, and then I said, 'But, Hawley, I thought you were dead.'

"'I am,' he answered. 'But why should a little thing like that stand between friends?'

"'It shouldn't, Hawley,' I answered, meekly; 'but it's condemnedly unusual, you know, for a man to associate even with his best friends fifteen years after they've died and been buried.'

"'Do you mean to say, Austin, that just because I was weak enough once to succumb to a bad cold, you, the dearest friend of my youth, the closest companion of my school-days, the partner of my childish joys, intend to go back on me here in a strange city?'

"'Hawley,' I answered, huskily, 'not a bit of it. My letter of credit, my room at the hotel, my dress suit, even my ticket to Coney Island, are at your disposal; but I think the partner of your childish joys ought first to be let in on the around-floor of this enterprise, and informed how the deuce you manage to turn up in New York fifteen years subsequent to your obsequies. Is New York the hereafter for boys of your kind, or is this some freak of my imagination?'

"That was an eminently proper question," I put in, just to show that while the story I was hearing terrified me, I was not altogether speechless.

"It was, indeed," said 5010; "and Hawley recognized it as such, for he replied at once.

"'Neither,' said he. 'Your imagination is all right, and New York is neither heaven nor the other place. The fact is, I'm spooking, and I can tell you, Austin, it's just about the finest kind of work there is. If you could manage to shuffle off your mortal coil and get in with a lot of ghosts, the way I have, you'd be playing in great luck.'

"'Thanks for the hint, Hawley,' I said, with a grateful smile; 'but, to tell you the truth, I do not find that life is entirely bad. I get my three meals a day, keep my pocket full of coin, and sleep eight hours every night on a couch that couldn't be

44

more desirable if it were studded with jewels and had mineral springs.'

"'That's your mortal ignorance, Austin,' he retorted. 'I lived long enough to appreciate the necessity of being ignorant, but your style of existence is really not to be mentioned in the same cycle with mine. You talk about three meals a day, as if that were an ideal; you forget that with the eating your labor is just begun; those meals have to be digested, every one of 'em, and if you could only understand it, it would appall you to see what a fearful wear and tear that act of digestion is. In my life you are feasting all the time, but with no need for digestion. You speak of money in your pockets; well, I have none, yet am I the richer of the two. I don't need money.

The world is mine. If I chose to I could pour the contents of that jeweller's window into your lap in five seconds, but cui bono? The gems delight my eye quite as well where they are; and as for travel, Austin, of which you have always been fond, the spectral method beats all. Just watch me!'

"I watched him as well as I could for a minute," said 5010; "and then he disappeared. In another minute he was before me again.

"'Well,' I said, 'I suppose you've been around the block in that time, eh?'

He roared with laughter. 'Around the block?' he ejaculated. 'I have done the Continent of Europe, taken a run through China, haunted the Emperor of Japan, and sailed around the Horn since I left you a minute ago.'

"He was a truthful boy in spite of his peculiarities, Hawley was," said Surrennes, quietly, "so I had to believe what he said. He abhorred lies."

"That was pretty fast travelling, though," said I. "He'd make a fine messenger-boy."

"That's so. I wish I'd suggested it to him," smiled my host. "But I can tell you, sir, I was astonished. 'Hawley,' I said, 'you always were a fast youth, but I never thought you would develop into this. I wonder you're not out of breath after such a journey.'

"'Another point, my dear Austin, in favor of my mode of existence. We spooks have no breath to begin with. Consequently, to get out of it is no deprivation. But, I say,' he added, 'whither are you bound?'

"'To Coney Island to see the sights,' I replied. 'Won't you join me?'

"'Not I,' he replied. 'Coney Island is tame. When I first joined the spectre band, it seemed to me that nothing could delight me more than an eternal round of gayety like that; but, Austin, I have changed. I have developed a good deal since you and I were parted at the grave.'

"'I should say you had,' I answered. 'I doubt if many of your old friends would know you.'

"'You seem to have had difficulty in so doing yourself, Austin,' he replied, regretfully, 'but see here, old chap, give up Coney Island, and spend the evening with me at the club. You'll have a good time, I can assure you.'

"'The club?' I said. 'You don't mean to say you visions have a club?'

"'I do indeed; the Ghost Club is the most flourishing association of choice spirits in the world. We have rooms in every city in creation; and the finest part of it is there are no dues to be paid. The membership list holds some of the finest names in history—Shakespeare, Milton, Chaucer, Napoleon Bonaparte, Cæsar, George Washington, Mozart, Frederick the Great, Marc Antony—Cassius was black-balled on Cæsar's account—Galileo, Confucius.'

"'You admit the Chinese, eh?' I queried.

"'Not always,' he replied. 'But Con was such a good fellow they hadn't the heart to keep him out; but you see, Austin, what a lot of fine fellows there are in it.'

45

Yes, it's a magnificent list, and I should say they made a pretty interesting set of fellows to hear talk,' I put in.

"'Well, rather,' Hawley replied. 'I wish you could have heard a debate between Shakespeare and Cæsar on the resolution, "The Pen is mightier than the Sword;" it was immense.'

"'I should think it might have been,' I said. 'Which won?'

"'The sword party. They were the best fighters; though on the merits of the argument Shakespeare was 'way ahead.'

If I thought I'd stand a chance of seeing spooks like that, I think I'd give up Coney Island and go with you,' I said.

"'Well,' replied Hawley, 'that's just the kind of a chance you do stand. They'll all be there tonight, and as this is ladies' day, you might meet Lucretia Borgia, Cleopatra, and a few other feminine apparitions of considerable note.'

"'That settles it. I am yours for the rest of the day,' I said, and so we adjourned to the rooms of the Ghost Club.

"These rooms were in a beautiful house on Fifth Avenue; the number of the house you will find on consulting the court records. I have forgotten it. It was a large, broad, brown-stone structure, and must have been over one hundred and fifty feet in depth. Such fittings I never saw before; everything was in the height of luxury, and I am quite certain that among beings to whom money is a measure of possibility no such magnificence is attainable. The paintings on the walls were by the most famous artists of our own and other days. The rugs on the superbly polished floors were worth fortunes, not only for their exquisite beauty, but also for their extreme rarity.

In keeping with these were the furniture and bric-à-brac. In short, my dear sir, I had never dreamed of anything so dazzlingly, so superbly magnificent as that apartment into which I was ushered by the ghost of my quondam friend Hawley Hicks.

"At first I was speechless with wonder, which seemed to amuse Hicks very much."

"'Pretty fine, eh?' he said, with a short laugh.

"'Well,' I replied, in a moment, 'considering that you can get along without money, and that all the resources of the world are at your disposal, it is not more than half bad. Have you a library?'

"I was always fond of books," explained 5010 in parenthesis to me, "and so was quite anxious to see what the club of ghosts could show in the way of literary treasures. Imagine my surprise when Hawley informed me that the club had no collection of the sort to appeal to the bibliophile.

"'No,' he answered, 'we have no library.'

"'Rather strange,' I said, 'that a club to which men like Shakespeare, Milton, Edgar Allan Poe, and other deceased literati belong should be deficient in that respect.'

"'Not at all,' said he. 'Why should we want books when we have the men themselves to tell their tales to us? Would you give a rap to possess a set of Shakespeare if William himself would sit down and rattle off the whole business to you any time you chose to ask him to do it? Would you follow Scott's printed narratives through their devious and tedious periods if Sir Walter in spirit would come to you on demand, and tell you all the old stories over again in a tenth part of the time it would take you to read the introduction to one of them?'

"'I fancy not,' I said. 'Are you in such luck?'

"'I am,' said Hawley; 'only personally I never send for Scott or Shakespeare. I prefer something lighter than either—Douglas Jerrold or Marryat. But best of all, I like to sit down and hear Noah swap animal stories with Davy Crockett. Noah's the brightest man of his age in the club. Adam's kind of slow.'

"'How about Solomon?' I asked, more to be flippant than with any desire for information. I was much amused to hear Hawley speak of these great spirits as if he and they were chums of long standing.

"'Solomon has resigned from the club,' he said, with a sad sigh. 'He was a good fellow, Solomon was, but he thought he knew it all until old Doctor Johnson got hold of him, and then he knuckled under. It's rather rough for a man to get firmly established in his belief that he is the wisest creature going, and then, after a couple of thousand years, have an Englishman come along and tell him things he never knew before, especially the way Sam Johnson delivers himself of his opinions. Johnson never cared whom he hurt, you know, and when he got after Solomon, he did it with all his might.'

"I wonder if Boswell was there?" I ventured, interrupting 5010 in his extraordinary narrative for an instant.

"Yes, he was there," returned the prisoner. "I met him later in the evening; but he isn't the spook he might be. He never had much spirit anyhow, and when he died he had to leave his nose behind him, and that settled him."

"Of course," I answered. "Boswell with no nose to stick into other people's affairs would have been like Othello with Desdemona left out. But go on. What did you do next?"

"Well," 5010 resumed, "after I'd looked about me, and drunk my fill of the magnificence on every hand, Hawley took me into the music-room, and introduced me to Mozart and Wagner and a few other great composers. In response to my request, Wagner played an impromptu version of 'Daisy Bell' on the organ. It was great; not much like 'Daisy Bell,' of course; more like a collision between a cyclone and a simoom in a tin-plate mining camp, in fact, but, nevertheless, marvellous. I tried to remember it afterwards, and jotted down a few notes, but I found the first bar took up seven sheets of fool's-cap, and so gave it up. Then Mozart tried his hand on a banjo for my amusement, Mendelssohn sang a half-dozen of his songs without words, and then Gottschalk played one of Poe's weird stories on the piano.

"Then Carlyle came in, and Hawley introduced me to him, he was a gruff old gentleman, and seemingly anxious to have Froude become an eligible, and I judged from the rather fierce manner in which he handled a club he had in his hand, that there were one or two other men of prominence still living he was anxious to meet. Dickens, too, was desirous of a two-minute interview with certain of his at present purely mortal critics; and, between you and me, if the wink that Bacon gave Shakespeare when I spoke of Ignatius Donnelly meant anything, the famous cryptogrammarian will do well to drink a bottle of the elixir of life every morning before breakfast, and stave off dissolution as long as he can. There's no getting around the fact, sir,"

Surrennes added, with a significant shake of the head, "that the present leaders of literary thought with critical tendencies are going to have the hardest kind of a time when they cross the river and apply for admission to the Ghost Club. I don't ask for any better fun than that of watching from a safe distance the initiation ceremonies of the next dozen who go over. And as an Englishman, sir, who thoroughly believes in and admires Lord Wolseley, if I were out of jail and able to do it. I'd write him a letter, and warn him that he would better revise his estimates of certain famous soldiers no longer living if he desires to find rest in that mysterious other world whither he must eventually betake himself. They've got their swords sharpened for him, and he'll discover an instance when he gets over there in which the sword is mightier than the pen.

"After that, Hawley took me up-stairs and introduced me to the spirit of Napoleon Bonaparte, with whom I passed about twenty-five minutes talking over his victories and defeats. He told me he never could understand how a man like Wellington came to defeat him at Waterloo, and added that he had sounded the Iron Duke on the subject, and found him equally ignorant.

"So the afternoon and evening passed. I met quite a number of famous ladies— Catherine, Marie Louise, Josephine, Queen Elizabeth, and others. Talked architecture with Queen Anne, and was surprised to learn that she never saw a Queen Anne cottage. I took Peg Woffington down to supper, and altogether had a fine time of it."

"But, my dear Surrennes," I put in at this point, "I fail to see what this has to do with your defence in your trial for stealing spoons."

"I am coming to that," said 5010, sadly. "I dwell on the moments passed at the club because they were the happiest of my life, and am loath to speak of what followed, but I suppose I must.

It was all due to Queen Isabella that I got into trouble. Peg Woffington presented me to Queen Isabella in the supper-room, and while her majesty and I were talking, I spoke of how beautiful everything in the club was, and admired especially a half-dozen old Spanish spoons upon the side-board. When I had done this, the Queen called to Ferdinand, who was chatting with Columbus on the other side of the room, to come to her, which he did with alacrity. I was presented to the King, and then my troubles began.

"'Mr. Surrennes admires our spoons, Ferdinand,' said the Queen.

The King smiled, and turning to me observed, 'Sir, they are yours. Er—waiter, just do these spoons up and give them to Mr. Surrennes.'

"Of course," said 5010, "I protested against this; whereupon the King looked displeased.

"It is a rule of our club, sir, as well as an old Spanish custom, for us to present to our guests anything that they may happen openly to admire. You are surely sufficiently well acquainted with the etiquette of club life to know that guests may not with propriety decline to be governed by the regulations of the club whose hospitality they are enjoying.'

"'I certainly am aware of that, my dear King,' I replied, 'and of course I accept the spoons with exceeding deep gratitude. My remonstrance was prompted solely by my desire to explain to you that I was unaware of any such regulation, and to assure you that when I ventured to inform your good wife that the spoons had excited my sincerest admiration, I was not hinting that it would please me greatly to be accounted their possessor.'

"'Your courtly speech, sir,' returned the King, with a low bow, 'is ample assurance of your sincerity, and I beg that you will put the spoons in your pocket and say no more. They are yours. Verb. sap.'

I thanked the great Spaniard and said no more, pocketing the spoons with no little exultation, because, having always been a lover of the quaint and beautiful, I was glad to possess such treasures, though I must confess to some misgivings as to the possibility of their being unreal.

Shortly after this episode I looked at my watch and discovered that it was getting well on towards eleven o'clock, and I sought out Hawley for the purpose of thanking him for a delightful evening and of taking my leave. I met him in the hall talking to Euripides on the subject of the amateur stage in the United States. What they said I did not stop to hear, but offering my hand to Hawley informed him of my intention to depart.

"'Well, old chap,' he said, affectionately, 'I'm glad you came. It's always a pleasure to see you, aid I hope we may meet again some time soon.' And then, catching sight of my bundle, he asked, 'What have you there?'

"I informed him of the episode in the supper-room, and fancied I perceived a look of annoyance on his countenance.

"'I didn't want to take them, Hawley,' I said; 'but Ferdinand insisted.'

"'Oh, it's all right!' returned Hawley. 'Only I'm sorry! You'd better get along home with them as quickly as you can and say nothing; and, above all, don't try to sell them.'

"'But why?' I asked. 'I'd much prefer to leave them here if there is any question of the propriety of my—'

"Here," continued 5010, "Hawley seemed to grow impatient, for he stamped his foot angrily, and bade me go at once or there might be trouble. I proceeded to obey him, and left the house instanter, slamming the door somewhat angrily behind me. Hawley's unceremonious way of speeding his parting guest did not seem to me to be exactly what I had a right to expect at the time. I see now what his object was, and acquit him of any intention to be rude, though I must say if I ever catch him again, I'll wring an explanation from him for having introduced me into such bad company.

"As I walked down the steps," said 5010, "the chimes of the neighboring church were clanging out the hour of eleven. I stopped on the last step to look for a possible hansom-cab, when a portly gentleman accompanied by a lady started to mount the stoop. The man eyed me narrowly for a moment, and then, sending the lady up the steps, he turned to me and said,

"'What are you doing here?'

"'I've just left the club,' I answered. 'It's all right. I was Hawley Hicks's guest. Whose ghost are you?'

"'What the deuce are you talking about?' he asked, rather gruffly, much to my surprise and discomfort.

"'I tried to give you a civil answer to your question,' I returned, indignantly.

"'I guess you're crazy—or a thief,' he rejoined.

"'See here, friend,' I put in, rather impressively, 'just remember one thing. You are talking to a gentleman, and I don't take remarks of that sort from anybody, spook or otherwise. I don't care if you are the ghost of the Emperor Nero, if you give me any more of your impudence I'll dissipate you to the four quarters of the universe—see?'

"Then he grabbed me and shouted for the police, and I was painfully surprised to find that instead of coping with a mysterious being from another world, I had two hundred and ten pounds of flesh and blood to handle. The populace began to gather. The million and a half of small boys of whom I have already spoken—mostly street gamins, owing to the lateness of the hour—sprang up from all about us. Hansom-cab drivers, attracted by the noise of our altercation, drew up to the sidewalk to watch developments, and then, after the usual fifteen or twenty minutes, the blue-coat emissary of justice appeared.

"'Phat's dthis?' he asked.

"'I have detected this man leaving my house in a suspicious manner,' said my adversary. 'I have reason to suspect him of thieving.'

"'Your house!' I ejaculated, with fine scorn. 'I've got you there; this is the house of the New York Branch of the Ghost Club. If you want it proved,' I added, turning to the policeman, 'ring the bell, and ask.'

"'Oi t'ink dthat's a fair prophosition,' observed the policeman. 'Is the motion siconded?'

"'Oh, come now!' cried my captor. 'Stop this nonsense, or I'll report you to the department. This is my house, and has been for twenty years. I want this man searched.'

"'Oi hov no warrant permithin' me to invistigate the contints ov dthe gintle-mon's clothes,' returned the intelligent member of the force. 'But av yez'll take yer solemn alibi dthat yez hov rayson t' belave the gintlemon has worked ony *habeas corpush* business on yure prophery, oi'll jug dthe blagyard.'

"'I'll be responsible,' said the alleged owner of the house. 'Take him to the sta-tion.'

"'I refuse to move,' I said.

"'Oi'll not carry yez,' said the policeman, 'and oi'd advoise ye to furnish yure own locomotion. Av ye don't, oi'll use me club. Dthot's th' ounly waa yez'll git dthe ambulanch.'

"'Oh, well, if you insist,' I replied, 'of course I'll go. I have nothing to fear.'

("You see," added 5010 to me, in parenthesis, "the thought suddenly flashed across my mind that if all was as my captor said, if the house was really his and not the Ghost Club's, and if the whole thing was only my fancy, the spoons themselves would turn out to be entirely fanciful; so I was all right—or at least I thought I was. So we trotted along to the police station. On the way I told the policeman the whole story, which impressed him so that he crossed himself a half-dozen times, and ut-tered numerous ejaculatory prayers—'Maa dthe shaints presharve us,' and 'Hivin hov mershy,' and others of a like import.)

"'Waz dthe ghosht ov Dan O'Connell dthere?' he asked.

"'Yes,' I replied. 'I shook hands with it.'

"'Let me shaak dthot hana,' he said, his voice trembling with emotion, and then he whispered in my ear: 'Oi belave yez to be innoshunt; but av yez ain't, for the love of Dan, oi'll let yez eshcape.'

"'Thanks, old fellow,' I replied. 'But I am innocent of wrong-doing, as I can prove.'

"Alas!" sighed the convict, "it was not to be so. When I arrived at the station-house, I was dumbfounded to learn that the spoons were all, too real. I told my story to the sergeant, and pointed to the monogram, 'G. C.,' on the spoons as evidence that my story was correct; but even that told against me, for the alleged owner's ini-tials were G. C.—his name I withhold—and the monogram only served to substan-tiate his claim to the spoons. Worst of all, he claimed that he had been robbed on several occasions before this, and by midnight I found myself locked up in a dirty cell to await trial.

"I got a lawyer, and, as I said before, even he declined to believe my story, and suggested the insanity dodge. Of course I wouldn't agree to that. I tried to get him to subpoena Ferdinand and Isabella and Euripides and Hawley Hicks in my behalf, and all he'd do was to sit there and shake his head at me. Then I suggested going up to the Metropolitan Opera-house some fearful night as the clock struck twelve, and try to serve papers on Wagner's spook—all of which he treated as unworthy of a moment's consideration. Then I was tried, convicted, and sentenced to live in this beastly hole; but I have one strong hope to buoy me up, and if that is realized, I'll be free tomorrow morning."

"What is that?" I asked.

"Why," he answered, with a sigh, as the bell rang summoning him to his supper —"why, the whole horrid business has been so weird and uncanny that I'm beginning to believe it's all a dream. If it is, why, I'll wake up, and find myself at home in bed; that's all. I've clung to that hope for nearly a year now, but it's getting weaker every minute."

"Yes, 5010," I answered, rising and shaking him by the hand in parting; "that's a mighty forlorn hope, because I'm pretty wide awake myself at this moment, and can't be a part of your dream. The great pity is you didn't try the insanity dodge."

"Tut!" he answered. "That is the last resource of a weak mind."

THE SHADOWS OF THE DEAD,
by Louis Becke

"It is bad to speak of the ghosts of the dead when their shadows may be near," said Tulpé, the professed Christian, but pure, unsophisticated heathen at heart; "no one but a fool—or a careless white man such as thee, Tenisoni—would do that."

Denison laughed, but Kusis, the stalwart husband of black-browed Tulpé, looked at him with grave reproval, and said in English, as he struck his paddle into the water—

"Tulpé speak true, Mr. Denison. This place is a bad place at night-time, suppose you no make fire before you sleep. Plenty men—white men—been die here, and now us native people only come here when plenty of us come together. Then we not feel much afraid. Oh, yes, these two little island very bad places; long time ago many white men die here in the night. And sometimes, if any man come here and sleep by himself, he hear the dead white men walk about and cry out."

* * * *

They—Denison, the supercargo of the *Leonora*, Kusis, the head man of the village near by and Tulpé, his wife, and little Kinia, their daughter—had been out fishing on the reef, but had met with but scant success; for in the deep coral pools that lay between the inner and outer reefs of the main island were hundreds of huge blue and gold striped leatherjackets, which broke their hooks and bit their lines. So they had ceased awhile, that they might rest till nightfall upon one of two little islets of palms, that like floating gardens raised their verdured heights from the deep waters of the slumbering lagoon.

Slowly they paddled over the glassy surface, and as the little craft cut her way noiselessly through the water, the dying sun turned the slopes of vivid green on Mont Buache to changing shades on gold and purple light, and the dark blue of the water of the reef-bound lagoon paled and shallowed and turned to bright transparent green with a bottom of shining snow-white sand—over which swift black shadows swept as startled fish fled seaward in affright beneath the slender hull of the light canoe. Then as the last booming notes of the great grey-plumaged mountain-pigeons echoed through the forest aisles, the sun touched the western sea-rim in a flood of misty golden haze, and plunging their paddles together in a last stroke they grounded upon the beach of a lovely little bay, scarce a hundred feet in curve from point to point; and whilst Kusis and Tulpé lit a fire to cook some fish for the white man, Denison clambered to the summit of the island and looked shoreward upon the purpling outline of the mainland a league away.

Half a mile distant he could see the sharp peaks of the grey-thatched houses in Leassé village still standing out plainly in the clear atmosphere, and from every house a slender streak of pale blue smoke rose straight up skywards, for the land-breeze had not yet risen, and the smoky haze of the rollers thundering westward hung like a filmy mantle of white over long, long lines of curving reef. Far inland, the great southern spur of the mountain that the Frenchman Duperrey had named Buache, had cloaked its sides in the shadows of the night, though its summit yet blazed with the last red shafts of gold from the sunken sun. And over the tops of the drooping palms of the little isle, Denison heard the low cries and homeward flight of ocean-roving birds as they sped shoreward to their rookeries among the dense mangrove shrubs behind Leassé. Some pure white, red-footed boatswain birds, whose home was among the foliage of the two islets, muttered softly about as they sank like flakes of falling snow among the branches of the palms and bread-fruit trees around him. All day long had they hovered high in air above the sweeping roll of the wide Pacific, and one by one they were coming back to rest, and Denison could see their white forms settling down on the drooping palm-branches, to rise with flapping wing and sharp, fretful croak as some belated wanderer fluttered noiselessly down and pushed his way to a perch amidst his companions, to nestle together till the bright rays of sunlight lit up the ocean blue once more.

At a little distance from the beach stood a tiny thatched roofed house with sides open to welcome the cooling breath of the land-breeze that, as the myriad stars came out, stole down from the mountains to the islet trees and then rippled the waters of the shining lagoon.

The house had been built by the people of Leassé, who used it as a rest-house when engaged in fishing in the vicinity of the village. Rolled up and placed over the cross-beams were a number of soft mats, and as Denison returned Kusis took these down and placed them upon the ground, which was covered with a thick layer of pebbles. Throwing himself down on the mats, Denison filled his pipe and smoked, while Tulpé and the child made an oven of heated stones to cook the fish they had caught. Kusis had already plucked some young drinking coconuts, and Denison heard their heavy fall as he threw them to the ground. And only that Kusis had brave blood in his veins, they had had nothing to drink that night, for no Strong's Islander would ascend a coconut tree there after dark, for devils, fiends, goblins, the ghosts of men long dead, and evil spirits flitted to and fro amid the boscage of the islet once night had fallen. And even Kusis, despite the long years he had spent among white men in his cruises in American whaleships in his younger days, chid his wife and child sharply for not hastening to him and carrying the nuts away as they fell.

Then, as Denison and Kusis waited for the oven to be opened, Tulpé and Kinia came inside the hut and sat down beside them, and listened to Kusis telling the white man of a deep, sandy-bottomed pool, near to the islets, which, when the tide came in over the reef at night-time, became filled with big fish, which preyed upon the swarms of minnows that made the pool their home.

"'Tis there, Tenisoni, that we shall go when we have eaten," he said, and he dropped his voice to a whisper, "and there shall we tell thee the story of the dead white men."

So, when the fish was cooked, Tulpé and Kinia hurriedly took it from the oven and carried to the canoe, in which they all sat and ate, and then pushing out into the lagoon again they paddled slowly along in shallow water till Denison saw the white sandy sides of a deep, dark pool glimmering under the starlight of the island night. Softly the girl Kinia lowered the stone anchor down till it touched bottom two fathoms below, on the very edge; and then payed out the kellick line whilst her father backed the canoe out from the quickly shelving sides into the centre, where she lay head-on to the gentle current.

For many hours they fished, and soon the canoe was half-filled with great pink and pearly-hued groper and blue-backed, silver-sided sea salmon, and then Denison, wearying of the sport, stretched himself upon the outrigger and smoked whilst Tulpé told him of the tale of the white men who had once lived and died on the little islets.

"'Twas long before the time that the two French fighting-ships came here and anchored in this harbour of Leassé. Other ships had come to Kusaie [Strong's Island], and white men had come ashore at Lêla and spoken with the king and chiefs, and made presents of friendship to them, and been given turtle and hogs in return. This was long before my mother was married, and then this place of Leassé, which is now so poor, and hath but so few people in it, was a great town, the houses of which covered all the flat land between the two points of the bay. She, too, was named I am—Tulpé—and came from a family that lived under the strong arm of the king at Lêla, where they had houses and many plantations. In those days there were three great chiefs on Kusaie, one at Lêla, from where my mother came, one at Utwe, and one here at Leassé. Peace had been between them all for nearly two years, so, when the news came here that there were two ships at anchor in the king's harbour, many of the people of Leassé went thither in their canoes to see the strangers, for these ships were the first the people had seen for, it may have been, twenty years. Among those that went from Leassé was a young man named Kasilak—Kasi the big or strong, for he was the tallest and strongest man on this side of the island, and a great wrestler. There were in all nearly two hundred men and women went from Leassé, and when they reached the narrow passage to Lêla, they saw that the harbour was covered with canoes full of the people from the great town there. These clustered about the ships so thickly that those that came from Leassé could not draw near enough to them to look at the white men, so they rested on their paddles and waited awhile. Presently there came out upon a high part of the ship a chief whose name was Malik. He was the king's foster-brother, and a great fighting-man, and was hated by the people of Leassé for having ravaged all the low-lying country from the mountains to the shore ten years before, slaying women and children as well as men, and casting their bodies into the flames of their burning houses.

"But now, because of the peace that was between Leassé and Lêla, he showed his white teeth in a smile of welcome, and, standing upon the high stern part of the ship, he called out, 'Welcome, O friends!' and bade them paddle their canoes to the shore, to the great houses of the king, his brother, where they would be made welcome, and where food would be prepared for them to eat.

"So, much as they desired to go on board the ships, they durst not offend such a man as Malik, and paddled to the shore, where they were met by the king's slaves, who drew their canoes high up on the beach, and covered them with mats to protect them from the sun, and then the king himself came to meet them with fair words and smiles of friendship.

"'Welcome, O men of Leassé,' he said. 'See, my people have covered thy canoes with mats from the sun, for now that there is no hate between us, ye shall remain here at Lêla with me for many days. And so that there shall be no more bloodletting between my people and thine, shall I give every young man among ye that is yet unmarried a wife from these people of mine. Come, now, and eat and drink.'

"So all the two hundred sat down in one of the king's houses, and while they ate and drank there came boats from the ships, and the white men, whom Malik led ashore, came into the house where they sat, and spoke to them. In those days there were but three or four of the Kusaie men who understood English, and these Malik kept by him, so that he could put words into their mouths when he desired to speak to the white strangers. These white men, so my mother said, wore short, broadbladed swords in sheaths made of thick black skins, and pistols were thrust through belts of skin around their waists. Their hair, too, was dressed like that of the men of

Kusaie—it hung down in a short, thick roll, and was tied at the end.

"Kasi, who was the father of this my husband, Kusis, sat a little apart from the rest of the Leassé people. Beside him was a young girl named Nehi, his cousin. She had never before left her home, and the strange faces of the men of Lêla made her so frightened that she clung to Kasi's arm in fear, and when the white men came into the house she flung her arms around her cousin's neck and laid her face against his naked chest. Presently, as the white men walked to and fro among the people, they stopped in front of Kasi and Nehi, and one of them, who was the captain of the largest of the two ships, desired Kasi to stand up so that he might see his great stature the better. So he stood up, and Nehi the girl, still clinging to his arm, stood up with him.

"'He is a brave-looking man,' said the white officer to Malik. 'Such men as he are few and far between. Only this man here,' and he touched a young white man who stood beside him on the arm, 'is his equal in strength and fine looks.' And with that the young white man, who was an officer of the smaller of the two ships, laughed, and held out his hand to Kasi, and then his eyes, blue, like the deep sea, fell upon the face of Nehi, whose dark ones looked wonderingly into his.

"'Who is this girl? Is she the big man's sister?' he asked of Malik. Then Malik told him, through the mouth of one of the three Kusaie men, who spoke English, that the girl's name was Nehi, and that with many of her people she had come from Leassé to see the fighting-ships.

"By and by the white men with Malik went away to talk and eat, and drank kava in the house of the king, his brother; but presently the younger white man came back with Rijon, a native who spoke English, and sat down beside Kasi and his cousin Nehi, and talked with them for a long time. And this he told them of himself. That he was the second chief of the little ship, that with but two masts; and because of the long months they had spent upon the sea, and of the bad blood between the common sailor men and the captain, he was wearied of the ship, and desired to leave it. Ten others were there on his own ship of a like mind, and more than a score on the larger ship, which had twenty-and-two great cannons on her deck. And then he and Rijon and Kasi talked earnestly together, and Kasi promised to aid him; and so that Rijon should not betray them to Malik or the two captains, the young white man promised to give him that night a musket and a pistol as an earnest of greater gifts, when he and others with him had escaped from the ships, and were under the roofs of the men of Leassé. So then he pressed the hand of Kasi, and again his eyes sought those of Nehi, the girl, as he turned away.

"Then Rijon, who stayed, drew near to Kasi, and said—

"'What shall be mine if I tell thee of a plan that is in the mind of a great man here to put thee and all those of Leassé with thee to death?'

"'Who is the man? Is it Malik?'

"'It is Malik.'

"'Then,' said Kasi, 'help me to escape from this trap, and thou shalt be to me as mine own brother; of all that I possess half shall be thine.'

"And then Rijon, who was a man who hated bloodshed, and thought it hard and cruel that Malik should slay so many unarmed people who came to him in peacetime, swore to help Kasi in his need. And the girl Nehi took his hand and kissed it, and wept.

"By and by, when Rijon had gone, there came into the big house where the people of Leassé were assembled a young girl named Tulpé—she who afterwards became my mother. And coming over to where Kasi and his cousin sat, she told them she brought a message from the king. That night, she said, there was to be a great feast, so that the white men from the ships might see the dancing and wrestling that were to follow; and the king had sent her to say that he much desired the people from Leassé to join in the feasting and dancing; and with the message he sent further gifts of baked fish and turtle meat and many baskets of fruit.

"Kasi, though he knew well that the king and Malik, his brother, meant to murder him and all his people, smiled at the girl, and said, 'It is good; we shall come, and I shall wrestle with the best man ye have here.'

"Then he struck the palm of his hand on the mat upon which he sat, and said to the girl Tulpé, 'Sit thou here, and eat with us,' for he was taken with her looks, and wanted speech with her.

"'Nay,' she said, with a smile, though her voice trembled strangely, and her eyes filled with tears as she spoke. 'Why ask me to sit with thee when thou hast so handsome a wife?' And she pointed to Nehi, whose hand lay upon her cousin's arm.

"''Tis but my sister Nehi, my father's brother's child,' he answered. 'No wife have I, and none do I want but thee. What is thy name?'

"'I am Tulpé, the daughter of Malik.'

"Then Kasi was troubled in his mind; for now he hated Malik, but yet was he determined to make Tulpé his wife, first because he desired her for her soft voice and gentle ways, and then because she might be a shield for the people of Leassé against her father's vengeance. So drawing her down beside him, he and Nehi made much of her; and Tulpé's heart went out to him; for he was a man whose deeds as a wrestler were known in every village on the island. But still as she tried to eat and drink and to smile at his words of love, the tears fell one by one, and she became very silent and sad; and presently, putting aside her food, she leant her face on Nehi's shoulder and sobbed.

"'Why dost thou weep, little one?' said Kasi, tenderly.

"She made no answer awhile, but then turned her face to him.

"'Because, O Kasi the Wrestler, of an evil dream which came to me in the night as I lay in my father's house.'

"'Tell me thy dream,' said Kasi.

"First looking around her to see that none but themselves could hear her, she took his hand in hers, and whispered—

"'Aye, Kasi, I will tell thee. This, then, was my dream: I saw the bodies of men and women and children, whose waists were girt about with red and yellow girdles of *oap*, floating upon a pool of blood. Strange faces were they all to me in my dream, but now two of them are not. And it is for this I weep; for those two faces were thine own and that of this girl by my side.'

"Then Kasi knew that she meant to warn him of her father's cruel plot, for only the people of Leassé wore girdles of the bark of the plant called *oap*. So then he told her of that which Rijon had spoken, and Tulpé wept again.

"'It is true,' she said, 'and I did but seek to warn thee, for no dream came to me in the night; yet do I know that even now my father is planning with his brother the king how that they may slaughter thee all tonight when ye sleep after the dance. What can I do to help thee?'

"They talked together again, and planned what should be done; and then Tulpé went quietly away lest Malik should grow suspicious of her. And Kasi went quickly about among his people telling them of the treachery of Malik, and bade them do what he should bid them when the time came. And then Rijon went to and fro between Kasi and the big white man, carrying messages and settling what was to be done.

"When darkness came great fires were lit in the dance-house and the town square, and the great feast began. And the king and Malik made much of Kasi and his people, and placed more food before them than even was given to their own people. Then when the feast was finished the two ship captains came on shore, and sat on a mat beside the king, and the women danced and the men wrestled. And Kasi, whose heart was bursting with rage though his lips smiled, was praised by Malik and the king for his great strength and skill, for he overcame all who stood up to wrestle with him.

"When the night was far gone, Kasi told Malik that he and his people were weary, and asked that they might sleep. And Malik, who only waited till they slept, said, 'Go, and sleep in peace.'

"But as soon as Kasi and those with him were away out of sight from the great swarm of people who still danced and wrestled in the open square, they ran quickly to the beach where their canoes were lying, and Kasi lit a torch and waved it thrice in the air towards the black shadows of the two ships. Then he waited.

"Suddenly on the ships there arose a great commotion and loud cries, and in a little time there came the sound of boats rowing quickly to the shore. And then came a great flash of light from the side of one of the ships and the thunder of a cannon's voice.

"'Quick,' cried Kasi; 'launch the canoes, lest we be slain here on the beach!' And ere the echoes of the cannon-shot had died away in the mountain caves of Lêla, the men of Leassé had launched their canoes and paddled swiftly out to meet the boats.

"As the boats and canoes drew near, Rijon stood up in the bows of the foremost boat, and the white sailors ceased rowing so that he and Kasi might talk. But there was but little time, for already the sound of the cannon and the cries and struggling on board the ships had brought a great many of the Lêla people to the beach; fires were lit, and conch shells were blown, and Malik and his men began to fire their muskets at the escaping canoes. Presently, too, the white men in the boats began to handle their muskets and fire back in return, when their leader bade them cease, telling them that it was but Malik's men firing at Kasi's people.

"'Now,' said he to Rijon, 'tell this man Kasi to lead the way with his canoes to the passage, and we in the boats shall follow closely, so that if Malik's canoes pursue and overtake us, we white men shall beat them back with our musket-fire.'

"So then Kasi turned his canoes seaward, and the boats followed; and as they rowed and paddled, all keeping closely together, the great cannons of the two ships flashed and thundered and the shot roared above them in the darkness. But yet was no one hurt, for the night was very dark; and soon they reached the deep waters of the passage, and rose and fell to the ocean swell, and still the iron cannon-shot hummed about them, and now and again struck the water near; and on the left-hand shore ran Malik's men with cries of rage, and firing as they ran, till at last they came to the point and could pursue no farther; and soon their cries grew fainter and fainter as the canoes and boats reached the open ocean. Then it happened that one of the white sailors, vexed that a last bullet had whistled near his head, raised his musket and fired into the dark shore whence it came.

"Thou fool!' cried his leader, and he struck the man senseless with the boat's tiller, and then told Rijon to call out to Kasi and his people to pull to the left for their lives, for the flash of the musket would be seen from the ships. Ah, he was a clever white man, for scarce had the canoes and boats turned to the left more than fifty fathoms, when there came a burst of flame from all the cannons on the ships, and a great storm of great iron shot and small leaden bullets lashed the black water into white foam just behind them. After that the firing ceased, and Rijon called out

57

that there was no more danger; for the cunning white man had told him that they could not be pursued—he had broken holes in all the boats that remained on the ships.

"When daylight came, the boats and canoes were far down the coast towards Leassé. Then, as the sun rose from the sea, the men in the boats ceased rowing, and the big white man stood up and beckoned to Kasi to bring his canoe alongside. And when the canoe lay beside the boat, the white man laughed and held out his hand to Kasi and asked for Nehi; and as Nehi rose from the bottom of Kasi's canoe, where she had been sleeping, and stood up beside her cousin, so did Tulpé, the daughter of Malik, stand up beside the white man in his boat, and the two girls threw their arms around each other's necks and wept glad tears. Then as the canoes and boats hoisted their sails to the wind of sunrise, the people saw that Tulpé sat beside Kasi in his canoe, and Nehi, his cousin, sat beside the white man in his boat, with her face covered with her hands so that no one should see her eyes.

"As they sailed along the coast, Tulpé told Kasi how she and Rijon had gone on board the smaller of the two ships, and seen the tall young white man whispering to some of the sailors. Then, when they saw the flash of Kasi's torch, how these sailors sprang upon the others and bound them hand and foot while a boat was lowered, and muskets and food and water put in. Then she and Rijon and the young white leader and some of the sailors got in, and Rijon stood in the bows and guided them to the shore to where Kasi and his people awaited them on the beach.

II

"For nearly three months these white men lived at Leassé, and the father of Kasi, who was chief of the town, made much of them, because they had muskets, and bullets, and powder in plenty, and this made him strong against Malik and the people of Lêla. The ships had sailed away soon after the night of the dance, but the two captains had given the king and Malik many muskets and much powder, and a small cannon, and urged him to pursue and kill all the white men who had deserted the ships.

"'By and by, I will kill them,' said Malik.

"The young white man took Nehi to wife, and was given a tract of land near Leassé, and Kasi became husband to Tulpé, and there grew a great friends hip between the two men. Then came warfare with Lêla again, and of the twenty and two white men ten were killed in a great fight at Utwé with Malik's people, who surprised them as they were building a vessel, for some of them were already weary of Kusaic, and wished to sail away to other lands.

"Soon those that were left began to quarrel among themselves and kill each other, till only seven, beside the husband of Nehi, were left. These, who lived in a village at the south point, seldom came to Leassé, for the big white man would have none of them, and naught but bitter words had passed between them for many months, for he hated their wild, dissolute ways, and their foul manners. Then, too, they had learnt to make grog from coconut toddy, and sometimes, when they were drunken with it, would stagger about from house to house, musket or sword in hand, and frighten the women and children.

"One day it came about that a girl named Luan, who was a blood relation of Nehi, and wife to one of these white men, was walking along a mountain-path, carrying her infant child, when her foot slipped, and she and the infant fell a great distance. When she came to she found that the child had a great wound in its forehead, and was cold and stiff in death. She lifted it up, and when she came to her husband's house she found him lying asleep, drunken with toddy, and when she roused him with her grief he did but curse her.

"Then Luan, with bitter scorn, pointed to the body of the babe and said, 'Oh, thou wicked and drunken father, dost thou not see that thy child is dead?'

"Then in his passion he seized his pistol and struck her on the head, so that she was stunned and fell as if dead.

"That night the people of Leassé saw the seven white men, with their wives and children, paddling over towards the two little islands, carrying all their goods with them, for the people had risen against them by reason of the cruelty of the husband of Luan, and driven them away.

"So there they lived for many weeks, making grog from the coconut trees, and drinking and fighting among themselves all day, and sleeping the sleep of the drunken at night. Their wives toiled for them all day, fishing on the reef, and bringing them taro, yams, and fruit from the mainland. But Luan alone could not work, for she grew weaker and weaker, and one day she died. Then her white husband went to the village from whence they were driven, and seizing the wife of a young man, bore her away to the two islets.

"The next day he whose wife had been stolen came to the husband of Nehi, and said, 'O white man, help me to get back my wife; help me for the sake of Luan, whom this dog slew, and whose blood cries out to thee for vengeance, for was she not a blood relation to Nehi, thy wife?'

"But though the husband of Nehi shook his head and denied the man the musket he asked for, he said naught when at night-time a hundred men, carrying knives and clubs in their hands, gathered together in the council-house, and talked of the evil lives of the seven white men, and agreed that the time had come for them to die.

"So in silence they rose up from the mats in the council-house and walked down to the beach, and launching their canoes, paddled across to the islands under cover of the darkness. It so happened that one woman was awake, but all the rest with the white men and their children slept. This woman belonged to Leassé, and had come to the beach to bathe, for the night was hot and windless. Suddenly the canoes surrounded her, and, fearing danger to her white husband, she sought to escape, but a strong hand caught her by the hair, and a voice bade her be silent.

"Now, the man who held her by the hair was her own sister's husband, and he desired to save her life, so he and two others seized and bound her, and quickly tied a waist-girdle over her mouth so that she could not cry out. But she was strong, and struggled so that the girdle slipped off, and she gave a loud cry. And then her sister's husband, lest his chief might say he had failed in his duty, and the white men escape, seized her throat in his hands and pressed it so that she all but died.

"Then the avengers of the blood of Luan sprang out upon the beach, and ran through the palm grove to where the white men's house stood. It was a big house, for they all lived together, and in the middle of the floor a lamp of coconut oil burned, and showed where the seven white men lay.

"And there as they slept were they speared and stabbed to death, although their wives threw their arms around the slayers and besought them to spare their husbands' lives. And long before dawn the canoes returned to Leassé with the wives and children of the slain men, and only the big white man, the husband of Nehi, was left alive out of the twenty and two who came from the ships at Lêla. So that is the story of the two islets, and of the evil men who dwelt there."

* * * *

Denison rose and stretched himself. "And what of the big white man—the husband of Nehi?" he asked; "doth his spirit, too, wander about at night?"

"Nay," said Tulpé, "why should it? There was no innocent blood upon his hand.

59

Both he and Nehi lived and died among us; and tomorrow it may be that Kinia shalt show thee the place whereon their house stood in the far-back years. And true are the words in the Book of Life—'He that sheddeth blood, by man shall his blood be shed.'"

THE ROOM IN THE TOWER,
by E. F. Benson

It is probable that everybody who is at all a constant dreamer has had at least one experience of an event or a sequence of circumstances which have come to his mind in sleep being subsequently realized in the material world. But, in my opinion, so far from this being a strange thing, it would be far odder if this fulfilment did not occasionally happen, since our dreams are, as a rule, concerned with people whom we know and places with which we are familiar, such as might very naturally occur in the awake and daylit world. True, these dreams are often broken into by some absurd and fantastic incident, which puts them out of court in regard to their subsequent fulfilment, but on the mere calculation of chances, it does not appear in the least unlikely that a dream imagined by anyone who dreams constantly should occasionally come true. Not long ago, for instance, I experienced such a fulfilment of a dream which seems to me in no way remarkable and to have no kind of psychical significance. The manner of it was as follows.

A certain friend of mine, living abroad, is amiable enough to write to me about once in a fortnight. Thus, when fourteen days or thereabouts have elapsed since I last heard from him, my mind, probably, either consciously or subconsciously, is expectant of a letter from him. One night last week I dreamed that as I was going upstairs to dress for dinner I heard, as I often heard, the sound of the postman's knock on my front door, and diverted my direction downstairs instead. There, among other correspondence, was a letter from him. Thereafter the fantastic entered, for on opening it I found inside the ace of diamonds, and scribbled across it in his well-known handwriting, "I am sending you this for safe custody, as you know it is running an unreasonable risk to keep aces in Italy." The next evening I was just preparing to go upstairs to dress when I heard the postman's knock, and did precisely as I had done in my dream. There, among other letters, was one from my friend. Only it did not contain the ace of diamonds. Had it done so, I should have attached more weight to the matter, which, as it stands, seems to me a perfectly ordinary coincidence. No doubt I consciously or subconsciously expected a letter from him, and this suggested to me my dream. Similarly, the fact that my friend had not written to me for a fortnight suggested to him that he should do so. But occasionally it is not so easy to find such an explanation, and for the following story I can find no explanation at all. It came out of the dark, and into the dark it has gone again.

All my life I have been a habitual dreamer: the nights are few, that is to say, when I do not find on awaking in the morning that some mental experience has been mine, and sometimes, all night long, apparently, a series of the most dazzling adventures befall me. Almost without exception these adventures are pleasant, though often merely trivial. It is of an exception that I am going to speak.

It was when I was about sixteen that a certain dream first came to me, and this is how it befell. It opened with my being set down at the door of a big red-brick house, where, I understood, I was going to stay. The servant who opened the door told me that tea was being served in the garden, and led me through a low dark-panelled hall, with a large open fireplace, on to a cheerful green lawn set round with flower beds. There were grouped about the tea-table a small party of people, but they were all strangers to me except one, who was a schoolfellow called Jack Stone, clearly the son of the house, and he introduced me to his mother and father and a couple of sisters. I was, I remember, somewhat astonished to find myself here, for the boy in question was scarcely known to me, and I rather disliked what I knew of him; moreover, he had left school nearly a year before. The afternoon was very hot, and an intolerable oppression reigned. On the far side of the lawn ran a red-brick wall, with an iron gate in its center, outside which stood a walnut tree. We sat in the shadow of the house opposite a row of long windows, inside which I could see a table with cloth laid, glimmering with glass and silver. This garden front of the house was very long, and at one end of it stood a tower of three stories, which looked to me much older than the rest of the building.

Before long, Mrs. Stone, who, like the rest of the party, had sat in absolute silence, said to me, "Jack will show you your room: I have given you the room in the tower."

Quite inexplicably my heart sank at her words. I felt as if I had known that I should have the room in the tower, and that it contained something dreadful and significant. Jack instantly got up, and I understood that I had to follow him. In silence we passed through the hall, and mounted a great oak staircase with many corners, and arrived at a small landing with two doors set in it. He pushed one of these open for me to enter, and without coming in himself, closed it after me. Then I knew that my conjecture had been right: there was something awful in the room, and with the terror of nightmare growing swiftly and enveloping me, I awoke in a spasm of terror.

Now that dream or variations on it occurred to me intermittently for fifteen years. Most often it came in exactly this form, the arrival, the tea laid out on the lawn, the deadly silence succeeded by that one deadly sentence, the mounting with Jack Stone up to the room in the tower where horror dwelt, and it always came to a close in the nightmare of terror at that which was in the room, though I never saw what it was. At other times I experienced variations on this same theme. Occasionally, for instance, we would be sitting at dinner in the dining-room, into the windows of which I had looked on the first night when the dream of this house visited me, but wherever we were, there was the same silence, the same sense of dreadful oppression and foreboding. And the silence I knew would always be broken by Mrs. Stone saying to me, "Jack will show you your room: I have given you the room in the tower." Upon which (this was invariable) I had to follow him up the oak staircase with many corners, and enter the place that I dreaded more and more each time that I visited it in sleep. Or, again, I would find myself playing cards still in silence in a drawing-room lit with immense chandeliers, that gave a blinding illumination. What the game was I have no idea; what I remember, with a sense of miserable anticipation, was that soon Mrs. Stone would get up and say to me, "Jack will show you your room: I have given you the room in the tower." This drawing-room where we played cards was next to the dining-room, and, as I have said, was always brilliantly illuminated, whereas the rest of the house was full of dusk and shadows. And yet, how often, in spite of those bouquets of lights, have I not pored over the cards that were dealt me, scarcely able for some reason to see them. Their designs, too, were strange: there were no red suits, but all were black, and among them there were certain cards which were black all over. I hated and dreaded those.

As this dream continued to recur, I got to know the greater part of the house. There was a smoking-room beyond the drawing-room, at the end of a passage with a green baize door. It was always very dark there, and as often as I went there I passed somebody whom I could not see in the doorway coming out. Curious developments, too, took place in the characters that peopled the dream as might happen to living persons. Mrs. Stone, for instance, who, when I first saw her, had been black-haired, became gray, and instead of rising briskly, as she had done at first when she said, "Jack will show you your room: I have given you the room in the tower," got up very feebly, as if the strength was leaving her limbs. Jack also grew up, and became a rather ill-looking young man, with a brown moustache, while one of the sisters ceased to appear, and I understood she was married.

Then it so happened that I was not visited by this dream for six months or more, and I began to hope, in such inexplicable dread did I hold it, that it had passed away for good. But one night after this interval I again found myself being shown out onto the lawn for tea, and Mrs. Stone was not there, while the others were all dressed in black. At once I guessed the reason, and my heart leaped at the thought that perhaps this time I should not have to sleep in the room in the tower, and though we usually all sat in silence, on this occasion the sense of relief made me talk and laugh as I had never yet done. But even then matters were not altogether comfortable, for no one else spoke, but they all looked secretly at each other. And soon the foolish stream of my talk ran dry, and gradually an apprehension worse than anything I had previously known gained on me as the light slowly faded.

Suddenly a voice which I knew well broke the stillness, the voice of Mrs. Stone, saying, "Jack will show you your room: I have given you the room in the tower." It seemed to come from near the gate in the red-brick wall that bounded the lawn, and looking up, I saw that the grass outside was sown thick with gravestones. A curious greyish light shone from them, and I could read the lettering on the grave nearest me, and it was, "In evil memory of Julia Stone." And as usual Jack got up, and again I followed him through the hall and up the staircase with many corners. On this occasion it was darker than usual, and when I passed into the room in the tower I could only just see the furniture, the position of which was already familiar to me. Also there was a dreadful odor of decay in the room, and I woke screaming.

The dream, with such variations and developments as I have mentioned, went on at intervals for fifteen years. Sometimes I would dream it two or three nights in succession; once, as I have said, there was an intermission of six months, but taking a reasonable average, I should say that I dreamed it quite as often as once in a month. It had, as is plain, something of nightmare about it, since it always ended in the same appalling terror, which so far from getting less, seemed to me to gather fresh fear every time that I experienced it. There was, too, a strange and dreadful consistency about it. The characters in it, as I have mentioned, got regularly older, death and marriage visited this silent family, and I never in the dream, after Mrs. Stone had died, set eyes on her again. But it was always her voice that told me that the room in the tower was prepared for me, and whether we had tea out on the lawn, or the scene was laid in one of the rooms overlooking it, I could always see her gravestone standing just outside the iron gate. It was the same, too, with the married daughter; usually she was not present, but once or twice she returned again, in company with a man, whom I took to be her husband. He, too, like the rest of them, was always silent. But, owing to the constant repetition of the dream, I had ceased to attach, in my waking hours, any significance to it. I never met Jack Stone again during all those years, nor did I ever see a house that resembled this dark house of my dream. And then something happened.

I had been in London in this year, up till the end of the July, and during the first week in August went down to stay with a friend in a house he had taken for the summer months, in the Ashdown Forest district of Sussex. I left London early, for John Clinton was to meet me at Forest Row Station, and we were going to spend the day golfing, and go to his house in the evening. He had his motor with him, and we set off, about five of the afternoon, after a thoroughly delightful day, for the drive, the distance being some ten miles. As it was still so early we did not have tea at the club house, but waited till we should get home. As we drove, the weather, which up till then had been, though hot, deliciously fresh, seemed to me to alter in quality, and become very stagnant and oppressive, and I felt that indefinable sense of ominous apprehension that I am accustomed to before thunder. John, however, did not share my views, attributing my loss of lightness to the fact that I had lost both my matches. Events proved, however, that I was right, though I do not think that the thunderstorm that broke that night was the sole cause of my depression.

Our way lay through deep high-banked lanes, and before we had gone very far I fell asleep, and was only awakened by the stopping of the motor. And with a sudden thrill, partly of fear but chiefly of curiosity, I found myself standing in the doorway of my house of dream. We went, I half wondering whether or not I was dreaming still, through a low oak-panelled hall, and out onto the lawn, where tea was laid in the shadow of the house. It was set in flower beds, a red-brick wall, with a gate in it, bounded one side, and out beyond that was a space of rough grass with a walnut tree. The facade of the house was very long, and at one end stood a three-storied tower, markedly older than the rest.

Here for the moment all resemblance to the repeated dream ceased. There was no silent and somehow terrible family, but a large assembly of exceedingly cheerful persons, all of whom were known to me. And in spite of the horror with which the dream itself had always filled me, I felt nothing of it now that the scene of it was thus reproduced before me. But I felt intensest curiosity as to what was going to happen.

Tea pursued its cheerful course, and before long Mrs. Clinton got up. And at that moment I think I knew what she was going to say. She spoke to me, and what she said was:

"Jack will show you your room: I have given you the room in the tower."

At that, for half a second, the horror of the dream took hold of me again. But it quickly passed, and again I felt nothing more than the most intense curiosity. It was not very long before it was amply satisfied.

John turned to me.

"Right up at the top of the house," he said, "but I think you'll be comfortable. We're absolutely full up. Would you like to go and see it now? By Jove, I believe that you are right, and that we are going to have a thunderstorm. How dark it has become."

I got up and followed him. We passed through the hall, and up the perfectly familiar staircase. Then he opened the door, and I went in. And at that moment sheer unreasoning terror again possessed me. I did not know what I feared: I simply feared. Then like a sudden recollection, when one remembers a name which has long escaped the memory, I knew what I feared. I feared Mrs. Stone, whose grave with the sinister inscription, "In evil memory," I had so often seen in my dream, just beyond the lawn which lay below my window. And then once more the fear passed so completely that I wondered what there was to fear, and I found myself, sober and quiet and sane, in the room in the tower, the name of which I had so often heard in my dream, and the scene of which was so familiar.

I looked around it with a certain sense of proprietorship, and found that nothing had been changed from the dreaming nights in which I knew it so well. Just to the left of the door was the bed, lengthways along the wall, with the head of it in the angle. In a line with it was the fireplace and a small bookcase; opposite the door the outer wall was pierced by two lattice-paned windows, between which stood the dressing-table, while ranged along the fourth wall was the washing-stand and a big cupboard. My luggage had already been unpacked, for the furniture of dressing and undressing lay orderly on the wash-stand and toilet-table, while my dinner clothes were spread out on the coverlet of the bed. And then, with a sudden start of unexplained dismay, I saw that there were two rather conspicuous objects which I had not seen before in my dreams: one a life-sized oil painting of Mrs. Stone, the other a black-and-white sketch of Jack Stone, representing him as he had appeared to me only a week before in the last of the series of these repeated dreams, a rather secret and evil-looking man of about thirty. His picture hung between the windows, looking straight across the room to the other portrait, which hung at the side of the bed. At that I looked next, and as I looked I felt once more the horror of nightmare seize me.

It represented Mrs. Stone as I had seen her last in my dreams: old and withered and white-haired. But in spite of the evident feebleness of body, a dreadful exuberance and vitality shone through the envelope of flesh, an exuberance wholly malign, a vitality that foamed and frothed with unimaginable evil. Evil beamed from the narrow, leering eyes; it laughed in the demon-like mouth. The whole face was instinct with some secret and appalling mirth; the hands, clasped together on the knee, seemed shaking with suppressed and nameless glee. Then I saw also that it was signed in the left-hand bottom corner, and wondering who the artist could be, I looked more closely, and read the inscription, "Julia Stone by Julia Stone."

There came a tap at the door, and John Clinton entered.

"Got everything you want?" he asked.

"Rather more than I want," said I, pointing to the picture.

He laughed.

"Hard-featured old lady," he said. "By herself, too, I remember. Anyhow she can't have flattered herself much."

"But don't you see?" said I. "It's scarcely a human face at all. It's the face of some witch, of some devil."

He looked at it more closely.

"Yes; it isn't very pleasant," he said. "Scarcely a bedside manner, eh? Yes; I can imagine getting the nightmare if I went to sleep with that close by my bed. I'll have it taken down if you like."

"I really wish you would," I said. He rang the bell, and with the help of a servant we detached the picture and carried it out onto the landing, and put it with its face to the wall.

"By Jove, the old lady is a weight," said John, mopping his forehead. "I wonder if she had something on her mind."

The extraordinary weight of the picture had struck me too. I was about to reply, when I caught sight of my own hand. There was blood on it, in considerable quantities, covering the whole palm.

"I've cut myself somehow," said I.

John gave a little startled exclamation.

"Why, I have too," he said.

Simultaneously the footman took out his handkerchief and wiped his hand with it. I saw that there was blood also on his handkerchief.

John and I went back into the tower room and washed the blood off; but neither on his hand nor on mine was there the slightest trace of a scratch or cut. It seemed to me that, having ascertained this, we both, by a sort of tacit consent, did not allude to it again. Something in my case had dimly occurred to me that I did not wish to think about. It was but a conjecture, but I fancied that I knew the same thing had occurred to him.

The heat and oppression of the air, for the storm we had expected was still undischarged, increased very much after dinner, and for some time most of the party, among whom were John Clinton and myself, sat outside on the path bounding the lawn, where we had had tea. The night was absolutely dark, and no twinkle of star or moon ray could penetrate the pall of cloud that overset the sky. By degrees our assembly thinned, the women went up to bed, men dispersed to the smoking or billiard room, and by eleven o'clock my host and I were the only two left. All the evening I thought that he had something on his mind, and as soon as we were alone he spoke.

"The man who helped us with the picture had blood on his hand, too, did you notice?" he said.

"I asked him just now if he had cut himself, and he said he supposed he had, but that he could find no mark of it. Now where did that blood come from?"

By dint of telling myself that I was not going to think about it, I had succeeded in not doing so, and I did not want, especially just at bedtime, to be reminded of it.

"I don't know," said I, "and I don't really care so long as the picture of Mrs. Stone is not by my bed."

He got up.

"But it's odd," he said. "Ha! Now you'll see another odd thing."

A dog of his, an Irish terrier by breed, had come out of the house as we talked. The door behind us into the hall was open, and a bright oblong of light shone across the lawn to the iron gate which led on to the rough grass outside, where the walnut tree stood. I saw that the dog had all his hackles up, bristling with rage and fright; his lips were curled back from his teeth, as if he was ready to spring at something, and he was growling to himself. He took not the slightest notice of his master or me, but stiffly and tensely walked across the grass to the iron gate. There he stood for a moment, looking through the bars and still growling. Then of a sudden his courage seemed to desert him: he gave one long howl, and scuttled back to the house with a curious crouching sort of movement.

"He does that half-a-dozen times a day," said John. "He sees something which he both hates and fears."

I walked to the gate and looked over it. Something was moving on the grass outside, and soon a sound which I could not instantly identify came to my ears. Then I remembered what it was: it was the purring of a cat. I lit a match, and saw the purrer, a big blue Persian, walking round and round in a little circle just outside the gate, stepping high and ecstatically, with tail carried aloft like a banner. Its eyes were bright and shining, and every now and then it put its head down and sniffed at the grass.

I laughed.

"The end of that mystery, I am afraid." I said. "Here's a large cat having Walpurgis night all alone."

"Yes, that's Darius," said John. "He spends half the day and all night there. But that's not the end of the dog mystery, for Toby and he are the best of friends, but the beginning of the cat mystery. What's the cat doing there? And why is Darius pleased, while Toby is terror-stricken?"

At that moment I remembered the rather horrible detail of my dreams when I saw through the gate, just where the cat was now, the white tombstone with the sinister inscription. But before I could answer the rain began, as suddenly and heavily as if a tap had been turned on, and simultaneously the big cat squeezed through the bars of the gate, and came leaping across the lawn to the house for shelter. Then it sat in the doorway, looking out eagerly into the dark. It spat and struck at John with its paw, as he pushed it in, in order to close the door.

Somehow, with the portrait of Julia Stone in the passage outside, the room in the tower had absolutely no alarm for me, and as I went to bed, feeling very sleepy and heavy, I had nothing more than interest for the curious incident about our bleeding hands, and the conduct of the cat and dog. The last thing I looked at before I put out my light was the square empty space by my bed where the portrait had been. Here the paper was of its original full tint of dark red: over the rest of the walls it had faded. Then I blew out my candle and instantly fell asleep.

My awaking was equally instantaneous, and I sat bolt upright in bed under the impression that some bright light had been flashed in my face, though it was now absolutely pitch dark. I knew exactly where I was, in the room which I had dreaded in dreams, but no horror that I ever felt when asleep approached the fear that now invaded and froze my brain. Immediately after a peal of thunder crackled just above the house, but the probability that it was only a flash of lightning which awoke me gave no reassurance to my galloping heart. Something I knew was in the room with me, and instinctively I put out my right hand, which was nearest the wall, to keep it away. And my hand touched the edge of a picture-frame hanging close to me.

I sprang out of bed, upsetting the small table that stood by it, and I heard my watch, candle, and matches clatter onto the floor. But for the moment there was no need of light, for a blinding flash leaped out of the clouds, and showed me that by my bed again hung the picture of Mrs. Stone. And instantly the room went into blackness again. But in that flash I saw another thing also, namely a figure that leaned over the end of my bed, watching me. It was dressed in some close-clinging white garment, spotted and stained with mold, and the face was that of the portrait.

Overhead the thunder cracked and roared, and when it ceased and the deathly stillness succeeded, I heard the rustle of movement coming nearer me, and, more horrible yet, perceived an odor of corruption and decay. And then a hand was laid on the side of my neck, and close beside my ear I heard quick-taken, eager breathing. Yet I knew that this thing, though it could be perceived by touch, by smell, by eye and by ear, was still not of this earth, but something that had passed out of the body and had power to make itself manifest. Then a voice, already familiar to me, spoke.

"I knew you would come to the room in the tower," it said. "I have been long waiting for you. At last you have come. Tonight I shall feast; before long we will feast together."

And the quick breathing came closer to me; I could feel it on my neck.

At that the terror, which I think had paralyzed me for the moment, gave way to the wild instinct of self-preservation. I hit wildly with both arms, kicking out at the same moment, and heard a little animal-squeal, and something soft dropped with a thud beside me. I took a couple of steps forward, nearly tripping up over whatever it was that lay there, and by the merest good-luck found the handle of the door. In another second I ran out on the landing, and had banged the door behind me. Almost at the same moment I heard a door open somewhere below, and John Clinton, candle in hand, came running upstairs.

"What is it?" he said. "I sleep just below you, and heard a noise as if—Good heavens, there's blood on your shoulder."

I stood there, so he told me afterwards, swaying from side to side, white as a sheet, with the mark on my shoulder as if a hand covered with blood had been laid there.

"It's in there," I said, pointing. "She, you know. The portrait is in there, too, hanging up on the place we took it from."

At that he laughed.

"My dear fellow, this is mere nightmare," he said.

He pushed by me, and opened the door, I standing there simply inert with terror, unable to stop him, unable to move.

"Phew! What an awful smell," he said.

Then there was silence; he had passed out of my sight behind the open door. Next moment he came out again, as white as myself, and instantly shut it.

"Yes, the portrait's there," he said, "and on the floor is a thing—a thing spotted with earth, like what they bury people in. Come away, quick, come away."

How I got downstairs I hardly know. An awful shuddering and nausea of the spirit rather than of the flesh had seized me, and more than once he had to place my feet upon the steps, while every now and then he cast glances of terror and apprehension up the stairs. But in time we came to his dressing-room on the floor below, and there I told him what I have here described.

The sequel can be made short; indeed, some of my readers have perhaps already guessed what it was, if they remember that inexplicable affair of the churchyard at West Fawley, some eight years ago, where an attempt was made three times to bury the body of a certain woman who had committed suicide. On each occasion the coffin was found in the course of a few days again protruding from the ground. After the third attempt, in order that the thing should not be talked about, the body was buried elsewhere in unconsecrated ground. Where it was buried was just outside the iron gate of the garden belonging to the house where this woman had lived. She had committed suicide in a room at the top of the tower in that house. Her name was Julia Stone.

Subsequently the body was again secretly dug up, and the coffin was found to be full of blood.

THE HAUNTED AND THE HAUNTERS,
by Lord Edward Bulwer-Lytton

A friend of mine, who is a man of letters and a philosopher, said to me one day, as if between jest and earnest, "Fancy! since we last met, I have discovered a haunted house in the midst of London."

"Really haunted?—and by what? ghosts?"

"Well, I can't answer that question: all I know is this—six weeks ago my wife and I were in search of a furnished apartment. Passing a quiet street, we saw on the window of one of the houses a hill, 'Apartments Furnished.' The situation suited us; we entered the house—liked the rooms—engaged them by the week—and left them the third day. No power on earth could have reconciled my wife to stay longer; and I don't wonder at it."

"What did you see?"

"Excuse me—I have no desire to be ridiculed as a superstitious dreamer—nor, on the other hand, could I ask you to accept on my affirmation what you would hold to be incredible without the evidence of your own senses. Let me only say this, it was not so much what we saw or heard (in which you might fairly suppose that we were the dupes of our own excited fancy, or the victims of imposture in others) that drove us away, as it was an undefinable terror which seized both of us whenever we passed by the door of a certain unfurnished room, in which we neither saw nor heard anything. And the strangest marvel of all was, that for once in my life I agreed with my wife, silly woman though she be—and allowed, after the third night, that it was impossible to stay a fourth in that house. Accordingly, on the fourth morning I summoned the woman who kept the house and attended on us, and told her that the rooms did not quite suit us, and we would not stay out our week. She said, dryly, 'I know why: you have stayed longer than any other lodger. Few ever stay a second night; none before you a third. But I take it they have been very kind to you.'

"'They—who?' I asked, affecting to smile.

"'Why, they who haunt the house, whoever they are. I don't mind them; I remember them from many years ago, when I lived in this house, not as a servant; but I know they will be the death of me some day. I don't care—I'm old, and must die soon anyhow; and then I shall be with them, and in this house still.' The woman spoke with so dreary a calmness, that really it was a sort of awe that prevented my conversing with her further. I paid for my week, and too happy were my wife and I to get off so cheaply."

"You excite my curiosity," said I; "nothing I should like better than to sleep in a haunted house. Pray give me the address of the one which you left so ignominiously."

My friend gave me the address; and when we parted, I walked straight towards the house thus indicated.

It is situated on the north side of oxford Street (in a dull but respectable thoroughfare). I found the house shut up—no bill at the window, and no response to my knock. As I was turning away, a beer-boy, collecting pewter pots at the neighbouring areas, said to me, "Do you want any one at that house, sir?"

"Yes, I heard it was to be let."

"Let!—why, the woman who kept it is dead—has been dead these three weeks, and no one can be found to stay there, though Mr. J—— offered ever so much. He offered Mother, who chars for him, a pound a week just to open and shut the windows, and she would not."

"Would not!—and why?"

"The house is haunted; and the old woman who kept it was found dead in her bed, with her eyes wide open. They say the devil strangled her."

"Pooh!—you speak of Mr. J——. Is he the owner of the house?"

"Yes."

"Where does he live?"

"What is he—in any business?"

"No, sir—nothing particular; a single gentleman."

I gave the pot-boy the gratuity earned by his liberal information, and proceeded to Mr. J——, in G—— Street, which was close by the street that boasted the haunted house. I was lucky enough to find Mr. J—— at home, an elderly man, with intelligent countenance and prepossessing manners.

I communicated my name and my business frankly. I said I heard the house was considered to be haunted—that I had a strong desire to examine a house with so equivocal a reputation—that I should be greatly obliged if he would allow me to hire it, though only for a night. I was willing to pay for that privilege whatever he might be inclined to ask. "Sir," said Mr. J——, with great courtesy, "the house is at your service, for as short or as long a time as you please. Rent is out of the question —the obligation will be on my side should you be able to discover the cause of the strange phenomena which at present deprive it of all value. I cannot let it, for I cannot even get a servant to keep it in order or answer the door. Unluckily the house is haunted, if I may use that expression, not only by night, but by day; though at night the disturbances are of a more unpleasant and sometimes of a more alarming character. The poor old woman who died in it three weeks ago was a pauper whom I took out of a workhouse, for in her childhood she had been known to some of my family, and had once been in such good circumstances that she had rented that house of my uncle. She was a woman of superior education and strong mind, and was the only person I could ever induce to remain in the house. Indeed, since her death, which was sudden, and the coroner's inquest, which gave it a notoriety in the neighbourhood, I have so despaired of finding any person to take charge of the house, much more a tenant, that I would willingly let it rent-free for a year to any one who would pay its rates and taxes."

"How long is it since the house acquired this sinister character?"

"That I can scarcely tell you, but very many years since. The old woman I spoke of said it was haunted when she rented it between thirty and forty years ago. The fact is, that my life has been spent in the East Indies, and in the civil service of the Company. I returned to England last year, on inheriting the fortune of an uncle, among whose possessions was the house in question. I found it shut up and uninhabited. I was told that it was haunted, that no one would inhabit it. I smiled at what seemed to be so idle a story. I spent some money in repairing it—added to its old-fashioned furniture a few modern articles—advertised it, and obtained a lodger for a year. He was a colonel retired on half-pay. He came in with his family, a son and a daughter, and four or five servants: they all left the house the next day; and, although each of them declared that he had seen something different from that which had scared the others, a something still was equally terrible to all. I really could not in conscience sue, nor even blame, the colonel for breach of agreement. Then I put in the old woman I have spoken of, and she was empowered to let the house in apartments. I never had one lodger who stayed more than three days. I do not tell you their stories—to no two lodgers have there been exactly the same phenomena repeated. It is better that you should judge for yourself, than enter the house with an imagination influenced by previous narratives; only be prepared to see and to hear something or other, and take whatever precautions you yourself please."

"Have you never had a curiosity yourself to pass a night in that house?"

"Yes. I passed not a night, but three hours in broad daylight alone in that house. My curiosity is not satisfied but it is quenched. I have no desire to renew the experiment. You cannot complain, you see, sir, that I am not sufficiently candid; and unless your interest be exceedingly eager and your nerves unusually strong, I honestly add, that I advise you not to pass a night in that house."

"My interest is exceedingly keen," said I, "and though only a coward will boast of his nerves in situations wholly unfamiliar to him, yet my nerves have been seasoned in such variety of danger that I have the right to rely on them—even in a haunted house."

Mr. J—— said very little more; he took the keys of the house out of his bureau, gave them to me—and, thanking him cordially for his frankness, and his urbane concession to my wish, I carried off my prize.

Impatient for the experiment, as soon as I reached home, I summoned my confident servant—a young man of gay spirits, fearless temper, and as free from superstitious prejudices as any one I could think of.

"F——," said I, "you remember in Germany how disappointed we were at not finding a ghost in that old castle, which was said to be haunted by a headless apparition? Well, I have heard of a house in London which, I have reason to hope, is decidedly haunted. I mean to sleep there tonight. From what I hear, there is no doubt that something will allow itself to be seen or to be heard—something, perhaps, excessively horrible. Do you think if I take you with me, I may rely on your presence of mind, whatever may happen?"

"Oh, sir! pray trust me," answered F——, grinning with delight.

"Very well; then here are the keys of the house—this is the address. Go now—select for me any bedroom you please; and since the house has not been inhabited for weeks, make up a good fire—air the bed well—see, of course, that there are candles as well as fuel. Take with you my revolver and my dagger—so much for my weapons—arm yourself equally well; and if we are not a match for a dozen ghosts, we shall be but a sorry couple of Englishmen."

I was engaged for the rest of the day on business so urgent that I had not leisure to think much on the nocturnal adventure to which I had plighted my honour. I dined alone, and very late, and while dining, read, as is my habit. I selected one of the volumes of Macaulay's *Essays*. I thought to myself that I would take the book with me; there was so much of the healthfulness in the style, and practical life in the subjects, that it would serve as an antidote against the influence of superstitious fancy.

Accordingly, about half-past nine, I put the book into my pocket, and strolled leisurely towards the haunted house. I took with me a favourite dog—an exceedingly sharp, bold and vigilant bull-terrier—a dog fond of prowling about strange ghostly corners and passages at night in search of rats—a dog of dogs for a ghost.

It was a summer night, but chilly, the sky somewhat gloomy and overcast. Still there was a moon—faintly and sickly, but still a moon—and if the clouds permitted, after midnight it would be brighter.

I reached the house, knocked, and my servant opened with a cheerful smile.

"All right, sir, and very comfortable."

"Oh!" said I, rather disappointed; "have you not seen nor heard anything remarkable?"

"Well, sir, I must own I have heard something queer."

"What—what?"

"The sound of feet pattering behind me; and once or twice small noises like whispers close at my ear—nothing more."

"You are not at all frightened?"

"I! not a bit of it, sir," and the man's bold look reassured me on one point—*viz.*, that happen what might, he would not desert me.

We were in the hall, the street-door closed, and my attention was now drawn to my dog. He had at first run in eagerly enough, but had sneaked back to the door, and was scratching and whining to get out. After patting him on the head, and encouraging him gently, the dog seemed to reconcile himself to the situation, and followed me and F—— through the house, but keeping close at my heels instead of hurrying inquisitively in advance, which was his usual and normal habit in all strange places. We first visited the subterranean apartments, the kitchen and other offices, and especially the cellars, in which last there were two or three bottles of wine still left in a bin, covered with cobwebs, and evidently, by their appearance, undisturbed for many years. It was clear that the ghosts were not wine-bibbers. For the rest we discovered nothing of interest. There was a gloomy little backyard with very high walls. The stones of this yard were very damp; and what with the damp, and what with the dust and smoke-grime on the pavement, our feet left a slight impression where we passed.

And now appeared the first strange phenomenon witnessed by myself in this strange abode. I saw, just before me, the print of a foot suddenly form itself, as it were. I stopped, caught hold of my servant, and pointed to it. In advance of that footprint as suddenly dropped another. We both saw it. I advanced quickly to the place; the footprint kept advancing before me, a small footprint—the foot of a child; the impression was too faint thoroughly to distinguish the shape, but it seemed to us both that it was the print of a naked foot. This phenomenon ceased when we arrived at the opposite wall, nor did it repeat itself on returning. We remounted the stairs, and entered the rooms on the ground floor, a dining parlour, a small back parlour, and a still smaller third room that had been probably appropriated to a footman—all still as death. We then visited the drawing-rooms, which seemed fresh and new. In the front room I seated myself in an armchair. F—— placed on the table the candlestick with which he had lighted us. I told him to shut the door. As he had turned to do so, a chair opposite to me moved from the wall quickly and noiselessly, and dropped itself about a yard from my own chair, immediately fronting it.

"Why, this is better than the turning tables," said I, with a half laugh; and as I laughed, my dog put back his head and howled.

F——, coming back, had not observed the movement of the chair. He employed himself now in stilling the dog. I continued to gaze on the chair, and fancied I saw on it a pale blue misty outline of a human figure, but an outline so indistinct that I could only distrust my own vision. The dog now was quiet.

"Put back that chair opposite me," said I to F——; "put it back to the wall."

F—— obeyed. "Was that you, sir?" said he, turning abruptly.

"I!—what?"

"Why, something struck me. I felt it sharply on the shoulder—just here."

"No," said I. "But we have jugglers present, and though we may not discover their tricks, we shall catch them before they frighten us."

We did not stay long in the drawing rooms—in fact, they felt so damp and so chilly that I was glad to get to the fire upstairs. We locked the doors of the drawing rooms—a precaution which, I should observe, we had taken with all the rooms we had searched below. The bedroom my servant had selected for me was the best on the floor—a large one, with two windows fronting the street. The four-posted bed, which took up no inconsiderable space, was opposite to the fire, which burned clear and bright; a door in the wall to the left, between the bed and the window, communicated with the room which my servant appropriated to himself. This last was a small room with a sofa bed, and had no communication with the landing-place—no other door but that which conducted to the bedroom I was to occupy. On either side of my fireplace was a cupboard, without locks, flush with the wall and covered with the same dull-brown paper. We examined these cupboards—only hooks to suspend female dresses—nothing else; we sounded the walls—evidently solid—the outer walls of the building. Having finished the survey of these apartments, warmed myself a few moments, and lighted my cigar, I then, still accompanied by F——, went forth to complete my reconnoitre. In the landing-place there was another door; it was closed firmly. "Sir," said my servant, in surprise, "I unlocked this door with all the others when I first came; it cannot have got locked from the inside, for—"

Before he had finished his sentence, the door, which neither of us then was touching, opened quietly of itself. We looked at each other a single instant. The same thought seized both—some human agency might be detected here. I rushed in first, my servant followed. A small blank dreary room without furniture—few empty boxes and hampers in a corner—a small window—the shutters closed—not even a fireplace—no other door than that by which we had entered—no carpet on the floor, and the floor seemed very old, uneven, worm-eaten, mended here and there, as was shown by the whiter patches on the wood; but no living being, and no visible place in which a living being could have hidden. As we stood gazing round, the door by which we had entered closed as quietly as it had before opened: we were imprisoned.

For the first time I felt a creep of undefinable horror. Not so my servant. "Why, they don't think to trap us, sir; I could break the trumpery door with a kick of my foot."

"Try first if it will open to your hand," said I, shaking off the vague apprehension that had seized me, "while I unclose the shutters and see what is without."

I unbarred the shutters—the window looked on the little back yard I have before described; there was no ledge without—nothing to break the sheer descent of the wall. No man getting out of that window would have found any footing till he had fallen on the stones below.

F——, meanwhile, was vainly attempting to open the door. He now turned round to me and asked my permission to use force. And I should here state, in justice to the servant, that, far from evincing any superstitious terrors, his nerve, composure, and even gayety amidst circumstances so extraordinary, compelled my admiration, and made me congratulate myself on having secured a companion in every way fitted to the occasion. I willingly gave him the permission he required. But though he was a remarkably strong man, his force was as idle as his milder efforts; the door did not even shake to his stoutest kick. Breathless and panting, he desisted. I then tried the door myself, equally in vain. As I ceased from the effort, again that creep of horror came over me; but this time it was more cold and stubborn. I felt as if some strange and ghastly exhalation were rising up from the chinks of that rugged floor, and filling the atmosphere with a venomous influence hostile to human life. The door now very slowly and quietly opened as of its own accord. We precipitated ourselves into the landing-place. We both saw a large pale light— as large as the human figure but shapeless and unsubstantial—move before us, and ascend the stairs that led from the landing into the attics. I followed the light, and my servant followed me. It entered, to the right of the landing, a small garret, of which the door stood open. I entered in the same instant. The light then collapsed into a small globule, exceedingly brilliant and vivid; rested a moment on a bed in the corner, quivered, and vanished.

We approached the bed and examined it—a half-tester, such as is commonly found in attics devoted to servants. On the drawers that stood near it we perceived an old faded silk kerchief, with the needle still left in a rent half repaired. The kerchief was covered with dust; probably it had belonged to the old woman who had died in that house, and this might have been her sleeping room. I had sufficient curiosity to open the drawers: there were a few odds and ends of female dress, and two letters tied round with a narrow ribbon of faded yellow. I took the liberty to possess myself of the letters. We found nothing else in the room worth noticing— nor did the light reappear; but we distinctly heard, as we turned to go, a pattering footfall on the floor—just before us. We went through the other attics (in all four), the footfall still preceding us. Nothing to be seen—nothing but the footfall heard. I had the letters in my hand: just as I was descending the stairs I distinctly felt my wrist seized, and a faint soft effort made to draw the letters from my clasp. I only held them the more tightly, and the effort ceased.

We regained the bedchamber appropriated to myself, and I then remarked that my dog had not followed us when we had left it. He was thrusting himself close to the fire, and trembling. I was impatient to examine the letters; and while I read them, my servant opened a little box in which he had deposited the weapons I had ordered him to bring; took them out, placed them on a table close at my bed-head, and then occupied himself in soothing the dog, who, however, seemed to heed him very little.

The letters were short—they were dated; the dates exactly thirty-five years ago. They were evidently from a lover to his mistress, or a husband to some young wife. Not only the terms of expression, but a distinct reference to a former voyage, indicated the writer to have been a seafarer. The spelling and handwriting were those of a man imperfectly educated, but still the language itself was forcible. In the expressions of endearment there was a kind of rough wild love; but here and there were dark and unintelligible hints at some secret not of love—some secret that seemed of crime. "We ought to love each other," was one of the sentences I remember, "for how every one else would execrate us if all was known." Again: "Don't let any one be in the same room with you at night—you talk in your sleep." And again: "What's done can't be undone; and I tell you there's nothing against us unless the dead could come to life." Here there was underlined in a better handwriting (a female's), "They do!" At the end of the letter latest in date the same female hand had written these words: "Lost at sea the 4th of June, the same day as—"

I put down the letters, and began to muse over their contents.

Fearing, however, that the train of thought into which I fell might unsteady my nerves, I fully determined to keep my mind in a fit state to cope with whatever of the marvellous the advancing night might bring forth. I roused myself—laid the letters on the table—stirred up the fire, which was still bright and cheering—and opened my volume of Macaulay. I read quietly enough till about half-past eleven. I then threw myself dressed upon the bed, and told my servant he might retire to his

74

own room, but must keep himself awake. I bade him leave open the doors between the two rooms. Thus alone, I kept two candles burning on the table by my bed-head. I placed my watch beside the weapons, and calmly resumed my Macaulay. Opposite to me the fire burned clear; and on the hearthrug, seemingly asleep, lay the dog. In about twenty minutes I felt an exceedingly cold air pass by my cheek, like a sudden draught. I fancied the door to my right, communicating with the landing-place, must have got open; but no—it was closed. I then turned my glance to my left, and saw the flame of the candles violently swayed as by a wind. At the same moment the watch beside the revolver softly slid from the table—softly, softly—no visible hand—it was gone. I sprang up, seizing the revolver with the one hand, the dagger with the other: I was not willing that my weapons should share the fate of the watch. Thus armed, I looked round the floor—no sign of the watch. Three slow, loud, distinct knocks were now heard at the bed-head; my servant called out, "Is that you, sir?"

"No; be on your guard."

The dog now roused himself and sat on his haunches, his ears moving quickly backwards and forwards. He kept his eyes fixed on me with a look so strange that he concentrated all my attention on himself. Slowly he rose up, all his hair bristling, and stood perfectly rigid, and with the same wild stare. I had no time, however, to examine the dog. Presently my servant emerged from his room; and if ever I saw horror in the human face, it was then. I should not have recognized him had we met in the street, so altered was every lineament. He passed by me quickly, saying in a whisper that seemed scarcely to come from his lips, "Run—run! it is after me!" He gained the door to the landing, pulled it open, and rushed forth. I followed him into the landing involuntarily, calling him to stop; but, without heeding me, he bounded down the stairs, clinging to the balusters, and taking several steps at a time. I heard, where I stood, the street-door open—heard it again clap to. I was left alone in the haunted house.

It was but for a moment that I remained undecided whether or not to follow my servant; pride and curiosity alike forbade so dastardly a flight. I re-entered my room, closing the door after me, and proceeded cautiously into the interior chamber. I encountered nothing to justify my servant's terror. I again carefully examined the walls, to see if there were any concealed door. I could find no trace of one—not even a seam in the dull brown paper with which the room was hung. How, then, had the THING, whatever it was, which had so scared him, obtained ingress except through my own chamber?

I returned to my room, shut and locked the door that opened upon the interior one, and stood on the hearth, expectant and prepared. I now perceived that the dog had slunk into an angle of the wall, and was pressing himself close against it, as if literally striving to force his way into it. I approached the animal and spoke to it; the poor brute was evidently beside itself with terror. It showed all its teeth, the slaver dropping from its jaws, and would certainly have bitten me if I had touched it. It did not seem to recognize me. Whoever has seen at the Zoological Gardens a rabbit fascinated by a serpent, cowering in a corner, may form some idea of the anguish which the dog exhibited. Finding all efforts to soothe the animal in vain, and fearing that his bite might be as venomous in that state as in the madness of hydrophobia, I left him alone, placed my weapons on the table beside the fire, seated myself, and recommenced my Macaulay.

Perhaps, in order not to appear seeking credit for a courage, or rather a coolness, which the reader may conceive I exaggerate, I may be pardoned if I pause to indulge in one or two egotistical remarks.

As I hold presence of mind, or what is called courage, to be precisely proportioned to familiarity with the circumstances that lead to it, so I should say that I had been long sufficiently familiar with all experiments that appertain to the Marvellous. I had witnessed many very extraordinary phenomena in various parts of the world—phenomena that would be either totally disbelieved if I stated them, or ascribed to supernatural agencies. Now, my theory is that the Supernatural is the Impossible, and that what is called supernatural is only a something in the laws of nature of which we have been hitherto ignorant. Therefore, if a ghost rise before me, I have not the right to say, "So, then, the supernatural is possible," but rather, "So, then, the apparition of a ghost is, contrary to received opinion, within the laws of nature—*i.e.*, not supernatural."

Now, in all that I had hitherto witnessed, and indeed in all the wonders which the amateurs of mystery in our age record as facts, a material living agency is always required. On the continent you will still find magicians who assert that they can raise spirits. Assume for the moment that they assert truly, still the living material form of the magician is present; and he is the material agency by which, from some constitutional peculiarities, certain strange phenomena are represented to your natural senses.

Accept, again, as truthful, the tales of spirit manifestation in America—musical or other sounds—writings on paper, produced by no discernible hand—articles of furniture moved without apparent human agency—or the actual sight and touch of hands, to which no bodies seem to belong—still there must be found the MEDIUM or living being, with constitutional peculiarities capable of obtaining these signs. In fine, in all such marvels, supposing even that there is no imposture, there must be a human being like ourselves by whom, or through whom, the effects presented to human beings are produced. It is so with the now familiar phenomena of mesmerism or electro-biology; the mind of the person operated on is affected through a material living agent. Nor, supposing it true that a mesmerized patient can respond to the will or passes of a mesmerizer a hundred miles distant, is the response less occasioned by a material fluid—call it Electric, call it Odic, call it what you will—which has the power of traversing space and passing obstacles, that the material effect is communicated from one to the other. Hence all that I had hitherto witnessed, or expected to witness, in this strange house, I believed to be occasioned through some agency or medium as mortal as myself: and this idea necessarily prevented the awe with which those who regard as supernatural things that are not within the ordinary operations of nature might have been impressed by the adventures of that memorable night.

As, then, it was my conjecture that all that was presented; or would be presented to my senses, must originate in some human being gifted by constitution with the power so to present them, and having some motive so to do, I felt an interest in my theory which, in its way, was rather philosophical than superstitious. And I can sincerely say that I was in as tranquil a temper for observation as any practical experimentalist could be in awaiting the effect of some rare, though perhaps perilous, chemical combination. Of course, the more I kept my mind detached from fancy, the more the temper fitted for observation would be obtained; and I therefore riveted eye and thought on the strong daylight sense in the page of my Macaulay.

I now became aware that something interposed between the page and the light—the page was overshadowed: I looked up, and I saw what I shall find very difficult, perhaps impossible, to describe.

It was a Darkness shaping itself forth from the air in very undefined outline. I cannot say it was of a human form, and yet it had more resemblance to a human form, or rather shadow, than to anything else. As it stood, wholly apart and distinct from the air and the light around it, its dimensions seemed gigantic, the summit nearly touching the ceiling. While I gazed, a feeling of intense cold seized me. An iceberg before me could not more have chilled me; nor could the cold of an iceberg have been more purely physical. I feel convinced that it was not the cold caused by fear. As I continued to gaze, I thought—but this I cannot say with precision—that I distinguished two eyes looking down on me from the height. One moment I fancied that I distinguished them clearly, the next they seemed gone; but still two rays of a pale-blue light frequently shot through the darkness, as from the height on which I half believed, half doubted, that I had encountered the eyes.

I strove to speak—my voice utterly failed me; I could only think to myself, "Is this fear? it is not fear!" I strove to rise—in vain; I felt as if weighed down by an irresistible force. Indeed, my impression was that of an immense and overwhelming Power opposed to any volition—that sense of utter inadequacy to cope with a force beyond man's, which one may feel physically in a storm at sea, in a conflagration, or when confronting some terrible wild beast, or rather, perhaps, the shark of the ocean, I felt morally. Opposed to my will was another will, as far superior to its strength as storm, fire, and shark are superior in material force to the force of man.

And now, as this impression grew on me—now came, at last, horror—horror to a degree that no words can convey. Still I retained pride, if not courage; and in my own mind I said, "This is horror, but it is not fear; unless I fear I cannot be harmed; my reason rejects this thing, it is an illusion—I do not fear." With a violent effort I succeeded at last in stretching out my hand towards the weapon on the table; as I did so, on the arm and shoulder I received a strange shock, and my arm fell to my side powerless. And now, to add to my horror, the light began slowly to wane from the candles; they were not, as it were, extinguished, but their flame seemed very gradually withdrawn; it was the same with the fire—the light was extracted from the fuel; in a few minutes the room was in utter darkness.

The dread that came over me, to be thus in the dark with that dark Thing, whose power was so intensely felt, brought a reaction of nerve. In fact, terror had reached that climax, that either my senses must have deserted me, or I must have burst through the spell. I did burst through it. I found voice, though the voice was a shriek. I remember that I broke forth with words like these—"I do not fear, my soul does not fear" and at the same time I found strength to rise. Still in that profound gloom I rushed to one of the windows—tore aside the curtain—flung open the shutters; my first thought was—*light*. And when I saw the moon high, clear, and calm, I felt a joy that almost compensated for the previous terror. There was the moon, there was also the light from the gas lamps in the deserted slumberous street. I turned to look back into the room; the moon penetrated its shadow very palely and partially—but still there was light. The dark Thing, whatever it might be, was gone —except that I could yet see a dim shadow, which seemed the shadow of that shade, against the opposite wall.

My eye now rested on the table, and from under the table (which was without cloth or cover—an old mahogany round table) there rose a hand, visible as far as the wrist. It was a hand, seemingly, as much of flesh and blood as my own, but the hand of an aged person—lean, wrinkled, small, too—a woman's hand. That hand very softly closed on the two letters that lay on the table: hand and letters both vanished. There then came the same three loud measured knocks I heard at the bed-head before this extraordinary drama had commenced.

As those sounds slowly ceased, I felt the whole room vibrate sensibly; and at the far end there rose, as from the floor, sparks or globules like bubbles of light, many-coloured—green, yellow, fire-red, azure. Up and down, to and fro, hither, thither, as tiny Will-o'-the-Wisps the sparks moved slow or swift, each at his own caprice. A chair (as in the drawing-room below) was now advanced from the wall without apparent agency, and placed at the opposite side of the table. Suddenly as forth from the chair, there grew a shape—a woman's shape. It was distinct as a shape of life—ghastly as a shape of death. The face was that of youth, with a strange mournful beauty: the throat and shoulders were bare, the rest of the form in a loose robe of cloudy white. It began sleeking its long yellow hair, which fell over its shoulders; its eyes were not turned towards me, but to the door; it seemed listening, watching, waiting. The shadow of the shade in the background grew darker; and again I thought I beheld the eyes gleaming out from the summit of the shadow—eyes fixed upon that shape.

As if from the door, though it did not open, there grew out another shape, equally distinct, equally ghastly—a man's shape—a young man's. It was in the dress of the last century, or rather in a likeness of such dress (for both the male shape and the female, though defined, were evidently unsubstantial, impalpable—simulacra—phantasms); and there was something incongruous, grotesque, yet fearful, in the contrast between the elaborate finery, the courtly precision of that old-fashioned garb, with its ruffles and lace and buckles, and the corpse-like aspect and ghostlike stillness of the flitting wearer. Just as the male shape approached the female, the dark shadow started from the wall, all three for a moment wrapped in darkness. When the pale light returned, the two phantoms were as in the grasp of the shadow that towered between them; and there was a bloodstain on the breast of the female; and the phantom male was leaning on its phantom sword, and blood seemed trickling fast from the ruffles, from the lace; and the darkness of the intermediate Shadow swallowed them up—they were gone. And again the bubbles of light shot, and sailed, and undulated, growing thicker and thicker and more wildly confused in their movements.

The closet door to the right of the fireplace now opened, and from the aperture there came the form of an aged woman. In her hand she held letters—the very letters over which I had seen the Hand close; and behind her I heard a footstep. She turned round as if to listen, and then she opened the letters and seemed to read; and over her shoulder I saw a livid face, the face as of a man long drowned—bloated, bleached, seaweed tangled in its dripping hair; and at her feet lay a form as of a corpse, and beside the corpse there cowered a child, a miserable squalid child, with famine in its cheeks and fear in its eyes. And as I looked in the old woman's face, the wrinkles and lines vanished and it became a face of youth—hard-eyed, stony, but still youth; and the Shadow darted forth, and darkened over these phantoms as it had darkened over the last.

Nothing now was left but the Shadow, and on that my eyes were intently fixed, till again eyes grew out of the Shadow—malignant, serpent eyes. And the bubbles of light again rose and fell, and in their disorder, irregular, turbulent maze, mingled with the wan moonlight. And now from these globules themselves, as from the shell of an egg, monstrous things burst out; the air grew filled with them; larvae so bloodless and so hideous that I can in no way describe them except to remind the reader of the swarming life which the solar microscope brings before his eyes in a drop of water—things transparent, supple, agile, chasing each other, devouring each other—forms like nought ever beheld by the naked eye. As the shapes were without symmetry, so their movements were without order. In their very vagrancies there was no sport; they came round me and round, thicker and faster and swifter, swarming over my head, crawling over my right arm, which was outstretched in involuntary command against all evil beings. Sometimes I felt myself touched, but not by them; invisible hands touched me. Once I felt the clutch as of cold soft fingers at my throat. I was still equally conscious that if I gave way to fear I should be in bodily peril; and I concentrated all my faculties in the single focus of resisting, stubborn will. And I turned my sight from the Shadow—above all, from those strange serpent eyes—eyes that had now become distinctly visible. For there, though in nought else round me, I was aware that there was a WILL, and a will of intense, creative, working evil, which might crush down on my own.

The pale atmosphere in the room began now to redden as if in the air of some near conflagration. The larvae grew lurid as things that live in fire. Again the room vibrated; again were heard the three measured knocks; and again all things were swallowed up in the darkness of the dark Shadow, as if out of that darkness all had come, into that darkness all returned.

As the gloom receded, the Shadow was wholly gone. Slowly as it had been withdrawn, the flame grew again into the candles on the table, again into the fuel in the grate. The whole room came once more calmly, healthfully into sight.

The two doors were still closed, the door communicating with the servant's room still locked. In the corner of the wall into which he had so convulsively niched himself, lay the dog. I called to him—no movement; I approached—the animal was dead; his eyes protruded; his tongue out of his mouth; the froth gathered round his jaws. I took him in my arms; I brought him to the fire, I felt acute grief for the loss of my poor favourite—acute self-reproach; I accused myself of his death; I imagined he had died of fright. But what was my surprise on finding that his neck was actually broken. Had this been done in the dark?—must it not have been by a hand human as mine?—must there not have been a human agency all the while in that room? Good cause to suspect it. I cannot tell. I cannot do more than state the fact fairly; the reader may draw his own inference.

Another surprising circumstance—my watch was restored to the table from which it had been so mysteriously withdrawn; but it had stopped at the very moment it was so withdrawn; nor, despite all the skill of the watchmaker, has it ever gone since—that is, it will go in a strange erratic way for a few hours, and then come to a dead stop—it is worthless.

Nothing more chanced for the rest of the night. Nor, indeed, had I long to wait before the dawn broke. Nor till it was broad daylight did I quit the haunted house. Before I did so, I revisited the little blind room in which my servant and myself had been for a time imprisoned. I had a strong impression—for which I could not account—that from that room had originated the mechanism of the phenomena—if I may use the term—which had been experienced in my chamber. And though I entered it now in the clear day, with the sun peering through the filmy window, I still felt, as I stood on its floor, the creep of the horror which I had first there experienced the night before, and which had been so aggravated by what had passed in my own chamber. I could not, indeed, bear to stay more than half a minute within those walls. I descended the stairs, and again I heard the footfall before me; and when I opened the street door, I thought I could distinguish a very low laugh. I gained my own home, expecting to find my runaway servant there. But he had not presented himself; nor did I hear more of him for three days, when I received a letter from him, dated from Liverpool to this effect:

HONOURED SIR—

I humbly entreat your pardon, though I can scarcely hope that you will think I deserve it, unless—which Heaven forbid—you saw what I did. I feel that it will be years before I can recover myself and as to being fit for service, it is out of the question. I am therefore going to my brother-in-law at Melbourne. The ship sails tomorrow. Perhaps the long voyage may set me up. I do nothing now but start and tremble, and fancy IT is behind me. I humbly beg you, honoured sir, to order my clothes, and whatever wages are due to me, to be sent to my mother's, at Walworth. John knows her address.

The letter ended with additional apologies, somewhat incoherent, and explanatory details as to effects that had been under the writer's charge.

This flight may perhaps warrant a suspicion that the man wished to go to Australia, and had been somehow or other fraudulently mixed up with the events of the night. I say nothing in refutation of that conjecture; rather, I suggest it as one that would seem to many persons the most probable solution of improbable occurrences. My belief in my own theory remained unshaken. I returned in the evening to the house, to bring away in a hack cab the things I had left up there, with my poor dog's body. In the task I was not disturbed, nor did any incident worth note befall me, except that still, on ascending and descending the stairs, I heard the same footfall in advance. On leaving the house, I went to Mr. J——'s. He was at home. I returned him the keys, told him that my curiosity was sufficiently gratified, and was about to relate quickly what had passed, when he stopped me, and said, though with much politeness, that he had no longer any interest in a mystery which none had ever solved.

I determined at least to tell him of the two letters in which I had read, as well as of the extraordinary manner in which they had disappeared, and I then inquired if he thought they had been addressed to the woman who had died in the house, and if there were anything in her early history which could possibly confirm the dark suspicions to which the letters gave rise. Mr. J—— seemed startled, and, after musing a few moments, answered, "I am but little acquainted with the woman's earlier history, except, as I before told you, that her family were known to mine. But you revive some vague reminiscences to her prejudice. I will make inquiries, and inform you of their result. Still, even if we could admit the popular superstition that a person who had been either the perpetrator or the victim of dark crimes in life could revisit, as a restless spirit, the scene in which those crimes had been committed, I should observe that the house was infested by strange sights and sounds before the old woman died—you smile—what would you say?"

"I would say this, that I am convinced, if we could get to the bottom of these mysteries, we should find a living human agency."

"What! you believe it is all an imposture? for what object?"

"Not an imposture in the ordinary sense of the word. If suddenly I were to sink into a deep sleep, from which you could not awake me, but in that sleep could answer questions with an accuracy which I could not pretend to when awake—tell you what money you had in your pocket—nay, describe your very thoughts—it is not necessarily an imposture, any more than it is necessarily supernatural. I should be, unconsciously to myself, under a mesmeric influence, conveyed to me from a distance by a human being who had acquired power over me by previous rapport."

"But if a mesmerizer could so affect another living being, can you suppose that a mesmerizer could also affect inanimate objects: move chairs—open and shut doors?"

"Or impress our senses with the belief in such effects—we never having been en rapport with the person acting on us? No. What is commonly called mesmerism could not do this; but there may be a power akin to mesmerism, and superior to it— the power that in the old days was called Magic. That such a power may extend to all inanimate objects of matter I do not say; but if so, it would not be against nature

—it would be only a rare power in nature which might be given to constitutions with certain peculiarities, and cultivated by practice to an extraordinary degree. That such a power might extend over the dead—that is, over certain thoughts and memories that the dead may still retain—and compel, not that which ought properly to be called the SOUL, and which is far beyond human reach, but rather a phantom of what has been most earth-stained on earth, to make itself apparent to our senses —is a very ancient though obsolete theory, upon which I will hazard no opinion. But I do not conceive the power would be supernatural. Let me illustrate what I mean from an experiment which Paracelsus describes as not difficult, and which the author of the *Curiosities of Literature* cites as credible: A flower perishes; you burn it. Whatever were the elements of that flower while it lived are gone, dispersed, you know not whither; you can never discover nor re-collect them. But you can, by chemistry, out of the burnt dust of that flower, raise a spectrum of the flower, just as it seemed in life. It may be the same with the human being. The soul has as much escaped you as the essence or elements of the flower. Still you may make a spectrum of it.

"And this phantom, though in the popular superstition it is held to be the soul of the departed, must not be confounded with the true soul; it is but an eidolon of the dead form. Hence, like the best attested stories of ghosts or spirits, the thing that most strikes us is the absence of what we hold to be soul; that is, of superior emancipated intelligence. These apparitions come for little or no object—they seldom speak when they do come; if they speak, they utter no ideas above those of an ordinary person on earth. American spirit-seers have published volumes of communications in prose and verse, which they assert to be given in the names of the most illustrious dead—Shakespeare, Bacon—heaven knows whom. Those communications, taking the best, are certainly not a whit of higher order than would be communications from living persons of fair talent and education; they are wondrously inferior to what Bacon, Shakespeare, and Plato said and wrote when on earth. Nor, what is more noticeable, do they ever contain an idea that was not on the earth before. Wonderful, therefore, as such phenomena may be (granting them to be truthful), I see much that philosophy may question, nothing that it is incumbent on philosophy to deny, *viz.*, nothing supernatural. They are but ideas conveyed somehow or other (we have not yet discovered the means) from one mortal brain to another. Whether, in so doing, tables walk of their own accord, or fiend-like shapes appear in a magic circle, or bodiless hands rise and remove material objects, or a Thing of Darkness, such as presented itself to me, freeze our blood—still am I persuaded that these are but agencies conveyed, as if by electric wires, to my own brain from the brain of another. In some constitutions there is a natural chemistry, and these constitutions may produce chemic wonders—in others a natural fluid, call it electricity, and these may produce electric wonders.

"But the wonders differ from Normal Science in this—they are alike objectless, purposeless, puerile, frivolous. They lead on to no grand results; and therefore the world does not heed, and true sages have not cultivated them. But sure I am, that of all I saw or heard, a man, human as myself, was the remote originator; and I believe unconsciously to himself as to the exact effects produced, for this reason: no two persons, you say, have ever told you that they experienced exactly the same thing. Well, observe, no two persons ever experience exactly the same dream. If this were an ordinary imposture, the machinery would be arranged for results that would but little vary; if it were a supernatural agency permitted by the Almighty, it would surely be for some definite end. These phenomena belong to neither class; my persuasion is, that they originate in some brain now far distant; that that brain had no distinct volition in anything that occurred; that what does occur reflects but its devi-ous, motley, ever-shifting, half-formed thoughts; in short, that it has been the dreams of such a brain put into action and invested with a semi-substance. That this brain is of immense power, that it can set matter into movement, that it is malignant and destructive, I believe; some material force must have killed my dog; the same force might, for ought I know, have sufficed to kill myself, had I been as subju-gated by terror as the dog—had my intellect or my spirit given me no countervail-ing resistance in my will."

"It killed your dog! that is fearful! indeed it is strange that no animal can be in-duced to stay in that house; not even a cat. Rats and mice are never found in it."

"The instincts of the brute creation detect influences deadly to their existence. Man's reason has a sense less subtle, because it has a resisting power more supreme. But enough; do you comprehend my theory?"

"Yes, though imperfectly—and I accept any crotchet (pardon the word), how-ever odd, rather than embrace at once the notion of ghosts and hob-goblins we im-bibed in our nurseries. Still, to my unfortunate house the evil is the same. What on earth can I do with the house?"

"I will tell you what I would do. I am convinced from my own internal feelings that the small unfurnished room at right angles to the door of the bedroom which I occupied, forms a starting point or receptacle for the influences which haunt the house; and I strongly advise you to have the walls opened, the floor removed—nay, the whole room pulled down. I observed that it is detached from the body of the house, built over the small back yard, and could be removed without injury to the rest of the building."

"And you think, if I did that—"

"You would cut off the telegraph wires. Try it. I am so persuaded that I am right, that I will pay half the expenses if you will allow me to direct the operations."

"Nay, I am well able to afford the cost; for the rest, allow me to write to you." About ten days afterwards I received a letter from Mr. J——, telling me that he had visited the house since I had seen him; that he had found the two letters I had de-scribed replaced in the drawer from which I had taken them; that he had read them with misgivings like my own; that he had instituted a cautious inquiry about the woman to whom I rightly conjectured they had been written. It seemed that thirty-six years ago (a year before the date of the letters) she had married, against the wish of her relations, an American of very suspicious character, in fact, he was generally believed to have been a pirate. She herself was the daughter of very respectable tradespeople, and had served in the capacity of nursery governess before her mar-riage. She had a brother, a widower, who was considered wealthy, and who had one child of about six years old. A month after the marriage, the body of this brother was found in the Thames, near London Bridge; there seemed some marks of vio-lence about his throat, but they were not deemed sufficient to warrant the inquest in any other verdict than that of "found drowned."

The American and his wife took charge of the little boy, the deceased brother having by his will left his sister the guardian of his only child—and in the event of the child's death, the sister inherited. The child died about six months afterwards—it was supposed to have been neglected and ill-treated. The neighbours deposed to have heard it shriek at night. The surgeon who had examined it after death said that it was emaciated as if from want of nourishment, and the body was covered with livid bruises. It seemed that one winter night the child had sought to escape—crept out into the back yard—tried to scale the wall—fallen back exhausted, and been found at morning on the stones in a dying state. But though there was some evidence of cruelty, there was none of murder; and the aunt and her husband had sought to palliate cruelty by alleging the exceeding stubbornness and perversity of the child, who was declared to be half-witted. Be that as it may, at the orphan's death the aunt inherited her brother's fortune. Before the first wedded year was out the American quitted England abruptly, and never returned to it. He obtained a cruising vessel, which was lost in the Atlantic two years afterwards. The widow was left in affluence; but reverses of various kinds had befallen her; a bank broke—an investment failed—she went into a small business and became insolvent—then she entered into the service, sinking lower and lower, from housekeeper down to maid-of-all work—never long retaining a place, though nothing decided against her character was ever alleged. She was considered sober, honest, and peculiarly quiet in her ways; still nothing prospered with her. And so she had dropped into the workhouse, from which Mr. J—— had taken her, to be placed in charge of the very house which she had rented as mistress in the first years of her wedded life.

Mr. J—— added that he had passed an hour alone in the unfurnished room which I had urged him to destroy, and that his impressions of dread while there were so great, though he had neither heard nor seen anything, that he was eager to have the walls bared and the floors removed as I had suggested. He had engaged persons for the work, and would commence any day I would name.

The day was accordingly fixed. I repaired to the haunted house—he went into the blind dreary room, took up the skirting, and then the floors. Under the rafters, covered with rubbish, was found a trap-door, quite large enough to admit a man. It was closely nailed down, with clamps and rivets of iron. On removing these we descended into a room below, the existence of which had never been suspected. In this room there had been a window and a flue, but they had been bricked over, evidently for many years. By the help of candles we examined this place; it still retained some mouldering furniture—three chairs, an oak settle, a table—all of the fashion of about eighty years ago. There was a chest of drawers against the wall, in which we found, half-rotted away, old-fashioned articles of a man's dress, such as might have been worn eighty or a hundred years ago by a gentleman of some rank—costly steel buckles and buttons, like those yet worn in court-dresses, a handsome court sword—in a waistcoat which had once been rich with gold-lace, but which was now blackened and foul with damp, we found five guineas, a few silver coins, and an ivory ticket, probably for some place of entertainment long since passed away. But our main discovery was in a kind of iron safe fixed to the wall, the lock of which it cost us much trouble to get picked.

In this safe were three shelves, and two small drawers. Ranged on the shelves were several bottles of crystal, hermetically stopped. They contained colourless volatile essences, of the nature of which I shall only say that they were not poisons—phosphor and ammonia entered into some of them. There were also some very curious glass tubes, and a small pointed rod of iron, with a large lump of rock-crystal, and another of amber—also a loadstone of great power.

In one of the drawers we found a miniature portrait set in gold, and retaining the freshness of its colours most remarkably, considering the length of time it had probably been there. The portrait was that of a man who might be somewhat advanced in middle life, perhaps forty-seven or forty-eight.

It was a remarkable face—a most impressive face. If you could fancy some mighty serpent transformed into a man, preserving in the human lineaments the old serpent type, you would have a better idea of that countenance than long descriptions can convey: the width and flatness of frontal—the tapering elegance of contour disguising the strength of the deadly jaw—the long, large, terrible eye, glittering and green as the emerald—and withal a certain ruthless calm, as if from the consciousness of an immense power.

Mechanically I turned round the miniature to examine the back of it, and on the back was engraved a pentacle; in the middle of the pentacle a ladder, and the third step of the ladder was formed by the date 1765. Examining still more minutely, I detected a spring; this, on being pressed, opened the back of the miniature as a lid. Withinside the lid were engraved, "Marianna to thee—be faithful in life and in death to———." Here follows a name that I will not mention, but it was not unfamiliar to me. I had heard it spoken by old men in my childhood as the name borne by a dazzling charlatan who had made a great sensation in London for a year or so, and had fled the country on the charge of a double murder within his own house—that of his mistress and his rival. I said nothing of this to Mr. J———, to whom reluctantly I resigned the miniature.

We had found no difficulty in opening the first drawer within the iron safe; we found great difficulty in opening the second: it was not locked, but it resisted all efforts, till we inserted in the chinks the edge of a chisel. When we had thus drawn it forth we found a very singular apparatus in the nicest order. Upon a small thin book, or rather tablet, was placed a saucer of crystal: this saucer was filled with a clear liquid—on that liquid floated a kind of compass, with a needle shifting rapidly round; but instead of the usual points of a compass were seven strange characters, not very unlike those used by astrologers to denote the planets.

A particular, but not strong nor displeasing odour came from this drawer, which was lined with a wood that we afterwards discovered to be hazel. Whatever the cause of this odour, it produced a material effect on the nerves. We all felt it, even the two workmen who were in the room—a creeping tingling sensation from the tips of the fingers to the roots of the hair. Impatient to examine the tablet, I removed the saucer. As I did so the needle of the compass went round and round with exceeding swiftness, and I felt a shock that ran through my whole frame, so that I dropped the saucer on the floor. The liquid was spilt—the saucer was broken—the compass rolled to the end of the room—and at that instant the walls shook to and fro, as if a giant had swayed and rocked them. The two workmen were so frightened that they ran up the ladder by which we had descended from the trapdoor; but seeing that nothing more happened, they were easily induced to return.

Meanwhile I had opened the tablet: it was bound in plain red leather, with a silver clasp; it contained but one sheet of thick vellum, and on that sheet were inscribed within a double pentacle, words in old monkish Latin, which are literally to be translated thus:

On all that it can reach within these walls—sentient or inanimate, living or dead—as moves the needle, so work my will! Accursed be the house, and restless be the dwellers therein.

We found no more. Mr. J——— burnt the tablet and its anathema. He razed to the foundations the part of the building containing the secret room with the chamber over it. He had then the courage to inhabit the house himself for a month, and a quieter, better-conditioned house could not be found in all London. Subsequently he let it to advantage, and his tenant has made no complaints.

THE MIDDLE BEDROOM,
by H. de Vere Stacpoole

Are all living creatures represented in the human race, so that we find shark men —or, at least, men with the instincts of sharks—sloth men, cat men, tiger men, and so on? Le Brun started the idea, I believe, and I take it up as bearing on the case of Sir Michael Carey, of Carey House, near Innis Town, on the west coast of Ireland.

I would ask another question before starting on my story: If a man were to give way to his natural instincts and retire from the world would he develop, or, rather, degenerate, along the line of his main instinct? Who can say? I only know that Sir Michael, the builder of the house that took his name, was known a hundred years ago amongst the illiterate peasantry as "the spider," that so dubbed on account of his mentality and general make-up, he lived alone in his house like a spider in a gloomy corner, that, according to legend, the devil came and took him one dark night, leaving neither rag nor bone of him and that his ghost was reputed to haunt Carey House and the country round, ever after.

The next of kin, Mr. Massy Pope, tried to live in the house. He left suddenly on account of the "loneliness" of the situation and succeeded in letting the place, with the shooting and fishing rights, to a hard-headed Englishman named Doubleday.

Doubleday didn't believe in ghosts nor care about them, snipe was his game and cock; he was a two-bottle man—it was in 1863—and if he had met with a ghost any time after ten o'clock he would scarcely have seen it, or seeing it, would not have cared. But his servants were the trouble. They left one day in a body, being soft-headed folk and unfortified and having a very good reason of their own. Then some years elapsed and the story of the next let, as told to me by Micky Feelan one day, out shooting, was as follows:

"When Mr. Doubleday had gone, sor, the house laid empty, spilin' the country for miles round, not a man would go into the groun's to trap a rabbit nor a woman enter its doors to lift a window, and Mr. Pope squanderin' his money to advertise it. That's the man he was, he wouldn't be bet by it, rowlin' in riches what did it matter to him whether it lay let or empty, not a brass farthin', but he wouldn't be bet by it, it was like a horse that wouldn't rise at a ditch and he'd canther it back and try it again and lather it over the head, squanderin' his money in the advertisin' till all of a sudden he got a rise out of a family be name of Leftwidge.

"Dublin people they were, with a grocer's shop in old Fishamble Street. There was a dozen of them, mostly childer and one red-headed strip of a girl to do the cookin'. Twenty pound a year was the rent, I've heard tell, and they lived mostly be trappin' rabbits, the boys doin' a bit of fishin' and the groceries comin' from the shop where the ould father stuck at work in his shirt sleeves while the rest of the lot was airin' themselves in the counthry.

"Be jabers, they were a crowd, ghosts! Little they cared about ghosts shamblin' about widout shoes or stockin's and the boys wid their sticks and catapults killin' hens be the sly and maltreatin' the country boys like Red Injuns, the shame of the county.

"Norah Driscol was the name of the redheaded slip and many a time me mother has seen her wid her apron over her head rockin' and cryin' wid the treatment of them boys and the botheration of the rest of them, for there was a matter of a dozen or more, rangin' like the pipes of an organ from Micky the eldest son six fut and as thin as a gas pipe, to Pat the youngest not the height of your knee.

"Well, sor, the ghost lay aisy at the sight of the lot of them and didn't let a word out of it for a full mouth. Then one day, Norah Driscoll was goin' along the top flure passage whin the band begin to play. The bedrooms was mostly on that passage and the house agent had warned them against havin' anythin' to do with the middle most bedroom, for, says he, there's rats there that can't be got rid of and that's the cause of all the trouble in the lettin' of the house, says he. It would be a hundred and twenty a year rent, only for them rats, says he, so they're worth a hundred a year to you if you just keep the door shut and don't bother about the noises they do be makin' at odd times—sometimes it's like as if they was sneezin' and blowin' their noses and sometimes it's like as if they was walkin' about with their brogues on and sometimes it's like as if they was cursin' and swearin'. Don't you mind them, he says, but keep sayin' over and over to yourself they're worth a hundred a year to me. That's what' he tould Mrs. Leftwidge.

"Well, sor, Norah was moonin' along the passage, sent to fetch duster or somethin' when she opened the dure of the middle bedroom be mistake. There was no furniture in it, not as much as a three-legged stool and the blind was down, but a shaft of the sun struck through be the side of the blind and there in the middle of the flure was sittin' a little old man dressed as they was dressed a hundred years ago in an ould brown coat wid brass buttons and all and the face of him under his hat topped the sight of him, for Norah said it wasn't a face, but more like one of those masks the childer make out of a bit of paper with holes in it.

"The screech she let out of her as she banged the dure to, brought the family runnin' from down-stairs, and the boys slammed open the door to get at the chap but there wasn't a speck of him.

"'It's a rat she saw,' says Mrs. Leftwidge, 'Down-stairs wid the lot of you or I'll give you the linth of me slipper—and open that dure again if you dare.'

"Down they went, Norah bawlin' and the old woman pushin' her and nothin' more happened that day till the night. Half a dozen of the little ones slep' in the same room with their mother to save the light and be under control, and gettin' on for twelve o'clock the old woman, snorin' wid her mouth wide, was woke from her slape be one of the childer.

"'Mummy,' says he, 'listen to the bagpipes.' She lifted herself on her elbow, but, faith, she could have heard it with her head; under the clothes, for the dhrone of the pipes filled the house comin' from the middle bedroom.

"Next minit the whole lither of them was in the passage, the old woman with a gutherin' candle in her hand, and as they stood there keepin' time with their teeth to the tune of the pipes, the noise of it suddenly let off and the handle of the middle bedroom dure began to turn.

"They didn't wait to see what was comin' out; no, your honor, you may bet your life they didn't, they was half of them under their beds the linth of that night and next mornin' they began to pack to go back to Dublin, gettin' their old traps together and strippin' the garden to take back wid them in hampers. Micky, the second boy, was sent runnin' to hire two cars to take them to the station, for the railway in those days had just come to Drumboyne, twelve miles away, and whilst he was gone they tore up the potatoes and cut the cabbages and faith they'd have taken the flurin' away if they'd had manes to shift it.

"Well, there they were strapped and ready to go when Mrs. Leftwidge, sittin' in her bonnet on the boxes and atin' a sandwidge, suddenly stops her chewin' and looks about her like a hen countin' her chickens:

"'Where's Pat?' says she.

"Pat was the youngest, as I've tould you, sor, a bit of a chap in petticoats, no size at all and always gettin' astray.

"'I don't know,' says one of the boys, 'but faith, I hear him shoutin' somewhere up-stairs.'

"Upstairs they all rushed led by the woman and they hadn't no sooner reached the top passage than they seen Pat bein' whisked through the open dure of the middle bedroom, dragged along be somebody's hand, and when they reached the dure, there was Pat bein' dragged up the chimney.

"It was one of them big ould chimneys a man could go up, and the heels of the child was disappearin' when Mrs. Leftwidge lays hold of a fut and pulls, bawlin' murder Irish, till the thing in the chimney let go its holt and Pat comes into the grater kickin' like a pup in the shtrangles and liftin' the roof off with the hullabaloo of him.

"She tuck him be one fut like a turkey and down she runs with him and into the garden and there when they'd soothed him he gives his story, how he'd been playin' in the passage when a little ould man, the funniest ould man he'd ever seen pokes his head out of the bedroom dure. Pat, poor divil, bein' sated at his play couldn't get his legs under him wid the fright, he could only sit and shout whilst the head of the little ould man pops in and out of the dure-way like the head of a tortoise from its shell.

"Then out he comes the whole of him and grabs the child be the hand and whisks him off into the bedroom and goes up the chimney heels and first haulin' Pat after him. Goes up like a spider.

"Well, they was sittin' about on the boxes they'd hauled out of the house waitin' for the cars and tryin' to squeeze more of the news out of Pat, when up comes the cars wid Sergeant Rafferty and Constable O'Halloran on wan of them, to see they weren't takin' the house away wid them—they'd got that bad name in the county.

"And when the sergeant heard the story, up he went to the bedroom and down he comes again.

"'Here,' says he to O'Halloran, 'take this lot off to the train and go to the barracks and fetch me two carbines wid buck shot ca'tridges—the same ould Forster used to shoot the boys with, bad luck to him—and look slippy,' says he, 'for I'm a brave man, but I don't want to be no longer here be myself than's needful.'

"Off the cars went wid the family packed like flies on them an' in a matter of a couple of hours back comes the constable wid the guns. Up they go to the bedroom.

"'Stick your head up the chimney,' says the sergeant.

"'I'll be damned if do,' says the other.

"'Well, then, shut it,' says the sergeant, 'and keep still.'

"They listened but they didn't hear nothing at all. Then the sergeant begins talkin' in a loud voice, winkin' at the other.

"'There's nothin' there,' says he, 'it was a ghost they saw and it's gettin' on easy I am meself. Let's get off back to Drumboyne and have a glass and lave the ould house to look afther itself.'

"'I'm wid you,' says the constable and downstairs they tramped, makin' as much noise wid their big boots as a rigiment of soldiers. Then in the hall they sits down and begins takin' off their boots.

"'All the same,' says the constable as he pulled the laces, 'I'd be just as aisy in me mind if I was three miles off trampin' on the road to Drumboyne.'

"'So would I,' says the sergeant, 'and it's there I'd be only I'm thinkin' of promotion."

"'I'm thinkin' of ghosts,' says the constable wid the boot-lace in his hand.

"'Go on unlacin' your boots,' says the other, 'and don't be a keyoward, this is no ghost. Ghosts can't pull childer up chimneys.'

"'Faith, you seem to know a lot about them,' says the constable, 'but it's I that am thinkin' it's holy water and Father Mooney ought to be on this job instead of you and me and guns.'

"'And how would you get holy water up the chimney?' axes the sergeant.

"'Wit a squirt,' replies him, 'and how else?'

"'Squirt yourself out of them boots,' Says the sergeant, 'or it's me ram-rod I'll take to you, and now follow me,' he says, 'and walk soft.'

"Wid the loaded guns in their hands up they wint makin' no more sound than shaddas in a wall, and when they got to the room down they squats one on each side of the chimney.

"They hears nothin' for a while, but the tickin' of the sergeant's watch and the sounds of their own hearts goin' lub-a-dub. Then comes a cough. It wasn't a right sort of cough, for, let alone that it was comin' down a chimney, it sounded to be the cough of a chap that had died for want of water and lain in a brick kiln afther.

"The constable said next day he'd have been up and off only the sound cut the legs from under him, the sergeant wasn't much better and there they sat sayin' their prayers and listenin' for more.

"They waited near an hour hearin' nothin', and then all at once began a noise, a scratchin' and a scrabblin' like a cat comin' down a drain pipe.

"'It's comin' down,' shouts the constable.

"'Begob it's not,' says the sergeant and wid that he shoves the muzzle of his gun up the flue and fires.

"He fired from fright to keep it up, so he said at the inquest, but, he jabers, he brought it down like a cock pheasant, turnblin' and clawin' and when they stretched it out on the flure it was a man right enough. A bit of an ould man as brown as a spider, and there he lay dead as a grouse wid the buck-shot holes in him and not a drop of blood no more than if he'd been made of cardboard.

"'Cover the face of him,' says the constable, for that was the sort of face he had, better than I can tell you, and havin' nothin' to cover it they turned him face down, and made off runnin' to Drumboyne for the residint magistrit.

"Well, sor, when they took that chimney down they found a room off it, all littered with bones and birds' feathers and rats' tails. It wouldn't do to be tellin' you of that room, more than it had no winda to it and had been built on purpose be Sir Michael Carey when he put the house up. He'd took to live in it, for that was the way his heart was, and at long last he took to live nowhere else, and that was how the sergeant brought him down and he must have been a matter of a hundred and tin years of age, they reckoned.

"He had his bagpipes to cheer him and frighten away tinints and he'd be out be nights scavengin' for food—they say they found the bones of childer in the room, but may be that was a lie got be him tryin' to drag Pat Leftwidge up the flue—but faith I wouldn't put it beyond him. For that chap was a spider, sor, they said his face was the face of a spider, and his arms and legs no better.

"He'd begun in the shape of a man, maybe, but the spider in him got the bether of him. Look, there's all there's left of the house, sor, thim walls beyond the trees. They set a light to it to get shut o f that room and if you knew the truth of it all, you wouldn't blame them."

THE DRUMMER GHOST,
by John William DeForest

A bit of village—we can hardly call it a street; at best, the mere fag-end of a street; six houses and a church spire in sight—one of the houses, brick.

This is by no means the whole of Johnsonville, for the greater number of its dwellings lie in a neighboring hollow, clustered industriously beside the mill-dam over the Wampoosue, or loafing, as it were, at the two ends of the wooden bridge, or straggling, like picnickers, down the course of the black streamlet. But as these are all hidden from us by trees, and are, moreover, of not the least consequence to our story, we will not invade their sequestered insignificance. A young man, and also, of course, a young woman, demand our instant attention.

"Your uncle's appearance quite interests me," says Mr. Adrian Underhill. "Isn't there something—I don't quite know how to express myself—something rather remarkable about him?"

"I don't perceive that there is, except his appetite for wives; he is just finishing his third."

To think of a girl of nineteen, and a blond, blue-eyed girl at that, making such a speech! But in Miss Marian Turner's auburn there was a slightly disquieting dash of red, and about the corners of her rosy mouth there was a flexible twist which reminded one of the snapper of a whip-lash.

Furthermore, she carried herself upright, in a knightly manner, always ready for joust; she had a quick, positive step, as if she knew to the ends of her little bootees what she wanted; and there was a look in her eyes which declared, "I always mean more than I say." Clearly, if she had not seen life, she had guessed more than enough of it.

"Is that speaking light-mindedly of uncles?" she added. "I don't remember that it is anywhere commanded to be reverential towards them. Well, I mustn't perplex you. Don't mention my queerness to anyone."

"Of course not," answered Mr. Underhill, meanwhile studying her with profound attention.

Just graduated from Winslow University, and from the quiet, bookish sociables of New Boston, he had fancied himself well read up in young ladies, and was almost awed at meeting one whom he could not understand. She said and did the most original things; that is, he considered them most original; and to him what was the difference? Moreover, she had a way of ordering him which was quite new in his experience, for he had been a bit of a Grandison among the female circles of New Boston, and at home he was an only son, the natural governor of his mother and sisters. What was still more curious, and what was even alarming, he had begun to perceive that he liked to be thus ordered.

"There he is," she resumed, nodding towards a tall, thin, haggard man of fifty-five, who just then appeared in the veranda of the brick house; "he looks as if he wanted to see one of us. It can't be me. You had better come in."

Underhill hesitated. Parents in New Boston had put it to him about his "intentions," and perhaps Mr. Joshua Turner was waiting to ask him what he meant to do for Marian. He was aware that he had paid the girl some undeniable courtship, and still he was perplexedly conscious that he did not as yet hanker for marriage. But he drifted along, as is the manner of his unwise sex, and so presently found himself in the veranda of the brick house.

While Marian walked haughtily into the dwelling, without speaking to or looking at her uncle, the latter arrested Underhill with a grim, skeleton-like shake of the hand. Although a landgoing citizen from his youth, Mr. Joshua Turner was as long and lean and brown as the Ancient Mariner, and had moreover somewhat of his ghostly expression of enchantment. A shock of tossled, iron-gray hair; a high, narrow, wrinkled, tawny forehead; hollow black eyes, surrounded with circle on circle of brown and yellow; a lofty Roman nose, looking across a wide, thin-lipped mouth at a projecting chin; cheeks so sunken and pitted that they put you in mind of the epithets weather-beaten and worm-eaten; the whole face discolored by bile, indigestions, and lack of exercise, and corroded by care; the expression eager, anxious, and troubled, to the verge of lunacy;—such was the awful head of Joshua Turner.

"Mr. Underhill, come into the parlor," he said, in a deep, tremulous voice. "I have something private, strictly private, to tell you."

Leading the way into a sombre, curtained room, rendered additionally funereal by that musty smell which country parlors are apt to have, he turned the key in the door, and, without inviting his guest to sit, commenced striding from corner to corner.

"Mr. Underhill, I am almost crazy," he said. "I don't know but I am quite crazy. If I am, it is the drummer—the invisible, ghostly, fiendish, infernal drummer—who has made me so. Who wouldn't be crazy with that unearthly, horrible rubadub-dub?"

Here he began to beat upon his left hip, in the manner of one drumming, meanwhile repeating rapidly, "Rubadub-dub, rubadub-dub, rubadub-dub."

Underhill looked on in amazement and some slight alarm, suspecting that the man was really insane. He mustered up what anecdotes he had heard of lunatics, glanced at the door and windows, in order to settle upon his best method of escape, and finally took a chair by the fireplace, so as to have the poker within easy reach.

"Yes, that is his devilish tune," resumed Turner. "He began it only three days ago, and it has already driven me nearly mad. You are a college man; perhaps you can explain it all. I will tell you the whole story. I was sitting there, in that very chair where you are sitting now, when I first heard him. I was reading a paper— reading about one of Sherman's battles—when he came drumming down the street. I thought it was a pack of boys, or a company of furloughed soldiers. But it stopped, or he stopped, or she stopped, whatever it may be, and drummed so long and loud that I laid down my candle and went to the window. I looked out; I could see the whole street by the bright moonlight; but there was no one there."

After two or three long sighs of profound depression, he resumed: "I thought that the boys or the soldiers had passed, and I went back to the fire. Then it began in the hall—softly, very softly—rubadub-dub. Thinking that some joker was playing pranks upon me, I rushed to the door and opened it. Nothing was there. I went through the hall; I ran upstairs and downstairs; I looked into every room;—nobody! But when I came back to the parlor, something quiet and cold, like a breath of winter wind, followed me. I slammed the door behind me, and I hoped that I had shut the thing out. Then I took up my paper and tried to read. But I was scarcely seated before I heard it again."

Here he stopped his march from corner to corner, and commenced circling a chair which stood in the centre of the room, his hands meanwhile beating gently on his breast.

"It started at the door," he continued, "and drummed straight up to me, rubadub-dub; then it drummed all around me, twice, in a circle, rubadub-dub, rubadub-dub; then it stood between me and the hearth, chilling me through, such a dub-dub, rubadub-dub, rubadub-dub. It had begun softly, but as it went on it beat louder and louder and louder, until at last it almost deafened me with its cursed uproar."

Once more he drummed violently on his hips, repeating in a hurried stammer, "Rubadub-dub, rubadub-dub, rubadub-dub."

Underhill, as may be supposed, was thinking fast without coming to any conclusion. He made a hasty muddle of the Stratford Mysteries, Rochester Knockings, Cock Lane Ghost, and Salem Witchcraft, and did not perceive that any light was thereby shed upon the case now brought under his consideration. Meanwhile he stared at Mr. Turner, and kept within arm's-length of the poker.

"Since then he has never left me for a day," resumed the Unafflicted. "I have struck at him, and kicked at him, and thrown books at him, without touching anything, or hearing anything escape. But he has drummed; O, how he has drummed! Nothing will stop his drumming. He will drum me out of my senses; he will drum me out of my life. That is my story, Mr. Underhill. Can you make anything of it?"

It is not judicious to tell a man that he is a maniac, especially when there is a likelihood that he is one. Instead of venturing on this slightly perilous discourtesy, our young friend meekly replied, "No, Mr. Turner, I can't at once make anything of it. My college education doesn't seem to come in play here," he added. "This sort of thing wasn't lectured upon by the professors. If I had only been a medical student! It does strike me, Mr. Turner, that this is a matter of nerves. Have you consulted your doctor? Why not call him in?

"My doctor is an old fool," exploded the haunted man. "He would give me a blue-pill or some morphine. What good would that do me? Do you suppose the drummer would care if I should take all the blue-pills in the universe? I won't have any medicine. I am a well man and a sane man, whatever you think to the contrary," he asseverated, loudly, his eyes glowing like fires within their deep, discolored hollows.

Although his expression was not reassuring, Underhill nodded assent to his declaration of sanity, being much guided at the moment by worldly wisdom.

"Come here tonight at ten o'clock, and you shall hear him for yourself," continued Turner. Then judge whether drugs will stop him."

The seance was agreed upon, and the young man departed. As he went out, he gave the house a keener glance of investigation than he had hitherto bestowed upon it. The plan was obvious at first sight: a broad hall running from front to rear, with two rooms on each side; the second story an almost pr' cise counterpart of the first; above, the usual pointed attic The flooring was of considerable extent, while the stories w. e not more than eight feet in height, giving to the edifice a flattened, squat appearance.

The material was brick, originally soft, and now very old, so that the exterior had become strangely haggard and pitted, as if from a complex attack of architectural consumption and smallpox. It seemed as if the building were not only infirm with age, but infected, disfigured, and unwholesome with disease. A coat of glaring red paint, put on within the last three or four years, reminded one of rouge on the wrinkled visage of a dowager. In spite of the fresh coloring without, and the new papering within, the building had a moldering look and a musty odor. Underhill could not help conceding that the nineteenth century, as it exists in the United States of America, rarely offers a more suitable haunting-place to a ghost.

At a quarter to ten in the evening, he returned to the house, and was received by Turner in the parlor.

"Excuse my wife for not seeing you," said the haunted man. "She has gone to bed. Her health is very feeble, and this mystery has nearly prostrated her. As for my niece, she has her own ways; I don't pretend to govern her. By the way, you may think it odd, Mr. Underhill, that I should make my niece earn her own living, in part, at least, as a school-teacher. I do it from principle, sir. Young people should learn how hard it is to get money; then they will know how to keep it. I understand that people talk about it; but what business is it of theirs? My conscience tells me that my course is the right one."

Underhill nodded; he rather thought that the young lady might make a better wife for a poor man because of this system of education; and he, just beginning the world, was a poor man, the very one that he was thinking of for her. Not finding it easy, however, to converse concerning Miss Marian, he asked: "Any more light as to the nature of your—your ghost?"

"Judge for yourself," replied Turner, with an anxious glance at the clock.

"Is he regular? Does he come at certain hours?"

"Not always. Morning and evening. He has been thrice at ten o'clock. There!"

Rubadub-dub! There was no doubt about it; a drum of some sort was being beaten upon by something; rubadub-dub, down the street, through the door-yard, and into the veranda; there it rattled furiously for a moment, and then stopped. Underhill was so startled by the sound—it so surprised and convinced, or deluded, his hitherto incredulous soul—that he felt his skin writhe and the roots of his hair shudder. Perhaps he would not have been so moved had he not seen all the yellowish and brownish patches of Turner's complexion bleach to an ash-color at the first sound of the ghostly tattoo. For a full minute the two sat motionless, staring at each other with an air of sentenced criminals. When the young man recovered himself, he sprang up, and stepped softly toward the door, his idea being to steal into the veranda, and surprise some practical joker. His companion arrested him with a wave of the hand, and a hoarse whisper, "It is coming in."

Did it come in? Underhill was not quite satisfied as to that point. The rattle of a drum entered, no doubt; it rolled through the parlor in a distressingly audible manner; but did the mysterious agency which produced it likewise find ingress? Turner evidently believed that the drummer, whoever or whatever it might be, was in the parlor; his ghastly glare said thus much, and he vehemently asserted it afterwards; but the younger man, healthy in body and soul, was even yet only half convinced.

Underhill's first impulse, however, was towards faith; he believed what he saw that his companion believed. For a minute it seemed to him that the drummer entered with a soft rat-tat-ta, the mere trembling of the sticks on the sheepskin; that within a few seconds thereafter he commenced beating a march at the door and continued it straight up to Turner; then came a circling around the haunted man, followed by a furious long roll between him and the fire. This was Underhill's first impression, and while it lasted it was a terrible one.

He had supposed that he was a radical unbeliever in spiritual manifestations; that, if phenomena purporting to be of that nature were presented to his attention, he would receive them with perfect coolness; that he would laugh the mystery to scorn and proceed to unravel it. But on the present occasion his soul did not work in this satisfactory fashion. He was almost paralyzed intellectually; he glared about the room wherever Turner glared; he was little less than thoroughly frightened.

Presently his mind swung back towards its normal rationality, and caught once more at the suspicion that the creator of the noise was in the hall. Rising softly and gliding to the door, he cautiously opened it. No one! nothing but the rolling of the drum; nothing but a clamor without a cause. Another remarkable fact was that the drumming did not seem quite so clear without as within. Unchecked by this observation, to which in fact he then hardly gave a thought, he walked to the lower end of the passage, severely shook a venerable overcoat which hung there upon a nail, returned as far as the foot of the stairway, and mounted to the upper hall.

It seemed to him now as if he were nearing the mystery; and finding another stairway, he pushed on to the garret, but there the uproar grew dull again. He had in his hand a candle which he had taken from the lower passage, and which answered in the Turner house the purpose of an entry lamp. By its light he glanced over the trunks, broken furniture, dismissed demijohns and bottles, fragments of carpets and other indescribable rubbish, which ordinarily encumber a garret, without discovering the smallest fraction of a band of music. Moreover the noise had ceased; it had died away as he set foot on the creaking garret floor; the house was as silent as a decrepit and sickly old mansion could be.

Now back to the second floor; and here he made a discovery. Marian Turner, dressed in her every-day guise and holding a lighted candle in her hand, met him with a mournful and stern countenance which put him in mind of Lady Macbeth.

"Tell my uncle," she whispered, "that my brother must be dead."

"Your brother?" he inquired. "I didn't know that you had a brother."

"I have none now," she answered, her voice shaking with unmistakable emotion. "You will learn yet that he is dead." After a brief hesitation she continued more firmly: "My uncle put him to a trade, and he hated it. Last year he ran away and joined the army as a drummer-boy. He would have been sixteen today, if he had lived."

Here her self-possession quite broke down, and she burst into a loud sobbing. Underhill tried to offer encouragement; he took her hand, and then he drew her towards him: indeed we have reason to suspect that she cried for a while upon his shoulder. At last she raised her head, and whispering, "Tell my uncle," slipped away to her own room.

Returning to the parlor, Underhill found Turner, his face buried in his hands, shivering in front of the fire. At the entry of the young man, the elder, without removing his bony fingers from his sunken eyes, inquired in a shuddering voice, "Did you find anything?"

"No. But perhaps I might, if you had gone with me. I didn't know the house and couldn't get about it fast enough."

"No use. I have been about it at full speed, like a madman. No use."

"Have you seen nothing?" inquired Underhill, wondering why Turner covered his eyes.

"No," answered the haunted man, dropping his hands, "I tell you there is nothing to be seen." After a moment he added, "I was afraid I might see something."

"O, I met your niece upstairs," said Underhill. "She told me to tell you—well, it is very unaccountable and painful; but she has a strong impression that her brother —a drummer-boy, she called him—that he is dead."

"Ah!" exclaimed Turner, springing to his feet and staring at the young man with an expression of intense horror. "What did you tell me that for? O my God! What did you say it for? Do you want to drive me into the grave? Don't you see that I can't bear such things?"

After walking about the room for a moment, he partially recovered his self-possession, and broke out peevishly: "What does the fool mean by such nonsense! I won't have it in my house—I won't have people under my roof talking such nonsense."

"I beg your pardon, Mr. Turner. I was in fault for telling you. Don't lay blame upon her. I assure you that she was quite beside herself with emotion."

As the only response to this was a groan, Underhill concluded that he could do little good by prolonging his stay, and, after a few words of useless sympathy, he took his departure.

During the next day, he learned something new about the Turners. It is time now to explain that he was a lawyer, and that he had set up his virgin shingle in Johnsonville, with the intention of removing to New Boston at the first flattering opportunity. Into his office strolled an elderly male gossip, one of those men who do the "heavy standing round" in villages, and who have discovered whispering galleries at certain sunny corners, where they can overhear all the marvels of the neighborhood.

"Curious goings-on at Josh Turner's, I understand," said this useful personage, dropping into one of Underhill's arm-chairs. "Sat up with 'em last night, I understand. Say he's troubled with a ghost. Pshaw! No ghosts nowadays; ain't legal tender; don't circulate. It's a bad conscience, that's what it is. Tell you, Josh Turner's got an awful sink-hole in one corner of his conscience. Hadn't treated those children right—brother's children, too—only brother. Sam Turner came home, seven years ago, with fifty thousand dollars and two motherless children. Sam died—left Josh executor—gardeen of the boy and girl. Where'd the money go to? Josh Turner can't tell. Sam's estate settled up for nothing, an' Josh Turner turned out rich. Never made enough before to lay up anything, and here he is rich, retired from business, investing in railroads, painting his house. Looks kind of ugly, don't it? Then he made the girl teach school, and 'prenticed the boy to a trade, and let him run off to the army. Can't say I'd take Josh Turner's conscience for all his money. Well, I must be going. Don't mention this, Mr. Underhill. A lawyer ought to know how to keep secrets. Good morning."

From other sources our young barrister learned further particulars. The four children who had been born to Joshua Turner by his first two wives were now all away from home, the two girls prosperously married, the boys in successful business. By his living wife he had another boy, at present five years old. In this youngster the whole affection of both father and mother seemed to have centered. They cared little for the other children; they cared nothing for the nephew and niece. It was currently reported in Johnsonville that little Jimmy Turner would inherit the whole, or nearly the whole, of the Josh Turner property.

"The old woman will bring that around certain," said Phineas Munson, the gossip above mentioned, during a second call on Underhill; "she won't let the old man catch his last breath till he makes out a will in favor of her Jimmy. Dunno why I call her old, though; ain't more than forty. S'pose I call her so because she's such a poor, sickly, faded creetur. She's in a decline, and coughs to kill. But, sick as she is, she's got a temper like a wildcat, and she governs Josh Turner at the first yelp. By the way, heard any more about the ghost? Say it's a drummer, and drums like sixty. Wonder if Freddy Turner's dead? However, I don't believe in ghosts. All fiddle-faddle. Haw, haw, haw," he laughed just here. "I said, all fiddle-faddle. No drumming, don't ye see? Fiddle-faddle. Didn't mean to joke, though. Good morning."

While Underhill was thus studying the shadows of the Turner past, the village was going mad about the ghost. The Johnsonville drummings ought long since to have taken their place, in the history of "spiritual manifestations," by the side of the Stratford Mysteries and the Rochester Knockings. The house was invaded by so many people, and they were there at times in such incommodious crowds, that the

94

Turners were nearly as much troubled by the living as by their spiritual visitant. What added to the excitement was the publication of a list of the casualties in one of Sherman's minor battles, wherein the name of Frederic Turner figured among the dead. Nothing could be more obvious than that the drummer was the ghost of Joshua Turner's ill-used nephew.

Of course, efforts were made to trace the disturbance to a human, or at least a physical origin. The village materialists, that is to say, the doctor, the apothecary, Phineas Munson, and two or three more, nosed about the house by day and watched it by night. One talked of a peculiar circulation in the chimney; another of a loose shingle on the roof which clattered in the wind; another suspected little Jimmy Turner, and wanted to tie him up. All these frantic hypotheses were laughed to scorn by the great majority of Johnsonvillians, who found it more rational to believe in a ghost, and far more amusing.

Curiously enough, Mrs. Turner was one of the most vehement of the unbelievers. This determined woman, feeble and ghastly under the prolonged gripe of consumption, searched the dwelling from garret to cellar, by day and by night, to discover the trick which she declared was being played upon her household. In this investigation she displayed a feverish eagerness which was attributed partly to her native fervor of character and partly to the nervous excitability of invalidism. Small, meager, and narrow-shouldered, her clothes hanging straight along her skeleton figure, her puny and pointed face of a uniform waxen yellow, her large, prominent, lusterless eyes wandering hurriedly from object to object, her shrunken, glassy forefinger beckoning here and there in tremulous suspicion, she was woeful and almost terrible to look upon. So anxious was she to dissipate the mystery, that, passionately as she loved her little boy, she threatened him and whipped him to make him avow that he did the drumming. Then, when convinced of his innocence, she cried and coughed over him until it seemed as if her flickering life would go out in the spasm.

Against the assumption that the noises were produced by Frederic Turner's ghost, she argued with praiseworthy energy though inexcusable logic. At first, she scouted the idea that the boy was dead, asserting that he would yet reappear to make trouble for his family. When further news demolished this supposition, she declared that the drummings had commenced a week after the decease, so that there could be no connection between the two facts. But popular credulity stepped in here to controvert her; people now remembered to have heard the mysterious uproar for some time back; one and another had been startled by it a week before Josh Turner complained of it; in short, the dates of the drumming and the death became identical. Even the cautious and intelligent were obliged to admit that the manifestations began several days before the news of the boy's decease reached the village, and to infer that this circumstance tended to disprove all supposition of trickery. Why should a person, who did not know that Fred Turner was dead, set out to counterfeit Fred Turner's ghost?

For the ear of her husband, Mrs. Turner had another theory which she did not care to make public. "It's that girl," she said. "It's your own niece, Marian Turner, that does it."

"But you've searched her room and found nothing," groaned the husband, as sick in soul as his wife in body. "You've searched the whole house."

"Yes, but I shall find something. She's precious sly and deep, but I shall find her out yet. I have my eye on her, every day, while I am talking about other things."

"But when the—the noises commenced, Marian didn't know about Freddy."

"Yes, she did. You believe me, Joshua Turner, she did. She had a letter or something. Then she knew that the news would get to us later, and she begun her tantrums. O, she's precious deep—precious deep! I wish she'd cleared out when her brother did."

"I wish he hadn't gone," moaned the husband. "I wish I'd treated him better, and kept him by us."

"Joshua Turner, you haven't got the spirit of a man. If you had half my spunk, sick and dying as I am, you wouldn't whimper that way. Everything has gone right, except that you are a coward—a poor, feeble, sick-headed creature—afraid of your own shadow. If you only would pluck up a spirit and let this thing worry itself out, everything would be right."

"Pluck up a spirit? I tell you I can't. It's killing me."

"Well," she gasped, laying her hand on her breast as if to aid the action of her withered lungs—"well, it's killing me, too. That is, you are killing me. But do I flinch? Just look at me and see how I bear it. I wish to Heavens," concluded this audacious woman, "that I could give you my courage."

"Sarah Turner, you have no conscience," he replied, in a tone which was not so much reproachful as horror-stricken.

"How dare you say that to me, Josh Turner? And you know who I am suffering for and slaving for! It isn't for myself that I care," she continued, coughing and crying. "It's for Jimmy. I want Jimmy to be well off. And you want to rob him—leave him a beggar!"

"O my God! my God!" groaned Turner, and walked from her without another word.

"See here," she called after him, suppressing her tears. "If I find that girl is doing it, will you turn her out of the house? Will you send her off?"

He hesitated, looking at her sternly, and at last sighed, "No; I have done harm enough to Sam's children."

She turned her back upon him and left him, with an ejaculation of anger and contempt.

Meanwhile the manifestations pursued their course, to the beatitude of the wonder-loving, and the perplexity of the philosophical. One noteworthy circumstance was that the drummer seemed to hate a crowd. He rarely vouchsafed his music to the swarms of curious who invaded the house, while he poured it forth without stint to enliven the solitude of the Turners. He drummed rarely on a Sunday, frequently on a Saturday, and almost always in the evening. His favorite place of recreation was the parlor, and the listener in whom he delighted was Joshua Turner. Nevertheless, he sometimes assailed little Jimmy with long rolls and tattoos which almost drove him out of his five-year-old senses. The poor child was hysterically afraid of the ghostly visitant, and, at the first murmur of spiritual sheepskin, would fly screaming to his mother.

"There! don't be scared at it," she was once heard to whisper, while looking in his face with the anxiety of ardent love. "If Jimmy won't mind it, he shall be very rich some day, and have all the pretty things he wants."

At last, Joshua Turner remarked, apropos of a clamor which had driven the boy into spasms, "Sarah, it is killing our child."

"I know it," she burst out with a despairing cry. "O, I wish you and I were both dead. Then it would stop."

"If justice were done it might stop," replied the man, solemnly.

"Joshua Turner, don't you do it!" she gasped, tottering up to him and putting her tallowy face close to his. "Don't you do what you're thinking of! If you do, I'll haunt you. I will. I'll haunt you to the grave, and beyond it."

Not long after this interview, Mrs. Turner began to hint to the neighbors that her husband's mind was failing. The charge seemed natural enough; it was countenanced by his extravagance of speech and violence of manner; at times, especially when he talked of the drummer, his conversation was little less than maniacal. For instance, he once broke out in the following fashion upon gossip Phineas Munson, meantime walking frantically round the rocking-chair in which that gentleman was blandly oscillating.

"What do you come here for? Rubadub-dub" (beating on his hip); "is that it? Like drumming? I'll drum for you. Rubadub-dub, rubadub-dub. I'll be your ghost, Mr. Munson, I'll furnish you with the music of the spheres; send the whole band around to your house every evening; give you a diabolical drumming serenade; give you one now. Rubadub-dub, rubadub-dub, rubadub-dub. Had enough of it, Mr. Munson? Now go to every house in the village and report that you have seen the ghost. Do you want anybody to look more like a ghost than I do? I tell you I shall be one shortly; I am being killed by this thing and these people. Why can't they let me bear my torment alone? Why can't you go home, Mr. Munson? Yes, *go home!*"

"Tell you I never was so insulted in my life," repeated Phineas to his fellow-citizens. "Begin to think the old woman's right. Turner must be cracked. Wouldn't 'a' pitched into me so, if he hadn't been. Ought to have a conservator and a keeper. If he ain't watched, there'll be more ghosts of his manufacture."

What was the attitude of Marian Turner during this grotesque and yet horrible drama? Underhill watched her narrowly, not so much in a spirit of philosophical investigation, as because he was on the verge of being in love with her. The theory which he had constructed for the girl was, that she knew that she had been plundered by her uncle, and that she was now engaged in terrifying the plunderer into a restitution. Looking at her from this point of view, he was astonished at the determination, the hardness of spirit, with which she persecuted this family. She was killing her uncle and his wife; she was driving her childish cousin into chronic hysteria; yet she did not flinch. Perhaps she excused herself on the ground that the two elders had been in a manner the slayers of her brother, and that it was not in reality she, but their own evil consciences, which put them to the torture. Nevertheless, he would have been glad to discover in her more of feminine gentleness and even feminine weakness. It must be admitted that man does not easily adore a self-helpful woman.

Meanwhile the girl fascinated him. In the first place, she was the belle of the village, and the belles of other places were too far away to counteract her attraction. In the second place, she was bright and strange; she had entertaining oddities of thought and utterance; she had what he considered dazzling flashes of sarcasm. On the whole, she was the most interesting and original girl that he had ever seen, even putting aside her supposed connection with the so-called spiritual manifestations.

"Talking of ghosts," she one day said to Underhill, "I only know of Mrs. Turner. Did you ever see another person in this world, who so evidently belonged in the next? Why don't she follow her two predecessors? How it must provoke them to see her linger so, and the house new painted and papered!"

"You have very little pity for her," replied Underhill, gravely.

"I haven't a particle. Why should I pity a woman who would marry such an inveterate woman-killer as my uncle? He reminds me of the returned missionaries who used to come to South Hadley School to pick out second and third wives. Why is it that missionaries have such a matrimonial hunger? I suppose it is living among cannibals that demoralizes them."

"I really don't like to hear you joke in this manner," Underhill ventured to protest, though in an imploring tone.

"People joke the most when they are most unhappy," she answered, coldly. "That is, some people. Do you suppose I am gay?" she continued, with energy. Here I am, earning my own living, liable to be homeless any day, and wearing black for my only brother. Think of it. How do you suppose I can be soft-hearted towards people who_ n

Here she stopped, as if she were saying more than was prudent; in another moment she pressed her hands to her face and began to sob. It is not difficult to believe that this interview might have ended in a very common and yet very efficacious sort of comforting; but just as Underhill had taken the girl's hand, a servant appeared in the veranda of the haunted house, and beckoned to them wildly.

They were soon at the door of Mrs. Turner's room; there was silence within, broken only by gurgling gasps for breath; the consumptive was stretched, pallid and quivering, on the bed; the husband was leaning over her, his face almost as cadaverous as hers. Marian Turner walked to the side of the dying woman, and looked at her steadily without speaking. Underhill hesitated, and then advanced, slowly, on tiptoe.

"Shall I call a doctor?" he whispered, while thinking, "It is too late."

"They have gone for him," replied Joshua Turner, without lifting his eyes from that incarnate spasm.

The invalid was struggling violently, not seemingly to live, but to speak. She rolled her glassy eyes frightfully; her dry, blue lips opened again and again, but only to gasp; her whole frame joined feebly in the wrestling for words. It was evident, from the dullness and the fixed direction of her eyes, that she did not see any one, and it is almost certain that she was not aware of the presence of Marian and Underhill. At last the utterance came; it was a kind of voiceless whispering; it merely breathed, "Don't do it, Joshua!"

"Here is Marian," replied the husband, doubtless fearing lest the ruling passion might avow too much. "Have you any word for her?"

A strange look crossed the dying face; it was an expression of many conflicting emotions; it hated, defied, implored, and wheedled. It said: "I detest you—don't rob my child; I have been your enemy—don't take advantage of my death."

But this look, and the emotion which writhed beneath it, exhausted her strength; she had not another word, or even another change of countenance, for any one on earth; the planning's, pleadings, and fightings of her feverish life were over. There was an air and almost a movement of sinking, and as it were flattening, into the calmness of dissolution. Expression slid from her lips; the waxen yellow of her skin turned ashy; the tremulous hands stiffened into peace;—she was gone.

The husband, already accustomed to such scenes, was the only one of the three spectators who instantly recognized the great change. He laid his ear upon the body, listened awhile for breathing, slowly raised his neglected head, shook it solemnly rather than sadly, and exhaled a profound sigh. The expression in his face, like that in the face of his wife, was mainly "long disquiet merged in rest." It seemed as if he were glad that the struggle was over, as if he were soothingly conscious of relief from oppression, as if he breathed freer because her breath had ceased.

Divining from his manner the presence of death, Marian Turner shuddered slightly and drew a pace backward. Then she stood like a statue, looking at the corpse askant and with slightly contracted eyes, as one sometimes watches an object of aversion while desiring to turn away from it. Her mien was that of distaste, and little less than disgust. Like her uncle, she did not utter a syllable.

Underhill was the only one who spoke; and his words were but a commonplace of announcement and surprise: She is—she is dead—good heavens!" This was the only utterance of emotion over the body of one who had just gasped out a life of passionate hatred and love. The child for whom this mother had plotted and throbbed was not even in the village, having been sent the day before on a visit to one of his half-sisters. So far as concerned the presence of affection and mourning, she died alone.

Underhill retired from the scene with exceedingly painful impressions. What struck him most disagreeably was, not the fact of dissolution, but the coldness with which it had been regarded. Not that he wondered and groaned over the widower: it seemed natural that the decease of a third wife should be endured with equanimity; moreover, the departed had been a wretched invalid, and the survivor was a man; finally, what did Underhill care for Joshua Turner?

But that Marian should firmly carry her dislikes up to the verge of the grave was a circumstance which filled him with alarm and almost with horror. A woman, and not a relenting tear; almost a child, and not a start of pity! He called up, over and over again, the sidelong gaze of aversion which she had bent upon the helpless corpse, itself at peace with all the world. "What sort of a wife will she make?" was the selfish but natural question of the young man as he strolled alone at midnight by the sluggish stream of the Wampoosue, as black, silent, and funereal as if it were a gigantic grave. He walked there at that hour because he could not sleep; and he groaned aloud over his doubt, without being able to solve it.

Death, however, brought one relieving change in this drama; from the time that he entered the household, the drummer left it. Not another ghostly reveille or tattoo or long roll gladdened the ears of the gossips and wonder-lovers who had hitherto delighted in such uproars. During the funeral, the dwelling was filled and surrounded by a dense crowd, attracted by the belief that extraordinary manifestations would mingle with the burial rites, and so regardless of decorum in its curiosity that not a room was left unvisited by stealthy feet and peering faces. At times the whisper and buzz of discussion rose so loudly as to drown the voice of the clergyman. At other moments a suspense of expectation seemed to settle upon every one, producing a sudden, universal, profound silence which was inexpressibly sombre. But amid all the debate, and through all the agony of listening, not a note came from the mysterious visitant whose advent was so desired. Probably the prevailing feeling at the funeral of Mrs. Turner was extreme disappointment.

During the following week Underhill did not see any of the Turners. He was afraid to meet Marian, lest he should be fascinated by her presence, and should offer himself as her husband, only to repent of it for life. While he admitted that the girl had had great provocations, and was still suffering under grievous injustice, he could not clear her of a suspicion of cruelty. If she were really the author of the mysterious noises, she might be charged with having hastened the death of her aunt, and that with the full knowledge of what she was doing. No one could have watched the wild excitement of the consumptive during the last three weeks, without perceiving that it was lessening her hold on life. On the other hand, the drumming had ceased with her death. That looked like compunction; in that there was some mercy of womanliness, and from it he drew a hope.

In the midst of his indecisions he received a message requesting him to call upon Mr. Turner. He found the widower much changed—no longer wild in manner and language, as during the whole course of the "manifestations"; with something, indeed, of his native excitability in the tones of his voice, but, on the whole, languid, melancholy, and meek.

"Mr. Underhill," he said, pointing to writing materials on the table, "I wish to make a new will. Can you do it here?"

The young man sat down, and prepared to write.

"Begin it thus," said the widower, bending his shaggy head low, as if in humiliation: "The last will and testament of Joshua Turner, the chief of sinners."

"Let us avoid expressions which may lead to doubts of sanity," remarked the lawyer. "There have been singular circumstances of late in your life. If your will is to be anywise unusual——"

"Leave it out then," interrupted Turner, with the abrupt pettishness of a sickly man. "So I must not even confess?"

After a moment, during which he bent his head almost to his lean knees, he resumed: "Here it is. Ten thousand dollars to my son, James Pettengill Turner. All the rest of my estate, real and personal, to my niece, Marian Turner, to her and to her heirs and assigns. That is all."

It was written; two neighbors were called in as witnesses; the testator affixed his signature. As soon as he was once more alone with Underhill, he walked feebly to the door, and called in a hoarse voice for his niece. Presently the girl entered, bowed gravely to the lawyer, and seated herself at a distance from her uncle, not even looking at him.

"Marian," said Turner, rising, and handing her the will, "read this through, and speak to me."

She read it, gradually flushing with emotion, and when it was finished, she raised her eyes to his face, but still without uttering a word. Evidently she was oppressed by surprise, and hampered by the presence of Underhill.

"The whole estate is sixty thousand dollars. Are you willing that James should have ten thousand?" asked the uncle, with an affecting humility. "If not, I will cross him out."

"I am willing," she replied.

"If you wish it," he continued, "I will give up the property at once, though I am dying."

"I do not wish it."

"And you can't say more?" he implored. "You can't forgive?"

Some hard barrier in the girl's heart gave way at once, and she threw herself into her uncle's arms, crying upon his neck. The outburst astonished the man who had called it forth; never before, probably, had any adult member of his family met him with tears and kisses; it was not thus that the Turners expressed themselves. His words were, "Marian, I thank you; Marian, you are a very strange girl"; and then he let her leave him. Underhill, differently educated in the language of emotion, was unspeakably delighted with the sight of this gush of tenderness, and stole away from the room with a haze of moisture across his eyelashes.

The very next day he heard that Joshua Turner was ill. He offered his services as a nurse, and for a fortnight was almost hourly in the house, watching the progress of an evidently hopeless malady. Through the clouds of a brain fever the invalid heard, and at times beheld, his old tormentor. He continually complained of the drummer; through the windows and down the chimney came the drummer; the street rang and the house trembled with the infernal music of the drummer; at the judgment-seat, ready to bear witness against him, stood the drummer.

The bemoanings and adjurations of the haunted man were horrible. "Has the demon come again?" he shouted, in a high, hard scream. "See him there, stepping through the wall. My nephew? Have I devils for nephews? How is that? Ah! I belong to him; I must go to him. O, hear him! Can nobody stop his beating? Is there no mercy for me?"

During a lucid interval, Underhill said to him, "You have been a little out of your head."

"I have been out of my head for months, for years," he returned, in the husky whisper which was now his only voice. "I have done only one sane thing in five years. Restitution! Restitution!"

"Do you still believe in the manifestations?" the young man ventured to add.

"Thank God that I did believe in them! That madness led me back to sanity."

When Underhill returned to the house on the following morning, Marian said to him, in a trembling whisper, "My poor uncle is dead."

He hailed the tone of sorrow and tenderness with such joy that he forgot the solemnity of the moment, and kissed her hand.

We must pass over six months; during their flight the hand was kissed many times again. Underhill and Marian Turner were engaged. She was greatly changed from what she was when he first knew her. Either prosperity, or penitence for some evil done, had divested her of her old bitterness, and even made her exceptionally gentle. She had taken her little cousin James to her heart, and was doing by him the part of a mother. In deep mourning for her brother, uncle, and aunt, she usually had a pensive gravity which befitted the garb, and she was handsomer than any one had ever before known her.

At last she was Mrs. Underhill. Among the many confessions which she doubtless made to her husband, did she admit a connection with the mystery of the drummings? No; not a word on that subject; not a response when it was mentioned. Nor did Underhill question her; he did not care to open old sorrows.

But one day he discovered, inside the lath and plaster casing of the parlor, a square tin pipe, four inches deep by seven or eight broad, the remnant of some ancient heating apparatus. The opening by which it had once communicated with the room was simply covered over with wall paper, while the upper extremity terminated in the closet of a chamber which, in the time of the manifestations, had been occupied by Marian Turner.

It struck him that a drum beaten in this closet might have sounded below as if in the parlor, and, beaten gently outside of a window, might have produced an illusion that it was coming down the street. A perturbed conscience, the imagination of a sickly man, and the epidemic power of popular credulity, might have completed the delusion. The mystery was as simple as a conundrum after you know it.

But he discovered no drum, and he put no queries concerning the drummer, so that we have a margin for charitable doubt as to Marian, and also a pleasing chance for faith in mysteries.

MISS JÉROMETTE AND THE CLERGYMAN,
by Wilkie Collins

I

My brother, the clergyman, looked over my shoulder before I was aware of him, and discovered that the volume which completely absorbed my attention was a collection of famous Trials, published in a new edition and in a popular form.

He laid his finger on the Trial which I happened to be reading at the moment. I looked up at him; his face startled me. He had turned pale. His eyes were fixed on the open page of the book with an expression which puzzled and alarmed me.

"My dear fellow," I said, "what in the world is the matter with you?"

He answered in an odd absent manner, still keeping his finger on the open page.

"I had almost forgotten," he said. "And this reminds me."

"Reminds you of what?" I asked. "You don't mean to say you know anything about the Trial?"

"I know this," he said. "The prisoner was guilty."

"Guilty?" I repeated. "Why, the man was acquitted by the jury, with the full approval of the judge! What call you possibly mean?"

"There are circumstances connected with that Trial," my brother answered, "which were never communicated to the judge or the jury—which were never so much as hinted or whispered in court. *I* know them—of my own knowledge, by my own personal experience. They are very sad, very strange, very terrible. I have mentioned them to no mortal creature. I have done my best to forget them. You—quite innocently—have brought them back to my mind. They oppress, they distress me. I wish I had found you reading any book in your library, except *that* book!"

My curiosity was now strongly excited. I spoke out plainly.

"Surely," I suggested, "you might tell your brother what you are unwilling to mention to persons less nearly related to you. We have followed different professions, and have lived in different countries, since we were boys at school. But you know you can trust me."

He considered a little with himself.

"Yes," he said. "I know I can trust you." He waited a moment, and then he surprised me by a strange question.

"Do you believe," he asked, "that the spirits of the dead can return to earth, and show themselves to the living?"

I answered cautiously—adopting as my own the words of a great English writer, touching the subject of ghosts.

"You ask me a question," I said, "which, after five thousand years, is yet undecided. On that account alone, it is a question not to be trifled with."

My reply seemed to satisfy him.

"Promise me," he resumed, "that you will keep what I tell you a secret as long as I live. After my death I care little what happens. Let the story of my strange experience be added to the published experience of those other men who have seen what I have seen, and who believe what I believe. The world will not be the worse, and may be the better, for knowing one day what I am now about to trust to your ear alone."

My brother never again alluded to the narrative which he had confided to me, until the later time when I was sitting by his deathbed. He asked if I still remembered the story of Jéromette. "Tell it to others," he said, "as I have told it to you."

I repeat it after his death—as nearly as I can in his own words.

II

On a fine summer evening, many years since, I left my chambers in the Temple, to meet a fellow-student, who had proposed to me a night's amusement in the public gardens at Cremorne.

You were then on your way to India; and I had taken my degree at Oxford. I had sadly disappointed my father by choosing the Law as my profession, in preference to the Church. At that time, to own the truth, I had no serious intention of following any special vocation. I simply wanted an excuse for enjoying the pleasures of a London life. The study of the Law supplied me with that excuse. And I chose the Law as my profession accordingly.

On reaching the place at which we had arranged to meet, I found that my friend had not kept his appointment. After waiting vainly for ten minutes, my patience gave way and I went into the Gardens by myself.

I took two or three turns round the platform devoted to the dancers without discovering my fellow-student, and without seeing any other person with whom I happened to be acquainted at that time.

For some reason which I cannot now remember, I was not in my usual good spirits that evening. The noisy music jarred on my nerves, the sight of the gaping crowd round the platform irritated me, the blandishments of the painted ladies of the profession of pleasure saddened and disgusted me. I opened my cigar-case, and turned aside into one of the quiet by-walks of the Gardens.

A man who is habitually careful in choosing his cigar has this advantage over a man who is habitually careless. He can always count on smoking the best cigar in his case, down to the last. I was still absorbed in choosing *my* cigar, when I heard these words behind me—spoken in a foreign accent and in a woman's voice:

"Leave me directly, sir! I wish to have nothing to say to you."

I turned round and discovered a little lady very simply and tastefully dressed, who looked both angry and alarmed as she rapidly passed me on her way to the more frequented part of the Gardens. A man (evidently the worse for the wine he had drunk in the course of the evening) was following her, and was pressing his tipsy attentions on her with the coarsest insolence of speech and manner. She was young and pretty, and she cast one entreating look at me as she went by, which it was not in manhood—perhaps I ought to say, in young-manhood—to resist.

I instantly stepped forward to protect her, careless whether I involved myself in a discreditable quarrel with a blackguard or not. As a matter of course, the fellow resented my interference, and my temper gave way. Fortunately for me, just as I lifted my hand to knock him down, at policeman appeared who had noticed that he was drunk, and who settled the dispute officially by turning him out of the Gardens.

I led her away from the crowd that had collected. She was evidently frightened —I felt her hand trembling on my arm—but she had one great merit; she made no fuss about it.

"If I can sit down for a few minutes," she said in her pretty foreign accent, "I shall soon be myself again, and I shall not trespass any further on your kindness. I thank you very much, sir, for taking care of me."

We sat down on a bench in a retired part of the Gardens, near a little fountain. A row of lighted lamps ran round the outer rim of the basin. I could see her plainly.

I have said that she was "a little lady." I could not have described her more correctly in three words.

Her figure was slight and small: she was a well-made miniature of a woman from head to foot. Her hair and her eyes were both dark. The hair curled naturally; the expression of the eyes was quiet, and rather sad; the complexion, as I then saw it, very pale; the little mouth perfectly charming. I was especially attracted, I remembered, by the carriage of her head; it was strikingly graceful and spirited; it distinguished her, little as she was and quiet as she was, among the thousands of other women in the Gardens, as a creature apart. Even the one marked defect in her —a slight "cast" in the left eye—seemed to add, in some strange way, to the quaint attractiveness of her face. I have already spoken of the tasteful simplicity of her dress. I ought now to add that it was not made of any costly material, and that she wore no jewels or ornaments of any sort. My little lady was not rich; even a man's eye could see that.

She was perfectly unembarrassed and unaffected. We fell as easily into talk as if we had been friends instead of strangers.

I asked how it was that she had no companion to take care of her. "You are too young and too pretty," I said in my blunt English way, "to trust yourself alone in such a place as this."

She took no notice of the compliment. She calmly put it away from her as if it had not reached her ears.

"I have no friend to take care of me," she said simply. "I was sad and sorry this evening, all by myself, and I thought I would go to the Gardens and hear the music, just to amuse me. It is not much to pay at the gate; only a shilling."

"No friend to take care of you?" I repeated. "Surely there must be one happy man who might have been here with you tonight?"

"What man do you mean?" she asked.

"The man," I answered thoughtlessly, "whom we call, in England, a Sweetheart."

I would have given worlds to have recalled those foolish words the moment they passed my lips. I felt that I had taken a vulgar liberty with her. Her face saddened; her eyes dropped to the ground. I begged her pardon.

"There is no need to beg my pardon," she said. "If you wish to know, sir—yes, I had once a sweetheart, as you call it in England. He has gone away and left me. No more of him, if you please. I am rested now. I will thank you again, and go home."

She rose to leave me.

I was determined not to part with her in that way. I begged to be allowed to see her safely back to her own door. She hesitated. I took a man's unfair advantage of her, by appealing to her fears. I said, "Suppose the blackguard who annoyed you should be waiting outside the gates?" That decided her. She took my arm. We went away together by the bank of the Thames, in the balmy summer night.

A walk of half an hour brought us to the house in which she lodged—a shabby little house in a by-street, inhabited evidently by very poor people.

She held out her hand at the door, and wished me good-night. I was too much interested in her to consent to leave my little foreign lady without the hope of seeing her again. I asked permission to call on her the next day. We were standing under the light of the street-lamp. She studied my face with a grave and steady attention before she made any reply.

"Yes," she said at last. "I think I do know a gentleman when I see him. You may come, sir, if you please, and call upon me tomorrow."

So we parted. So I entered—doubting nothing, foreboding nothing—on a scene in my life which I now look back on with unfeigned repentance and regret.

III

I am speaking at this later time in the position of a clergyman, and in the character of a man of mature age. Remember that; and you will understand why I pass as rapidly as possible over the events of the next year of my life—why I say as little as I can of the errors and the delusions of my youth.

I called on her the next day. I repeated my visits during the days and weeks that followed, until the shabby little house in the by-street had become a second and (I say it with shame and self-reproach) a dearer home to me.

All of herself and her story which she thought fit to confide to me under these circumstances may be repeated to you in few words.

The name by which letters were addressed to her was "Mademoiselle Jéromette." Among the ignorant people of the house and the small tradesmen of the neighborhood—who found her name not easy of pronunciation by the average English tongue—she was known by the friendly nickname of "The French Miss." When I knew her, she was resigned to her lonely life among strangers. Some years had elapsed since she had lost her parents, and had left France. Possessing a small, very small, income of her own, she added to it by coloring miniatures for the photographers. She had relatives still living in France; but she had long since ceased to correspond with them. "Ask me nothing more about my family," she used to say. "I am as good as dead in my own country and among my own people."

This was all—literally all—that she told me of herself. I have never discovered more of her sad story from that day to this.

She never mentioned her family name—never even told me what part of France she came from or how long she had lived in England. That she was by birth and breeding a lady, I could entertain no doubt; her manners, her accomplishments, her ways of thinking and speaking, all proved it. Looking below the surface, her character showed itself in aspects not common among young women in these days. In her quiet way she was an incurable fatalist, and a firm believer in the ghostly reality of apparitions from the dead. Then again in the matter of money, she had strange views of her own. Whenever my purse was in my hand, she held me resolutely at a distance from first to last. She refused to move into better apartments; the shabby little house was clean inside, and the poor people who lived in it were kind to her— and that was enough. The most expensive present that she ever permitted me to offer her was a little enameled ring, the plainest and cheapest thing of the kind in the jeweler's shop. In all relations with me she was sincerity itself. On all occasions, and under all circumstances, she spoke her mind (as the phrase is) with the same uncompromising plainness.

"I like you," she said to me; "I respect you; I shall always be faithful to you while you are faithful to me. But my love has gone from me. There is another man who has taken it away with him, I know not where."

Who was the other man?

She refused to tell me. She kept his rank and his name strict secrets from me. I never discovered how he had met with her, or why he had left her, or whether the guilt was his of making of her an exile from her country and her friends. She despised herself for still loving him; but the passion was too strong for her—she owned it and lamented it with the frankness which was so preeminently a part of her character. More than this, she plainly told me, in the early days of our acquaintance, that she believed he would return to her. It might be tomorrow, or it might be years hence. Even if he failed to repent of his own cruel conduct, the man would still miss her, as something lost out of his life; and, sooner or later, he would come back.

"And will you receive him if he does come back?" I asked.

"I shall receive him," she replied, "against my own better judgment—in spite of my own firm persuasion that the day of his return to me will bring with it the darkest days of my life."

I tried to remonstrate with her.

"You have a will of your own," I said. "Exert it if he attempts to return to you."

"I have no will of my own," she answered quietly, "where *he* is concerned. It is my misfortune to love him." Her eyes rested for a moment on mine, with the utter self-abandonment of despair. "We have said enough about this," she added abruptly. "Let us say no more."

From that time we never spoke again of the unknown man. During the year that followed our first meeting, she heard nothing of him directly or indirectly. He might be living, or he might be dead. There came no word of him, or from him. I was fond enough of her to be satisfied with this—he never disturbed us.

IV

The year passed—and the end came. Not the end as you may have anticipated it, or as I might have foreboded it.

You remember the time when your letters from home informed you of the fatal termination of our mother's illness? It is the time of which I am now speaking. A few hours only before she breathed her last, she called me to her bedside, and desired that we might be left together alone. Reminding me that her death was near, she spoke of my prospects in life; she noticed my want of interest in the studies which were then supposed to be engaging my attention, and she ended by entreating me to reconsider my refusal to enter the Church.

"Your father's heart is set upon it," she said. "Do what I ask of you, my dear, and you will help to comfort him when I am gone."

Her strength failed her: she could say no more. Could I refuse the last request she would ever make to me? I knelt at the bedside, and took her wasted hand in mine, and solemnly promised her the respect which a son owes to his mother's last wishes.

Having bound myself by this sacred engagement, I had no choice but to accept the sacrifice which it imperatively exacted from me. The time had come when I must tear myself free from all unworthy associations. No matter what the effort cost me, I must separate myself at once and forever from the unhappy woman who was not, who never could be, my wife.

At the close of a dull foggy day I set forth with a heavy heart to say the words which were to part us forever.

Her lodging was not far from the banks of the Thames. As I drew near the place the darkness was gathering, and the broad surface of the river was hidden from me in a chill white mist. I stood for a while, with my eyes fixed on the vaporous shroud that brooded over the flowing water—I stood and asked myself in despair the one dreary question: "What am I to say to her?"

The mist chilled me to the bones. I turned from the river-bank, and made my way to her lodgings hard by. "It must be done!" I said to myself, as I took out my key and opened the house door.

She was not at her work, as usual, when I entered her little sitting-room. She was standing by the fire, with her head down and with an open letter in her hand.

The instant she turned to meet me, I saw in her face that something was wrong. Her ordinary manner was the manner of an unusually placid and self-restrained person. Her temperament had little of the liveliness which we associate in England with the French nature. She was not ready with her laugh; and in all my previous experience, I had never yet known her to cry. Now, for the first time, I saw the quiet face disturbed; I saw tears in the pretty brown eyes. She ran to meet me, and laid her head on my breast, and burst into a passionate fit of weeping that shook her from head to foot.

Could she by any human possibility have heard of the coming change in my life? Was she aware, before I had opened my lips, of the hard necessity which had brought me to the house?

It was simply impossible; the thing could not be.

I waited until her first burst of emotion had worn itself out. Then I asked—with an uneasy conscience, with a sinking heart—what had happened to distress her.

She drew herself away from me, sighing heavily, and gave me the open letter which I had seen in her hand.

"Read that," she said. "And remember I told you what might happen when we first met."

I read the letter.

It was signed in initials only; but the writer plainly revealed himself as the man who had deserted her. He had repented; he had returned to her. In proof of his penitence he was willing to do her the justice which he had hitherto refused—he was willing to marry her, on the condition that she would engage to keep the marriage a secret, so long as his parents lived. Submitting this proposal, he waited to know whether she would consent, on her side, to forgive and forget.

I gave her back the letter in silence. This unknown rival had done me the service of paving the way for our separation. In offering her the atonement of marriage, he had made it, on my part, a matter of duty to *her*, as well as to myself, to say the parting words. I felt this instantly. And yet, I hated him for helping me.

She took my hand, and led me to the sofa. We sat down, side by side. Her face was composed to a sad tranquillity. She was quiet; she was herself again.

"I have refused to see him," she said, "until I had first spoken to you. You have read his letter. What do you say?"

I could make but one answer. It was my duty to tell her what my own position was in the plainest terms. I did my duty—leaving her free to decide on the future for herself. Those sad words said, it was useless to prolong the wretchedness of our separation. I rose, and took her hand for the last time.

I see her again now, at that final moment, as plainly as if it had happened yesterday. She had been suffering from an affection of the throat; and she had a white silk handkerchief tied loosely round her neck. She wore a simple dress of purple merino, with a black-silk apron over it. Her face was deadly pale; her fingers felt icily cold as they closed round my hand.

"Promise me one thing," I said, "before I go. While I live, I am your friend—if I am nothing more. If you are ever in trouble, promise that you will let me know it."

She started, and drew back from me as if I had struck her with a sudden terror.

"Strange!" she said, speaking to herself. "*He* feels as I feel. He is afraid of what may happen to me, in my life to come."

I attempted to reassure her. I tried to tell her what was indeed the truth—that I had only been thinking of the ordinary chances and changes of life, when I spoke.

She paid no heed to me; she came back and put her hands on my shoulders and thoughtfully and sadly looked up in my face.

"My mind is not your mind in this matter," she said. "I once owned to you that I had my forebodings, when we first spoke of this man's return. I may tell you now, more than I told you then. I believe I shall die young, and die miserably. If I am right, have you interest enough still left in me to wish to hear of it?"

She paused, shuddering—and added these startling words:

"You *shall* hear of it."

The tone of steady conviction in which she spoke alarmed and distressed me. My face showed her how deeply and how painfully I was affected.

"There, there!" she said, returning to her natural manner; "don't take what I say too seriously. A poor girl who has led a lonely life like mine thinks strangely and talks strangely—sometimes. Yes; I give you my promise. If I am ever in trouble, I will let you know it. God bless you—you have been very kind to me—good-by!"

A tear dropped on my face as she kissed me. The door closed between us. The dark street received me.

It was raining heavily. I looked up at her window, through the drifting shower. The curtains were parted: she was standing in the gap, dimly lit by the lamp on the table behind her, waiting for our last look at each other. Slowly lifting her hand, she waved her farewell at the window, with the unsought native grace which had charmed me on the night when we first met. The curtain fell again—she disappeared—nothing was before me, nothing was round me, but the darkness and the night.

V

In two years from that time, I had redeemed the promise given to my mother on her deathbed. I had entered the Church.

My father's interest made my first step in my new profession an easy one. After serving my preliminary apprenticeship as a curate, I was appointed, before I was thirty years of age, to a living in the West of England.

My new benefice offered me every advantage that I could possibly desire—with the one exception of a sufficient income. Although my wants were few, and although I was still an unmarried man, I found it desirable, on many accounts, to add to my resources. Following the example of other young clergymen in my position, I determined to receive pupils who might stand in need of preparation for a career at the Universities. My relatives exerted themselves; and my good fortune still befriended me. I obtained two pupils to start with. A third would complete the number which I was at present prepared to receive. In course of time, this third pupil made his appearance, under circumstances sufficiently remarkable to merit being mentioned in detail.

It was the summer vacation; and my two pupils had gone home. Thanks to a neighboring clergyman, who kindly undertook to perform my duties for me, I too obtained a fortnight's holiday, which I spent at my father's house in London.

During my sojourn in the metropolis, I was offered an opportunity of preaching in a church, made famous by the eloquence of one of the popular pulpit-orators of our time. In accepting the proposal, I felt naturally anxious to do my best, before the unusually large and unusually intelligent congregation which would be assembled to hear me.

At the period of which I am now speaking, all England had been startled by the discovery of a terrible crime, perpetrated under circumstances of extreme provocation. I chose this crime as the main subject of my sermon. Admitting that the best among us were frail mortal creatures, subject to evil promptings and provocations like the worst among us, my object was to show how a Christian man may find his certain refuge from temptation in the safeguards of his religion. I dwelt minutely on the hardship of the Christian's first struggle to resist the evil influence—on the help which his Christianity inexhaustibly held out to him in the worst relapses of the weaker and viler part of his nature—on the steady and certain gain which was the ultimate reward of his faith and his firmness—and on the blessed sense of peace and happiness which accompanied the final triumph. Preaching to this effect, with the fervent conviction which I really felt, I may say for myself, at least, that I did no discredit to the choice which had placed me in the pulpit. I held the attention of my congregation, from the first word to the last.

While I was resting in the vestry on the conclusion of the service, a note was brought to me written in pencil. A member of my congregation—a gentleman—wished to see me, on a matter of considerable importance to himself. He would call on me at any place, and at any hour, which I might choose to appoint. If I wished to be satisfied of his respectability, he would beg leave to refer me to his father, with whose name I might possibly be acquainted.

The name given in the reference was undoubtedly familiar to me, as the name of a man of some celebrity and influence in the world of London. I sent back my card, appointing an hour for the visit of my correspondent on the afternoon of the next day.

VI

The stranger made his appearance punctually. I guessed him to be some two or three years younger than myself. He was undeniably handsome; his manners were the manners of a gentleman—and yet, without knowing why, I felt a strong dislike to him the moment he entered the room.

After the first preliminary words of politeness had been exchanged between us, my visitor informed me as follows of the object which he had in view.

"I believe you live in the country, sir?" he began.

"I live in the West of England," I answered.

"Do you make a long stay in London?"

"No. I go back to my rectory tomorrow."

"May I ask if you take pupils?"

"Yes."

"Have you any vacancy?"

"I have one vacancy."

"Would you object to let me go back with you tomorrow, as your pupil?"

The abruptness of the proposal took me by surprise. I hesitated.

In the first place (as I have already said), I disliked him. In the second place, he was too old to be a fit companion for my other two pupils—both lads in their teens. In the third place, he had asked me to receive him at least three weeks before the vacation came to an end. I had my own pursuits and amusements in prospect during that interval, and saw no reason why I should inconvenience myself by setting them aside.

He noticed my hesitation, and did not conceal from me that I had disappointed him.

"I have it very much at heart," he said, "to repair without delay the time that I have lost. My age is against me, I know. The truth is—I have wasted my opportunities since I left school, and I am anxious, honestly anxious, to mend my ways, before it is too late. I wish to prepare myself for one of the Universities—I wish to show, if I can, that I am not quite unworthy to inherit my father's famous name. You are the man to help me, if I can only persuade you to do it. I was struck by your sermon yesterday; and, if I may venture to make the confession in your presence, I took a strong liking to you. Will you see my father, before you decide to say No? He will be able to explain whatever may seem strange in my present application; and he will be happy to see you this afternoon, if you can spare the time. As to the question of terms, I am quite sure it can be settled to your entire satisfaction."

He was evidently in earnest—gravely, vehemently in earnest. I unwillingly consented to see his father.

Our interview was a long one. All my questions were answered fully and frankly.

The young man had led an idle and desultory life. He was weary of it, and ashamed of it. His disposition was a peculiar one. He stood sorely in need of a guide, a teacher, and a friend, in whom he was disposed to confide. If I disappointed the hopes which he had centered in me, he would be discouraged, and he would relapse into the aimless and indolent existence of which he was now ashamed. Any terms for which I might stipulate were at my disposal if I would consent to receive him, for three months to begin with, on trial.

Still hesitating, I consulted my father and my friends.

They were all of opinion (and justly of opinion so far) that the new connection would be an excellent one for me. They all reproached me for taking a purely capricious dislike to a well-born and well-bred young man, and for permitting it to influence me, at the outset of my career, against my own interests. Pressed by these considerations, I allowed myself to be persuaded to give the new pupil a fair trial. He accompanied me, the next day, on my way back to the rectory.

VII

Let me be careful to do justice to a man whom I personally disliked. My senior pupil began well: he produced a decidedly favorable impression on the persons attached to my little household.

The women, especially, admired his beautiful light hair, his crisply-curling beard, his delicate complexion, his clear blue eyes, and his finely shaped hands and feet. Even the inveterate reserve in his manner, and the downcast, almost sullen, look which had prejudiced *me* against him, aroused a common feeling of romantic enthusiasm in my servants' hall. It was decided, on the high authority of the housekeeper herself, that "the new gentleman" was in love—and, more interesting still, that he was the victim of an unhappy attachment which had driven him away from his friends and his home.

For myself, I tried hard, and tried vainly, to get over my first dislike to the senior pupil.

I could find no fault with him. All his habits were quiet and regular; and he devoted himself conscientiously to his reading. But, little by little, I became satisfied that his heart was not in his studies. More than this, I had my reasons for suspecting that he was concealing something from me, and that he felt painfully the reserve on his own part which he could not, or dared not, break through. There were moments when I almost doubted whether he had not chosen my remote country rectory as a safe place of refuge from some person or persons of whom he stood in dread.

For example, his ordinary course of proceeding, in the matter of his correspondence, was, to say the least of it, strange.

He received no letters at my house. They waited for him at the village post office. He invariably called for them himself, and invariably forbore to trust any of my servants with his own letters for the post. Again, when we were out walking together, I more than once caught him looking furtively over his shoulder, as if he suspected some person of following him, for some evil purpose. Being constitutionally a hater of mysteries, I determined, at an early stage of our intercourse, on making an effort to clear matters up. There might be just a chance of my winning the senior pupil's confidence, if I spoke to him while the last days of the summer vacation still left us alone together in the house.

"Excuse me for noticing it," I said to him one morning, while we were engaged over our books—"I cannot help observing that you appear to have some trouble on your mind. Is it indiscreet, on my part, to ask if I can be of any use to you?"

He changed color—looked up at me quickly—looked down again at his book—struggled hard with some secret fear or secret reluctance that was in him—and suddenly burst out with this extraordinary question: "I suppose you were in earnest when you preached that sermon in London?"

"I am astonished that you should doubt it," I replied.

He paused again; struggled with himself again; and startled me by a second outbreak, even stranger than the first.

"I am one of the people you preached at in your sermon," he said. "That's the true reason why I asked you to take me for your pupil. Don't turn me out! When you talked to your congregation of tortured and tempted people, you talked of Me."

I was so astonished by the confession, that I lost my presence of mind. For the moment, I was unable to answer him.

"Don't turn me out!" he repeated. "Help me against myself. I am telling you the truth. As God is my witness, I am telling you the truth!"

"Tell me the *whole* truth," I said; "and rely on my consoling and helping you—rely on my being your friend."

In the fervor of the moment, I took his hand. It lay cold and still in mine; it mutely warned me that I had a sullen and a secret nature to deal with.

"There must be no concealment between us," I resumed. "You have entered my house, by your own confession, under false pretenses. It is your duty to me, and your duty to yourself, to speak out."

The man's inveterate reserve—cast off for the moment only—renewed its hold on him. He considered, carefully considered, his next words before he permitted them to pass his lips.

"A person is in the way of my prospects in life," he began slowly, with his eyes cast down on his book. "A person provokes me horribly. I feel dreadful temptations (like the man you spoke of in your sermon) when I am in the person's company. Teach me to resist temptation. I am afraid of myself, if I see the person again. You are the only man who can help me. Do it while you can."

He stopped, and passed his handkerchief over his forehead.

"Will that do?" he asked—still with his eyes on his book.

"It will *not* do," I answered. "You are so far from really opening your heart to me, that you won't even let me know whether it is a man or a woman who stands in the way of your prospects in life. You used the word 'person,' over and over again —rather than say 'he' or 'she' when you speak of the provocation which is trying you. How can I help a man who has so little confidence in me as that?"

My reply evidently found him at the end of his resources. He tried, tried desperately, to say more than he had said yet. No! The words seemed to stick in his throat. Not one of them would pass his lips.

"Give me time," he pleaded piteously. "I can't bring myself to it, all at once. I mean well. Upon my soul, I mean well. But I am slow at this sort of thing. Wait till tomorrow."

Tomorrow came—and again he put it off.

"One more day!" he said. "You don't know how hard it is to speak plainly. I am half afraid; I am half ashamed. Give me one more day."

I had hitherto only disliked him. Try as I might (and did) to make merciful allowance for his reserve, I began to despise him now.

<h2 style="text-align:center">VIII</h2>

The day of the deferred confession came, and brought an event with it, for which both he and I were alike unprepared. Would he really have confided in me but for that event? He must either have done it, or have abandoned the purpose which had led him into my house.

We met as usual at the breakfast-table. My housekeeper brought in my letters of the morning. To my surprise, instead of leaving the room again as usual, she walked round to the other side of the table, and laid a letter before my senior pupil —the first letter, since his residence with me, which had been delivered to him under my roof.

He started, and took up the letter. He looked at the address. A spasm of suppressed fury passed across his face; his breath came quickly; his hand trembled as it held the letter. So far, I said nothing. I waited to see whether he would open the envelope in my presence or not.

He was afraid to open it in my presence. He got on his feet; he said, in tones so low that I could barely hear him: "Please excuse me for a minute"—and left the room.

I waited for half an hour—for a quarter of an hour after that—and then I sent to ask if he had forgotten his breakfast.

In a minute more, I heard his footstep in the hall. He opened the breakfast-room door, and stood on the threshold, with a small traveling-bag in his hand.

"I beg your pardon," he said, still standing at the door. "I must ask for leave of absence for a day or two. Business in London."

"Can I be of any use?" I asked. "I am afraid your letter has brought you bad news?"

"Yes," he said shortly. "Bad news. I have no time for breakfast."

"Wait a few minutes," I urged. "Wait long enough to treat me like your friend— to tell me what your trouble is before you go."

He made no reply. He stepped into the hall and closed the door—then opened it again a little way, without showing himself.

"Business in London," he repeated—as if he thought it highly important to inform me of the nature of his errand. The door closed for the second time. He was gone.

I went into my study, and carefully considered what had happened.

The result of my reflections is easily described. I determined on discontinuing my relations with my senior pupil. In writing to his father (which I did, with all due courtesy and respect, by that day's post), I mentioned as my reason for arriving at this decision:—First, that I had found it impossible to win the confidence of his son. Secondly, that his son had that morning suddenly and mysteriously left my house for London, and that I must decline accepting any further responsibility toward him, as the necessary consequence.

I had put my letter in the post-bag, and was beginning to feel a little easier after having written it, when my housekeeper appeared in the study, with a very grave face, and with something hidden apparently in her closed hand.

"Would you please look, sir, at what we have found in the gentleman's bed-room, since he went away this morning?"

I knew the housekeeper to possess a woman's full share of that amicable weak-ness of the sex which goes by the name of "Curiosity." I had also, in various indi-rect ways, become aware that my senior pupil's strange departure had largely in-creased the disposition among the women of my household to regard him as the victim of an unhappy attachment. The time was ripe, as it seemed to me, for check-ing any further gossip about him, and any renewed attempts at prying into his af-fairs in his absence.

"Your only business in my pupil's bedroom," I said to the housekeeper, "is to see that it is kept clean, and that it is properly aired. There must be no interference, if you please, with his letters, or his papers, or with anything else that he has left behind him. Put back directly whatever you may have found in his room."

The housekeeper had her full share of a woman's temper as well as of a woman's curiosity. She listened to me with a rising color, and a just perceptible toss of the head.

"Must I put it back, sir, on the floor, between the bed and the wall?" she in-quired, with an ironical assumption of the humblest deference to my wishes. *"That's* where the girl found it when she was sweeping the room. Anybody can see for themselves," pursued the housekeeper indignantly, "that the poor gentleman has gone away broken-hearted. And there, in my opinion, is the hussy who is the cause of it!"

With those words, she made me a low curtsey, and laid a small photographic portrait on the desk at which I was sitting.

I looked at the photograph.

In an instant, my heart was beating wildly—my head turned giddy—the house-keeper, the furniture, the walls of the room, all swayed and whirled round me.

The portrait that had been found in my senior pupil's bedroom was the portrait of Jéromette!

IX

I had sent the housekeeper out of my study. I was alone, with the photograph of the Frenchwoman on my desk.

There could surely be little doubt about the discovery that had burst upon me. The man who had stolen his way into my house, driven by the terror of a tempta-tion that he dared not reveal, and the man who had been my unknown rival in the by-gone time, were one and the same!

Recovering self-possession enough to realize this plain truth, the inferences that followed forced their way into my mind as a matter of course. The unnamed person who was the obstacle to my pupil's prospects in life, the unnamed person in whose company he was assailed by temptations which made him tremble for himself, stood revealed to me now as being, in all human probability, no other than Jéromette. Had she bound him in the fetters of the marriage which he had himself proposed? Had she discovered his place of refuge in my house? And was the letter that had been delivered to him of her writing? Assuming these questions to be an-swered in the affirmative, what, in that case, was his "business in London"? I re-membered how he had spoken to me of his temptations, I recalled the expression that had crossed his face when he recognized the handwriting on the letter—and the conclusion that followed literally shook me to the soul. Ordering my horse to be saddled, I rode instantly to the railway-station.

The train by which he had traveled to London had reached the terminus nearly an hour since. The one useful course that I could take, by way of quieting the dreadful misgivings crowding one after another on my mind, was to telegraph to Jéromette at the address at which I had last seen her. I sent the subjoined message —prepaying the reply:

"If you are in any trouble, telegraph to me. I will be with you by the first train. Answer, in any case."

There was nothing in the way of the immediate dispatch of my message. And yet the hours passed, and no answer was received. By the advice of the clerk, I sent a second telegram to the London office, requesting an explanation. The reply came back in these terms:

"Improvements in street. Houses pulled down. No trace of person named in telegram."

I mounted my horse, and rode back slowly to the rectory.

"The day of his return to me will bring with it the darkest days of my life." ... "I shall die young, and die miserably. Have you interest enough still left in me to wish to hear of it?" ... "You *shall* hear of it." Those words were in my memory while I rode home in the cloudless moonlight night. They were so vividly present to me that I could hear again her pretty foreign accent, her quiet clear tones, as she spoke them. For the rest, the emotions of that memorable day had worn me out. The answer from the telegraph office had struck me with a strange and stony despair. My mind was a blank. I had no thoughts. I had no tears.

I was about half-way on my road home, and I had just heard the clock of a village church strike ten, when I became conscious, little by little, of a chilly sensation slowly creeping through and through me to the bones. The warm, balmy air of a summer night was abroad. It was the month of July. In the month of July, was it possible that any living creature (in good health) could feel cold? It was *not* possible—and yet, the chilly sensation still crept through and through me to the bones.

I looked up. I looked all round me.

My horse was walking along an open highroad. Neither trees nor waters were near me. On either side, the flat fields stretched away bright and broad in the moonlight.

I stopped my horse, and looked round me again.

Yes: I saw it. With my own eyes I saw it. A pillar of white mist—between five and six feet high, as well as I could judge—was moving beside me at the edge of the road, on my left hand. When I stopped, the white mist stopped. When I went on, the white mist went on. I pushed my horse to a trot—the pillar of mist was with me. I urged him to a gallop—the pillar of mist was with me. I stopped him again—the pillar of mist stood still.

The white color of it was the white color of the fog which I had seen over the river—on the night when I had gone to bid her farewell. And the chill which had then crept through me to the bones was the chill that was creeping through me now.

I went on again slowly. The white mist went on again slowly—with the clear bright night all round it.

I was awed rather than frightened. There was one moment, and one only, when the fear came to me that my reason might be shaken. I caught myself keeping time to the slow tramp of the horse's feet with the slow utterances of these words, repeated over and over again: "Jéromette is dead. Jéromette is dead." But my will was still my own: I was able to control myself, to impose silence on my own muttering lips. And I rode on quietly. And the pillar of mist went quietly with me.

My groom was waiting for my return at the rectory gate. I pointed to the mist, passing through the gate with me.

"Do you see anything there?" I said.

The man looked at me in astonishment.

I entered the rectory. The housekeeper met me in the hall. I pointed to the mist, entering with me.

"Do you see anything at my side?" I asked.

The housekeeper looked at me as the groom had looked at me.

"I am afraid you are not well, sir," she said. "Your color is all gone—you are shivering. Let me get you a glass of wine."

I went into my study, on the ground-floor, and took the chair at my desk. The photograph still lay where I had left it. The pillar of mist floated round the table, and stopped opposite to me, behind the photograph.

The housekeeper brought in the wine. I put the glass to my lips, and set it down again. The chill of the mist was in the wine. There was no taste, no reviving spirit in it. The presence of the housekeeper oppressed me. My dog had followed her into the room. The presence of the animal oppressed me. I said to the woman: "Leave me by myself, and take the dog with you."

They went out, and left me alone in the room.

I sat looking at the pillar of mist, hovering opposite to me.

It lengthened slowly, until it reached to the ceiling. As it lengthened, it grew bright and luminous. A time passed, and a shadowy appearance showed itself in the center of the light. Little by little, the shadowy appearance took the outline of a human form. Soft brown eyes, tender and melancholy, looked at me through the unearthly light in the mist. The head and the rest of the face broke next slowly on my view. Then the figure gradually revealed itself, moment by moment, downward and downward to the feet. She stood before me as I had last seen her, in her purple-merino dress, with the black-silk apron, with the white handkerchief tied loosely round her neck. She stood before me, in the gentle beauty that I remembered so well; and looked at me as she had looked when she gave me her last kiss—when her tears had dropped on my cheek.

I fell on my knees at the table. I stretched out my hands to her imploringly. I said: "Speak to me—O, once again speak to me, Jéromette."

Her eyes rested on me with a divine compassion in them. She lifted her hand, and pointed to the photograph on my desk, with a gesture which bade me turn the card. I turned it. The name of the man who had left my house that morning was inscribed on it, in her own handwriting.

I looked up at her again, when I had read it. She lifted her hand once more, and pointed to the handkerchief round her neck. As I looked at it, the fair white silk changed horribly in color—the fair white silk became darkened and drenched in blood.

A moment more—and the vision of her began to grow dim. By slow degrees, the figure, then the face, faded back into the shadowy appearance that I had first seen. The luminous inner light died out in the white mist. The mist itself dropped slowly downward—floated a moment in airy circles on the floor—vanished. Nothing was before me but the familiar wall of the room, and the photograph lying face downward on my desk.

X

The next day, the newspapers reported the discovery of a murder in London. A Frenchwoman was the victim. She had been killed by a wound in the throat. The crime had been discovered between ten and eleven o'clock on the previous night.

I leave you to draw your conclusion from what I have related. My own faith in the reality of the apparition is immovable. I say, and believe, that Jéromette kept her word with me. She died young, and died miserably. And I heard of it from herself.

Take up the Trial again, and look at the circumstances that were revealed during the investigation in court. His motive for murdering her is there.

You will see that she did indeed marry him privately; that they lived together contentedly, until the fatal day when she discovered that his fancy had been caught by another woman; that violent quarrels took place between them, from that time to the time when my sermon showed him his own deadly hatred toward her, reflected in the case of another man; that she discovered his place of retreat in my house, and threatened him by letter with the public assertion of her conjugal rights; lastly, that a man, variously described by different witnesses, was seen leaving the door of her lodgings on the night of the murder. The Law—advancing no further than this—may have discovered circumstances of suspicion, but no certainty. The Law, in default of direct evidence to convict the prisoner, may have rightly decided in letting him go free.

But *I* persisted in believing that the man was guilty. *I* declare that he, and he alone, was the murderer of Jéromette. And now, you know why.

THE SPECTRE BRIDE,
by William Harrison Ainsworth

The castle of Hernswolf, at the close of the year 1655, was the resort of fashion and gaiety. The baron of that name was the most powerful nobleman in Germany, and equally celebrated for the patriotic achievements of his sons, and the beauty of his only daughter. The estate of Hernswolf, which was situated in the centre of the Black Forest, had been given to one of his ancestors by the gratitude of the nation, and descended with other hereditary possessions to the family of the present owner. It was a castellated, gothic mansion, built according to the fashion of the times, in the grandest style of architecture, and consisted principally of dark winding corridors, and vaulted tapestry rooms, magnificent indeed in their size, but ill-suited to private comfort, from the very circumstance of their dreary magnitude. A dark grove of pine and mountain ash encompassed the castle on every side, and threw an aspect of gloom around the scene, which was seldom enlivened by the cheering sunshine of heaven.

* * * *

The castle bells rung out a merry peal at the approach of a winter twilight, and the warder was stationed with his retinue on the battlements, to announce the arrival of the company who were invited to share the amusements that reigned within the walls. The Lady Clotilda, the baron's only daughter, had but just attained her seventeenth year, and a brilliant assembly was invited to celebrate the birthday. The large vaulted apartments were thrown open for the reception of the numerous guests, and the gaieties of the evening had scarcely commenced when the clock from the dungeon tower was heard to strike with unusual solemnity, and on the instant a tall stranger, arrayed in a deep suit of black, made his appearance in the ballroom. He bowed courteously on every side, but was received by all with the strictest reserve. No one knew who he was or whence he came, but it was evident from his appearance, that he was a nobleman of the first rank, and though his introduction was accepted with distrust, he was treated by all with respect. He addressed himself particularly to the daughter of the baron, and was so intelligent in his remarks, so lively in his sallies, and so fascinating in his address, that he quickly interested the feelings of his young and sensitive auditor. In fine, after some hesitation on the part of the host, who, with the rest of the company, was unable to approach the stranger with indifference, he was requested to remain a few days at the castle, an invitation which was cheerfully accepted.

The dead of the night drew on, and when all had retired to rest, the dull heavy bell was heard swinging to and fro in the grey tower, though there was scarcely a breath to move the forest trees. Many of the guests, when they met the next morning at the breakfast table, averred that there had been sounds as of the most heavenly music, while all persisted in affirming that they had heard awful noises, proceeding, as it seemed, from the apartment which the stranger at that time occupied. He soon, however, made his appearance at the breakfast circle, and when the circumstances of the preceding night were alluded to, a dark smile of unutterable meaning played round his saturnine features, and then relapsed into an expression of the deepest melancholy. He addressed his conversation principally to Clotilda, and when he talked of the different climes he had visited, of the sunny regions of Italy, where the very air breathes the fragrance of flowers, and the summer breeze sighs over a land of sweets; when he spoke to her of those delicious countries, where the smile of the day sinks into the softer beauty of the night, and the loveliness of heaven is never for an instant obscured, he drew tears of regret from the bosom of his fair auditor, and for the first time she regretted that she was yet at home

Days rolled on, and every moment increased the fervour of the inexpressible sentiments with which the stranger had inspired her. He never discoursed of love, but he looked it in his language, in his manner, in the insinuating tones of his voice, and in the slumbering softness of his smile, and when he found that he had succeeded in inspiring her with favourable sentiments, a sneer of the most diabolical meaning spoke for an instant, and died again on his dark featured countenance. When he met her in the company of her parents, he was at once respectful and submissive, and it was only when alone with her, in her ramble through the dark recesses of the forest, that he assumed the guise of the more impassioned admirer.

As he was sitting one evening with the baron in the wainscotted apartment of the library, the conversation happened to turn upon supernatural agency. The stranger remained reserved and mysterious during the discussion, but when the baron in a jocular manner denied the existence of spirits, and satirically mocked their appearance, his eyes glowed with unearthly lustre, and his form seemed to dilate to more than its natural dimensions. When the conversation had ceased, a fearful pause of a few seconds and a chorus of celestial harmony was heard pealing through the dark forest glade. All were entranced with delight, but the stranger was disturbed and gloomy; he looked at his noble host with compassion, and something like a tear swam in his dark eye. After the lapse of a few seconds, the music died gently in the distance, and all was hushed as before. The baron soon after quitted the apartment, and was followed almost immediately by the stranger. He had not long been absent, when an awful noise, as of a person in the agonies of death, was heard, and the Baron was discovered stretched dead along the corridors. His countenance was convulsed with pain, and the grip of a human hand was visible on his blackened throat. The alarm was instantly given, the castle searched in every direction, but the stranger was seen no more. The body of the baron, in the meantime, was quietly committed to the earth, and the remembrance of the dreadful transaction, recalled but as a thing that once was.

* * * *

After the departure of the stranger, who had indeed fascinated her very senses, the spirits of the gentle Clotilda evidently declined. She loved to walk early and late in the walks that he had once frequented, to recall his last words; to dwell on his sweet smile; and wander to the spot where she had once discoursed with him of love. She avoided all society, and never seemed to be happy but when left alone in the solitude of her chamber. It was then that she gave vent to her affliction in tears; and the love that the pride of maiden modesty concealed in public, burst forth in the hours of privacy. So beauteous, yet so resigned was the fair mourner, that she seemed already an angel freed from the trammels of the world, and prepared to take her flight to heaven.

As she was one summer evening rambling to the sequestered spot that had been selected as her favourite residence, a slow step advanced towards her. She turned round, and to her infinite surprise discovered the stranger. He stepped gaily to her side, and commenced an animated conversation. "You left me," exclaimed the delighted girl; "and I thought all happiness was fled from me for ever; but you return, and shall we not again be happy?"—"Happy," replied the stranger, with a scornful burst of derision, "Can I ever be happy again—can there—but excuse the agitation, my love, and impute it to the pleasure I experience at our meeting. Oh! I have many things to tell you; aye! and many kind words to receive; is it not so, sweet one? Come, tell me truly, have you been happy in my absence? No! I see in that sunken eye, in that pallid cheek, that the poor wanderer has at least gained some slight interest in the heart of his beloved. I have roamed to other climes, I have seen other nations; I have met with other females, beautiful and accomplished, but I have met with but one angel, and she is here before me. Accept this simple offering of my affection, dearest," continued the stranger, plucking a heath-rose from its stem; "it is beautiful as the wild flowers that deck thy hair, and sweet as is the love I bear thee."—"It is sweet, indeed," replied Clotilda, "but its sweetness must wither ere night closes around. It is beautiful, but its beauty is short-lived, as the love evinced by man. Let not this, then, be the type of thy attachment; bring me the delicate evergreen, the sweet flower that blossoms throughout the year, and I will say, as I wreathe it in my hair, 'The violets have bloomed and died—the roses have flourished and decayed; but the evergreen is still young, and so is the love of heart!/— you will not—cannot desert me. I live but in you; you are my hopes, my thoughts, my existence itself: and if I lose you, I lose my all—I was but a solitary wild flower in the wilderness of nature, until you transplanted me to a more genial soil; and can you now break the fond heart you first taught to glow with passion?"—"Speak not thus," returned the stranger, "it rends my very soul to hear you; leave me—forget me—avoid me for ever—or your eternal ruin must ensue. I am a thing abandoned of God and man—and did you but see the scared heart that scarcely beats within this moving mass of deformity, you would flee me, as you would an adder in your path. Here is my heart, love, feel how cold it is; there is no pulse that betrays its emotion; for all is chilled and dead as the friends I once knew."—"You are unhappy, love, and your poor Clotilda shall stay to succour you. Think not I can abandon you in your misfortunes. No! I will wander with thee through the wide world, and be thy servant, thy slave, if thou wilt have it so. I will shield thee from the night winds, that they blow not too roughly on thy unprotected head. I will defend thee from the tempest that howls around; and though the cold world may devote thy name to scorn—though friends may fall off, and associates wither in the grave, there shall be one fond heart who shall love thee better in thy misfortune, and cherish thee, bless thee still." She ceased, and her blue eyes swam in tears, as she turned it glistening with affection towards the stranger. He averted his head from her gaze, and a scornful sneer of the darkest, the deadliest malice passed over his fine countenance. In an instant, the expression subsided; his fixed glassy eye resumed its unearthly chillness, and he turned once again to his companion. "It is the hour of sunset," he exclaimed; "the soft, the beauteous hour, when the hearts of lovers are happy, and nature smiles in unison with their feelings; but to me it will smile no longer—ere the morrow dawns I shall very far, from the house of my beloved; from the scenes where my heart is enshrined, as in a sepulchre. But must I leave thee, dearest flower of the wilderness, to be the sport of a whirlwind, the prey of the mountain blast?"—"No, we will not part," replied the impassioned girl; "where thou goest, will I go; thy home shall be my home; and thy God shall be my God."—"Swear it, swear it," resumed the stranger, wildly grasping her by the hand; "swear to the fearful oath I shall dictate." He then desired her to kneel, and holding his right hand in a menacing attitude towards heaven, and throwing back his dark raven locks, exclaimed in a strain of bitter imprecation with the ghastly smile of an incarnate fiend, "May the curses of an offended God," he cried, "haunt thee, cling to thee for ever in the tempest and in the calm, in the day and in the night, in sickness and in sorrow, in life and in death, shouldst thou swerve from the promise thou hast here made to be mine. May the dark spirits of the damned howl in thine ears the accursed chorus of fiends—may the air rack thy bosom with the quenchless flames of hell! May thy soul be as the lazar-house of corruption, where the ghost of departed pleasure sits enshrined, as in a grave: where the hundred-headed worm never dies where the fire is never extinguished. May a spirit of evil lord it over thy brow, and proclaim, as thou passest by, '*This is the abandoned of God and man*;' may fearful spectres haunt thee in the night season; may thy dearest friends drop day by day into the grave, and curse thee with their dying breath: may all that is most horrible in human nature, more solemn than language can frame, or lips can utter, may this, and more than this, be thy eternal portion, shouldst thou violate the oath that thou has taken." He ceased—hardly knowing what she did, the terrified girl acceded to the awful adjuration, and promised eternal fidelity to him who was henceforth to be her lord. "Spirits of the damned, I thank thee for thine assistance," shouted the stranger; "I have wooed my fair bride bravely. She is mine—mine for ever.—Aye, body and soul both mine; mine in life, and mine in death. What in tears, my sweet one, ere yet the honeymoon is past? Why! indeed thou hast cause for weeping: but when next we meet we shall meet to sign the nuptial bond." He then imprinted a cold salute on the cheek of his young bride, and softening down the unutterable horrors of his countenance, requested her to meet him at eight o'clock on the ensuing evening in the chapel adjoining to the castle of Hernswolf. She turned round to him with a burning sigh, as if to implore protection from himself, but the stranger was gone.

On entering the castle, she was observed to be impressed with deepest melancholy. Her relations vainly endeavoured to ascertain the cause of her uneasiness; but the tremendous oath she had sworn completely paralysed her faculties, and she was fearful of betraying herself by even the slightest intonation of her voice, or the least variable expression of her countenance. When the evening was concluded, the family retired to rest; but Clotilda, who was unable to take repose, from the restlessness of her disposition, requested to remain alone in the library that adjoined her apartment.

All was now deep midnight; every domestic had long since retired to rest, and the only sound that could be distinguished was the sullen howl of the ban-dog as he bayed, the waning moon Clotilda remained in the library in an attitude of deep meditation. The lamp that burnt on the table, where she sat, was dying away, and the lower end of the apartment was already more than half obscured. The clock from the northern angle of the castle tolled out the hour of twelve, and the sound echoed dismally in the solemn stillness of the night. Sudden the oaken door at the farther end of the room was gently lifted on its latch, and a bloodless figure, apparelled in the habiliments of the grave, advanced slowly up the apartment. No sound heralded its approach, as it moved with noiseless steps to the table where the lady was stationed. She did not at first perceive it, till she felt a death-cold hand fast grasped in her own, and heard a solemn voice whisper in her ear, "Clotilda." She looked up, a dark figure was standing beside her; she endeavoured to scream, but her voice was unequal to the exertion; her eye was fixed, as if by magic, on the form which, slowly removed the garb that concealed its countenance, and disclosed the livid eyes and skeleton shape of her father. It seemed to gaze on her with pity, an regret, and mournfully exclaimed—"Clotilda, the dresses and the servants are ready, the church bell has tolled, and the priest is at the altar, but where is the affianced bride? There is room for her in the grave, and tomorrow shall she be with me."—

"Tomorrow?" faltered out the distracted girl; "the spirits of hell shall have registered it, and tomorrow must the bond be cancelled." The figure ceased—slowly retired, and was soon lost in the obscurity of distance.

The morning—evening—arrived; and already as the hall clock struck eight, Clotilda was on her road to the chapel. It was a dark, gloomy night, thick masses of dun clouds sailed across the firmament, and the roar of the winter wind echoed awfully through the forest trees. She reached the appointed place; a figure was in waiting for her—it advanced—and discovered the features of the stranger. "Why! this is well, my bride," he exclaimed, with a sneer; "and well will I repay thy fondness. Follow me." They proceeded together in silence through the winding avenues of the chapel, until they reached the adjoining cemetery. Here they paused for an instant; and the stranger, in a softened tone, said, "But one hour more, and the struggle will be over. And yet this heart of incarnate malice can feel, when it devotes so young, so pure a spirit to the grave. But it must—it must be," he proceeded, as the memory of her past love rushed on her mind; "for the fiend whom I obey has so willed it. Poor girl, I am leading thee indeed to our nuptials; but the priest will be death, thy parents the mouldering skeletons that rot in heaps around; and the witnesses to our union, the lazy worms that revel on the carious bones of the dead. Come, my young bride, the priest is impatient for his victim." As they proceeded, a dim blue light moved swiftly before them, and displayed at the extremity of the churchyard the portals of a vault. It was open, and they entered it in silence. The hollow wind came rushing through the gloomy abode of the dead; and on every side were piled the mouldering remnants of coffins, which dropped piece by piece upon the damp mud. Every step they took was on a dead body; and the bleached bones rattled horribly beneath their feet. In the centre of the vault rose a heap of unburied skeletons, whereon was seated, a figure too awful even for the darkest imagination to conceive. As they approached it, the hollow vault rung with a hellish peal of laughter; and every mouldering corpse seemed endued with unholy life. The stranger paused, and as he grasped his victim in his hand, one sigh burst from his heart—one tear glistened in his eye. It was but for an instant; the figure frowned awfully at his vacillation, and waved his gaunt hand.

The stranger advanced; he made certain mystic circles in the air, uttered unearthly words, and paused in excess of terror. On a sudden he raised his voice and wildly exclaimed—"Spouse of the spirit of darkness, a few moments are yet thine; that thou may'st know to whom thou hast consigned thyself. I am the undying spirit of the wretch who curst his Saviour on the cross. He looked at me in the closing hour of his existence, and that look hath not yet passed away, for I am curst above all on earth. I am eternally condemned to hell and I must cater for my master's taste till the world is parched as is a scroll, and the heavens and the earth have passed away. I am he of whom thou may'st have read, and of whose feats thou may'st have heard. A million souls has my master condemned me to ensnare, and then my penance is accomplished, and I may know the repose of the grave. Thou art the thousandth soul that I have damned. I saw thee in thine hour of purity, and I marked thee at once for my home. Thy father did I murder for his temerity, and permitted to warn thee of thy fate; and myself have I beguiled for thy simplicity. Ha! the spell works bravely, and thou shall soon see, my sweet one, to whom thou hast linked thine undying fortunes, for as long as the seasons shall move on their course of nature—as long as the lightning shall flash, and the thunders roll, thy penance shall be eternal. Look below! and see to what thou art destined." She looked, the vault split in a thousand different directions; the earth yawned asunder; and the roar of mighty waters was heard. A living ocean of molten fire glowed in the abyss beneath her, and blending with the shrieks of the damned, and the triumphant shouts of the fiends, rendered horror more horrible than imagination. Ten millions of souls were writhing in the fiery flames, and as the boiling billows dashed them against the blackened rocks of adamant, they cursed with the blasphemies of despair; and each curse echoed in thunder cross the wave. The stranger rushed towards his victim. For an instant he held her over the burning vista, looked fondly in her face and wept as he were a child. This was but the impulse of a moment; again he grasped her in his arms, dashed her from him with fury; and as her last parting glance was cast in kindness on his face, shouted aloud, "not mine is the crime, but the religion that thou professest; for is it not said that there is a fire of eternity prepared for the souls of the wicked; and hast not thou incurred its torments?" She, poor girl, heard not, heeded not the shouts of the blasphemer. Her delicate form bounded from rock to rock, over billow, and over foam; as she fell, the ocean lashed itself as it were in triumph to receive her soul, and as she sunk deep in the burning pit, ten thousand voices reverberated from the bottomless abyss, "Spirit of evil! here indeed is an eternity of torments prepared for thee; for here the worm never dies, and the fire is never quenched."

THE TAPESTRIED CHAMBER;
or, The Lady in the Square,
by Sir Walter Scott

About the end of the American war, when the officers of Lord Cornwallis's army which surrendered at Yorktown, and others, who had been made prisoners during the impolitic and ill-fated controversy, were returning to their own country, to relate their adventures and repose themselves after their fatigues, there was amongst them a general officer, to whom Miss S. gave the name of Browne, but merely, as I understood, to save the inconvenience of introducing a nameless agent in the narrative. He was an officer of merit, as well as a gentleman of high consideration for family and attainments.

Some business had carried General Browne upon a tour through the western counties, when, in the conclusion of a morning stage, he found himself in the vicinity of a small country town, which presented a scene of uncommon beauty and of a character peculiarly English.

The little town, with its stately old church whose tower bore testimony to the devotion of ages long past, lay amidst pasture and corn-fields of small extent, but bounded and divided with hedgerow timber of great age and size. There were few marks of modern improvement. The environs of the place intimated neither the solitude of decay, nor the bustle of novelty; the houses were old, but in good repair; and the beautiful little river murmured freely on its way to the left of the town, neither restrained by a dam, nor bordered by a towing-path.

Upon a gentle eminence, nearly a mile to the southward of the town, were seen amongst many venerable oaks and tangled thickets the turrets of a castle, as old as the wars of York and Lancaster, but which seemed to have received important alterations during the age of Elizabeth and her successors. It had not been a place of great size; but whatever accommodation it formerly afforded, was, it must be supposed, still to be obtained within its walls; at least, such was the inference which General Browne drew from observing the smoke arise merrily from several of the ancient wreathed and carved chimney-stalks.

The wall of the park ran alongside of the highway for two or three hundred yards, and, through the different points by which the eye found glimpses into the woodland scenery, it seemed to be well stocked. Other points of view opened in succession; now a full one, of the front of the old castle, and now a side glimpse at its particular towers; the former rich in all the bizarrerie of the Elizabethan school, while the simple and solid strength of other parts of the building seemed to show that they had been raised more for defence than ostentation.

Delighted with the partial glimpses which he obtained of the castle through the woods and glades by which this ancient feudal fortress was surrounded, our military traveller was determined to inquire whether it might not deserve a nearer view, and whether it contained family pictures or other objects of curiosity worthy of a stranger's visit, when, leaving the vicinity of the park, he rolled through a clean and well-paved street, and stopped at the door of a well-frequented inn.

Before ordering horses to proceed on his journey, General Browne made inquiries concerning the proprietor of the château which had so attracted his admiration, and was equally surprised and pleased at hearing in reply a nobleman named whom we shall call Lord Woodville. How fortunate! Much of Browne's early recollections, both at school and at college, had been connected with young Woodville, whom, by a few questions, he now ascertained to be the same with the owner of this fair domain. He had been raised to the peerage by the decease of his father a few months before, and, as the General learned from the landlord, the term of mourning being ended, was now taking possession of his paternal estate in the jovial season of merry autumn, accompanied by a select party of friends to enjoy the sports of a country famous for game.

This was delightful news to our traveller. Frank Woodville had been Richard Browne's fag at Eton, and his chosen intimate at Christ Church; their pleasures and their tasks had been the same; and the honest soldier's heart warmed to find his early friend in possession of so delightful a residence, and of an estate, as the landlord assured him with a nod and a wink, fully adequate to maintain and add to his dignity. Nothing was more natural than that the traveller should suspend a journey, which there was nothing to render hurried, to pay a visit to an old friend under such agreeable circumstances.

The fresh horses, therefore, had only the brief task of conveying the General's travelling-carriage to Woodville Castle. A porter admitted them at a modern Gothic lodge, built in that style to correspond with the castle itself, and at the same time rang a bell to give warning of the approach of visitors. Apparently the sound of the bell had suspended the separation of the company, bent on the various amusements of the morning; for, on entering the court of the château, several young men were lounging about in their sporting-dresses, looking at, and criticizing, the dogs which the keepers held in readiness to attend their pastime.

As General Browne alighted, the young lord came to the gate of the hall, and for an instant gazed, as at a stranger, upon the countenance of his friend, on which war, with its fatigues and its wounds, had made a great alteration. But the uncertainty lasted no longer than till the visitor had spoken, and the hearty greeting which followed was such as can only be exchanged betwixt those who have passed together merry days of careless boyhood or early youth.

"If I could have formed a wish, my dear Browne," said Lord Woodville, "it would have been to have you here, of all men, upon this occasion, which my friends are good enough to hold as a sort of holiday. Do not think you have been unwatched during the years you have been absent from us. I have traced you through your dangers, your triumphs, your misfortunes, and was delighted to see that, whether in victory or defeat, the name of my old friend was always distinguished with applause."

The General made a suitable reply, and congratulated his friend on his new dignities, and the possession of a place and domain so beautiful.

"Nay, you have seen nothing of it as yet," said Lord Woodville, "and I trust you do not mean to leave us till you are better acquainted with it. It is true, I confess, that my present party is pretty large, and the old house, like other places of the kind, does not possess so much accommodation as the extent of the outward walls appears to promise. But we can give you a comfortable old-fashioned room, and I venture to suppose that your campaigns have taught you to be glad of worse quarters."

The General shrugged his shoulders, and laughed. "I presume," he said, "the worst apartment in your château is considerably superior to the old tobacco-cask, in which I was fain to take up my night's lodging when I was in the Bush, as the Virginians call it, with the light corps. There I lay, like Diogenes himself, so delighted with my covering from the elements, that I made a vain attempt to have it rolled on to my next quarters; but my commander for the time would give way to no such luxurious provision, and I took farewell of my beloved cask with tears in my eyes."

"Well, then, since you do not fear your quarters," said Lord Woodville "you will stay with me a week at least. Of guns, dogs, fishing-rods, flies, and means of sport by sea and land, we have enough and to spare: you cannot pitch on an amusement, but we will pitch on the means of pursuing it. But if you prefer the gun and pointers, I will go with you myself, and see whether you have mended your shooting since you have been amongst the Indians of the back settlements."

The General gladly accepted his friendly host's proposal in all its points. After a morning of manly exercise, the company met at dinner, where it was the delight of Lord Woodville to conduce to the display of the high properties of his recovered friend, so as to recommend him to his guests, most of whom were persons of distinction. He led General Browne to speak of the scenes he had witnessed; and as every word marked alike the brave officer and the sensible man, who retained possession of his cool judgement under the most imminent dangers, the company looked upon the soldier with general respect, as on one who had proved himself possessed of an uncommon portion of personal courage—that attribute, of all others, of which everybody desires to be thought possessed.

The day at Woodville Castle ended as usual in such mansions. The hospitality stopped within the limits of good order; music, in which the young lord was a proficient, succeeded to the circulation of the bottle; cards and billiards, for those who preferred such amusements, were in readiness; but the exercise of the morning required early hours, and not long after eleven o'clock the guests began to retire to their several apartments.

The young lord himself conducted his friend, General Browne, to the chamber destined for him, which answered the description he had given of it, being comfortable, but old-fashioned. The bed was of the massive form used in the end of the seventeenth century, and the curtains of faded silk, heavily trimmed with tarnished gold. But then the sheets, pillows, and blankets looked delightful to the campaigner, when he thought of his "mansion, the cask."

There was an air of gloom in the tapestry hangings which, with their worn-out graces, curtained the walls of the little chamber, and gently undulated as the autumnal breeze found its way through the ancient lattice-window, which pattered and whistled as the air gained entrance. The toilet too, with its mirror, turbaned, after the manner of the beginning of the century, with a coiffure of murrey-coloured silk, and its hundred strange-shaped boxes, providing for arrangements which had been obsolete for more than fifty years, had an antique, and in so far a melancholy, aspect. But nothing could blaze more brightly and cheerfully than the two large wax candles; or if aught could rival them, it was the flaming bickering fagots in the chimney, that sent at once their gleam and their warmth through the snug apartment; which, notwithstanding the general antiquity of its appearance, was not wanting in the least convenience that modern habits rendered either necessary or desirable.

"This is an old-fashioned sleeping apartment, General," said the young lord; "but I hope you will find nothing that makes you envy your old tobacco-cask."

"I am not particular respecting my lodgings," replied the General; "yet were I to make any choice, I would prefer this chamber by many degrees, to the gayer and more modern rooms of your family mansion. Believe me that when I unite its modern air of comfort with its venerable antiquity, and recollect that it is your lord-ship's property, I shall feel in better quarters here, than if I were in the best hotel London could afford."

"I trust—I have no doubt—that you will find yourself as comfortable as I wish you, my dear General," said the young nobleman; and once more bidding his guest good night, he shook him by the hand and withdrew.

The General once more looked round him, and internally congratulating himself on his return to peaceful life, the comforts of which were endeared by the recollec-tion of the hardships and dangers he had lately sustained, undressed himself, and prepared himself for a luxurious night's rest.

Here, contrary to the custom of this species of tale, we leave the General in pos-session of his apartment until the next morning.

The company assembled for breakfast at an early hour, but without the appear-ance of General Browne, who seemed the guest that Lord Woodville was desirous of honouring above all whom his hospitality had assembled around him. He more than once expressed surprise at the General's absence, and at length sent a servant to make inquiry after him. The man brought back information that General Browne had been walking abroad since an early hour of the morning, in defiance of the weather, which was misty and ungenial.

"The custom of a soldier," said the young nobleman to his friends: "many of them acquire habitual vigilance, and cannot sleep after the early hour at which their duty usually commands them to be alert."

Yet the explanation which Lord Woodville thus offered to the company seemed hardly satisfactory to his own mind, and it was in a fit of silence and abstraction that he awaited the return of the General. It took place near an hour after the break-fast-bell had rung. He looked fatigued and feverish. His hair, the powdering and arrangement of which was at this time one of the most important occupations of a man's whole day, and marked his fashion as much as, in the present time, the tying of a cravat or the want of one, was dishevelled, uncurled, void of powder, and dank with dew. His clothes were huddled on with a careless negligence, remarkable in a military man, whose real or supposed duties are usually held to include some atten-tion to the toilet; and his looks were haggard and ghastly in a peculiar degree.

"So you have stolen a march upon us this morning, my dear General," said Lord Woodville; "or you have not found your bed so much to your mind as I had hoped and you seemed to expect. How did you rest last night?"

"Oh, excellently well—remarkably well—never better in my life!" said General Browne rapidly, and yet with an air of embarrassment which was obvious to his friend. He then hastily swallowed a cup of tea, and, neglecting or refusing whatever else was offered, seemed to fall into a fit of abstraction.

"You will take the gun today, General?" said his friend and host, but had to re-peat the question twice ere he received the abrupt answer, "No, my Lord; I am sorry I cannot have the honour of spending another day with your lordship; my post horses are ordered, and will be here directly."

All who were present showed surprise, and Lord Woodville immediately replied, "Post horses, my good friend! What can you possibly want with them, when you promised to stay with me quietly for at least a week?"

"I believe," said the General, obviously much embarrassed, "that I might, in the pleasure of my first meeting with your lordship, have said something about stop-ping here a few days; but I have since found it altogether impossible."

"That is very extraordinary," answered the young nobleman. "You seemed quite disengaged yesterday, and you cannot have had a summons today; for our post has

126

not come up from the town, and therefore you cannot have received any letters."

General Browne, without giving any further explanation, muttered something of indispensable business, and insisted on the absolute necessity of his departure in a manner which silenced all opposition on the part of his host, who saw that his resolution was taken, and forbore further importunity.

"At least, however," he said, "permit me, my dear Browne, since go you will or must, to show you the view from the terrace, which the mist that is now rising, will soon display."

He threw open a sash-window, and stepped down upon the terrace as he spoke. The General followed him mechanically, but seemed little to attend to what his host was saying, as, looking across an extended and rich prospect, he pointed out the different objects worthy of observation. Thus they moved on till Lord Woodville had attained his purpose of drawing his guest entirely apart from the rest of the company, when, turning round upon him with an air of great solemnity, he addressed him thus:

"Richard Browne, my old and very dear friend, we are now alone. Let me conjure you to answer me upon the word of a friend, and the honour of a soldier. How did you in reality rest during last night?"

"Most wretchedly indeed, my lord," answered the General, in the same tone of solemnity; "so miserably, that I would not run the risk of such a second night, not only for all the lands belonging to this castle, but for all the country which I see from this elevated point of view."

"This is most extraordinary," said the young lord, as if speaking to himself; "then there must be something in the reports concerning that apartment." Again turning to the General, he said, "For God's sake, my dear friend, be candid with me, and let me know the disagreeable particulars which have befallen you under a roof where, with consent of the owner, you should have met nothing save comfort."

The General seemed distressed by this appeal, and paused a moment before he replied. "My dear lord," he at length said, "what happened to me last night is of nature so peculiar and so unpleasant, that I could hardly bring myself to detail it even to your lordship, were it not that, independent of my wish to gratify any request of yours, I think that sincerity on my part may lead to some explanation about a circumstance equally painful and mysterious. To others, the communications I am about to make, might place me in the light of a weak-minded, superstitious fool who suffered his own imagination to delude and bewilder him; but you have known me in childhood and youth, and will not suspect me of having adopted in manhood the feelings and frailties from which my early years were free." Here he paused, and his friend replied:

"Do not doubt my perfect confidence in the truth of your communication, however strange it may be," replied Lord Woodville. "I know your firmness of disposition too well, to suspect you could be made the object of imposition, and am aware that your honour and your friendship will equally deter you from exaggerating whatever you may have witnessed."

"Well then," said the General, "I will proceed with my story as well as I can, relying upon your candour; and yet distinctly feeling that I would rather face a battery than recall to my mind the odious recollections of last night."

He paused a second time, and then perceiving that Lord Woodville remained silent and in an attitude of attention, he commenced, though not without obvious reluctance, the history of his night's adventures in the Tapestried Chamber.

"I undressed and went to bed, so soon as your lordship left me yesterday evening; but the wood in the chimney, which nearly fronted my bed, blazed

127

brightly and cheerfully, and, aided by a hundred exciting recollections of my child-hood and youth, which had been recalled by the unexpected pleasure of meeting your lordship, prevented me from falling immediately asleep. I ought, however, to say that these reflections were all of a pleasant and agreeable kind, grounded on a sense of having for a time exchanged the labour, fatigues, and dangers of my profession, for the enjoyments of a peaceful life, and the reunion of those friendly and affectionate ties which I had torn asunder at the rude summons of war.

"While such pleasing reflections were stealing over my mind, and gradually lulling me to slumber, I was suddenly aroused by a sound like that of the rustling of a silken gown, and the tapping of a pair of high-heeled shoes, as if a woman were walking in the apartment. Ere I could draw the curtain to see what the matter was, the figure of a little woman passed between the bed and the fire. The back of this form was turned to me, and I could observe, from the shoulders and neck, it was that of an old woman, whose dress was an old-fashioned gown, which, I think, ladies call a sacque—that is, a sort of robe, completely loose in the body, but gathered into broad plaits upon the neck and shoulders, which fall down to the ground, and terminate in a species of train.

"I thought the intrusion singular enough, but never harboured for a moment the idea that what I saw was anything more than the mortal form of some old woman about the establishment, who had a fancy to dress like her grandmother, and who, having perhaps (as your lordship mentioned that you were rather straitened for room) been dislodged from her chamber for my accommodation, had forgotten the circumstance, and returned by twelve to her old haunt. Under this persuasion I moved myself in bed and coughed a little, to make the intruder sensible of my being in possession of the premises. She turned slowly round, but gracious Heaven! My lord, what a countenance did she display to me!

"There was no longer any question what she was, or any thought of her being a living being. Upon a face which wore the fixed features of a corpse, were imprinted the traces of the vilest and most hideous passions which had animated her while she lived. The body of some atrocious criminal seemed to have been given up from the grave, and the soul restored from the penal fire, in order to form, for a space, a union with the ancient accomplice of its guilt. I started up in bed, and sat upright, supporting myself on my palms, as I gazed on this horrible spectre. The hag made, as it seemed, a single and swift stride to the bed where I lay, and squatted herself down upon it, in precisely the same attitude which I had assumed in the extremity of horror, advancing her diabolical countenance within half a yard of mine, with a grin which seemed to intimate the malice and the derision of an incarnate fiend."

Here General Browne stopped, and wiped from his brow the cold perspiration with which the recollection of his horrible vision had covered it.

"My lord," he said, "I am no coward. I have been in all the mortal dangers incidental to my profession, and I may truly boast that no man ever knew Richard Browne dishonour the sword he wears; but in these horrible circumstances, under the eyes, and as it seemed, almost in the grasp of an incarnation of an evil spirit, all firmness forsook me, all manhood melted from me like wax in the furnace, and I felt my hair individually bristle. The current of my life-blood ceased to flow, and I sank back in a swoon, as very a victim to panic terror as ever was a village girl or a child of ten years old. How long I lay in this condition I cannot pretend to guess.

"But I was roused by the castle clock striking one, so loud that it seemed as if it were in the very room. It was some time before I dared open my eyes, lest they should again encounter the horrible spectacle. When, however, I summoned courage to look up, she was no longer visible. My first idea was to pull my bell, wake the servants, and remove to a garret or a hay-loft, to be ensured against a second visitation. Nay, I will confess the truth, that my resolution was altered, not by the shame of exposing myself, but by the very fear that, as the bell-cord hung by the chimney, I might, in making my way to it, be again crossed by the fiendish hag, who, I figured to myself, might be still lurking about some corner of the apartment.

"I will not pretend to describe what hot and cold fever-fits tormented me for the rest of the night, through broken sleep, weary vigils, and that dubious state which forms the neutral ground between them. An hundred terrible objects appeared to haunt me; but there was the great difference betwixt the vision which I have described, and those which followed, that I knew the last to be deceptions of my own fancy and overexcited nerves.

"Day at last appeared, and I rose from my bed ill in health, and humiliated in mind. I was ashamed of myself as a man and a soldier, and still more so, at feeling my own extreme desire to escape from the haunted apartment, which, however, conquered all other considerations; so that, huddling on my clothes with the most careless haste, I made my escape from your lordship's mansion, to seek in the open air some relief to my nervous system, shaken as it was by this horrible rencounter with a visitant, for such I must believe her, from the other world. Your lordship has now heard the cause of my discomposure, and of my sudden desire to leave your hospitable castle. In other places I trust we may often meet; but God protect me from ever spending a second night under that roof!"

Strange as the General's tale was, he spoke with such a deep air of conviction, that it cut short all the usual commentaries which are made on such stories. Lord Woodville never once asked him if he was sure he did not dream of the apparition, or suggested any of the possibilities by which it is fashionable to explain supernatural appearances, as wild vagaries of the fancy or deceptions of the optic nerves. On the contrary, he seemed deeply impressed with the truth and reality of what he had heard; and, after a considerable pause, regretted, with much appearance of sincerity, that his early friend should in his house have suffered so severely.

"I am the more sorry for your pain, my dear Browne," he continued, "that it is the unhappy, though most unexpected, result of an experiment of my own. You must know that, for my father and grandfather's time, at least, the apartment which was assigned to you last night had been shut on account of reports that it was disturbed by supernatural sights and noises. When I came, a few weeks since, into possession of the estate, I thought the accommodation which the castle afforded for my friends was not extensive enough to permit the inhabitants of the invisible world to retain possession of a comfortable sleeping-apartment. I therefore caused the Tapestried Chamber, as we call it, to be opened; and without destroying its air of antiquity, I had such new articles of furniture placed in it as became the modern times.

"Yet, as the opinion that the room was haunted very strongly prevailed among the domestics, and was also known in the neighbourhood and to many of my friends, I feared some prejudice might be entertained by the first occupant of the Tapestried Chamber, which might tend to revive the evil report which it had laboured under, and so disappoint my purpose of rendering it a useful part of the house. I must confess, my dear Browne, that your arrival yesterday, agreeable to me for a thousand reasons besides, seemed the most favourable opportunity of removing the unpleasant rumours which attached to the room, since your courage was indubitable, and your mind free of any preoccupation on the subject. I could not, therefore, have chosen a more fitting subject for my experiment."

"Upon my life," said General Browne, somewhat hastily, "I am infinitely obliged to your lordship—very particularly indebted indeed. I am likely to remember for some time the consequences of the experiment, as your lordship is pleased to call it."

"Nay, now you are unjust, my dear friend," said Lord Woodville. "You have only to reflect for a single moment, in order to be convinced that I could not augur the possibility of the pain to which you have been so unhappily exposed. I was yesterday morning a complete sceptic on the subject of supernatural appearances. Nay, I am sure that, had I told you what was said about that room, those very reports would have induced you, by your own choice, to select it for your accommodation. It was my misfortune, perhaps my error, but really cannot be termed my fault, that you have been afflicted so strangely."

"Strangely indeed!" said the General, resuming his good temper; "and I acknowledge that I have no right to be offended with your lordship for treating me like what I used to think myself, a man of some firmness and courage. But I see my post-horses are arrived, and I must not detain your lordship from your amusement."

"Nay, my old friend," said Lord Woodville, "since you cannot stay with us another day, which, indeed, I can no longer urge, give me at least half an hour more. You used to love pictures, and I have a gallery of portraits, some of them by Vandyke, representing ancestry to whom this property and castle formerly belonged. I think that several of them will strike you as possessing merit."

General Browne accepted the invitation, though somewhat unwillingly. It was evident he was not to breathe freely or at ease until he left Woodville Castle far behind him. He could not refuse his friend's invitation, however; and the less so, that he was a little ashamed of the peevishness which he had displayed towards his well-meaning entertainer.

The general, therefore, followed Lord Woodville through several rooms, into a long gallery hung with pictures, which the latter pointed out to his guest, telling the names, and giving some account, of the personages whose portraits presented themselves in progression. General Browne was but little interested in the details which these accounts conveyed to him. They were, indeed, of the kind which are usually found in an old family gallery. Here was a cavalier who had ruined the estate in the royal cause; there, a fine lady who had reinstated it by contracting a match with a wealthy Roundhead. There hung a gallant who had been in danger for corresponding with the exiled court at St. Germain's; here, one who had taken arms for William at the Revolution; and there, a third that had thrown his weight alternately into the scale of Whig and Tory.

While Lord Woodville was cramming these words into his guest's ear, "against the stomach of his sense," they gained the middle of the gallery, when he beheld General Browne suddenly start, and assume an attitude of the utmost surprise, not unmixed with fear, as his eyes were caught and suddenly riveted by a portrait of an old lady in a sacque, the fashionable dress of the end of the 17th century.

"There she is!" he exclaimed—"there she is, in form and features, though inferior in demoniac expression to the accursed hag who visited me last night!"

"If that be the case," said the young nobleman, "there can remain no longer any doubt of the horrible reality of your apparition. That is the picture of a wretched ancestress of mine, of whose crimes a black and fearful catalogue is recorded in a family history in my charter-chest. The recital of them would be too horrible; it is enough to say, that in yon fatal apartment incest and unnatural murder were committed. I will restore it to the solitude to which the better judgement of those who preceded me had consigned it; and never shall any one, so long as I can prevent it, be exposed to a repetition of the supernatural horrors which could shake such courage as yours."

Thus the friends, who had met with such glee, parted in a very different mood— Lord Woodville to command the Tapestried Chamber to be unmantled and the door built up; and General Browne to seek in some less beautiful country, and with some less dignified friend, forgetfulness of the painful night which he had passed in Woodville Castle.

THE OLD NURSE'S STORY,
by Elizabeth Gaskell

You know, my dears, that your mother was an orphan, and an only child; and I dare say you have heard that your grand-father was a clergyman up in Westmoreland, where I come from. I was just a girl in the village school, when, one day, your grandmother came in to ask the mistress if there was any scholar there who would do for a nurse-maid; and mighty proud I was, I can tell ye, when the mistress called me up, and spoke to my being a good girl at my needle, and a steady, honest girl, and one whose parents were very respectable, though they might be poor I thought I should like nothing better than to serve the pretty, young lady, who was blushing as deep as I was, as she spoke of the coming baby, and what I should have to do with it. However, I see you don't care so much for this part of my story, as for what you think is to come, so I'll tell you at once. I was engaged and settled at the parsonage before Miss Rosamond (that was the baby, who is now your mother) was born. To be sure, I had little enough to do with her when she came, for she was never out of her mother's arms, and slept by her all night long; and proud enough was I sometimes when missis trusted her to me. There never was such a baby before or since, though you've all of you been fine enough in your turns; but for sweet, winning ways, you've none of you come up to your mother. She took after her mother, who was a real lady born; a Miss Furnivall, a granddaughter of Lord Furnivall's, in Northumberland. I believe she had neither brother nor sister, and had been brought up in my lord's family till she had married your grandfather, who was just a curate, son to a shopkeeper in Carlisle—but a clever, fine gentleman as ever was—and one who was a right-down hard worker in his parish, which was very wide, and scattered all abroad over the Westmoreland Fells. When your mother, little Miss Rosamond, was about four or five years old, both her parents died in a fortnight—one after the other. Ah! that was a sad time. My pretty young mistress and me was looking for another baby, when my master came home from one of his long rides, wet, and tired, and took the fever he died of; and then she never held up her head again, but lived just to see her dead baby, and have it laid on her breast before she sighed away her life. My mistress had asked me, on her death-bed, never to leave Miss Rosamond; but if she had never spoken a word, I would have gone with the little child to the end of the world.

The next thing, and before we had well stilled our sobs, the executors and guardians came to settle the affairs. They were my poor young mistress's own cousin, Lord Furnivall, and Mr. Esthwaite, my master's brother, a shopkeeper in Manchester; not so well to do then, as he was afterwards, and with a large family rising about him. Well! I don't know if it were their settling, or because of a letter my mistress wrote on her death-bed to her cousin, my lord; but somehow it was settled that Miss Rosamond and me were to go to Furnivall Manor House, in Northumberland, and my lord spoke as if it had been her mother's wish that she should live with his family, and as if he had no objections, for that one or two more or less could make no difference in so grand a household. So, though that was not the way in which I should have wished the coming of my bright and pretty pet to have been looked at—who was like a sunbeam in any family, be it never so grand —I was well pleased that all the folks in the Dale should stare and admire, when they heard I was going to be young lady's maid at my Lord Furnivall's at Furnivall Manor.

But I made a mistake in thinking we were to go and live where my lord did. It turned out that the family had left Furnivall Manor House fifty years or more. I could not hear that my poor young mistress had ever been there, though she had been brought up in the family; and I was sorry for that, for I should have liked Miss Rosamond's youth to have passed where her mother's had been.

My lord's gentleman, from whom I asked as many questions as I durst, said that the Manor House was at the foot of the Cumberland Fells, and a very grand place; that an old Miss Furnivall, a great-aunt of my lord's, lived there, with only a few servants; but that it was a very healthy place, and my lord had thought that it would suit Miss Rosamond very well for a few years, and that her being there might perhaps amuse his old aunt.

I was bidden by my lord to have Miss Rosamond's things ready by a certain day. He was a stern proud man, as they say all the Lords Furnivall were; and he never spoke a word more than was necessary. Folk did say he had loved my young mistress; but that, because she knew that his father would object, she would never listen to him, and married Esthwaite; but I don't know. He never married at any rate. But he never took much notice of Miss Rosamond; which I thought he might have done if he had cared for her dead mother. He sent his gentleman with us to the Manor House, telling him to join him at Newcastle that same evening; so there was no great length of time for him to make us known to all the strangers before he, too, shook us off; and we were left, two lonely young things (I was not eighteen), in the great old Manor House. It seems like yesterday that we drove there. We had left our own dear parsonage very early, and we had both cried as if our hearts would break, though we were travelling in my lord's carriage, which I thought so much of once. And now it was long past noon on a September day, and we stopped to change horses for the last time at a little, smoky town, all full of colliers and miners. Miss Rosamond had fallen asleep, but Mr. Henry told me to waken her, that she might see the park and the Manor House as we drove up. I thought it rather a pity; but I did what he bade me, for fear he should complain of me to my lord. We had left all signs of a town, or even a village, and were then inside the gates of a large, wild park—not like the parks here in the south, but with rocks, and the noise of running water, and gnarled thorn-trees, and old oaks, all white and peeled with age.

The road went up about two miles, and then we saw a great and stately house, with many trees close around it, so close that in some places their branches dragged against the walls when the wind blew; and some hung broken down; for no one seemed to take much charge of the place;—to lop the wood, or to keep the moss-covered carriage-way in order. Only in front of the house all was clear. The great oval drive was without a weed; and neither tree nor creeper was allowed to grow over the long, many-windowed front; at both sides of which a wing projected, which were each the ends of other side fronts; for the house, although it was so desolate, was even grander than I expected. Behind it rose the Fells, which seemed unenclosed and bare enough; and on the left hand of the house, as you stood facing it, was a little, old-fashioned flower-garden, as I found out afterwards. A door opened out upon it from the west front; it had been scooped out of the thick dark wood for some old Lady Furnivall; but the branches of the great forest trees had grown and overshadowed it again, and there were very few flowers that would live there at that time. When we drove up to the great front entrance, and went into the hall I thought we should be lost—it was so large, and vast, and grand. There was a chandelier all of bronze, hung down from the middle of the ceiling; and I had never seen one before, and looked at it all in amaze. Then, at one end of the hall, was a great fire-place, as large as the sides of the houses in my country, with massy andirons and dogs to hold the wood; and by it were heavy, old-fashioned sofas. At the opposite end of the hall, to the left as you went in—on the western side—was an organ built into the wall, and so large that it filled up the best part of that end. Beyond it, on the same side, was a door; and opposite, on each side of the fire-place, were also doors leading to the east front; but those I never went through as long as I stayed in the house, so I can't tell you what lay beyond.

The afternoon was closing in and the hall, which had no fire lighted in it, looked dark and gloomy, but we did not stay there a moment. The old servant, who had opened the door for us bowed to Mr. Henry, and took us in through the door at the further side of the great organ, and led us through several smaller halls and passages into the west drawing-room, where he said that Miss Furnivall was sitting. Poor little Miss Rosamond held very tight to me, as if she were scared and lost in that great place, and as for myself, I was not much better. The west drawing-room was very cheerful-looking, with a warm fire in it, and plenty of good, comfortable furniture about. Miss Furnivall was an old lady not far from eighty, I should think, but I do not know. She was thin and tall, and had a face as full of fine wrinkles as if they had been drawn all over it with a needle's point. Her eyes were very watchful to make up, I suppose, for her being so deaf as to be obliged to use a trumpet. Sitting with her, working at the same great piece of tapestry, was Mrs. Stark, her maid and companion, and almost as old as she was. She had lived with Miss Furnivall ever since they both were young, and now she seemed more like a friend than a servant; she looked so cold, and grey, and stony, as if she had never loved or cared for any one; and I don't suppose she did care for any one, except her mistress; and, owing to the great deafness of the latter, Mrs. Stark treated her very much as if she were a child. Mr. Henry gave some message from my lord, and then he bowed good-bye to us all,—taking no notice of my sweet little Miss Rosamond's outstretched hand—and left us standing there, being looked at by the two old ladies through their spectacles.

I was right glad when they rung for the old footman who had shown us in at first, and told him to take us to our rooms. So we went out of that great drawing-room, and into another sitting-room, and out of that, and then up a great flight of stairs, and along a broad gallery—which was something like a library, having books all down one side, and windows and writing-tables all down the other—till we came to our rooms, which I was not sorry to hear were just over the kitchens; for I began to think I should be lost in that wilderness of a house. There was an old nursery, that had been used for all the little lords and ladies long ago, with a pleasant fire burning in the grate, and the kettle boiling on the bob, and tea things spread out on the table; and out of that room was the night-nursery, with a little crib for Miss Rosamond close to my bed. And old James called up Dorothy, his wife, to bid us welcome; and both he and she were so hospitable and kind, that by and by Miss Rosamond and me felt quite at home; and by the time tea was over, she was sitting on Dorothy's knee, and chattering away as fast as her little tongue could go. I soon found out that Dorothy was from Westmoreland, and that bound her and me together, as it were; and I would never wish to meet with kinder people than were old James and his wife. James had lived pretty nearly all his life in my lord's family, and thought there was no one so grand as they. He even looked down a little on his wife; because, till he had married her, she had never lived in any but a farmer's household. But he was very fond of her, as well he might be. They had one servant under them, to do all the rough work. Agnes they called her; and she and me, and James and Dorothy, with Miss Furnivall and Mrs. Stark, made up the family; always remembering my sweet little Miss Rosamond! I used to wonder what they had done before she came, they thought so much of her now. Kitchen and drawing-room, it was all the same. The hard, sad Miss Furnivall, and the cold Mrs. Stark, looked pleased when she came fluttering in like a bird, playing and pranking hither and thither, with a continual murmur, and pretty prattle of gladness. I am sure, they were sorry many a time when she flitted away into the kitchen, though they were too proud to ask her to stay with them, and were a little surprised at her taste; though to be sure, as Mrs. Stark said, it was not to be wondered at, remembering what stock her father had come of. The great, old rambling house was a famous place for little Miss Rosamond. She made expeditions all over it, with me at her heels; all, except the east wing, which was never opened, and whither we never thought of going. But in the western and northern part was many a pleasant room; full of things that were curiosities to us, though they might not have been to people who had seen more. The windows were darkened by the sweeping boughs of the trees, and the ivy which had overgrown them: but, in the green gloom, we could manage to see old China jars and carved ivory boxes, and great, heavy books, and, above all, the old pictures!

Once, I remember, my darling would have Dorothy go with us to tell us who they all were; for they were all portraits of some of my lord's family, though Dorothy could not tell us the names of every one. We had gone through most of the rooms, when we came to the old state drawing-room over the hall, and there was a picture of Miss Furnivall; or, as she was called in those days, Miss Grace, for she was the younger sister. Such a beauty she must have been! but with such a set, proud look, and such scorn looking out of her handsome eyes, with her eyebrows just a little raised, as if she wondered how any one could have the impertinence to look at her; and her lip curled at us, as we stood there gazing. She had a dress on, the like of which I had never seen before, but it was all the fashion when she was young: a hat of some soft, white stuff like beaver, pulled a little over her brows, and a beautiful plume of feathers sweeping round it on one side; and her gown of blue satin was open in front to a quilted, white stomacher.

"Well, to be sure!" said I, when I had gazed my fill. "Flesh is grass, they do say; but who would have thought that Miss Furnivall had been such an out-and-out beauty, to see her now?"

"Yes," said Dorothy. "Folks change sadly. But if what my master's father used to say was true, Miss Furnivall, the elder sister, was handsomer than Miss Grace. Her picture is here somewhere; but, if I show it you, you must never let on, even to James, that you have seen it. Can the little lady hold her tongue, think you?" asked she.

I was not so sure, for she was such a little, sweet, bold, open-spoken child, so I set her to hide herself; and then I helped Dorothy to turn a great picture, that leaned with its face towards the wall, and was not hung up as the others were. To be sure, it beat Miss Grace for beauty; and, I think, for scornful pride, too, though in that matter it might be hard to choose. I could have looked at it an hour, but Dorothy seemed half frightened at having shown it to me, and hurried it back again, and bade me run and find Miss Rosamond, for that there were some ugly places about the house, where she should like ill for the child to go. I was a brave, high-spirited girl, and thought little of what the old woman said, for I liked hide-and-seek as well as any child in the parish; so off I ran to find my little one.

135

As winter drew on, and the days grew shorter, I was sometimes almost certain that I heard a noise as if some one was playing on the great organ in the hall. I did not hear it every evening; but, certainly, I did very often; usually when I was sitting with Miss Rosamond, after I had put her to bed, and keeping quite still and silent in the bed-room. Then I used to hear it booming and swelling away in the distance. The first night, when I went down to my supper, I asked Dorothy who had been playing music, and James said very shortly that I was a gowk to take the wind soughing among the trees for music: but I saw Dorothy look at him very fearfully, and Agnes, the kitchen-maid, said something beneath her breath, and went quite white. I saw they did not like my question, so I held my peace till I was with Dorothy alone, when I knew I could get a good deal out of her. So, the next day, I watched my time, and I coaxed and asked her who it was that played the organ; for I knew that it was the organ and not the wind well enough, for all I had kept silence before James. But Dorothy had had her lesson I'll warrant, and never a word could I get from her. So then I tried Agnes, though I had always held my head rather above her, as I was even to James and Dorothy, and she was little better than their servant. So she said I must never, never tell; and if I ever told, I was never to say *she* had told me; but it was a very strange noise, and she had heard it many a time, but most of all on winter nights, and before storms; and folks did say, it was the old lord playing on the great organ in the hall, just as he used to do when he was alive; but who the old lord was, or why he played, and why he played on stormy winter evenings in particular, she either could not or would not tell me. Well! I told you I had a brave heart; and I thought it was rather pleasant to have that grand music rolling about the house, let who would be the player; for now it rose above the great gusts of wind, and wailed and triumphed just like a living creature, and then it fell to a softness most complete; only it was always music, and tunes, so it was nonsense to call it the wind I thought at first, that it might be Miss Furnivall who played, unknown to Agnes; but, one day when I was in the hall by myself, I opened the organ and peeped all about it and around it, as I had done to the organ in Crosthwaite Church once before, and I saw it was all broken and destroyed inside, though it looked so brave and fine; and then, though it was noon-day, my flesh began to creep a little, and I shut it up, and run away pretty quickly to my own bright nursery; and I did not like hearing the music for some time after that, any more than James and Dorothy did. All this time Miss Rosamond was making her-self more and more beloved. The old ladies liked her to dine with them at their early dinner; James stood behind Miss Furnivall's chair, and I behind Miss Rosa-mond's all in state; and, after dinner, she would play about in a corner of the great drawing-room, as still as any mouse, while Miss Furnivall slept, and I had my din-ner in the kitchen. But she was glad enough to come to me in the nursery after-wards; for, as she said, Miss Furnivall was so sad, and Mrs. Stark so dull; but she and I were merry enough; and, by-and-by, I got not to care for that weird rolling music, which did one no harm, if we did not know where it came from.

That winter was very cold. In the middle of October the frosts began, and lasted many, many weeks. I remember, one day at dinner, Miss Furnivall lifted up her sad, heavy eyes, and said to Mrs. Stark, "I am afraid we shall have a terrible winter," in a strange kind of meaning way. But Mrs. Stark pretended not to hear, and talked very loud of something else. My little lady and I did not care for the frost; not we! As long as it was dry we climbed up the steep brows, behind the house, and went up on the Fells, which were bleak, and bare enough, and there we ran races in the fresh, sharp air; and once we came down by a new path that took us past the two old, gnarled holly-trees, which grew about half-way down by the east side of the house. But the days grew shorter, and shorter; and the old lord, if it was he, played away more, and more stormily and sadly on the great organ. One Sunday afternoon, —it must have been towards the end of November—I asked Dorothy to take charge of little Missey when she came out of the drawing-room, after Miss Furnivall had had her nap; for it was too cold to take her with me to church, and yet I wanted to go. And Dorothy was glad enough to promise, and was so fond of the child that all seemed well; and Agnes and I set off very briskly, though the sky hung heavy and black over the white earth, as if the night had never fully gone away; and the air, though still, was very biting and keen.

"We shall have a fall of snow," said Agnes to me. And sure enough, even while we were in church, it came down thick, in great, large flakes, so thick it almost darkened the windows. It had stopped snowing before we came out, but it lay soft, thick and deep beneath our feet, as we tramped home. Before we got to the hall the moon rose, and I think it was lighter then,—what with the moon, and what with the white dazzling snow—than it had been when we went to church, between two and three o'clock. I have not told you that Miss Furnivall and Mrs. Stark never went to church: they used to read the prayers together, in their quiet, gloomy way; they seemed to feel the Sunday very long without their tapestry-work to be busy at. So when I went to Dorothy in the kitchen, to fetch Miss Rosamond and take her up-stairs with me, I did not much wonder when the old woman told me that the ladies had kept the child with them, and that she had never come to the kitchen, as I had bidden her, when she was tired of behaving pretty in the drawing-room. So I took off my things and went to find her, and bring her to her supper in the nursery. But when I went into the best drawing-room, there sate the two old ladies, very still and quiet, dropping out a word now and then, but looking as if nothing so bright and merry as Miss Rosamond had ever been near them. Still I thought she might be hid-ing from me; it was one of her pretty ways; and that she had persuaded them to look as if they knew nothing about her; so I went softly peeping under this sofa, and behind that chair, making believe I was sadly frightened at not finding her.

"What's the matter, Hester?" said Mrs. Stark sharply. I don't know if Miss Fur-nivall had seen me, for, as I told you, she was very deaf, and she sate quite still, idly staring into the fire, with her hopeless face. "I'm only looking for my little Rosy-Posy," replied I, still thinking that the child was there, and near me, though I could not see her.

"Miss Rosamond is not here," said Mrs. Stark. "She went away more than an hour ago to find Dorothy." And she too turned and went on looking into the fire.

My heart sank at this, and I began to wish I had never left my darling. I went back to Dorothy and told her. James was gone out for the day, but she and me and Agnes took lights and went up into the nursery first, and then we roamed over the great large house, calling and entreating Miss Rosamond to come out of her hiding place, and not frighten us to death in that way. But there was no answer; no sound.

"Oh!" said I at last. "Can she have got into the east wing and hidden there?"

But Dorothy said it was not possible, for that she herself had never been in there; that the doors were always locked, and my lord's steward had the keys, she be-lieved; at any rate, neither she nor James had ever seen them: so, I said I would go back, and see if, after all, she was not hidden in the drawing-room, unknown to the old ladies; and if I found her there, I said, I would whip her well for the fright she had given me; but I never meant to do it. Well, I went back to the west drawing-room, and I told Mrs. Stark we could not find her anywhere, and asked for leave to look all about the furniture there, for I thought now, that she might have fallen asleep in some warm, hidden corner; but no! we looked, Miss Furnivall got up and looked, trembling all over, and she was no where there; then we set off again, every one in the house, and looked in all the places we had searched before, but we could not find her. Miss Furnivall shivered and shook so much, that Mrs. Stark took her back into the warm drawing-room; but not before they had made me promise to bring her to them when she was found. Well-a-day! I began to think she never would be found, when I bethought me to look out into the great front court, all covered with snow. I was up-stairs when I looked out; but, it was such dear moonlight, I could see quite plain two little footprints, which might be traced from the hall door, and round the corner of the east wing. I don't know how I got down, but I tugged open the great, stiff hall door; and, throwing the skirt of my gown over head for a cloak, I ran out. I turned the east corner, and there a black shadow fell on the snow; but when I came again into the moonlight, there were the little footmarks going up—up to the Fells. It was bitter cold; so cold that the air almost took the skin off my face as I ran, but I ran on, crying to think how my poor little darling must be perished, and frightened. I was within sight of the holly-trees, when I saw a shepherd coming down the hill, bearing something in his arms wrapped in his maud. He shouted to me, and asked me if I had lost a bairn; and, when I could not speak for crying, he bore towards me, and I saw my wee bairnie lying still, and white, and stiff, in his arms, as if she had been dead. He told me he had been up the Fells to gather in his sheep, before the deep cold of night came on, and that under the holly-trees (black marks on the hill-side, where no other bush was for miles around) he had found my little lady—my lamb—my queen—my darling—stiff, and cold, in the terrible sleep which is frost-begotten. Oh! the joy, and the tears, of having her in my arms once again! for I would not let him carry her; but took her, maud and all, into my own arms, and held her near my own warm neck, and heart, and felt the life stealing slowly back again into her little, gentle limbs. But she was still insensible when we reached the hall, and I had no breath for speech. We went in by the kitchen door.

"Bring the warming-pan," said I; and I carried her up-stairs and began undressing her by the nursery fire, which Agnes had kept up. I called my little lammie all the sweet and playful names I could think of,—even while my eyes were blinded by my tears; and at last, oh! at length she opened her large, blue eyes. Then I put her into her warm bed, and sent Dorothy down to tell Miss Furnivall that all was well; and I made up my mind to sit by my darling's bedside the live-long night. She fell away into a soft sleep as soon as her pretty head had touched the pillow, and I watched by her till morning light; when she wakened up bright and clear—or so I thought at first—and, my dears, so I think now.

She said, that she had fancied that she should like to go to Dorothy, for that both the old ladies were asleep, and it was very dull in the drawing-room; and that, as she was going through the west lobby, she saw the snow through the high window falling—falling—soft and steady; but she wanted to see it lying pretty and white on the ground; so she made her way into the great hall; and then, going to the window, she saw it bright and soft upon the drive; but while she stood there, she saw a little girl, not as old as she was, "but so pretty," said my darling, "and this little girl beckoned to me to come out; and oh, she was so pretty and so sweet, I could not choose but go." And then this other little girl had taken her by the hand, and side by side the two had gone round the east corner.

"Now, you are a naughty little girl, and telling stories," said I. "What would your good mamma, that is in heaven, and never told a story in her life, say to her little Rosamond, if she heard her—and I dare say she does—telling stories!"

"Indeed, Hester," sobbed out my child, "I'm telling you true. Indeed I am."

"Don't tell me!" said I, very stern. "I tracked you by your foot-marks through the snow; there were only yours to be seen: and if you had had a little girl to go hand-in-hand with you up the hill, don't you think the foot-prints would have gone along with yours?"

"I can't help it, dear, dear Hester," said she, crying, "if they did not; I never looked at her feet, but she held my hand fast and tight in her little one, and it was very, very cold. She took me up the Fell-path, up to the holly trees; and there I saw a lady weeping and crying; but when she saw me, she hushed her weeping, and smiled very proud and grand, and took me on her knee, and began to lull me to sleep; and that's all, Hester—but that is true; and my dear mamma knows it is," said she, crying. So I thought the child was in a fever, and pretended to believe her, as she went over her story—over and over again, and always the same. At last Dorothy knocked at the door with Miss Rosamond's breakfast; and she told me the old ladies were down in the eating parlour, and that they wanted to speak to me. They had both been into the night-nursery the evening before, but it was after Miss Rosamond was asleep; so they had only looked at her—not asked me any questions.

"I shall catch it," thought I to myself, as I went along the north gallery. "And yet," I thought, taking courage, "it was in their charge I left her; and it's they that's to blame for letting her steal away unknown and unwatched." So I went in boldly, and told my story. I told it all to Miss Furnivall, shouting it close to her ear; but when I came to the mention of the other little girl out in the snow, coaxing and tempting her out, and her up to the grand and beautiful lady by the holly-tree, she threw her arms up—her old and withered arms—and cried aloud, "Oh! Heaven, forgive! Have mercy!"

Mrs. Stark took hold of her; roughly enough, I thought; but she was past Mrs. Stark's management, and spoke to me, in a kind of wild warning and authority.

"Hester! keep her from that child! It will lure her to her death! That evil child! Tell her it is a wicked, naughty child." Then, Mrs. Stark hurried me out of the room; where, indeed, I was glad enough to go; but Miss Furnivall kept shrieking out, "Oh! have mercy! Wilt Thou never forgive! It is many a long year ago—"

I was very uneasy in my mind after that. I durst never leave Miss Rosamond, night or day, for fear lest she might slip off again, after some fancy or other; and all the more, because I thought I could make out that Miss Furnivall was crazy, from their odd ways about her; and I was afraid lest something of the same kind (which might be in the family, you know) hung over my darling. And the great frost never ceased all this time; and, whenever it was a more stormy night than usual, between the gusts, and through the wind, we heard the old lord playing on the great organ. But, old lord, or not, wherever Miss Rosamond went, there I followed; for my love for her, pretty, helpless orphan, was stronger than my fear for the grand and terrible sound. Besides, it rested with me to keep her cheerful and merry, as beseemed her age. So we played together, and wandered together, here and there, and every-where; for I never dared to lose sight of her again in that large and rambling house. And so it happened, that one afternoon, not long before Christmas day, we were playing together on the billiard-table in the great hall (not that we knew the right way of playing, but she liked to roll the smooth ivory balls with her pretty hands, and I liked to do whatever she did); and, by-and-by, without our noticing it, it grew dusk indoors, though it was still light in the open air, and I was thinking of taking her back into the nursery, when, all of sudden, she cried out,—

"Look, Hester! look! there is my poor little girl out in the snow!"

I turned towards the long, narrow windows, and there, sure enough, I saw a little girl, less than my Miss Rosamond dressed all unfit to be out-of-doors such a bitter night—crying, and beating against the window-panes, as if she wanted to be let in. She seemed to sob and wail, till Miss Rosamond could bear it no longer, and was flying to the door to open it, when, all of a sudden, and close upon us, the great organ pealed out so loud and thundering, it fairly made me tremble; and all the more, when I remembered me that, even in the stillness of that dead-cold weather, I had heard no sound of little battering hands upon the window-glass, although the Phantom Child had seemed to put forth all its force; and, although I had seen it wail and cry, no faintest touch of sound had fallen upon my ears. Whether I remembered all this at the very moment, I do not know; the great organ sound had so stunned me into terror; but this I know, I caught up Miss Rosamond before she got the hall-door opened, and clutched her, and carried her away, kicking and screaming, into the large, bright kitchen, where Dorothy and Agnes were busy with their mince-pies.

"What is the matter with my sweet one?" cried Dorothy, as I bore in Miss Rosamond, who was sobbing as if her heart would break.

"She won't let me open the door for my little girl to come in; and she'll die if she is out on the Fells all night. Cruel, naughty Hester," she said, slapping me; but she might have struck harder, for I had seen a look of ghastly terror on Dorothy's face, which made my very blood run cold.

"Shut the back kitchen door fast, and bolt it well," said she to Agnes. She said no more; she gave me raisins and almonds to quiet Miss Rosamond: but she sobbed about the little girl in the snow, and would not touch any of the good things. I was thankful when she cried herself to sleep in bed. Then I stole down to the kitchen, and told Dorothy I had made up my mind I would carry my darling back to my father's house in Applethwaite; where, if we lived humbly, we lived at peace. I said I had been frightened enough with the old lord's organ-playing; but now that I had seen for myself this little, moaning child, all decked out as no child in the neighbourhood could be, beating and battering to get in, yet always without any sound or noise—with the dark wound on its right shoulder; and that Miss Rosamond had known it again for the phantom that had nearly lured her to her death (which Dorothy knew was true); I would stand it no longer.

I saw Dorothy change colour once or twice. When I had done, she told me she did not think I could take Miss Rosamond with me, for that she was my lord's ward, and I had no right over her; and she asked me, would I leave the child that I was so fond of, just for sounds and sights that could do me no harm; and that they had all had to get used to in their turns? I was all in a hot, trembling passion; and I said it was very well for her to talk, that knew what these sights and noises betokened, and that had, perhaps, had something to do with the Spectre-Child while it was alive. And I taunted her so, that she told me all she knew, at last; and then I wished I had never been told, for it only made me more afraid than ever.

She said she had heard the tale from old neighbours, that were alive when she was first married; when folks used to come to the hall sometimes, before it had got such a bad name on the country side: it might not be true, or it might, what she had been told.

The old lord was Miss Furnivall's father—Miss Grace, as Dorothy called her, for Miss Maude was the elder, and Miss Furnivall by rights. The old lord was eaten up with pride. Such a proud man was never seen or heard of; and his daughters were like him. No one was good enough to wed them, although they had choice enough; for they were the great beauties of their day, as I had seen by their portraits, where they hung in the state drawing-room. But, as the old saying is, "Pride will have a fall"; and these two haughty beauties fell in love with the same man, and he no better than a foreign musician, whom their father had down from London to play music with him at the Manor House. For, above all things, next to his pride, the old lord loved music. He could play on nearly every instrument that ever was heard of: and it was a strange thing it did not soften him; but he was a fierce, dour, old man, and had broken his poor wife's heart with his cruelty, they said. He was mad after music, and would pay any money for it. So he got this foreigner to come; who made such beautiful music, that they said the very birds on the trees stopped their singing to listen. And, by degrees, this foreign gentleman got such a hold over the old lord, that nothing would serve him but that he must come every year; and it was he that had the great organ brought from Holland, and built up in the hall, where it stood now. He taught the old lord to play on it; but many and many a time, when Lord Furnivall was thinking of nothing but his fine organ, and his finer music, the dark foreigner was walking abroad in the woods with one of the young ladies; now Miss Maude, and then Miss Grace.

Miss Maude won the day and carried off the prize, such as it was; and he and she were married, all unknown to any one; and before he made his next yearly visit, she had been confined of a little girl at a farm-house on the Moors, while her father and Miss Grace thought she was away at Doncaster Races. But though she was a wife and a mother, she was not a bit softened, but as haughty and as passionate as ever; and perhaps more so for she was jealous of Miss Grace, to whom her foreign husband paid a deal of court—by way of blinding her—as he told his wife. But Miss Grace triumphed over Miss Maude, and Miss Maude grew fiercer and fiercer, both with her husband and with her sister; and the former who could easily shake off what was disagreeable, and hide himself in foreign countries—went away a month before his usual time that summer, and half-threatened that he would never come back again. Meanwhile, the little girl was left at the farm-house, and her mother used to have her horse saddled and gallop wildly over the hills to see her once every week, at the very least—for where she loved, she loved; and where she hated, she hated. And the old lord went on playing—playing on his organ; and the servants thought the sweet music he made had soothed down his awful temper, of which (Dorothy said) some terrible tales could be told. He grew infirm too, and had to walk with a crutch; and his son—that was the present Lord Furnivall's father—was with the army in America, and the other son at sea; so Miss Maude had it pretty much her own way, and she and Miss Grace grew colder and bitterer to each other every day; till at last they hardly ever spoke, except when the old lord was by. The foreign musician came again the next summer, but it was for the last time; for they led him such a life with their jealousy and their passions, that he grew weary, and went away, and never was heard of again. And Miss Maude, who had always meant to have her marriage acknowledged when her father should be dead, was left now a deserted wife—whom nobody knew to have been married—with a child that she dared not own, although she loved it to distraction; living with a father whom she feared, and a sister whom she hated. When the next summer passed over and the dark foreigner never came, both Miss Maude and Miss Grace grew gloomy and sad; they had a haggard look about them, though they looked handsome as ever. But by-and-by Miss Maude brightened; for her father grew more and more infirm, and more than ever carried away by his music; and she and Miss Grace lived almost entirely apart, having separate rooms, the one on the west side, Miss Maude on the east—those very rooms which were now shut up. So she thought she might have her little girl with her, and no one need ever know except those who dared not speak about it, and were bound to believe that it was, as she said, a cottager's child she had taken a fancy to. All this Dorothy said, was pretty well known; but what

141

came afterwards no one knew, except Miss Grace, and Mrs. Stark, who was even then her maid, and much more of a friend to her than ever her sister had been. But the servants supposed, from words that were dropped, that Miss Maude had triumphed over Miss Grace, and told her that all the time the dark foreigner had been mocking her with pretended love—he was her own husband; the colour left Miss Grace's cheek and lips that very day for ever, and she was heard to say many a time that sooner or later she would have her revenge; and Mrs. Stark was for ever spying about the east rooms.

One fearful night, just after the New Year had come in, when the snow was lying thick and deep, and the flakes were still falling—fast enough to blind any one who might be out and abroad—there was a great and violent noise heard, and the old lord's voice above all, cursing and swearing awfully,—and the cries of a little child,—and the proud defiance of a fierce woman,—and the sound of a blow,—and a dead stillness,—and moans and wailing's dying away on the hill-side! Then the old lord summoned all his servants, and told them, with terrible oaths, and words more terrible, that his daughter had disgraced herself, and that he had turned her out of doors,—her, and her child,—and that if ever they gave her help,—or food,—or shelter,—he prayed that they might never enter Heaven. And, all the while, Miss Grace stood by him, white and still as any stone; and when he had ended she heaved a great sigh, as much as to say her work was done, and her end was accomplished. But the old lord never touched his organ again, and died within the year; and no wonder! for, on the morrow of that wild and fearful night, the shepherds, coming down the Fell-side, found Miss Maude sitting, all crazy and smiling, under the holly-trees, nursing a dead child,—with a terrible mark on its right shoulder. "But that was not what killed it," said; "it was the frost and the cold;—every wild creature was in its hole, and every beast in its fold,—while the child and its mother were turned out to wander on the Fells! And now you know all! and I wonder if you are less frightened now?"

I was more frightened than ever; but I said I was not. I wished Miss Rosamond and myself well out of that dreadful house for ever; but I would not leave her, and I dared not take her away. But oh! how I watched her, and guarded her! We bolted the doors, and shut the window-shutters fast, an hour or more before dark, rather than leave them open five minutes too late. But my little lady still heard the weird child crying and mourning; and not all we could do or say, could keep her from wanting to go to her, and let her in from the cruel wind and the snow. All this time, I kept away from Miss Furnivall and Mrs. Stark, as much as ever I could; for I feared them—I knew no good could be about them, with their grey hard faces, and their dreamy eyes, looking back into the ghastly years that were gone. But, even in my fear, I had a kind of pity—for Miss Furnivall, at least. Those gone down to the pit can hardly have a more hopeless look than that which was ever on her face. At last I even got so sorry for her—who never said a word but what was quite forced from her—that I prayed for her; and I taught Miss Rosamond to pray for one who had done a deadly sin; but often when she came to those words, she would listen, and start up from her knees, and say, "I hear my little girl plaining and crying very sad—Oh! let her in, or she will die!"

One night—just after New Year's Day had come at last, and the long winter had taken a turn, as I hoped—I heard the west drawing-room bell ring three times, which was the signal for me. I would not leave Miss Rosamond alone, for all she was asleep—for the old lord had been playing wilder than ever—and I feared lest my darling should waken to hear the spectre child; see her I knew she could not. I had fastened the windows too well for that. So, I took her out of her bed and wrapped her up in such outer clothes as were most handy, and carried her down to the drawing-room, where the old ladies sate at their tapestry work as usual. They looked up when I came in, and Mrs. Stark asked, quite astounded, "Why did I bring Miss Rosamond there, out of her warm bed?" I had begun to whisper, "Because I was afraid of her being tempted out while I was away, by the wild child in the snow," when she stopped me short (with a glance at Miss Furnivall), and said Miss Furnivall wanted me to undo some work she had done wrong, and which neither of them could see to unpick. So, I laid my pretty dear on the sofa, and sate down on a stool by them, and hardened my heart against them, as I heard the wind rising and howling.

Miss Rosamond slept on sound, for all the wind blew so; and Miss Furnivall said never a word, nor looked round when the gusts shook the windows. All at once she started up to her full height, and put up one hand, as if to bid us listen.

"I hear voices!" said she. "I hear terrible screams—I hear my father's voice!"

Just at that moment, my darling wakened with a sudden start: "My little girl is crying, oh, how she is crying!" and she tried to get up and go to her, but she got her feet entangled in the blanket, and I caught her up; for my flesh had begun to creep at these noises, which they heard while we could catch no sound. In a minute or two the noises came, and gathered fast, and filled our ears; we, too, heard voices and screams, and no longer heard the winter's wind that raged abroad. Mrs. Stark looked at me, and I at her, but we dared not speak. Suddenly Miss Furnivall went towards the door, out into the ante-room, through the west lobby, and opened the door into the great hall. Mrs. Stark followed, and I durst not be left, though my heart almost stopped beating for fear. I wrapped my darling tight in my arms, and went out with them. In the hall the screams were louder than ever; they sounded to come from the east wing—nearer and nearer—close on the other side of the locked-up doors—close behind them. Then I noticed that the great bronze chandelier seemed all alight, though the hall was dim, and that a fire was blazing in the vast hearth-place, though it gave no heat; and I shuddered up with terror, and folded my darling closer to me. But as I did so, the east door shook, and she, suddenly struggling to get free from me, cried, "Hester! I must go! My little girl is there; I hear her; she is coming! Hester, I must go!"

I held her tight with all my strength; with a set will, I held her. If I had died, my hands would have grasped her still, I was so resolved in my mind. Miss Furnivall stood listening, and paid no regard to my darling, who had got down to the ground, and whom I, upon my knees now, was holding with both my arms clasped round her neck; she still striving and crying to get free.

All at once, the east door gave way with a thundering crash, as if torn open in a violent passion, and there came into that broad and mysterious light, the figure of a tall, old man, with grey hair and gleaming eyes. He drove before him, with many a relentless gesture of abhorrence, a stern and beautiful woman, with a little child clinging to her dress.

"Oh Hester! Hester!" cried Miss Rosamond. "It's the lady! the lady below the holly-trees; and my little girl is with her. Hester! Hester! let me go to her; they are drawing me to them. I feel them—I feel them. I must go!"

Again she was almost convulsed by her efforts to get away; but I held her tighter and tighter, till I feared I should do her a hurt; but rather that than let her go towards those terrible phantoms. They passed along towards the great hall-door, where the winds howled and ravened for their prey; but before they reached that, the lady turned; and I could see that she defied the old man with a fierce and proud defiance; but then she quailed—and then she threw her arms wildly and piteously to save her child—her little child—from a blow from his uplifted crutch.

And Miss Rosamond was torn as by a power stronger than mine, and writhed in my arms, and sobbed (for by this time the poor darling was growing faint).

"They want me to go with them on to the Fells—they are drawing me to them. Oh, my little girl! I would come, but cruel, wicked Hester holds me very tight." But when she saw the uplifted crutch she swooned away, and I thanked God for it. Just at this moment—when the tall, old man, his hair streaming as in the blast of a furnace, was going to strike the little, shrinking child—Miss Furnivall, the old woman by my side, cried out, "Oh, father! father! spare the little, innocent child!" But just then I saw—we all saw—another phantom shape itself, and grow clear out of the blue and misty light that filled the hall; we had not seen her till now, for it was another lady who stood by the old man, with a look of relentless hate and triumphant scorn. That figure was very beautiful to look upon, with a soft, white hat drawn down over the proud brows, and a red and curling lip. It was dressed in an open robe of blue satin. I had seen that figure before. It was the likeness of Miss Furnivall in her youth; and the terrible phantoms moved on, regardless of old Miss Furnivall's wild entreaty, and the uplifted crutch fell on the right shoulder of the little child, and the younger sister looked on, stony and deadly serene. But at that moment, the dim lights, and the fire that gave no heat, went out of themselves, and Miss Furnivall lay at our feet stricken down by the palsy—death-stricken.

Yes! she was carried to her bed that night never to rise again. She lay with her face to the wall, muttering low, but muttering always: "Alas! alas! what is done in youth can never be undone in age! what is done in youth can never be undone in age!"

THE JUDGE'S HOUSE,
by Bram Stoker

When the time for his examination drew near Malcolm Malcolmson made up his mind to go somewhere to read by himself. He feared the attractions of the seaside, and also he feared completely rural isolation, for of old he knew its charms, and so he determined to find some unpretentious little town where there would be nothing to distract him. He refrained from asking suggestions from any of his friends, for he argued that each would recommend some place of which he had knowledge, and where he had already acquaintances. As Malcolmson wished to avoid friends he had no wish to encumber himself with the attention of friends' friends and so he determined to look out for a place for himself. He packed a portmanteau with some clothes and all the books he required, and then took ticket for the first name on the local time-table which he did not know.

When at the end of three hours' journey he alighted at Benchurch, he felt satisfied that he had so far obliterated his tracks as to be sure of having a peaceful opportunity of pursuing his studies. He went straight to the one inn which the sleepy little place contained, and put up for the night. Benchurch was a market town, and once in three weeks was crowded to excess, but for the reminder of the twenty-one days it was as attractive as a desert. Malcolmson looked around the day after his arrival to try to find quarters more isolated than even so quiet an inn as "The Good Traveller" afforded. There was only one place which took his fancy, and it certainly satisfied his wildest ideas regarding quiet; in fact, quiet was not the proper word to apply to it—desolation was the only term conveying any suitable idea of its isolation. It was an old, rambling, heavy-built house of the Jacobean style, with heavy gables and windows, unusually small, and set higher than was customary in such houses, and was surrounded with a high brick wall massively built. Indeed, on examination, it looked more like a fortified house than an ordinary dwelling. But all these things pleased Malcolmson. "Here," he thought, "is the very spot I have been looking for, and if I can only get opportunity of using it I shall be happy." His joy was increased when he realized beyond doubt that it was not at present inhabited.

From the post-office he got the name of the agent, who was rarely surprised at the application to rent a part of the old house. Mr. Carnford, the local lawyer and agent, was a genial old gentleman, and frankly confessed his delight at anyone being willing to live in the house.

"To tell you the truth," said he, "I should be only too happy, on behalf of the owners, to let anyone have the house rent free, for a term of years if only to accustom the people here to see it inhabited. It has been so long empty that some kind of absurd prejudice has grown up about it, and this can be best put down by its occupation—if only," he added with a sly glance at Malcolmson, "by a scholar like yourself, who wants its quiet for a time."

Malcolmson thought it needless to ask the agent about the "absurd prejudice"; he knew he would get more information, if he should require it, on that subject from other quarters. He paid his three months' rent, got a receipt, and the name of an old woman who would probably undertake to "do" for him, and came away with the keys in his pocket. He then went to the landlady of the inn, who was a cheerful and most kindly person, and asked her advice as to such stores and provisions as he would be likely to require. She threw up her hands in amazement when he told her where he was going to settle himself.

"Not in the Judge's House!" she said, and grew pale as she spoke. He explained the locality of the house, saying that he did not know its name. When he had finished she answered:

"Aye, sure enough—sure enough the very place! It is the Judge's House sure enough." He asked her to tell him about the place, why so called, and what there was against it. She told him that it was so called locally because it had been many years before—how long she could not say, as she was herself from another part of the country, but she thought it must have been a hundred years or more—the abode of a judge who was held in great terror on account of his harsh sentences and his hostility to prisoners at Assizes. As to what there was against the house she could not tell. She had often asked, but no one could inform her, but there was a general feeling that there was *something*, and for her own part she would not take all the money in Drinkwater's Bank and stay in the house an hour by herself. Then she apologized to Malcolmson for her disturbing talk.

"It is too bad of me, sir, and you—and a young gentleman, too—if you will pardon me saying it, going to live there all alone. If you were my boy—and you'll excuse me for saying it—you wouldn't sleep there a night, not if I had to go there myself and pull the big alarm bell that's on the roof!" The good creature was so manifestly in earnest, and was so kindly in her intentions, that Malcolmson, although amused, was touched. He told her kindly how much he appreciated her interest in him, and added:

"But, my dear Mrs. Witham, indeed you need not be concerned about me! A man who is reading for the Mathematical Tripos has too much to think of to be disturbed by any of these mysterious 'somethings,' and his work is of too exact and prosaic a kind to allow of his having any order in his mind for mysteries of any kind. Harmonical Progression, Permutations and Combinations, and Elliptic Functions have sufficient mysteries for me!" Mrs. Witham kindly undertook to see after his commissions, and he went himself to look for the old woman who had been recommended to him. When he turned to the Judge's House with her, after an interval of a couple of hours, he found Mrs. Witham herself waiting with several men and boys carrying parcels, and an upholsterer's man with a bed in a cart, for she said, though table and chairs might be all very well, a bed that hadn't been aired for maybe fifty years was not proper for young ones to lie on. She was evidently curious to see the inside of the house, and though manifestly so afraid of the 'somethings' that at the slightest sound she clutched on to Malcolmson, whom she never left for a moment, went over the whole place.

After his examination of the house, Malcolmson decided to take up his abode in the great dining-room, which was big enough to serve for all his requirements, and Mrs. Witham, with the aid of the charwoman, Mrs. Dempster, proceeded to arrange matters. When the hampers were brought in and unpacked, Malcolmson saw that with much kind forethought she had sent from her own kitchen sufficient provisions to last for a few days. Before going she expressed all sorts of kind wishes, and at the door turned and said:

"And perhaps, sir, as the room is big and draughty it might be well to have one of those big screens put round your bed at night—though truth to tell, I would die myself if I were to be so shut in with all kinds of—of 'things,' that put their heads round the sides or over the top, and look on me!" The image which she had called

146

up was too much for her nerves and she fled incontinently.

Mrs. Dempster sniffed in a superior manner as the landlady disappeared, and remarked that for her own part she wasn't afraid of all the bogies in the kingdom.

"I'll tell you what it is, sir," she said, "bogies is all kinds and sorts of things—except bogies! Rats and mice, and beetles and creaky doors, and loose slates, and broken panes, and stiff drawer handles, that stay out when you pull them and then fall down in the middle of the night. Look at the wainscot of the room! It is old—hundreds of years old! Do you think there's no rats and beetles there? And do you imagine, sir, that you won't see none of them? Rats is bogies, I tell you, and bogies is rats, and don't you get to think anything else!"

"Mrs. Dempster," said Malcolmson gravely, making her a polite bow, "you know more than a Senior Wrangler! And let me say that, as a mark of esteem for your indubitable soundness of head and heart, I shall, when I go, give you possession of this house, and let you stay here by yourself for the last two months of my tenancy, for four weeks will serve my purpose."

"Thank you kindly, sir!" she answered, "but I couldn't sleep away from home a night. I am in Greenhow's Charity, and if I slept a night away from my rooms I should lose all I have got to live on. The rules is very strict, and there's too many watching for a vacancy for me to run any risks in the matter. Only for that, sir, I'd gladly come here and attend on you altogether during your stay."

"My good woman," said Malcolmson hastily, "I have come here on a purpose to obtain solitude, and believe me that I am grateful to the late Greenhow for having organized his admirable charity—whatever it is—that I am perforce denied the opportunity of suffering from such a form of temptation! Saint Anthony himself could not be more rigid on the point!"

The old woman laughed harshly. "Ah, you young gentlemen," she said, "you don't fear for nought, and belike you'll get all the solitude you want here." She set to work with her cleaning, and by nightfall, when Malcolmson returned from his walk—he always had one of his books to study as he walked—he found the room swept and tidied, a fire burning on the old hearth, the lamp lit, and the table spread for supper with Mrs. Witham's excellent fare. "This is comfort indeed," he said, and rubbed his hands.

When he had finished his supper, and lifted the tray to the other end of the great oak dining-table, he got out his books again, put fresh wood on the fire, trimmed his lamp, and set himself down to a spell of real hard work. He went on without a pause till about eleven o'clock, when he knocked off for a bit to fix his fire and lamp, and to make himself a cup of tea. He had always been a tea-drinker, and during his college life had sat late at work and had taken tea late. The rest was a great luxury to him, and he enjoyed it with a sense of delicious voluptuous ease. The renewed fire leaped and sparkled, and threw quaint shadows through the great old room, and as he sipped his hot tea he revelled in the sense of isolation from his kind. Then it was that he began to notice for the first time what a noise the rats were making.

"Surely," he thought, "they cannot have been at it all the time I was reading. Had they been, I must have noticed it!" Presently, when the noise increased, he satisfied himself that it was really new. It was evident that at first the rats had been frightened at the presence of a stranger, and the light of fire and lamp, but that as the time went on they had grown bolder and were now disporting themselves as was their wont.

How busy they were—and hark to the strange noises! Up and down the old wainscot, over the ceiling and under the floor they raced, and gnawed, and scratched! Malcolmson smiled to himself as he recalled to mind the saying of Mrs. Dempster, "Bogies is rats, and rats is bogies!" The tea began to have its effect of intellectual and nervous stimulus, he saw with joy another long spell of work to be done before the night was past, and in the sense of security which it gave him, he allowed himself the luxury of a good look round the room. He took his lamp in one hand, and went all round, wondering that so quaint and beautiful an old house had been so long neglected. The carving of the oak on the panels of the wainscot was fine, and on and round the doors and windows it was beautiful and of rare merit. There were some old pictures on the walls, but they were coated so thick with dust and dirt that he could not distinguish any detail of them, though he held his lamp as high as he could over his head. Here and there as he went round he saw some crack or hole blocked for a moment by the face of a rat with its bright eyes glittering in the light, but in an instant it was gone, and a squeak and a scamper followed. The thing that most struck him, however, was the rope of the great alarm bell on the roof, which hung down in a corner of the room on the right-hand side of the fireplace. He pulled up close to the hearth a great high-backed carved oak chair, and sat down to his last cup of tea. When this was done he made up the fire, and went back to his work, sitting at the corner of the table, having the fire to his left. For a little while the rats disturbed him somewhat with their perpetual scampering, but he got accustomed to the noise as one does to the ticking of the clock or to the roar of moving water, and he became so immersed in his work that everything in the world, except the problem which he was trying to solve, passed away from him.

He suddenly looked up, his problem was still unsolved, and there was in the air that sense of the hour before the dawn, which is so dread to doubtful life. The noise of the rats had ceased. Indeed it seemed to him that it must have ceased but lately and that it was the sudden cessation which had disturbed him. The fire had fallen low, but still it threw out a deep red glow. As he looked he started in spite of his *sang froid*.

There, on the great high-backed carved oak chair by the right side of the fireplace sat an enormous rat, steadily glaring at him with baleful eyes. He made a motion to it as though to hunt it away, but it did not stir. Then he made the motion of throwing something. Still it did not stir, but showed its great white teeth angrily, and its cruel eyes shone in the lamplight with an added vindictiveness.

Malcolmson felt amazed, and seizing the poker from the hearth ran at it to kill it. Before, however, he could strike it the rat, with a squeak that sounded like the concentration of hate, jumped upon the floor, and, running up the rope of the alarm bell, disappeared in the darkness beyond the range of the green-shaded lamp. Instantly, strange to say, the noisy scampering of the rats in the wainscot began again.

By this time Malcolmson's mind was quite off the problem, and as a shrill cock-crow outside told him of the approach of morning, he went to bed and to sleep.

He slept so sound that he was not even waked by Mrs. Dempster coming in to make up his room. It was only when she had tided up the place and got his breakfast ready and tapped on the screen which closed in his bed that he woke. He was a little tired still after his night's hard work, but a strong cup of tea soon freshened him up and, taking his book, he went out for his morning walk, bringing with him a few sandwiches lest he should not care to return till dinner-time. He found a quiet walk between high elms some way outside the town, and here he spent the greater part of the day studying his Laplace. On his return he looked in to see Mrs. Witham and to thank her for her kindness. When she saw him coming through the diamond-paned bay window of her sanctum she came out to meet him and asked him in. She looked at him searchingly and shook her head as she said:

"You must not overdo it, sir. You are paler this morning than you should be. Too late hours and too hard work on the brains isn't good for any man! But tell me, sir, how did you pass the night? Well, I hope? But, my heart! sir, I was glad when Mrs. Dempster told me this morning that you were all right and sleeping sound when she went in."

"Oh, I was all right," he answered smiling, "The 'somethings' didn't worry me, as yet. Only the rats, and they had a circus, I tell you, all over the place. There was one wicked-looking old devil that sat up on my own chair by the fire, and wouldn't go till I took the poker to him, and then he ran up the rope of the alarm bell and got to somewhere up the wall or the ceiling—I couldn't see where, it was so dark."

"Mercy on us," said Mrs. Witham, "an old devil, and sitting on a chair by the fireside! Take care, sir! take care! There's many a true word spoken in jest."

"How do you mean? 'Pon my word, I don't understand."

"An old devil! The old devil, perhaps. There! sir, you needn't laugh," for Malcolmson had broken into a hearty peal. "You young folks think it easy to laugh at things that makes older ones shudder. Never mind, sir! never mind! Please God, you'll laugh all the time. It's what I wish you myself!" and the good lady beamed all over in sympathy with his enjoyment, her fears gone for a moment.

"Oh, forgive me," said Malcolmson presently. "Don't think me rude, but the idea was too much for me—that the old devil himself was on the chair last night!" And at the thought he laughed again. Then he went home to dinner.

This evening the scampering of the rats began earlier, indeed it had been going on before his arrival, and only ceased whilst his presence by its freshness disturbed them. After dinner he sat by the fire for a while and had a smoke, and then, having cleared his table, began to work as before. Tonight the rats disturbed him more than they had done on the previous night.

How they scampered up and down and under and over! How they squeaked and scratched and gnawed! How they, getting bolder by degrees, came to the mouths of their holes and to the chinks and cracks and crannies in the wainscoting till their eyes shone like tiny lamps as the firelight rose and fell. But to him, now doubtless accustomed to them, their eyes were not wicked, only their playfulness touched him. Sometimes the boldest of them made sallies out on the floor or along the mouldings of the wainscot. Now and again as they disturbed him Malcolmson made a sound to frighten them, smiting the table with his hand or giving a fierce "Hsh, hsh," so that they fled straightway to their holes.

And so the early part of the night wore on, and despite the noise Malcolmson got more and more immersed in his work.

All at once he stopped, as on the previous night, being overcome by a sudden silence. There was not the faintest sound of gnaw, or scratch, or squeak. The silence was as of the grave.

He remembered the odd occurrence of the previous night, and instinctively he looked at the chair standing close by the fireside. And then a very odd sensation thrilled through him.

There, on the great old high-backed carved oak chair beside the fireplace sat the same enormous rat, steadily glaring at him with baleful eyes.

Instinctively he took the nearest thing to his hand, a book of logarithms, and flung it at it. The book was badly aimed and the rat did not stir, so again the poker performance of the previous night was repeated, and again the rat, being closely pursued, fled up the rope of the alarm bell. Strangely, too, the departure of this rat was instantly followed by the renewal of the noise made by the general rat community. On this occasion, as on the previous one, Malcolmson could not see at what part of the room the rat disappeared, for the green shade of his lamp left the upper part of the room in darkness and the fire had burned low.

On looking at his watch he found it was close on midnight, and, not sorry for the *divertissement*, he made up his fire and made himself his nightly pot of tea. He had got through a good spell of work, and thought himself entitled to a cigarette, and so he sat on the great carved oak chair before the fire and enjoyed it. Whilst smoking he began to think that he would like to know where the rat disappeared to, for he had certain ideas for the morrow not entirely disconnected with a rat-trap. Accordingly he lit another lamp and placed it so that it would shine well into the right-hand corner of the wall by the fireplace. Then he got all the books he had with him, and placed them handy to throw at the vermin. Finally he lifted the rope of the alarm bell and placed the end of it on the table, fixing the extreme end under the lamp. As he handled it he could not help noticing how pliable it was, especially for so strong a rope and one not in use. "You could hang a man with it," he thought to himself. When his preparations were made he looked around, and said complacently:

"There now, my friend, I think we shall learn something of you this time!" He began his work again, and though, as before, somewhat disturbed at first by the noise of the rats, soon lost himself in his proposition and problems.

Again he was called to his immediate surroundings suddenly. This time it might not have been the sudden silence only which took his attention; there was a slight movement of the rope, and the lamp moved. Without stirring, he looked to see if his pile of books was within range, and then cast his eye along the rope. As he looked he saw the great rat drop from the rope on the oak arm-chair and sit there glaring at him. He raised a book in his right hand, and taking careful aim, flung it at the rat. The latter, with a quick movement, sprang aside and dodged the missile. Then he took another book, and a third, and flung them one after the other at the rat, but each time unsuccessfully. At last, as he stood with a book poised in his hand to throw, the rat squeaked and seemed afraid. This made Malcolmson more than ever eager to strike, and the book flew and struck the rat a resounding blow. It gave a terrified squeak, and turning on his pursuer a look of terrible malevolence, ran up the chair-back and made a great jump to the rope of the alarm bell and ran up it like lightning. The lamp rocked under the sudden strain, but it was a heavy one and did not topple over. Malcolmson kept his eyes on the rat, and saw it by the light of the second lamp leap to a moulding of the wainscot and disappear through a hole in one of the great pictures which hung on the wall, obscured and invisible through its coating of dirt and dust.

"I shall look up my friend's habitation in the morning," said the student, as he went over to collect his books. "The third picture from the fireplace, I shall not forget." He picked up the books one by one, commenting on them as he lifted them. *Conic Sections* he does not mind, nor *Cycloid Oscillations*, nor the Principia, nor *Quaternions*, nor *Thermodynamics*. Now for a look at the book that fetched him!" Malcolmson took it up and looked at it. As he did so he started, and a sudden pallor overspread his face. He looked round uneasily and shivered slightly, as he murmured to himself:

"The Bible my mother gave me! What an odd coincidence." He sat down to work again, and the rats in the wainscot renewed their gambols. They did not disturb him, however; somehow their presence gave him a sense of companionship. But he could not attend to his work, and after striving to master the subject on which he was engaged gave it up in despair, and went to bed as the first streak of dawn stole in through the eastern window.

He slept heavily but uneasily, and dreamed much, and when Mrs. Dempster woke him late in the morning he seemed ill at ease, and for a few minutes did not seem to realize exactly where he was. His first request rather surprised the servant.

"Mrs. Dempster, when I am out today I wish you would get the steps and dust or wash those pictures—specially that one the third from the fireplace—I want to see what they are."

Late in the afternoon Malcolmson worked at his books in the shaded walk, and the cheerfulness of the previous day came back to him as the day wore on, and he found that his reading was progressing well. He had worked out to a satisfactory conclusion all the problems which had as yet baffled him, and it was in a state of jubilation that he paid a visit to Mrs. Witham at "The Good Traveller." He found a stranger in the cosy sitting-room with the landlady, who was introduced to him as Dr. Thornhill. She was not quite at ease, and this, combined with the doctor's plunging at once into a series of questions, made Malcolmson come to the conclusion that his presence was not an accident, so without preliminary he said:

"Dr. Thornhill, I shall with pleasure answer you any question you may choose to ask me if you will answer me one question first."

The doctor seemed surprised, but he smiled and answered at once, "Done! What is it?"

"Did Mrs. Witham ask you to come here and see me and advise me?"

Dr. Thornhill for a moment was taken aback, and Mrs. Witham got fiery red and turned away, but the doctor was a frank and ready man, and he answered at once and openly:

"She did, but she didn't intend you to know it. I suppose it was my clumsy haste that made you suspect. She told me that she did not like the idea of your being in that house all by yourself, and that she thought you took too much strong tea. In fact, she wants me to advise you, if possible, to give up the tea and the very late hours. I was a keen student in my time, so I suppose I may take the liberty of a college man, and without offence, advise you not quite as a stranger."

Malcolmson with a bright smile held out his hand. "Shake—as they say in America," he said. "I must thank you for your kindness, and Mrs. Witham too, and your kindness deserves a return on my part. I promise to take no more strong tea—no tea at all till you let me—and I shall go to bed tonight at one o'clock at latest. Will that do?"

"Capital," said the doctor. "Now tell us all that you noticed in the old house," and so Malcolmson then and there told in minute detail all that had happened in the last two nights. He was interrupted every now and then by some exclamation from Mrs. Witham, till finally when he told of the episode of the Bible the landlady's pent-up emotions found vent in a shriek, and it was not till a stiff glass of brandy and water had been administered that she grew composed again. Dr. Thornhill listened with a face of growing gravity, and when the narrative was complete and Mrs. Witham had been restored he asked:

"The rat always went up the rope of the alarm bell?"

"Always."

"I suppose you know," said the Doctor after a pause, "what that rope is?"

"No?"

"It is," said the Doctor slowly, "the very rope which the hangman used for all the victims of the Judge's judicial rancour!" Here he was interrupted by another scream from Mrs. Witham, and steps had to be taken for her recovery. Malcolmson having looked at his watch, and found that it was close to his dinner-hour, had gone home before her complete recovery.

When Mrs. Witham was herself again she almost assailed the Doctor with angry questions as to what he meant by putting such horrible ideas into the poor young man's mind. "He has quite enough there already to upset him," she added.

Dr. Thornhill replied:

"My dear madam, I had a distinct purpose in it! I wanted to draw his attention to the bell-rope, and to fix it there. It may be that he is in a highly over-wrought state, and has been studying too much, although I am bound to say that he seems as sound and healthy a young man, mentally and bodily, as ever I saw—but then the rats—and that suggestion of the devil." The doctor shook his head and went on. "I would have offered to go and stay the first night with him but that I felt sure it would have been a cause of offence. He may get in the night some strange fright or hallucination, and if he does I want him to pull that rope. All alone as he is it will give us warning, and we may reach him in time to be of service. I shall be sitting up pretty late tonight and shall keep my ears open. Do not be alarmed if Benchurch gets a surprise before morning."

"Oh, Doctor, what do you mean? What do you mean?"

"I mean this, that possibly—nay, more probably—we shall hear the great alarm-bell from the Judge's House tonight," and the Doctor made about an effective an exit as could be thought of.

When Malcolmson arrived home he found that it was a little after his usual time, and Mrs. Dempster had gone away—the rules of Greenhow's Charity were not to be neglected. He was glad to see that the place was bright and tidy with a cheerful fire and a well-trimmed lamp. The evening was colder than might have been expected in April, and a heavy wind was blowing with such rapidly-increasing strength that there was every promise of a storm during the night. For a few minutes after his entrance the noise of the rats ceased, but so soon as they became accustomed to his presence they began again. He was glad to hear them, for he felt once more the feeling of companionship in their noise, and his mind ran back to the strange fact that they only ceased to manifest themselves when the other—the great rat with the baleful eyes—came upon the scene. The reading-lamp only was lit and its green shade kept the ceiling and the upper part of the room in darkness so that the cheerful light from the hearth spreading over the floor and shining on the white cloth laid over the end of the table was warm and cheery. Malcolmson sat down to his dinner with a good appetite and a buoyant spirit. After his dinner and a cigarette he sat steadily down to work, determined not to let anything disturb him, for he remembered his promise to the doctor, and made up his mind to make the best of the time at his disposal.

For an hour or so he worked all right, and then his thoughts began to wander from his books. The actual circumstances around him, and the calls on his physical attention, and his nervous susceptibility were not to be denied. By this time the wind had become a gale, and the gale a storm. The old house, solid though it was, seemed to shake to its foundation, and the storm roared and raged through its many chimneys and its queer old gables, producing strange, unearthly sounds in the empty rooms and corridors. Even the great alarm-bell on the roof must have felt the force of the wind, for the rope rose and fell slightly, as though the bell were moved a little from time to time, and the limber rope fell on the oak floor with a hard and hollow sound.

As Malcolmson listened to it he bethought himself of the doctor's words, "It is the rope which the hangman used for the victims of the Judge's judicial rancour," and he went over to the corner of the fireplace and took it in his hand to look at it. There seemed a sort of deadly interest in it, and as he stood there he lost himself for a moment in speculation as to who these victims were, and the grim wish of the Judge to have such a ghastly relic ever under his eyes. As he stood there the swaying of the bell on the roof still lifted the rope now and again, but presently there came a new sensation—a sort of tremor in the rope, as though something was moving along it.

Looking up instinctively Malcolmson saw the great rat coming slowly down towards him, glaring at him steadily. He dropped the rope and started back with a muttered curse, and the rat turning ran up the slope again and disappeared, and at the same instant Malcolmson became conscious that the noise of the other rats, which had ceased for a while, began again.

All this set him thinking, and it occurred to him that he had not investigated the lair of the rat or looked at the pictures, as he had intended. He lit the other lamp without the shade, and, holding it up went and stood opposite the third picture from the fireplace on the right-hand side where he had seen the rat disappear on the previous night.

At the first glance he started back so suddenly that he almost dropped the lamp, and a deadly pallor overspread his face.

His knees shook, and heavy drops of sweat came on his forehead, and he trembled like an aspen. But he was young and plucky, and pulled himself together, and after the pause of a few seconds stepped forward again, raised the lamp, and examined the picture which had been dusted and washed, and now stood out clearly.

It was of a judge dressed in his robes of scarlet and ermine. His face was strong and merciless, evil, crafty and vindictive, with a sensual mouth, hooked nose of ruddy colour, and shaped like the beak of a bird of prey. The rest of the face was of a cadaverous colour. The eyes were of peculiar brilliance and with a terribly malignant expression. As he looked at them, Malcolmson grew cold, for he saw there the very counterpart of the eyes of the great rat. The lamp almost fell from his hand, he saw the rat with its baleful eyes peering out through the hole in the corner of the picture, and noted the sudden cessation of the noise of the other rats. However, he pulled himself together, and went on with his examination of the picture.

The Judge was seated in a great high-backed carved oak chair, on the right-hand side of a great stone fireplace where, in the corner, a rope hung down from the ceiling, its end lying coiled on the floor. With a feeling of something like horror, Malcolmson recognized the scene of the room as it stood, and gazed around him in an awestruck manner as though he expected to find some strange presence behind him. Then he looked over to the corner of the fireplace—and with a loud cry he let the lamp fall from his hand.

There, in the judge's arm-chair, with the rope hanging behind, sat the rat with the Judge's baleful eyes, now intensified as with a fiendish leer. Save for the howling of the storm without there was silence.

The fallen lamp recalled Malcolmson to himself. Fortunately it was of metal, and so the oil was not spilt. However, the practical need of attending to it settled at once his nervous apprehensions. When he had turned it out, he wiped his brow and thought for a moment.

"This will not do," he said to himself. "If I go on like this I shall become a crazy fool. This must stop! I promised the doctor I would not take tea. Faith, he was pretty right! My nerves must have been getting into a queer state. Funny I did not notice it. I never felt better in my life. However, it is all right now, and I shall not be such a fool again."

Then he mixed himself a good stiff glass of brandy and water and resolutely sat down to his work.

It was nearly an hour when he looked up from his book, disturbed by the sudden stillness. Without, the wind howled and roared louder then ever, and the rain drove in sheets against the windows, beating like hail on the glass, but within there was no sound whatever save the echo of the wind as it roared in the great chimney, and now and then a hiss as a few raindrops found their way down the chimney in a lull of the storm. The fire had fallen low and had ceased to flame, though it threw out a red glow. Malcolmson listened attentively, and presently heard a thin, squeaking noise, very faint. It came from the corner of the room where the rope hung down, and he thought it was the creaking of the rope on the floor as the swaying of the bell raised and lowered it. Looking up, however, he saw in the dim light the great rat clinging to the rope and gnawing it. The rope was already nearly gnawed through—he could see the lighter colour where the strands were laid bare. As he looked the job was completed, and the severed end of the rope fell clattering on the oaken floor, whilst for an instant the great rat remained like a knob or tassel at the end of the rope, which now began to sway to and fro. Malcolmson felt for a moment another pang of terror as he thought that now the possibility of calling the outer world to his assistance was cut off, but an intense anger took its place, and seizing the book he was reading he hurled it at the rat. The blow was well-aimed, but before the missile could reach him the rat dropped off and struck the floor with a soft thud. Malcolmson instantly rushed over towards him, but it darted away and disappeared in the darkness of the shadows of the room. Malcolmson felt that his work was over for the night, and determined then and there to vary the monotony of the proceedings by a hunt for the rat, and took off the green shade of the lamp so as to insure a wider spreading light. As he did so the gloom of the upper part of the room was relieved, and in the new flood of light, great by comparison with the previous darkness, the pictures on the wall stood out boldly.

From where he stood, Malcolmson saw right opposite to him the third picture on the wall from the right of the fireplace. He rubbed his eyes in surprise, and then a great fear began to come upon him.

In the centre of the picture was a great irregular patch of brown canvas, as fresh as when it was stretched on the frame. The background was as before, with chair and chimney-corner and rope, but the figure of the Judge had disappeared.

Malcolmson, almost in a chill of horror, turned slowly round, and then he began to shake and tremble like a man in a palsy. His strength seemed to have left him, and he was incapable of action or movement, hardly even of thought. He could only see and hear.

There, on the great high-backed carved oak chair sat the judge in his robes of scarlet and ermine, with his baleful eyes glaring vindictively, and a smile of triumph on the resolute cruel mouth, as he lifted with his hands a *black cap*. Malcolmson felt as if the blood was running from his heart, as one does in moments of prolonged suspense. There was a singing in his ears. Without, he could hear the roar and howl of the tempest, and through it, swept on the storm, came the striking of midnight by the great chimes in the market-place. He stood for a space of time that seemed to him endless still as a statue, and with wide-open, horror-struck eyes, breathless. As the clock struck, so the smile of triumph on the Judge's face intensified, and at the last stroke of midnight he placed the black cap on his head.

Slowly and deliberately the Judge rose from his chair and picked up the piece of rope of the alarm bell which lay on the floor, drew it through his hands as if he enjoyed its touch and then deliberately began to knot one end of it, fashioning it into a noose. This he tightened and tested with his foot, pulling hard at it till he was satisfied and then making a running noose of it, which he held in his hand. Then he

154

began to move along the table on the opposite side of Malcolmson keeping his eyes on him until he had passed him, when with a quick movement he stood in front of the door. Malcolmson then began to feel that he was trapped, and tried to think of what he should do. There was some fascination in the Judge's eyes, which he never took off him, and he had, perforce, to look. He saw the Judge approach—still keeping between him and the door—and raise the noose and throw it towards him as if to entangle him. With a great effort he made a quick movement to one side, and saw the rope fall beside him, and heard it strike the oaken floor. Again the Judge raised the noose and tried to ensnare him, ever keeping his baleful eyes fixed on him, and each time by a mighty effort the student just managed to evade it. So this went on for many times, the Judge seeming never discouraged nor discomposed at failure, but playing as a cat does with a mouse. At last in despair, which had reached its climax, Malcolmson cast a quick glance round him. The lamp seemed to have blazed up, and there was a fairly good light in the room. At the many rat-holes and in the chinks and crannies of the wainscot he saw the rats' eyes, and this aspect, that was purely physical, gave him a gleam of comfort. He looked round and saw that the rope of the great alarm bell was laden with rats. Every inch of it was covered with them, and more and more were pouring through the small circular hole in the ceiling whence it emerged, so that with their weight the bell was beginning to sway.

Hark! it had swayed till the clapper had touched the bell. The sound was but a tiny one, but the bell was only beginning to sway, and it would increase.

At the sound the Judge, who had been keeping his eyes fixed on Malcolmson, looked up, and a scowl of diabolical anger overspread his face. His eyes fairly glowed like hot coals, and he stamped his foot with a sound that seemed to make the house shake. A dreadful peal of thunder broke overhead as he raised the rope again, whilst the rats kept running up and down the rope as though working against time. This time, instead of throwing it, he drew close to his victim, and held open the noose as he approached. As he came closer there seemed something paralyzing in his very presence, and Malcolmson stood rigid as a corpse. He felt the Judge's icy fingers touch his throat as he adjusted the rope. The noose tightened—tightened. Then the Judge, taking the rigid form of the student in his arms, carried him over and placed him standing in the oak chair, and stepping up beside him, put his hand up and caught the end of the swaying rope of the alarm-bell. As he raised his hand the rats fled squeaking and disappeared through the hole in the ceiling. Taking the end of the noose which was round Malcolmson's neck, he tied it to the hanging bell-rope, and then descending pulled away the chair.

* * * *

When the alarm-bell of the Judge's House began to sound a crowd soon assembled. Lights and torches of various kinds appeared, and soon a silent crowd was hurrying to the spot. They knocked loudly at the door, but there was no reply. Then they burst in the door, and poured into the great dining-room, the doctor at the head.

There at the end of the rope of the great alarm-bell hung the body of the student, and on the face of the Judge in the picture was a malignant smile.

AT THE END OF THE PASSAGE,
by Rudyard Kipling

The sky is lead and our faces are red,
And the gates of Hell are opened and riven,
And the winds of Hell are loosened and driven,
And the dust flies up in the face of Heaven,
And the clouds come down in a fiery sheet,
Heavy to raise and hard to be borne.

And the soul of man is turned from his meat,
Turned from the trifles for which he has striven
Sick in his body, and heavy hearted,
And his soul flies up like the dust in the sheet
Breaks from his flesh and is gone and departed,
As the blasts they blow on the cholera-horn.

—Himalayan

* * * *

Four men, each entitled to "life, liberty, and the pursuit of happiness," sat at a table playing whist. The thermometer marked—for them—one hundred and one degrees of heat. The room was darkened till it was only just possible to distinguish the pips of the cards and the very white faces of the players. A tattered, rotten punkah of whitewashed calico was puddling the hot air and whining dolefully at each stroke. Outside lay gloom of a November day in London. There was neither sky, sun, nor horizon—nothing but a brown purple haze of heat. It was as though the earth were dying of apoplexy.

From time to time clouds of tawny dust rose from the ground without wind or warning, flung themselves tablecloth-wise among the tops of the parched trees, and came down again. Then a-whirling dust-devil would scutter across the plain for a couple of miles, break, and fall outward, though there was nothing to check its flight save a long low line of piled railway-sleepers white with the dust, a cluster of huts made of mud, condemned rails, and canvas, and the one squat four-roomed bungalow that belonged to the assistant engineer in charge of a section of the Gaudhari State line then under construction.

The four, stripped to the thinnest of sleeping-suits, played whist crossly, with wranglings as to leads and returns. It was not the best kind of whist, but they had taken some trouble to arrive at it. Mottram of the Indian Survey had ridden thirty and railed one hundred miles from his lonely post in the desert since the night before; Lowndes of the Civil Service, on special duty in the political department, had come as far to escape for an instant the miserable intrigues of an impoverished native State whose king alternately fawned and blustered for more money from the pitiful revenues contributed by hard-wrung peasants and despairing camel-breeders; Spurstow, the doctor of the line, had left a cholera-stricken camp of coolies to look after itself for forty-eight hours while he associated with white men once more. Hummil, the assistant engineer, was the host. He stood fast and received his friends thus every Sunday if they could come in. When one of them failed to appear, he would send a telegram to his last address, in order that he might know whether the defaulter were dead or alive. There are very many places in the East where it is not good or kind to let your acquaintances drop out of sight even for one short week.

The players were not conscious of any special regard for each other. They squabbled whenever they met; but they ardently desired to meet, as men without water desire to drink. They were lonely folk who understood the dread meaning of loneliness. They were all under thirty years of age—which is too soon for any man to possess that knowledge.

"Pilsener?" said Spurstow, after the second rubber, mopping his forehead.

"Beer's out, I'm sorry to say, and there's hardly enough soda-water for tonight," said Hummil.

"What filthy bad management!" Spurstow snarled.

"Can't help it. I've written and wired; but the trains don't come through regularly yet. Last week the ice ran out—as Lowndes knows."

"Glad I didn't come. I could ha' sent you some if I had known, though. Phew! it's too hot to go on playing bumblepuppy." This with a savage scowl at Lowndes, who only laughed. He was a hardened offender.

Mottram rose from the table and looked out of a chink in the shutters.

"What a sweet day!" said he.

The company yawned all together and betook themselves to an aimless investigation of all Hummil's possessions—guns, tattered novels, saddlery, spurs, and the like. They had fingered them a score of times before, but there was really nothing else to do.

"Got anything fresh?" said Lowndes.

"Last week's *Gazette of India*, and a cutting from a home paper. My father sent it out. It's rather amusing."

"One of those vestrymen that call 'emselves M.P.s again, is it?" said Spurstow, who read his newspapers when he could get them.

"Yes. Listen to this. It's to your address, Lowndes. The man was making a speech to his constituents, and he piled it on. Here's a sample, 'And I assert unhesitatingly that the Civil Service in India is the preserve—the pet preserve—of the aristocracy of England. What does the democracy—what do the masses—get from that country, which we have step by step fraudulently annexed? I answer, nothing whatever. It is farmed with a single eye to their own interests by the scions of the aristocracy. They take good care to maintain their lavish scale of incomes, to avoid or stifle any inquiries into the nature and conduct of their administration, while they themselves force the unhappy peasant to pay with the sweat of his brow for all the luxuries in which they are lapped.'" Hummil waved the cutting above his head. "''Ear! 'ear!" said his audience.

Then Lowndes, meditatively, "I'd give—I'd give three months' pay to have that gentleman spend one month with me and see how the free and independent native prince works things. Old Timbersides"—this was his flippant title for an honoured and decorated feudatory prince—"has been wearing my life out this week past for money. By Jove, his latest performance was to send me one of his women as a bribe!"

"Good for you! Did you accept it?" said Mottram.

"No. I rather wish I had, now. She was a pretty little person, and she yarned away to me about the horrible destitution among the king's women-folk. The darlings haven't had any new clothes for nearly a month, and the old man wants to buy a new drag from Calcutta—solid silver railings and silver lamps, and trifles of that

157

kind. I've tried to make him understand that he has played the deuce with the revenues for the last twenty years and must go slow. He can't see it."

"But he has the ancestral treasure-vaults to draw on. There must be three millions at least in jewels and coin under his palace," said Hummil.

"Catch a native king disturbing the family treasure! The priests forbid it except as the last resort. Old Timbersides has added something like a quarter of a million to the deposit in his reign."

"Where the mischief does it all come from?" said Mottram.

"The country. The state of the people is enough to make you sick. I've known the taxmen wait by a milch-camel till the foal was born and then hurry off the mother for arrears. And what can I do? I can't get the court clerks to give me any accounts; I can't raise anything more than a fat smile from the commander-in-chief when I find out the troops are three months in arrears; and old Timbersides begins to weep when I speak to him. He has taken to the King's Peg heavily, liqueur brandy for whisky, and Heidsieck for soda-water."

"That's what the Rao of Jubela took to. Even a native can't last long at that," said Spurstow. "He'll go out."

"And a good thing, too. Then I suppose we'll have a council of regency, and a tutor for the young prince, and hand him back his kingdom with ten years' accumulations."

"Whereupon that young prince, having been taught all the vices of the English, will play ducks and drakes with the money and undo ten years' work in eighteen months. I've seen that business before," said Spurstow. "I should tackle the king with a light hand if I were you, Lowndes. They'll hate you quite enough under any circumstances.

"That's all very well. The man who looks on can talk about the light hand; but you can't clean a pig-sty with a pen dipped in rose-water. I know my risks; but nothing has happened yet. My servant's an old Pathan, and he cooks for me. They are hardly likely to bribe him, and I don't accept food from my true friends, as they call themselves. Oh, but it's weary work! I'd sooner be with you, Spurstow. There's shooting near your camp."

"Would you? I don't think it. About fifteen deaths a day don't incite a man to shoot anything but himself. And the worst of it is that the poor devils look at you as though you ought to save them. Lord knows, I've tried everything. My last attempt was empirical, but it pulled an old man through. He was brought to me apparently past hope, and I gave him gin and Worcester sauce with cayenne. It cured him; but I don't recommend it."

"How do the cases run generally?" said Hummil.

"Very simply indeed. Chlorodyne, opium pill, chlorodyne, collapse, nitre, bricks to the feet, and then—the burning-ghaut. The last seems to be the only thing that stops the trouble. It's black cholera, you know. Poor devils! But, I will say, little Bunsee Lal, my apothecary, works like a demon. I've recommended him for promotion if he comes through it all alive."

"And what are your chances, old man?" said Mottram.

"Don't know; don't care much; but I've sent the letter in. What are you doing with yourself generally?"

"Sitting under a table in the tent and spitting on the sextant to keep it cool," said the man of the survey. "Washing my eyes to avoid ophthalmia, which I shall certainly get, and trying to make a sub-surveyor understand that an error of five degrees in an angle isn't quite so small as it looks. I'm altogether alone, y' know, and shall be till the end of the hot weather."

"Hummil's the lucky man," said Lowndes, flinging himself into a long chair. "He has an actual roof-torn as to the ceiling-cloth, but still a roof-over his head. He sees one train daily. He can get beer and soda-water and ice 'em when God is good. He has books, pictures—they were torn from the *Graphic*—and the society of the excellent sub-contractor Jevins, besides the pleasure of receiving us weekly."

Hummil smiled grimly. "Yes, I'm the lucky man, I suppose. Jevins is luckier."

"How? Not—"

"Yes. Went out. Last Monday."

"By his own hand?" said Spurstow quickly, hinting the suspicion that was in everybody's mind. There was no cholera near Hummil's section. Even fever gives a man at least a week's grace, and sudden death generally implied self-slaughter.

"I judge no man this weather," said Hummil. "He had a touch of the sun, I fancy; for last week, after you fellows had left, he came into the verandah and told me that he was going home to see his wife, in Market Street, Liverpool, that evening.

"I got the apothecary in to look at him, and we tried to make him lie down. After an hour or two he rubbed his eyes and said he believed he had had a fit, hoped he hadn't said anything rude. Jevins had a great idea of bettering himself socially. He was very like Chucks in his language."

"Well?"

"Then he went to his own bungalow and began cleaning a rifle. He told the servant that he was going to shoot buck in the morning. Naturally he fumbled with the trigger, and shot himself through the head—accidentally. The apothecary sent in a report to my chief; and Jevins is buried somewhere out there. I'd have wired to you, Spurstow, if you could have done anything."

"You're a queer chap," said Mottram. "If you'd killed the man yourself you couldn't have been more quiet about the business."

"Good Lord! what does it matter?" said Hummil calmly. "I've got to do a lot of his overseeing work in addition to my own. I'm the only person that suffers. Jevins is out of it, by pure accident, of course, but out of it. The apothecary was going to write a long screed on suicide. Trust a babu to drivel when he gets the chance."

"Why didn't you let it go in as suicide?" said Lowndes.

"No direct proof. A man hasn't many privileges in his country, but he might at least be allowed to mishandle his own rifle. Besides, some day I may need a man to smother up an accident to myself. Live and let live. Die and let die."

"You take a pill," said Spurstow, who had been watching Hummil's white face narrowly. "Take a pill, and don't be an ass. That sort of talk is skittles. Anyhow, suicide is shirking your work. If I were Job ten times over, I should be so interested in what was going to happen next that I'd stay on and watch."

"Ah! I've lost that curiosity," said Hummil.

"Liver out of order?" said Lowndes feelingly.

"No. Can't sleep. That's worse."

"By Jove, it is!" said Mottram. "I'm that way every now and then, and the fit has to wear itself out. What do you take for it?"

"Nothing. What's the use? I haven't had ten minutes' sleep since Friday morning."

"Poor chap! Spurstow, you ought to attend to this," said Mottram. "Now you mention it, your eyes are rather gummy and swollen."

Spurstow, still watching Hummil, laughed lightly. "I'll patch him up, later on. Is it too hot, do you think, to go for a ride?"

"Where to?" said Lowndes wearily. "We shall have to go away at eight, and there'll be riding enough for us then. I hate a horse when I have to use him as a necessity. Oh, heavens! what is there to do?"

"Begin whist again, at chick points [a 'chick' is supposed to be eight shillings] and a gold mohur on the rub," said Spurstow promptly.

"Poker. A month's pay all round for the pool—no limit—and fifty-rupee raises. Somebody would be broken before we got up," said Lowndes.

"Can't say that it would give me any pleasure to break any man in this company," said Mottram. "There isn't enough excitement in it, and it's foolish." He crossed over to the worn and battered little camp-piano—wreckage of a married household that had once held the bungalow—and opened the case.

"It's used up long ago," said Hummil. "The servants have picked it to pieces."

The piano was indeed hopelessly out of order, but Mottram managed to bring the rebellious notes into a sort of agreement, and there rose from the ragged keyboard something that might once have been the ghost of a popular music-hall song. The men in the long chairs turned with evident interest as Mottram banged the more lustily.

"That's good!" said Lowndes. "By Jove! the last time I heard that song was in '79, or thereabouts, just before I came out."

"Ah!" said Spurstow with pride, "I was home in '8o." And he mentioned a song of the streets popular at that date.

Mottram executed it roughly. Lowndes criticized and volunteered emendations. Mottram dashed into another ditty, not of the music-hall character, and made as if to rise.

"Sit down," said Hummil. "I didn't know that you had any music in your composition. Go on playing until you can't think of anything more. I'll have that piano tuned up before you come again. Play something festive."

Very simple indeed were the tunes to which Mottram's art and the limitations of the piano could give effect, but the men listened with pleasure, and in the pauses talked all together of what they had seen or heard when they were last at home. A dense dust-storm sprung up outside, and swept roaring over the house, enveloping it in the choking darkness of midnight, but Mottram continued unheeding, and the crazy tinkle reached the ears of the listeners above the flapping of the tattered ceiling-cloth.

In the silence after the storm he glided from the more directly personal songs of Scotland, half humming them as he played, into the Evening Hymn.

"Sunday," said he, nodding his head.

"Go on. Don't apologize for it," said Spurstow.

Hummil laughed long and riotously. "Play it, by all means. You're full of surprises today. I didn't know you had such a gift of finished sarcasm. How does that thing go?"

Mottram took up the tune.

"Too slow by half. You miss the note of gratitude," said Hummil. "It ought to go to the *Grasshopper's Polka*—this way." And he chanted, prestissimo,

> *"Glory to thee, my God, this night,*
> *For all the blessings of the light.*

That shows we really feel our blessings. How does it go on?—

> *If in the night I sleepless lie,*
> *My soul with sacred thoughts supply;*
> *May no ill dreams disturb my rest,—*

Quicker, Mottram!—

Or powers of darkness me molest!"

"Bah! what an old hypocrite you are!"

"Don't be an ass," said Lowndes. "You are at full liberty to make fun of anything else you like, but leave that hymn alone. It's associated in my mind with the most sacred recollections—"

"Summer evenings in the country, stained-glass window, light going out, and you and she jamming your heads together over one hymnbook," said Mottram.

"Yes, and a fat old cockchafer hitting you in the eye when you walked home. Smell of hay, and a moon as big as a bandbox sitting on the top of a haycock; bats, roses, milk and midges," said Lowndes.

"Also mothers. I can just recollect my mother singing me to sleep with that when I was a little chap," said Spurstow.

The darkness had fallen on the room. They could hear Hummil squirming in his chair.

"Consequently," said he testily, "you sing it when you are seven fathom deep in Hell! It's an insult to the intelligence of the Deity to pretend we're anything but tortured rebels."

"Take *two* pills," said Spurstow; "that's tortured liver."

"The usually placid Hummil is in a vile bad temper. I'm sorry for his coolies tomorrow," said Lowndes, as the servants brought in the lights and prepared the table for dinner.

As they were settling into their places about the miserable goat-chops, and the smoked tapioca pudding, Spurstow took occasion to whisper to Mottram, "Well done, David!"

"Look after Saul, then," was the reply.

"What are you two whispering about?" said Hummil suspiciously.

"Only saying that you are a damned poor host. This fowl can't be cut," returned Spurstow with a sweet smile. "Call this a dinner?"

"I can't help it. You don't expect a banquet, do you?"

Throughout that meal Hummil contrived laboriously to insult directly and pointedly all his guests in succession, and at each insult Spurstow kicked the aggrieved persons under the table; but he dared not exchange a glance of intelligence with either of them. Hummil's face was white and pinched, while his eyes were unnaturally large. No man dreamed for a moment of resenting his savage personalities, but as soon as the meal was over they made haste to get away.

"Don't go. You're just getting amusing, you fellows. I hope I haven't said anything that annoyed you. You're such touchy devils." Then, changing the note into one of almost abject entreaty, Hummil added, "I say, you surely aren't going?"

"In the language of the blessed Jorrocks, where I dines I sleeps," said Spurstow. "I want to have a look at your coolies tomorrow, if you don't mind. You can give me a place to lie down in, I suppose?"

The others pleaded the urgency of their several duties next day, and, saddling up, departed together, Hummil begging them to come next Sunday. As they jogged off, Lowndes unbosomed himself to Mottram—

"... And I never felt so like kicking a man at his own table in my life. He said I cheated at whist, and reminded me I was in debt! Told you you were as good as a liar to your face! You aren't half indignant enough over it."

"Not I," said Mottram. "Poor devil! Did you ever know old Hummy behave like that before or within a hundred miles of it?"

"That's no excuse. Spurstow was hacking my shin all the time, so I kept a hand on myself. Else I should have—"

"No, you wouldn't. You'd have done as Hummy did about Jevins; judge no man this weather. By Jove! the buckle of my bridle is hot in my hand! Trot out a bit, and 'ware rat-holes."

Ten minutes' trotting jerked out of Lowndes one very sage remark when he pulled up, sweating from every pore—

"Good thing Spurstow's with him tonight."

"Ye-es. Good man, Spurstow. Our roads turn here. See you again next Sunday, if the sun doesn't bowl me over."

"S'pose so, unless old Timbersides' finance minister manages to dress some of my food. Goodnight, and—God bless you!"

"What's wrong now?"

"Oh, nothing." Lowndes gathered up his whip, and, as he flicked Mottram's mare on the flank, added, "You're not a bad little chap, that's all." And the mare bolted half a mile across the sand, on the word.

In the assistant engineer's bungalow Spurstow and Hummil smoked the pipe of silence together, each narrowly watching the other. The capacity of a bachelor's establishment is as elastic as its arrangements are simple. A servant cleared away the dining-room table, brought in a couple of rude native bedsteads made of tape strung on a light wood frame, flung a square of cool Calcutta matting over each, set them side by side, pinned two towels to the punkah so that their fringes should just sweep clear of the sleeper's nose and mouth, and announced that the couches were ready.

The men flung themselves down, ordering the punkah-coolies by all the powers of Hell to pull. Every door and window was shut, for the outside air was that of an oven. The atmosphere within was only 104 degrees, as the thermometer bore witness, and heavy with the foul smell of badly-trimmed kerosene lamps; and this stench, combined with that of native tobacco, baked brick, and dried earth, sends the heart of many a strong man down to his boots, for it is the smell of the Great Indian Empire when she turns herself for six months into a house of torment. Spurstow packed his pillows craftily so that he reclined rather than lay, his head at a safe elevation above his feet. It is not good to sleep on a low pillow in the hot weather if you happen to be of thick-necked build, for you may pass with lively snores and gugglings from natural sleep into the deep slumber of heat-apoplexy.

"Pack your pillows," said the doctor sharply, as he saw Hummil preparing to lie down at full length.

The night-light was trimmed; the shadow of the punkah wavered across the room, and the "*flick*" of the punkah-towel and the soft whine of the rope through the wall-hole followed it. Then the punkah flagged, almost ceased. The sweat poured from Spurstow's brow. Should he go out and harangue the coolie? It started forward again with a savage jerk, and a pin came out of the towels. When this was replaced, a tomtom in the coolie-lines began to beat with the steady throb of a swollen artery inside some brain-fevered skull. Spurstow turned on his side and swore gently. There was no movement on Hummil's part. The man had composed himself as rigidly as a corpse, his hands clinched at his sides. The respiration was too hurried for any suspicion of sleep. Spurstow looked at the set face. The jaws were clinched, and there was a pucker round the quivering eyelids.

"He's holding himself as tightly as ever he can," thought Spurstow. "What in the world is the matter with him?—Hummil!"

"Yes," in a thick constrained voice.

"Can't you get to sleep?"

"No."

"Head hot? Throat feeling bulgy? or how?"

"Neither, thanks. I don't sleep much, you know."

"Feel pretty bad?"

"Pretty bad, thanks. There is a tomtom outside, isn't there? I thought it was my head at first.... Oh, Spurstow, for pity's sake give me something that will put me asleep, sound asleep, if it's only for six hours!" He sprang up, trembling from head to foot. "I haven't been able to sleep naturally for days, and I can't stand it! I can't stand it!"

"Poor old chap!"

"That's no use. Give me something to make me sleep. I tell you I'm nearly mad. I don't know what I say half my time. For three weeks I've had to think and spell out every word that has come through my lips before I dared say it. Isn't that enough to drive a man mad? I can't see things correctly now, and I've lost my sense of touch. My skin aches—my skin aches! Make me sleep. Oh, Spurstow, for the love of God make me sleep sound. It isn't enough merely to let me dream. Let me sleep!"

"All right, old man, all right. Go slow; you aren't half as bad as you think."

The flood-gates of reserve once broken, Hummil was clinging to him like a frightened child. "You're pinching my arm to pieces."

"I'll break your neck if you don't do something for me. No, I didn't mean that. Don't be angry, old fellow." He wiped the sweat off himself as he fought to regain composure. "I'm a bit restless and off my oats, and perhaps you could recommend some sort of sleeping mixture—bromide of potassium."

"Bromide of skittles! Why didn't you tell me this before? Let go of my arm, and I'll see if there's anything in my cigarette-case to suit your complaint." Spurstow hunted among his day-clothes, turned up the lamp, opened a little silver cigarette-case, and advanced on the expectant Hummil with the daintiest of fairy squirts.

"The last appeal of civilization," said he, "and a thing I hate to use. Hold out your arm. Well, your sleeplessness hasn't ruined your muscle; and what a thick hide it is! Might as well inject a buffalo subcutaneously. Now in a few minutes the morphia will begin working. Lie down and wait."

A smile of unalloyed and idiotic delight began to creep over Hummil's face. "I think," he whispered,—"I think I'm going off now. Gad! it's positively heavenly! Spurstow, you must give me that case to keep; you—" The voice ceased as the head fell back.

"Not for a good deal," said Spurstow to the unconscious form. "And now, my friend, sleeplessness of your kind being very apt to relax the moral fibre in little matters of life and death, I'll just take the liberty of spiking your guns."

He paddled into Hummil's saddle-room in his bare feet and uncased a twelve-bore rifle, an express, and a revolver. Of the first he unscrewed the nipples and hid them in the bottom of a saddlery-case; of the second he abstracted the lever, kicking it behind a big wardrobe. The third he merely opened, and knocked the doll-head bolt of the grip up with the heel of a riding-boot.

"That's settled," he said, as he shook the sweat off his hands. "These little precautions will at least give you time to turn. You have too much sympathy with gun-room accidents."

And as he rose from his knees, the thick muffled voice of Hummil cried in the doorway, "You fool!"

Such tones they use who speak in the lucid intervals of delirium to their friends a little before they die.

Spurstow started, dropping the pistol. Hummil stood in the doorway, rocking with helpless laughter.

"That was awf'ly good of you, I'm sure," he said, very slowly, feeling for his words. "I don't intend to go out by my own hand at present. I say, Spurstow, that stuff won't work. What shall I do? What shall I do?" And panic terror stood in his eyes.

"Lie down and give it a chance. Lie down at once."

"I daren't. It will only take me half-way again, and I shan't be able to get away this time. Do you know it was all I could do to come out just now? Generally I am as quick as lightning; but you had clogged my feet. I was nearly caught."

"Oh yes, I understand. Go and lie down."

"No, it isn't delirium; but it was an awfully mean trick to play on me. Do you know I might have died?"

As a sponge rubs a slate clean, so some power unknown to Spurstow had wiped out of Hummil's face all that stamped it for the face of a man, and he stood at the doorway in the expression of his lost innocence. He had slept back into terrified childhood.

"Is he going to die on the spot?" thought Spurstow. Then, aloud, "All right, my son. Come back to bed, and tell me all about it. You couldn't sleep; but what was all the rest of the nonsense?"

"A place, a place down there," said Hummil, with simple sincerity. The drug was acting on him by waves, and he was flung from the fear of a strong man to the fright of a child as his nerves gathered sense or were dulled.

"Good God! I've been afraid of it for months past, Spurstow. It has made every night hell to me; and yet I'm not conscious of having done anything wrong."

"Be still, and I'll give you another-dose. We'll stop your nightmares, you unutterable idiot!"

"Yes, but you must give me so much that I can't get away. You must make me quite sleepy, not just a little sleepy. It's so hard to run then."

"I know it; I know it. I've felt it myself. The symptoms are exactly as you describe."

"Oh, don't laugh at me, confound you! Before this awful sleeplessness came to me I've tried to rest on my elbow and put a spur in the bed to sting me when I fell back. Look!"

"By Jove! the man has been rowelled like a horse! Ridden by the nightmare with a vengeance! And we all thought him sensible enough. Heaven send us understanding! You like to talk, don't you?"

"Yes, sometimes. Not when I'm frightened. *Then* I want to run. Don't you?"

"Always. Before I give you your second dose try to tell me exactly what your trouble is."

Hummil spoke in broken whispers for nearly ten minutes, whilst Spurstow looked into the pupils of his eyes and passed his hand before them once or twice.

At the end of the narrative the silver cigarette-case was produced, and the last words that Hummil said as he fell back for the second time were, "Put me quite to sleep; for if I'm caught I die, I die!"

"Yes, yes; we all do that sooner or later, thank Heaven who has set a term to our miseries," said Spurstow, settling the cushions under the head. "It occurs to me that unless I drink something I shall go out before my time. I've stopped sweating, and —I wear a seventeen-inch collar." He brewed himself scalding hot tea, which is an excellent remedy against heat-apoplexy if you take three or four cups of it in time. Then he watched the sleeper.

"A blind face that cries and can't wipe its eyes, a blind face that chases him down corridors! H'm! Decidedly, Hummil ought to go on leave as soon as possible; and, sane or otherwise, he undoubtedly did rowel himself most cruelly. Well, Heaven send us understanding!"

At mid-day Hummil rose, with an evil taste in his mouth, but an unclouded eye and a joyful heart.

"I was pretty bad last night, wasn't I?" said he.

"I have seen healthier men. You must have had a touch of the sun. Look here: if I write you a swinging medical certificate, will you apply for leave on the spot?"

"No."

"Why not? You want it."

"Yes, but I can hold on till the weather's a little cooler."

"Why should you, if you can get relieved on the spot?"

"Burkett is the only man who could be sent; and he's a born fool."

"Oh, never mind about the line. You aren't so important as all that. Wire for leave, if necessary."

Hummil looked very uncomfortable.

"I can hold on till the Rains," he said evasively.

"You can't. Wire to headquarters for Burkett."

"I won't. If you want to know why, particularly, Burkett is married, and his wife's just had a kid, and she's up at Simla, in the cool, and Burkett has a very nice billet that takes him into Simla from Saturday to Monday. That little woman isn't at all well. If Burkett was transferred she'd try to follow him. If she left the baby behind she'd fret herself to death. If she came—and Burkett's one of those selfish little beasts who are always talking about a wife's place being with her husband—she'd die. It's murder to bring a woman here just now. Burkett hasn't the physique of a rat. If he came here he'd go out; and I know she hasn't any money, and I'm pretty sure she'd go out too. I'm salted in a sort of way, and I'm not married. Wait till the Rains, and then Burkett can get thin down here. It'll do him heaps of good."

"Do you mean to say that you intend to face—what you have faced, till the Rains break?"

"Oh, it won't be so bad, now you've shown me a way out of it. I can always wire to you. Besides, now I've once got into the way of sleeping, it'll be all right. Anyhow, I shan't put in for leave. That's the long and the short of it."

"My great Scott! I thought all that sort of thing was dead and done with."

"Bosh! You'd do the same yourself. I feel a new man, thanks to that cigarette-case. You're going over to camp now, aren't you?"

"Yes; but I'll try to look you up every other day, if I can."

"I'm not bad enough for that. I don't want you to bother. Give the coolies gin and ketchup."

"Then you feel all right?"

"Fit to fight for my life, but not to stand out in the sun talking to you. Go along, old man, and bless you!"

Hummil turned on his heel to face the echoing desolation of his bungalow, and the first thing he saw standing in the verandah was the figure of himself. He had met a similar apparition once before, when he was suffering from overwork and the strain of the hot weather.

"This is bad—already," he said, rubbing his eyes. "If the thing slides away from me all in one piece, like a ghost, I shall know it is only my eyes and stomach that are out of order. If it walks—my head is going."

He approached the figure, which naturally kept at an unvarying distance from him, as is the use of all spectres that are born of overwork. It slid through the house and dissolved into swimming specks within the eyeball as soon as it reached the burning light of the garden. Hummil went about his business till even. When he came in to dinner he found himself sitting at the table. The vision rose and walked out hastily. Except that it cast no shadow it was in all respects real.

No living man knows what that week held for Hummil. An increase of the epidemic kept Spurstow in camp among the coolies, and all he could do was to telegraph to Mottram, bidding him go to the bungalow and sleep there. But Mottram was forty miles away from the nearest telegraph, and knew nothing of anything save the needs of the survey till he met, early on Sunday morning, Lowndes and Spurstow heading towards Hummil's for the weekly gathering.

"Hope the poor chap's in a better temper," said the former, swinging himself off his horse at the door. "I suppose he isn't up yet."

"I'll just have a look at him," said the doctor. "If he's asleep there's no need to wake him."

And an instant later, by the tone of Spurstow's voice calling upon them to enter, the men knew what had happened. There was no need to wake him.

The punkah was still being pulled over the bed, but Hummil had departed this life at least three hours.

The body lay on its back, hands clinched by the side, as Spurstow had seen it lying seven nights previously. In the staring eyes was written terror beyond the expression of any pen.

Mottram, who had entered behind Lowndes, bent over the dead and touched the forehead lightly with his lips. "Oh, you lucky, lucky devil!" he whispered.

But Lowndes had seen the eyes, and withdrew shuddering to the other side of the room.

"Poor chap! poor old chap! Arid the last time I met him I was angry. Spurstow, we should have watched him. Has he—?"

Deftly Spurstow continued his investigations, ending by a search round the room.

"No, he hasn't," he snapped. "There's no trace of anything. Call the servants."

They came, eight or ten of them, whispering and peering over each other's shoulders.

"When did your Sahib go to bed?" said Spurstow.

"At eleven or ten, we think," said Hummil's personal servant.

"He was well then? But how should you know?"

"He was not ill, as far as our comprehension extended. But he had slept very little for three nights. This I know, because I saw him walking much, and specially in the heart of the night."

As Spurstow was arranging the sheet, a big straight-necked hunting-spur tumbled on the ground. The doctor groaned. The personal servant peeped at the body.

"What do you think, Chuma?" said Spurstow, catching the look on the dark face.

"Heaven-born, in my poor opinion, this that was my master has descended into the Dark Places, and there has been caught because he was not able to escape with sufficient speed. We have the spur for evidence that he fought with Fear. Thus have I seen men of my race do with thorns when a spell was laid upon them to overtake them in their sleeping hours and they dared not sleep."

"Chuma, you're a mud-head. Go out and prepare seals to be set on the Sahib's property."

"God has made the Heaven-born. God has made me. Who are we, to enquire into the dispensations of God? I will bid the other servants hold aloof while you are reckoning the tale of the Sahib's property. They are all thieves, and would steal."

"As far as I can make out, he died from—oh, anything; stoppage of the heart's action, heat-apoplexy, or some other visitation," said Spurstow to his companions. "We must make an inventory of his effects, and so on."

"He was scared to death," insisted Lowndes. "Look at those eyes! For pity's sake don't let him be buried with them open!"

"Whatever it was, he's clear of all the trouble now," said Mottram softly. Spurstow was peering into the open eyes.

"Come here," said he. "Can you see anything there?"

"I can't face it!" whimpered Lowndes. "Cover up the face! Is there any fear on earth that can turn a man into that likeness? It's ghastly. Oh, Spurstow, cover it up!"

"No fear—on earth," said Spurstow. Mottram leaned over his shoulder and looked intently.

"I see nothing except some grey blurs in the pupil. There can be nothing there, you know."

"Even so. Well, let's think. It'll take half a day to knock up any sort of coffin; and he must have died at midnight. Lowndes, old man, go out and tell the coolies to break ground next to Jevins's grave. Mottram, go round the house with Chuma and see that the seals are put on things. Send a couple of men to me here, and I'll arrange."

The strong-armed servants when they returned to their own kind told a strange story of the doctor Sahib vainly trying to call their master back to life by magic arts —to wit, the holding of a little green box that clicked to each of the dead man's eyes, and of a bewildered muttering on the part of the doctor Sahib, who took the little green box away with him.

The resonant hammering of a coffin-lid is no pleasant thing to hear, but those who have experience maintain that much more terrible is the soft swish of the bed-linen, the reeving and unreeving of the bed-tapes, when he who has fallen by the roadside is apparelled for burial, sinking gradually as the tapes are tied over, till the swaddled shape touches the floor and there is no protest against the indignity of hasty disposal.

At the last moment Lowndes was seized with scruples of conscience. "Ought you to read the service, from beginning to end?" said he to Spurstow.

"I intend to. You're my senior as a civilian. You can take it if you like."

"I didn't mean that for a moment. I only thought if we could get a chaplain from somewhere, I'm willing to ride anywhere, and give poor Hummil a better chance. That's all."

"Bosh!" said Spurstow, as he framed his lips to the tremendous words that stand at the head of the burial service.

* * * *

After breakfast they smoked a pipe in silence to the memory of the dead. Then Spurstow said absently—

"'Tisn't medical science."

"What?"

"Things in a dead man's eye."

"For goodness' sake leave that horror alone!" said Lowndes. "I've seen a native die of pure fright when a tiger chivied him. I know what killed Hummil."

"The deuce you do! I'm going to try to see." And the doctor retreated into the bathroom with a Kodak camera. After a few minutes there was the sound of something being hammered to pieces, and he emerged, very white indeed.

"Have you got a picture?" said Mottram. "What does the thing look like?"

"It was impossible, of course. You needn't look, Mottram. I've torn up the films. There was nothing there. It was impossible."

"That," said Lowndes, very distinctly, watching the shaking hand striving to re-light the pipe, "is a damned lie."

Mottram laughed uneasily. "Spurstow's right," he said. "We're all in such a state now that we'd believe anything. For pity's sake let's try to be rational."

There was no further speech for a long time. The hot wind whistled without, and the dry trees sobbed. Presently the daily train, winking brass, burnished steel, and spouting steam, pulled up panting in the intense glare. "We'd better go on that," said Spurstow. "Go back to work. I've written my certificate. We can't do any more good here, and work'll keep our wits together. Come on."

No one moved. It is not pleasant to face railway journeys at mid-day in June. Spurstow gathered up his hat and whip, and, turning in the doorway, said—

"There may be Heaven-there must be Hell.
Meantime, there is our life here. We-ell?"

Neither Mottram nor Lowndes had any answer to the question.

THE WITHERED ARM,
by Thomas Hardy

I
A Lorn Milkmaid

It was an eighty-cow dairy, and the troop of milkers, regular and supernumerary, were all at work; for, though the time of year was as yet but early April, the feed lay entirely in water-meadows, and the cows were "in full pail." The hour was about six in the evening, and three-fourths of the large, red, rectangular animals having been finished off, there was opportunity for a little conversation.

"He do bring home his bride tomorrow, I hear. They've come as far as Anglebury today."

The voice seemed to proceed from the belly of the cow called Cherry, but the speaker was a milking-woman, whose face was buried in the flank of that motionless beast.

"Hav' anybody seen her?" said another.

There was a negative response from the first. "Though they say she's a rosy-cheeked, tisty-tosty little body enough," she added; and as the milkmaid spoke she turned her face so that she could glance past her cow's tail to the other side of the barton, where a thin, fading woman of thirty milked somewhat apart from the rest.

"Years younger than he, they say," continued the second, with also a glance of reflectiveness in the same direction.

"How old do you call him, then?"

"Thirty or so."

"More like forty," broke in an old milkman near, in a long white pinafore or "wropper," and with the brim of his hat tied down, so that he looked like a woman. "A was born before our Great Weir was builded, and I hadn't man's wages when I laved water there."

The discussion waxed so warm that the purr of the milk streams became jerky, till a voice from another cow's belly cried with authority, "Now then, what the Turk do it matter to us about Farmer Lodge's age, or Farmer Lodge's new mis'ess? I shall have to pay him nine pound a year for the rent of every one of these milchers, whatever his age or hers. Get on with your work, or 'twill be dark afore we have done. The evening is pinking in a'ready." This speaker was the dairyman himself, by whom the milkmaids and men were employed.

Nothing more was said publicly about Farmer Lodge's wedding, but the first woman murmured under her cow to her next neighbour. "'Tis hard for she," signifying the thin worn milkmaid aforesaid.

"O no," said the second. "He ha'n't spoke to Rhoda Brook for years."

When the milking was done they washed their pails and hung them on a many-forked stand made as usual of the peeled limb of an oak-tree, set upright in the earth, and resembling a colossal antlered horn. The majority then dispersed in various directions homeward. The thin woman who had not spoken was joined by a boy of twelve or thereabout, and the twain went away up the field also.

Their course lay apart from that of the others, to a lonely spot high above the water-meads, and not far from the border of Egdon Heath, whose dark countenance was visible in the distance as they drew nigh to their home.

"They've just been saying down in barton that your father brings his young wife home from Anglebury tomorrow," the woman observed. "I shall want to send you for a few things to market, and you'll be pretty sure to meet 'em."

"Yes, Mother," said the boy. "Is Father married then?"

"Yes.... You can give her a look, and tell me what she's like, if you do see her."

"Yes, Mother."

"If she's dark or fair, and if she's tall—as tall as I. And if she seems like a woman who has ever worked for a living, or one that has been always well off, and has never done anything, and shows marks of the lady on her, as I expect she do."

"Yes."

They crept up the hill in the twilight and entered the cottage. It was built of mud-walls, the surface of which had been washed by many rains into channels and depressions that left none of the original flat face visible, while here and there in the thatch above a rafter showed like a bone protruding through the skin.

She was kneeling down in the chimney-corner, before two pieces of turf laid together with the heather inwards, blowing at the red-hot ashes with her breath till the turves flamed. The radiance lit her pale cheek, and made her dark eyes, that had once been handsome, seem handsome anew. "Yes," she resumed, "see if she is dark or fair, and if you can, notice if her hands be white; if not, see if they look as though she had ever done housework, or are milker's hands like mine."

The boy again promised, inattentively this time, his mother not observing that he was cutting a notch with his pocket-knife in the beech-backed chair.

II
The Young Wife

The road from Anglebury to Holmstoke is in general level, but there is one place where a sharp ascent breaks its monotony. Farmers homeward-hound from the former market-town, who trot all the rest of the way, walk their horses up this short incline.

The next evening while the sun was yet bright a handsome new gig, with a lemon-coloured body and red wheels, was spinning westward along the level highway at the heels of a powerful mare. The driver was a yeoman in the prime of life, cleanly shaven like an actor, his face being toned to that bluish-vermilion hue which so often graces a thriving farmer's features when returning home after successful dealings in the town. Beside him sat a woman, many years his junior—almost, indeed, a girl. Her face too was fresh in colour, but it was of a totally different quality—soft and evanescent, like the light under a heap of rose-petals.

Few people travelled this way, for it was not a main road; and the long white riband of gravel that stretched before them was empty, save of one small scarce-moving speck, which presently resolved itself into the figure of a boy, who was creeping on at a snail's pace, and continually looking behind him—the heavy bundle he carried being some excuse for, if not the reason of, his dilatoriness. When the bouncing gig-party slowed at the bottom of the incline above mentioned, the pedestrian was only a few yards in front. Supporting the large bundle by putting one hand on his hip, he turned and looked straight at the farmer's wife as though he would read her through and through, pacing along abreast of the horse.

The low sun was full in her face, rendering every feature, shade, and colour distinct, from the curve of her little nostril to the colour of her eyes. The farmer, though he seemed annoyed at the boy's persistent presence, did not order him to get out of the way; and thus the lad preceded them, his hard gaze never leaving her, till they reached the top of the ascent, when the farmer trotted on with relief in his lineaments having taken no outward notice of the boy whatever.

"How that poor lad stared at me!" said the young wife.

"Yes, dear; I saw that he did."

"He is one of the village, I suppose?"

"One of the neighbourhood. I think he lives with his mother a mile or two off."

"He knows who we are, no doubt?"

"O yes. You must expect to be stared at just at first, my pretty Gertrude."

"I do—though I think the poor boy may have looked at us in the hope we might relieve him of his heavy load, rather than from curiosity."

"O no," said her husband off-handedly. "These country lads will carry a hundredweight once they get it on their backs; besides his pack had more size than weight in it. Now, then, another mile and I shall be able to show you our house in the distance—if it is not too dark before we get there." The wheels spun round, and particles flew from their periphery as before, till a white house of ample dimensions revealed itself, with farm-buildings and ricks at the back.

Meanwhile the boy had quickened his pace, and turning up a by-lane some mile-and-a-half short of the white farmstead, ascended towards the leaner pastures, and so on to the cottage of his mother.

She had reached home after her day's milking at the outlying dairy, and was washing cabbage at the doorway in the declining light. "Hold up the net a moment," she said, without preface, as the boy came up.

He flung down his bundle, held the edge of the cabbage-net, and as she filled its meshes with the dripping leaves she went on, "Well, did you see her?"

"Yes; quite plain."

"Is she ladylike?"

"Yes; and more. A lady complete."

"Is she young?"

"Well, she's growed up, and her ways be quite a woman's."

"Of course. What colour is her hair and face?"

"Her hair is lightish, and her face as comely as a live doll's."

"Her eyes, then, are not dark like mine?"

"No—of a bluish turn, and her mouth is very nice and red; and when she smiles, her teeth show white."

"Is she tall?" said the woman sharply.

"I couldn't see. She was sitting down."

"Then do you go to Holmstoke church tomorrow morning: she's sure to be there. Go early and notice her walking in, and come home and tell me if she's taller than I."

"Very well, Mother. But why don't you go and see for yourself?"

"*I* go to see her! I wouldn't look up at her if she were to pass my window this instant. She was with Mr. Lodge, of course. What did he say or do?"

"Just the same as usual."

"Took no notice of you?"

"None."

Next day the mother put a clean shirt on the boy, and started him off for Holmstoke church. He reached the ancient little pile when the door was just being opened, and he was the first to enter. Taking his seat by the font, he watched all the parishioners file in. The well-to-do Farmer Lodge came nearly last; and his young wife, who accompanied him, walked up the aisle with the shyness natural to a modest woman who had appeared thus for the first time. As all other eyes were fixed upon her, the youth's stare was not noticed now.

When he reached home his mother said, "Well?" before he had entered the room.

"She is not tall. She is rather short," he replied.

"Ah!" said his mother, with satisfaction.

"But she's very pretty—very. In fact, she's lovely." The youthful freshness of the yeoman's wife had evidently made an impression even on the somewhat hard nature of the boy.

"That's all I want to hear," said his mother quickly. "Now, spread the table-cloth. The hare you wired is very tender; but mind nobody catches you. You've never told me what sort of hands she had."

"I have never seen 'em. She never took off her gloves."

"What did she wear this morning?"

"A white bonnet and a silver-coloured gownd. It whewed and whistled so loud when it rubbed against the pews that the lady coloured up more than ever for very shame at the noise, and pulled it in to keep it from touching; but when she pushed into her seat, it whewed more than ever. Mr. Lodge, he seemed pleased, and his waistcoat stuck out, and his great golden seals hung like a lord's; but she seemed to wish her noisy gownd anywhere but on her."

"Not she! However, that will do now."

These descriptions of the newly married couple were continued from time to time by the boy at his mother's request, after any chance encounter he had had with them. But Rhoda Brook, though she might easily have seen young Mrs. Lodge for herself by walking a couple of miles, would never attempt an excursion towards the quarter where the farmhouse lay. Neither did she, at the daily milking in the dairyman's yard on Lodge's outlying second farm, ever speak on the subject of the recent marriage. The dairyman, who rented the cows of Lodge, and knew perfectly the tall milkmaid's history, with manly kindness always kept the gossip in the cowbarton from annoying Rhoda. But the atmosphere thereabout was full of the subject the first days of Mrs. Lodge's arrival; and fom her boy's description and the casual words of the other milkers, Rhoda Brook could raise a mental image of the unconscious Mrs. Lodge that was realistic as a photograph.

III

A Vision

One night, two or three weeks after the bridal return, when the boy had gone to bed, Rhoda sat a long time over the turf ashes that she had raked out in front of her to extinguish them. She contemplated so intently the new wife, as presented to her in her mind's eye over the embers, that she forgot the lapse of time. At last, wearied by her day's work, she too retired.

But the figure which had occupied her so much during this and the previous days was not to be banished at night. For the first time Gertrude Lodge visited the supplanted woman in her dreams. Rhoda Brook dreamed—since her assertion that she really saw, before falling asleep, was not to be believed—that the young wife, in the pale silk dress and white bonnet, but with features shockingly distorted, and wrinkled as by age, was sitting upon her chest as she lay. The pressure of Mrs.

Lodge's person grew heavier; the blue eyes peered cruelly into her face: and then the figure thrust forward its left hand mockingly, so as to make the wedding-ring it wore glitter in Rhoda's eyes. Maddened mentally, and nearly suffocated by pressure, the sleeper struggled; the incubus, still regarding her, withdrew to the foot of the bed, only, however, to come forward by degrees, resume her seat, and flash her left hand as before.

Gasping for breath, Rhoda, in a last desperate effort, swung out her right hand, seized the confronting spectre by its obtrusive left arm, and whirled it backward to the floor, starting up herself as she did so with a low cry.

"O, merciful heaven!" she cried, sitting on the edge of the bed in a cold sweat; "that was not a dream—she was here!"

She could feel her antagonist's arm within her grasp even now—the very flesh and bone of it, as it seemed. She looked on the floor whither she had whirled the spectre, but there was nothing to be seen.

Rhoda Brook slept no more that night, and when she went milking at the next dawn they noticed how pale and haggard she looked. The milk that she drew quivered into the pail; her hand had not calmed even yet. and still retained the feel of the arm, She came home to breakfast as wearily as if it had been supper-time.

"What was that noise in your chimmer, mother, last night?" said her son. "You fell off the bed. surely?"

"Did you hear anything fall? At what time?"

"Just when the clock struck two."

She could not explain, and when the meal was done went silently about her household works, the boy assisting her, for he hated going afield on the farms, and she indulged his reluctance. Between eleven and twelve the garden-gate clicked, and she lifted her eyes to the window. At the bottom of the garden, within the gate, stood the woman of her vision. Rhoda seemed transfixed.

"Ah, she said she would come!" exclaimed the boy, also observing her.

"Said so—when? How does she know us?"

"I have seen and spoken to her. I talked to her yesterday."

"I told you," said the mother, flushing indignantly, "never to speak to anybody in that house, or go near the place."

"I did not speak to her till she spoke to me. And I did not go near the place. I met her in the road."

"What did you tell her?"

"Nothing. She said, 'Are you the poor boy who had to bring the heavy load from market?' And she looked at my hoots, and said they would not keep my feet dry if it came on wet, because they were so cracked. I told her I lived with my mother, and we had enough to do to keep ourselves, and that's how it was; and she said then: 'I'll come and bring you some better hoots, and see your mother.' She gives away things to other folks in the meads besides us."

Mrs. Lodge was by this time close to the door—not in her silk, as Rhoda had dreamt of in the bed-chamber, but in a morning hat, and gown of common light material, which became her better than silk. On her arm she carried a basket.

The impression remaining from the night's experience was still strong. Brook had almost expected to see the wrinkles, the scorn and the cruelty on her visitor's face. She would have escaped an interview, had escape been possible. There was, however, no backdoor to the cottage, and in an instant the boy had lifted the latch to Mrs. Lodge's gentle knock.

"I see I have come to the right house," said she, glancing at the lad, and smiling. "But I was not sure till you opened the door."

The figure and action were those of the phantom; but her voice was so indescribably sweet, her glance so winning, her smile so tender, so unlike that of Rhoda's midnight visitant, that the latter could hardly believe the evidence of her senses. She was truly glad that she had not hidden away in sheer aversion, as she had been inclined to do. In her basket Mrs. Lodge brought the pair of boots that she had promised to the boy, and other useful articles.

At these proofs of a kindly feeling towards her and hers Rhoda's heart reproached her bitterly. This innocent young thing should have her blessing and not her curse. When she left them a light seemed gone from the dwelling. Two days later she came again to know if the boots fitted; and less than a fortnight after paid Rhoda another call. On this occasion the boy was absent.

"I walk a good deal," said Mrs. Lodge, "and your house is the nearest outside our own parish. I hope you are well. You don't look quite well."

Rhoda said she was well enough; and, indeed, though the paler of the two, there was more of the strength that endures in her well-defined features and large frame than in the soft-cheeked young woman before her. The conversation became quite confidential as regarded their powers and weaknesses; and when Mrs. Lodge was leaving, Rhoda said, "I hope you will find this air agree with you, ma'am, and not suffer from the damp of the water-meads."

The younger one replied that there was not much doubt of her general health being usually good. "Though, now you remind me," she added, "I have one little ailment which puzzles me. It is nothing serious, but I cannot make it out."

She uncovered her left hand and arm; and their outline confronted Rhoda's gaze as the exact original of the limb she had beheld and seized in her dream. Upon the pink round surface of the arm were faint marks of an unhealthy colour, as if produced by a rough grasp. Rhoda's eyes became riveted on the discolorations; she fancied that she discerned in them the shape of her own four fingers.

"How did it happen?" she said mechanically.

"I cannot tell," replied Mrs. Lodge, shaking her head. "One night when I was sound asleep, dreaming I was away in some strange place, a pain suddenly shot into my arm there, and was so keen as to awaken me. I must have struck it in the daytime, I suppose, though I don't remember doing so." She added, laughing, "I tell my dear husband that it looks just as if he had flown into a rage and struck me there. O, I daresay it will soon disappear."

"Ha, ha! Yes.... On what night did it come?"

Mrs. Lodge considered, and said it would be a fortnight ago on the morrow. "When I awoke I could not remember where I was," she added, "till the clock striking two reminded me."

She had named the night and hour of Rhoda's spectral encounter, and Brook felt like a guilty thing. The artless disclosure startled her; she did not reason on the freaks of coincidence; and all the scenery of that ghastly night returned with double vividness to her mind.

"O, can it be," she said to herself, when her visitor had departed, "that I exercise a malignant power over people against my own will?" She knew that she had been slyly called a witch since hey fall; but never having understood why that particular stigma had been attached to her, it had passed disregarded. Could this be the explanation, and had such things as this ever happened before?

IV

A Suggestion

174

The summer drew on, and Rhoda Brook almost dreaded to meet Mrs. Lodge again, notwithstanding that her feeling for the young wife amounted well-nigh to affection. Something in her own individuality seemed to convict Rhoda of crime. Yet a fatality sometimes would direct the steps of the latter to the outskirts of Holmstoke whenever she left her house for any other purpose than her daily work; and hence it happened that their next encounter was out of doors. Rhoda could not avoid the subject which had so mystified her, and after the first few words she stammered, "I hope your—arm is well again, ma'am?" She had perceived with consternation that Gertrude Lodge carried her left arm stiffly.

"No; it not quite well. Indeed it is no better at all; it is rather worse. It pains me dreadfully sometimes."

"Perhaps you had better go to a doctor, ma'am."

She replied that she had already seen a doctor. Her husband had insisted upon her going to one. But the surgeon had not seemed to understand the afflicted limb at all; he had told her to bathe it in hot water, and she had bathed it, but the treatment had done no good.

"Will you let me see it?" said the milkwoman.

Mrs. Lodge pushed up her sleeve and disclosed the place, which was a few inches above the wrist. As soon as Rhoda Brook saw it, she could hardly preserve her composure. There was nothing of the nature of a wound, but the arm at that point had a shrivelled look, and the outline of the four fingers appeared more distinct than at the former Moreover, she fancied that they were imprinted in precisely the relative position of her clutch upon the arm in the trance; the first linger towards Gertrude's wrist, and the fourth towards her elbow.

What the impress resembled seemed to have struck Gertrude herself since their last meeting. "It looks almost like finger marks," she said; adding with a faint laugh, "my husband says it is as if some witch, or the devil himself, had taken hold of me there, and blasted the flesh."

Rhoda shivered. "That's fancy," she said hurriedly. "I wouldn't mind it, if I were you."

"I shouldn't so much mind it," said the younger, with hesitation, "if—if I hadn't a notion that it makes my husband dislike me—no, love me less. Men think so much of personal appearance."

"Some do—he for one."

"Yes; and he was very proud of mine, at first."

"Keep your arm covered from his sight."

"Ah—he knows the disfigurement is there!" She tried to hide the tears that filled her eyes.

"Well, ma'am, I earnestly hope it will go away soon."

And so the milkwoman's mind was chained anew to the subject by a horrid sort of spell as she returned home. The sense of having been guilty of an act of malignity increased, affect as she might to ridicule her superstition. In her secret heart Rhoda did not altogether object to a slight diminution of her successor's beauty, by whatever means it had come about; but she did not wish to inflict upon her physical pain. For though this pretty young woman had rendered impossible any reparation which Lodge might have made Rhoda for his past conduct, everything like resentment at the unconscious usurpation had quite passed away from the elder's mind.

If the sweet and kindly Gertrude Lodge only knew of the dream-scene in the bed-chamber, what would she think? Not to inform her of it seemed treachery in the presence of her friendliness; but tell she could not of her own accord neither could she devise a remedy.

She mused upon the matter the greater part of the night; and the next day, after the morning milking, set out to obtain another glimpse of Gertrude Lodge if she could, being held to her by a gruesome fascination. By watching the house from a distance the milkmaid was presently able to discern the farmer's wife in a ride she was taking alone—probably to join her husband in some distant field. Mrs. Lodge perceived her, and cantered in her direction.

"Good morning, Rhoda!" Gertrude said, when she had come up. "I was going to call."

Rhoda noticed that Mrs. Lodge held the reins with some difficulty.

"I hope—the bad arm," said Rhoda.

"They tell me there is possibly one way by which I might be able to find out the cause, and so perhaps the cure of it," replied the other anxiously. "It is by going to some clever man over in Egdon Heath. They did not know if he was still alive—and I cannot remember his name at this moment; but they said that you knew more of his movements than anybody else hereabout, and could tell me if he were still to be consulted. Dear me what was his name? But you know."

"Not Conjuror Trendle?" said her thin companion, turning pale.

"Trendle—yes. Is he alive?"

"I believe so," said Rhoda, with reluctance.

"Why do you call him conjuror?"

"Well—they say—they used to say he was a—he had powers other folks have not."

"O, how could my people be so superstitious as to recommend a man of that sort! I thought they meant some medical man. I shall think no more of him."

Rhoda looked relieved, and Mrs. Lodge rode on. The milkwoman had inwardly seen, from the moment she heard of her having been mentioned as a reference for this man, that there must exist a sarcastic feeling among the work-folk that a sorceress would know the whereabouts of the exorcist. They suspected her, then. A short time ago this would have given no concern to a woman of her common sense. But she had a haunting reason to be superstitious now; and she had been seized with sudden dread that this Conjuror Trendle might name her as the malignant influence which was blasting the fair person of Gertrude, and so lead her friend to hate her for ever, and to treat her as some fiend in human shape.

But all was not over. Two days after, a shadow intruded into the window-pattern thrown on Rhoda Brook's floor by the afternoon sun. The woman opened the door at once, almost breathlessly.

"Are you alone?" said Gertrude. She seemed to be no less harassed and anxious than Brook herself.

"Yes," said Rhoda.

"The place on my arm seems worse, and troubles me!" the young farmer's wife went on. "It is so mysterious! I do hope it will not be an incurable wound. I have again been thinking of what they said about Conjuror Trendle. I don't really believe in such men, but I should not mind just visiting him, from curiosity—though on no account must my husband know. Is it far to where he lives?"

"Yes—five miles," said Rhoda backwardly. "In the heart of Egdon."

"Well, I should have to walk. Could not you go with me to show me the way—say tomorrow afternoon?"

"O, not I; that is—," the milkwoman murmured, with a start of dismay. Again the dread seized her that something to do with her fierce act in the dream might be revealed, and her character in the eyes of the most useful friend she had ever had be ruined irretrievably.

Mrs. Lodge urged, and Rhoda finally assented, though with much misgiving. Sad as the journey would be to her, she could not conscientiously stand in the way of a possible remedy for her patron's strange affliction. It was agreed that, to escape suspicion of their mystic intent, they should meet at the edge of the heath at the corner of a plantation which was visible from the spot where they now stood.

V

Conjuror Trendle

By the next afternoon Rhoda would have done anything to escape this inquiry. But she had promised to go. Moreover, there was a horrid fascination at times in becoming instrumental in throwing such possible light on her own character as would reveal her to be something greater in the occult world than she had ever herself suspected.

She started just before the time of day mentioned between them, and half an hour's brisk walking brought her to the south-eastern extension of the Egdon tract of country, where the fir plantation was. A slight figure, cloaked and veiled; was already there. Rhoda recognized, almost with a shudder, that Mrs. Lodge bore her left arm in a sling.

They hardly spoke to each other, and immediately set out on their climb into the interior of this solemn, country, which stood high above the rich alluvial soil they had left half an hour before. It was a long walk; thick clouds made the atmosphere dark, though it was as yet only early afternoon; and the wind howled dismally over the slopes of the heath—not improbably the same heath which had witnessed the agony of the Wessex King Ina, presented to after-ages as Lear. Gertrude Lodge talked most, Rhoda replying with monosyllabic preoccupation. She had a strange dislike to walking on the side of her companion where hung the afflicted arm, moving round to the other when inadvertently near it. Much heather had been brushed by their feet when they descended upon a cart-track, beside which stood the house of the man they sought.

He did not profess his remedial practices openly, or care anything about their continuance, his direct interests being those of a dealer in furze, turf, "sharp sand," and other local products. Indeed, he affected not to believe largely in his own powers, and when watts that had been shown him for cure miraculously disappeared—which it must be owned they infallibly did—he would say lightly, "O, I only drink a glass of grog upon 'em at your expense—perhaps it's all chance," and immediately turn the subject.

He was at home when they arrived, having in fact seen them descending into his valley. He was a grey-bearded man, with a reddish face, and he looked singularly at Rhoda the first moment he beheld her. Mrs. Lodge told him her errand; and then with words of self-disparagement he examined her arm.

"Medicine can't cure it," he said promptly. "'Tis the work of an enemy."

Rhoda shrank into herself, and drew back.

"An enemy? What enemy?" asked Mrs. Lodge.

He shook his head. "That's best known to yourself," he said. "If you like, I can show the person to you, though I shall not myself know who it is. I can do no more; and don't wish to do that."

She pressed him; on which he told Rhoda to wait outside where she stood, and took Mrs. Lodge into the room. It opened immediately from the door; and, as the latter remained ajar, Rhoda Brook could see the proceedings without taking part in them. He brought a tumbler from the dresser, nearly filled it with water, and fetching an egg, prepared it in some private way; after which he broke it on the edge of the glass, so that the white went in and the yolk remained. As it was getting gloomy, he took the glass and its contents to the window, and told Gertrude to watch the mixture closely. They leant over the table together, and the milkwoman could see the opaline hue of the egg-fluid changing form as it sank in the water, but she was not near enough to define the shape that it assumed.

"Do you catch the likeness of any face or figure as you look?" demanded the conjuror of the young woman.

She murmured a reply, in tones so low as to be inaudible to Rhoda, and continued to gaze intently into the glass. Rhoda turned, and walked a few steps away.

When Mrs. Lodge came out, and her face was met by the light, it appeared exceedingly pale—as pale as Rhoda's—against the sad dun shades of the upland's garniture. Trendle shut the door behind her, and they at once started homeward together. But Rhoda perceived that her companion had quite changed.

"Did he charge much?" she asked tentatively.

"Oh, no—nothing. He would not take a farthing," said Gertrude.

"And what did you see?" inquired Rhoda.

"Nothing I—care to speak of." The constraint in her manner was remarkable; her face was so rigid as to wear an oldened aspect, faintly suggestive of the face in Rhoda's bed-chamber.

"Was it you who first proposed coming here?" Mrs. Lodge suddenly inquired, after a long pause. "How very odd, if you did!"

"No. But I am not very sorry we have come, all things considered," she replied. For the first time a sense of triumph possessed her, and she did not altogether deplore that the young thing at her side should learn that their lives had been antagonized by other influences than their own.

The subject was no more alluded to during the long and dreary walk home. But in some way or other a story was whispered about the many-dairied lowland that winter that Mrs. Lodge's gradual loss of the use of her left arm was owing to her being "overlooked" by Rhoda Brook. The latter kept her own counsel about the incubus, but her face grew sadder and thinner; and in the spring she and her boy disappeared from the neighbourhood of Holmstoke.

VI

A Second Attempt

Half a dozen years passed away. and Mr. and Mrs. Lodge's married experience sank into prosiness, and worse. The farmer was usually gloomy and silent: the woman whom he had wooed for her grace and beauty was contorted and disfigured in the left limb; moreover, she had brought him no child, which rendered it likely that he would be the last of a family who had occupied that valley for some two hundred years. He thought of Rhoda Brook and her son; and feared this might be a judgement from heaven upon him.

The once blithe-hearted and enlightened Gertrude was changing into an irritable, superstitious woman, whose whole time was given to experimenting upon her ailment with every quack remedy she came across. She was honestly attached to her husband, and was ever secretly hoping against hope to win back his heart again by regaining some at least of her personal beauty. Hence it arose that her closet was lined with bottles, packets, and ointment-pots of every description—nay, bunches of mystic herbs, charms, and books of necromancy, which in her schoolgirl time she would have ridiculed as folly.

178

"Damned if you won't poison yourself with these apothecary messes and witch mixtures some time or other," said her husband, when his eye chanced to fall upon the multitudinous array.

She did not reply, but turned her sad, soft glance upon him in such heart-swollen reproach that he looked sorry for his words, and added, "I only meant it for your good, you know, Gertrude."

"I'll clear out the whole lot, and destroy them," said she huskily, "and try such remedies no more!"

"You want somebody to cheer you," he observed. "I once thought of adopting a boy; but he is too old now. And he is gone away I don't know where."

She guessed to whom he alluded; for, Rhoda Brook's story had in the course of years become known to her; though not a, word had ever passed between her husband and herself on the subject. Neither had she ever spoken to him of her visit to Conjuror Trendle, and of what was revealed to her, or she thought was revealed to her, by that solitary heathman.

She was now five-and-twenty; but she seemed older. "Six years of marriage, and only a few months of love," she sometimes whispered to herself. And then she thought of the apparent cause, and said, with a tragic glance at her withering limb, "If I could only be again as I was when he first saw me!"

She obediently destroyed her nostrums and charms; but there remained a hankering wish to try something else—some other sort of cure altogether. She had never revisited Trendle since she had been conducted to the house of the solitary by Rhoda against her will; but it now suddenly occurred to Gertrude that she would, in a last desperate effort at deliverance from this seeming curse, again seek out the man, if he yet lived. He was entitled to a certain credence, for the indistinct form he had raised in the glass had undoubtedly resembled the only woman in the world who—as she now knew, though not then—could have a reason for bearing her ill-will. The visit should be paid.

This time she went alone, though she nearly got lost on the heath, and roamed a considerable distance out of her way. Trendle's house was reached at last, however: he was not indoors, and instead of waiting at the cottage. she went to where his bent figure was pointed out to her at work a long way off. Trendle remembered her, and laying down the handful of furze-roots which he was gathering and throwing into a heap, he offered to accompany her in the homeward direction, as the distance was considerable and the days were short. So they walked together, his head bowed nearly to the earth, and his form of a colour with it.

"You can send away warts and other excrescences, I know," she said; "why can't you send away this?" And the arm was uncovered.

"You think too much of my powers!" said Trendle; "and I am old and weak now, too. No, no; it is too much for me to attempt in my own person. What have ye tried?"

She named to him some of the hundred medicaments and counterspells which she had adopted from time to time. He shook his head.

"Some were good enough," he said approvingly; "but not many of them for such as this. This is of the nature of a blight, not of the nature of a wound; and if you ever do throw it off, it will be all at once."

"If I only could!"

"There is only one chance of doing it known to me. It has never failed in kindred afflictions—that I can declare. But it is hard to carry out, and especially for a woman."

"Tell me!" said she.

179

"You must touch with the limb the neck of a man who's been hanged."

She started a little at the image he had raised.

"Before he's cold—just after he's cut down," continued the conjuror impassively.

"How can that do good?"

"It will turn the blood and change the constitution. But, as I say, to do it is hard. You must go to the jail when there's a hanging, and wait for him when he's brought off the gallows. Lots have done it, though perhaps not such pretty women as you. I used to send dozens for skin complaints. But that was in former times. The last I sent was in '13—near twelve years ago."

He had no more to tell her; and, when he had put her into a straight track homeward, turned and left her, refusing all money as at first.

VII

A Ride

The communication sank deep into Gertrude's mind. Her nature was rather a timid one; and probably of all remedies that the white wizard could have suggested there was not one which would have filled her with so much aversion as this, not to speak of the immense obstacles in the way of its adoption.

Casterbridge, the county-town, was a dozen or fifteen miles off; and though in those days, when men were executed for horse-stealing, arson, and burglary, an assize seldom passed without a hanging, it was not likely that she could get access to the body of the criminal unaided. And the fear of her husband's anger made her reluctant to breathe a word of Trendle's suggestion to him or to anybody about him.

She did nothing for months, and patiently bore her disfigurement as before. But her woman's nature, craving for renewed love, through the medium of renewed beauty (she was but twenty-five), was ever stimulating her to try what, at any rate, could hardly do her any harm. "What came by a spell will go by a spell surely," she would say. Whenever her imagination pictured the act she shrank in terror from the possibility of it: then the words of the conjuror, "It will turn your blood," were seen to be capable of a scientific no less than ghastly interpretation; the mastering desire returned;. and urged her on again.

There was at this time but one county paper, and that her husband only occasionally borrowed. But old-fashioned days had old-fashioned means, and news was extensively conveyed by word of mouth from market to market, or from fair to fair, so that, whenever such an event as an execution was about to take place, few within a radius of twenty miles were ignorant of the coming sight; and, so far as Holmstoke was concerned, some enthusiasts had been known to walk all the way to Casterbridge and back in one day, solely to witness the spectacle. The next assizes were in March; and when Gertrude Lodge heard that they had been held, she inquired stealthily at the inn as to the result, as soon as she could find opportunity.

She was, however, too late. The time at which the sentences were to be carried out had arrived, and to make the journey and obtain permission at such short notice required at least her husband's assistance. She dared not tell him, for she had found by delicate experiment that these smouldering village beliefs made him furious if mentioned, partly because he half entertained them himself. It was therefore necessary to wait for another opportunity.

Her determination received a fillip from learning that two epileptic children had attended from this very village of Holmstoke many years before with beneficial results, though the experiment had been strongly condemned by the neighbouring clergy. April, May, June, passed; and it is no overstatement to say that by the end of the last-named month Gertrude well-nigh longed for the death of a fellow-creature. Instead of her formal prayers each night, her unconscious prayer was, "O Lord, hang some guilty or innocent person soon!"

This time she made earlier inquiries, and was altogether more systematic in her proceedings. Moreover the season was summer, between the haymaking and the harvest, and in the leisure thus afforded him her husband had been holiday-taking away from home.

The assizes were in July, and she went to the inn as before. There was to be one execution—only one—for arson.

Her greatest problem was not how to get to Casterbridge, but what means she should adopt for obtaining admission to the jail. Though access for such purposes had formerly never been denied, the custom had fallen into desuetude; and in contemplating her possible difficulties, she was again almost driven to fall back upon her husband. But, on sounding him about the assizes, he was so uncommunicative, so more than usually cold, that she did not proceed, and decided that whatever she did she would do alone.

Fortune, obdurate hitherto, showed her unexpected favour. On the Thursday before the Saturday fixed for the execution, Lodge remarked to her that he was going away from home for another day or two on business at a fair, and that he was sorry he could not take her with him.

She exhibited on this occasion so much readiness to stay at home that he looked at her in surprise. Time had been when she would have shown deep disappointment at the loss of such a jaunt. However, he lapsed into his usual taciturnity, and on the day named left Holmstoke.

It was now her turn. She at first had thought of driving, but on reflection held that driving would not do, since it would necessitate her keeping to the turnpike-road, and so increase by tenfold the risk of her ghastly errand being found out. She decided to ride, and avoid the beaten track, notwithstanding that in her husband's stables there was no animal just at present which by any stretch of imagination could be considered a lady's mount, in spite of his promise before marriage to always keep a mare for her. He had, however, many cart-horses, fine ones of their kind; and among the rest was a serviceable creature, an equine Amazon, with a back as broad as a sofa, on which Gertrude had occasionally taken an airing when unwell. This horse she chose.

On Friday afternoon one of the men brought it round. She was dressed, and before going down looked at her shrivelled arm. "Ah!" she said to it, "if it had not been for you this terrible ordeal would have been saved me!"

When strapping up the bundle in which she carried a few articles of clothing, she took occasion to say to the servant, "I take these in case I should not get back tonight from the person I am going to visit. Don't be alarmed if I am not in by ten, and close up the house as usual. I shall be home tomorrow for certain." She meant then to tell her husband privately: the deed accomplished was not like the deed projected. He would almost certainly forgive her.

And then the pretty palpitating Gertrude Lodge went from her husband's homestead; but though her goal was Casterbridge she did not take the direct route thither through Stickleford. Her cunning course at first was in precisely the opposite direction. As soon as she was out of sight, however, she turned to the left, by a road which led into Egdon, and on entering the heath wheeled round, and set out in the true course, due westerly. A more private way down the county could not be imagined; and as to direction, she had merely to keep her horse's head to a point a little to the right of the sun. She knew that she would light upon a furze-cutter or cottager of some sort from time to time, from whom she might correct her bearing.

Though the date was comparatively recent, Egdon was much less fragmentary in character than now. The attempts—successful and otherwise—at cultivation on the lower slopes, which intrude and break up the original heath Into small detached heaths, had not been carried far; Enclosure Acts had not taken effect, and the banks and fences which now exclude the cattle of those villagers who formerly enjoyed rights of commonage thereon, and the carts of those who had turbary privileges which kept them in firing all the year round, were not erected. Gertrude, therefore, rode along with no other obstacles than the prickly furze-bushes, the mats of heather, the white water-courses, and the natural steeps and declivities of the ground.

Her horse was sure, if heavy-footed and slow, and though a draught animal, was easy-paced; had it been otherwise, she was not a woman who could have ventured to ride over such a bit of country with a half-dead arm. It was therefore nearly eight o'clock when she drew rein to breathe her bearer on the last outlying high point of heath-land towards Casterbridge, previous to leaving Egdon for the cultivated valleys.

She halted before a pool called Rushy-pond, flanked by the ends of two hedges; a railing ran through the centre of the pond, dividing h in half. Over the railing she saw the low green country; over the green trees the roofs of the town; over the roofs a white flat façade, denoting the entrance to the county jail. On the roof of this front specks were moving about; they seemed to be workmen erecting something. Her flesh crept. She descended slowly, and was soon amid corn-fields and pastures In another half-hour, when it was almost dusk, Gertrude reached the White Hart, the first inn of the town on that side.

Little surprise was excited by her arrival; farmers' wives rode on horseback then more than they do now; though, for that matter, Mrs. Lodge was not imagined to be a wife at all; the innkeeper supposed her some harum-skarum young woman who had come to attend "hang-fair" next day. Neither her husband nor herself ever dealt in Casterbridge market, so that she was unknown. While dismounting she beheld a crowd of boys standing at the door of a harness-maker's shop just above the inn, looking inside it with deep interest.

"What is going on there?" she asked of the ostler.

"Making the rope for tomorrow."

She throbbed responsively, and contracted her arm.

"'Tis sold by the inch afterwards," the man continued. "I could get you a bit, miss, for nothing, if you'd like?"

She hastily repudiated any such wish, all the more from a curious creeping feeling that the condemned wretch's destiny was becoming interwoven with her own; and having engaged a room for the night, sat down to think.

Up to this time she had formed but the vaguest notions about her means of obtaining access to the prison. The words of the cunning-man returned to her mind. He had implied that she should use her beauty, impaired though it was, as a pass-key, In her inexperience she knew little about jail functionaries; she had heard of a high-sheriff and an under-sheriff, but dimly only. She knew, however, that there must be a hangman, and to the hangman she determined to apply.

VIII
A Water-side Hermit

182

At this date, and for several years after, there was a hangman to almost every jail. Gertrude found, on inquiry, that the Casterbridge official dwelt in. a lonely cottage by a deep slow river flowing under the cliff on which the prison buildings were situate—the stream being the self-same one, though she did not know it, which watered the Stickleford and Holmstoke meads lower down in its course.

Having changed her dress, and before she had eaten or drunk—for she could not take her ease till she had ascertained some particulars—Gertrude pursued her way by a path along the water-side to the cottage indicated. Passing thus the outskirts of the jail, she discerned on the level roof over the gateway three rectangular lines against the sky, where the specks had been moving in her distant view; she recognized what the erection was, and passed quickly on. Another hundred yards brought her to the executioner's house, which a boy pointed out. It stood close to the same stream, and was hard by a weir, the waters of which emitted a steady roar.

While she stood hesitating the door opened, and an old man came forth shading a candle with one hand. Locking the door on the outside, he turned to a flight of wooden steps fixed against the end of the cottage, and began to ascend them, this being evidently the staircase to his bedroom. Gertrude hastened forward, but by the time she reached the foot of the ladder he was at the top. She called to him loudly enough to be heard above the roar of the weir; he looked down and said, "What d'ye want here?"

"To speak to you a minute."

The candle-light, such as it was, fell upon her imploring, pale, upturned face, and Davies (as the hangman was called) backed down the ladder. "I was just going to bed," he said; "Early to bed and early to rise, but I don't mind stopping a minute for such a one as you. Come into house." He reopened the door, and preceded her to the room within.

The implements of his daily work, which was that of a jobbing gardener, stood in a corner, and seeing probably that she looked rural, he said, "If you want me to undertake country work I can't come, for I never leave Casterbridge for gentle nor simple—not I. My real calling is officer of justice," he added formally.

"Yes, yes! That's it. Tomorrow!"

"Ah! I thought so. Well, what's the matter about that? 'Tis no use to come here about the knot—folks do come continually, but I tell 'em one knot is as merciful as another if ye keep it under the ear. Is the unfortunate man a relation; or, I should say, perhaps" (looking at her dress) "a person who's been in your employ?"

"No. What time is the execution?"

"The same as usual—twelve o'clock, or as soon after as the London mail-coach gets in. We always wait for that, in case of a reprieve."

"O—a reprieve—I hope not!" she said involuntarily.

"Well,—hee, hee!—as a matter of business, so do I! But still, if ever a young fellow deserved to be let off, this one does; only just turned eighteen, and only present by chance when the rick was fired. Howsomever, there's not much risk of that, as they are obliged to make an example of him, there having been so much destruction of property that way lately."

"I mean," she explained, "that I want to touch him for a charm, a cure of an affliction, by the advice of a man who has proved the virtue of the remedy."

"O yes, miss! Now I understand. I've had such people come in past years. But it didn't strike me that you looked of a sort to require blood-turning. What's the complaint? The wrong kind for this, I'll be bound."

"My arm." She reluctantly showed the withered skin.

"Ah!—'tis all a-scram!" said the hangman, examining it.

"Yes," said she.

"Well," he continued, with interest, "that is the class o' subject, I'm bound to admit! I like the look of the wownd; it is as suitable for the cure as any I ever saw. 'Twas a knowing-man that sent 'ee, whoever he was."

"You can contrive for me all that's necessary?" she said breathlessly.

"You should really have gone to the governor of the jail, and your doctor with 'ee, and given your name and address—that's how it used to be done, if I recollect. Still, perhaps, I can manage it for a trifling fee."

"O, thank you! I would rather do it this way, as I should like it kept private."

"Lover not to know, eh?"

"No—husband."

"Aha! Very well. I'll get 'ee a touch of the corpse."

"Where is it now?" she said, shuddering.

"It?—*he*, you mean; he's living yet. Just inside that little small winder up there in the glum." He signified the jail on the cliff above.

She thought of her husband and her friends. "Yes, of course," she said; "and how am I to proceed?"

He took her to the door. "Now, do you be waiting at the little wicket in the wall, that you'll find up there in the lane, not later than one o'clock. I will open it from the inside, as I shan't come home to dinner till he's cut down. Goodnight. Be punctual; and if you don't want anybody to know 'ee, wear a veil. Ah—once I had such a daughter as you!"

She went away, and climbed the path above, to assure herself that she would be able to find the wicket next day. Its outline was soon visible to her—a narrow opening in the outer wall of the prison precincts. The steep was so great that, having reached the wicket, she stopped a moment to breathe: and, looking back upon the water-side cot, saw the hangman again ascending his outdoor staircase. He entered the loft or chamber to which it led, and in a few minutes extinguished his light.

The town clock struck ten, and she returned to the White Hart as she had come.

IX

A Rencounter

It was one o'clock on Saturday. Gertrude Lodge, having been admitted to the jail as above described, was sitting in a waiting-room within the second gate, which stood under a classic archway of ashlar, then comparatively modern, and bearing the inscription, 'COVNTY JAIL: 1793.' This had been the façade she saw from the heath the day before. Near at hand was a passage to the roof on which the gallows stood.

The town was thronged, and the market suspended; but Gertrude had seen scarcely a soul. Having kept her room till the hour of the appointment, she had proceeded to the spot by a way which avoided the open space below the cliff where the spectators had gathered; but she could, even now, hear the multitudinous babble of their voices, out of which rose at intervals the hoarse croak of a single voice uttering the words, "Last dying speech and confession!" There had been no reprieve, and the execution was over; but the crowd still waited to see the body taken down.

Soon the persistent woman heard a trampling overhead, then a hand beckoned to her, and, following directions, she went out and crossed the inner paved court beyond the gate-house, her knees trembling so that she could scarcely walk. One of her arms was out of its sleeve, and only covered by her shawl.

On the spot at which she had now arrived were two trestles, and before she could think of their purpose she heard, heavy feet descending stairs somewhere at her back. Turn her head she would not, or could not, and, rigid in this position, she was conscious of a rough coffin passing her borne by four men. It was open, and in it lay the body of a young man, wearing the smockfrock of a rustic, and fustian breeches. The corpse had been thrown into the coffin so hastily that the skirt of the smockfrock was hanging over. The burden was temporarily deposited on the trestles.

By this time the young woman's state was such that a grey mist seemed to float before her eyes, on account of which, and the veil she wore, she could scarcely discern anything: it was as though she had nearly died, but was held up by a sort of galvanism.

"Now!" said a voice close at hand, and she was just conscious that the word had been addressed to her.

By a last strenuous effort she advanced, at the same time hearing persons approaching behind her. She bared her poor curst arm; and Davies, uncovering the face of the corpse, took Gertrude's hand, and held it so that her arm lay across the dead man's neck, upon a line the colour of an unripe blackberry, which surrounded it.

Gertrude shrieked: "the turn o' the blood," predicted by the conjuror, had taken place. But at that moment a second shriek rent the air of the enclosure: it was not Gertrude's, and its effect upon her was to make her start round.

Immediately behind her stood Rhoda Brook, her face drawn, and her eyes red with weeping. Behind Rhoda stood Gertrude's own husband; his countenance lined, his eyes dim, but without a tear.

"Damn you! what are you doing here?" he said hoarsely.

"Hussy—to come between us and our child now!" cried Rhoda. "This is the meaning of what Satan showed me in the vision! You are like her at last!" And clutching the bare arm of the younger woman, she pulled her unresistingly back against the wall. Immediately Brook had loosened her hold the fragile young Gertrude slid down against the feet of her husband. When he lifted her up she was unconscious.

The mere sight of the twain had been enough to suggest to her that the dead young man was Rhoda's son. At that time the relatives of an executed convict had the privilege of claiming the body for burial, if they chose to do so; and it was for this purpose that Lodge was awaiting the inquest with Rhoda. He had been summoned by her as soon as the young man was taken in the crime, and at different times since; and he had attended in court during the trial. This was the "holiday" he had been indulging in of late. The two wretched parents had wished to avoid exposure; and hence had come themselves for the body, a wagon and sheet for its conveyance and covering being in waiting outside.

Gertrude's case was so serious that it was deemed advisable to call to her the surgeon who was at hand. She was taken out of the jail into the town; but she never reached home alive. Her delicate vitality, sapped perhaps by the paralysed arm, collapsed under the double shock that followed the severe strain, physical and mental, to which she had subjected herself during the previous twenty-four hours. Her blood had been "turned" indeed—too far. Her death took place in the town three days after.

Her husband was never seen in Casterbridge again; once only in the old market-place at Anglebury, which he had so much frequented, and very seldom in public anywhere Burdened at first with moodiness and remorse, he eventually changed for the better, and appeared as a chastened and thoughtful man. Soon after attending the funeral of his poor wife he took steps towards giving up the farms in Holmstoke and the adjoining parish, and, having sold every head of his stock, he went away to Port-Bredy, at the other end of the county, living there in solitary lodgings till his death two years later of a painless decline. It was then found that he had bequeathed the whole of his not inconsiderable property to a reformatory for boys, subject to the payment of a small annuity to Rhoda Brook, if she could be found to claim it.

For some time she could not be found; but eventually she reappeared in her old parish—absolutely refusing, however, to have anything to do with the provision made for her. Her monotonous milking at the dairy was resumed, and followed for many long years, till her form became bent, and her once abundant dark hair white and worn away at the forehead—perhaps by long pressure against the cows. Here, sometimes, those who knew her experiences would stand and observe her, and wonder what sombre thoughts were beating inside that impassive, wrinkled brow, to the rhythm of the alternating milk-streams.

JOHN CHARRINGTON'S WEDDING,
by Edith Nesbit

No one ever thought that May Forster would marry John Charrington; but he thought differently, and things which John Charrington intended had a queer way of coming to pass. He asked her to marry him before he went up to Oxford. She laughed and refused him. He asked her again next time he came home. Again she laughed, tossed her dainty blonde head and again refused. A third time he asked her; she said it was becoming a confirmed bad habit, and laughed at him more than ever.

John was not the only man who wanted to marry her: she was the belle of our village coterie, and we were all in love with her more or less; it was a sort of fashion, like masher collars or Inverness capes. Therefore we were as much annoyed as surprised when John Charrington walked into our little local Club—we held it in a loft over the saddler's, I remember—and invited us all to his wedding.

"Your wedding?"

"You don't mean it?"

"Who's the happy pair? When's it to be?"

John Charrington filled his pipe and lighted it before he replied. Then he said:

"I'm sorry to deprive you fellows of your only joke—but Miss Forster and I are to be married in September."

"You don't mean it?"

"He's got the mitten again, and it's turned his head."

"No," I said, rising, "I see it's true. Lend me a pistol, someone—or a first-class fare to the other end of Nowhere. Charrington has bewitched the only pretty girl in our twenty-mile radius. Was it mesmerism, or a love-potion, Jack?"

"Neither, sir, but a gift you'll never have—perseverance—and the best luck a man ever had in this world."

There was something in his voice that silenced me, and all chaff of the other fellows failed to draw him further.

The queer thing about it was that when we congratulated Miss Forster, she blushed and smiled and dimpled, for all the world as though she were in love with him, and had been in love with him all the time. Upon my word, I think she had. Women are strange creatures.

We were all asked to the wedding. In Brixham everyone who was anybody knew everybody else who was anyone. My sisters were, I truly believe, more interested in the trousseau than the bride herself, and I was to be best man. The coming marriage was much canvassed at afternoon tea-tables, and at our little Club over the saddler's, and the question was always asked, "Does she care for him?"

I used to ask that question myself in the early days of their engagement, but after a certain evening in August I never asked it again. I was coming home from the Club through the churchyard. Our church is on a thyme-grown hill, and the turf about it is so thick and soft that one's footsteps are noiseless.

I made no sound as I vaulted the low lichened wall, and threaded my way between the tombstones. It was at the same instant that I heard John Charrington's voice, and saw her. May was sitting on a low flat gravestone, her face turned towards the full splendour of the western sun. Its expression ended, at once and for ever, any question of love for him; it was transfigured to a beauty I should not have believed possible, even to that beautiful little face.

John lay at her feet, and it was his voice that broke the stillness of the golden August evening.

"My dear, my dear, I believe I should come back from the dead if you wanted me!"

I coughed at once to indicate my presence, and passed on into the shadow fully enlightened.

The wedding was to be early in September. Two days before I had to run up to town on business. The train was late, of course, for we are on the South-Eastern, and as I stood grumbling with my watch in my hand, whom should I see but John Charrington and May Forster. They were walking up and down the unfrequented end of the platform, arm in arm, looking into each other's eyes, careless of the sympathetic interest of the porters.

Of course I knew better than to hesitate a moment before burying myself in the booking-office, and it was not till the train drew up at the platform, that I obtrusively passed the pair with my Gladstone, and took the corner in a first-class smoking-carriage. I did this with as good an air of not seeing them as I could assume. I pride myself on my discretion, but if John were travelling alone I wanted his company. I had it.

"Hullo, old man," came his cheery voice as he swung his bag into my carriage; "here's luck; I was expecting a dull journey!"

"Where are you off to?" I asked, discretion still bidding me turn my eyes away, though I saw, without looking, that hers were red-rimmed.

"To old Branbridge's," he answered, shutting the door and leaning out for a last word with his sweetheart.

"Oh, I wish you wouldn't go, John," she was saying in a low, earnest voice. "I feel certain something will happen."

"Do you think I should let anything happen to keep me, and the day after tomorrow our wedding day?"

"Don't go," she answered, with a pleading intensity which would have sent my Gladstone onto the platform and me after it. But she wasn't speaking to me. John Charrington was made differently: he rarely changed his opinions, never his resolutions.

He only stroked the little ungloved hands that lay on the carriage door.

"I must, May. The old boy's been awfully good to me, and now he's dying I must go and see him, but I shall come home in time for—" the rest of the parting was lost in a whisper and in the rattling lurch of the starting train.

"You're sure to come?" she spoke as the train moved.

"Nothing shall keep me," he answered; and we steamed out. After he had seen the last of the little figure on the platform he leaned back in his corner and kept silence for a minute.

When he spoke it was to explain to me that his godfather, whose heir he was, lay dying at Peasmarsh Place, some fifty miles away, and had sent for John, and John had felt bound to go.

"I shall be surely back tomorrow," he said, "or, if not, the day after, in heaps of time. Thank heaven, one hasn't to get up in the middle of the night to get married nowadays!"

"And suppose Mr. Branbridge dies?"

"Alive or dead I mean to be married on Thursday!" John answered, lighting a cigar and unfolding The Times.

At Peasmarsh station we said "goodbye," and he got out, and I saw him ride off; I went on to London, where I stayed the night.

When I got home the next afternoon, a very wet one, by the way, my sister greeted me with:

"Where's Mr. Charrington?"

"Goodness knows," I answered testily. Every man, since Cain, has resented that kind of question.

"I thought you might have heard from him," she went on, "as you're to give him away tomorrow."

"Isn't he back?" I asked, for I had confidently expected to find him at home.

"No, Geoffrey," my sister Fanny always had a way of jumping to conclusions, especially such conclusions as were least favourable to her fellow-creatures—"he has not returned, and, what is more, you may depend upon it he won't. You mark my words, there'll be no wedding tomorrow."

My sister Fanny has a power of annoying me which no other human being possesses.

"You mark my words," I retorted with asperity, "you had better give up making such a thundering idiot of yourself. There'll be more wedding tomorrow than ever you'll take the first part in." A prophecy which, by the way, came true.

But though I could snarl confidently to my sister, I did not feel so comfortable when late that night, I, standing on the doorstep of John's house, heard that he had not returned. I went home gloomily through the rain. Next morning brought a brilliant blue sky, gold sun, and all such softness of air and beauty of cloud as go to make up a perfect day. I woke with a vague feeling of having gone to bed anxious, and of being rather averse to facing that anxiety in the light of full wakefulness.

But with my shaving-water came a note from John which relieved my mind and sent me up to the Forsters with a light heart.

May was in the garden. I saw her blue gown through the hollyhocks as the lodge gates swung to behind me. So I did not go up to the house, but turned aside down the turfed path.

"He's written to you too," she said, without preliminary greeting, when I reached her side.

"Yes, I'm to meet him at the station at three, and come straight on to the church."

Her face looked pale, but there was a brightness in her eyes, and a tender quiver about the mouth that spoke of renewed happiness.

"Mr. Branbridge begged him so to stay another night that he had not the heart to refuse," she went on. "He is so kind, but I wish he hadn't stayed."

I was at the station at half past two. I felt rather annoyed with John. It seemed a sort of slight to the beautiful girl who loved him, that he should come as it were out of breath, and with the dust of travel upon him, to take her hand, which some of us would have given the best years of our lives to take.

But when the three o'clock train glided in, and glided out again having brought no passengers to our little station, I was more than annoyed. There was no other train for thirty-five minutes; I calculated that, with much hurry, we might just get to the church in time for the ceremony; but, oh, what a fool to miss that first train! What other man could have done it?

That thirty-five minutes seemed a year, as I wandered round the station reading the advertisements and the timetables, and the company's bye-laws, and getting more and more angry with John Charrington. This confidence in his own power of getting everything he wanted the minute he wanted it was leading him too far. I hate waiting. Everyone does, but I believe I hate it more than anyone else. The three thirty-five was late, of course.

I ground my pipe between my teeth and stamped with impatience as I watched the signals. Click. The signal went down. Five minutes later I flung myself into the carriage that I had brought for John.

"Drive to the church!" I said, as someone shut the door. "Mr. Charrington hasn't come by this train."

Anxiety now replaced anger. What had become of the man? Could he have been taken suddenly ill? I had never known him have a day's illness in his life. And even so he might have telegraphed. Some awful accident must have happened to him. The thought that he had played her false never—no, not for a moment—entered my head. Yes, some thing terrible had happened to him, and on me lay the task of telling his bride. I almost wished the carriage would upset and break my head so that someone else might tell her, not I, who—but that's nothing to do with this story.

It was five minutes to four as we drew up at the churchyard gate. A double row of eager onlookers lined the path from lychgate to porch. I sprang from the carriage and passed up between them. Our gardener had a good front place near the door. I stopped.

"Are they waiting still, Byles?" I asked, simply to gain time, for of course I knew they were by the waiting crowd's attentive attitude.

"Waiting, sir? No, no, sir; why, it must be over by now."

"Over! Then Mr. Charrington's come?"

"To the minute, sir; must have missed you somehow, and I say, sir," lowering his voice, "I never see Mr. John the least bit so afore, but my opinion is he's been drinking pretty free. His clothes was all dusty and his face like a sheet. I tell you I didn't like the looks of him at all, and the folks inside are saying all sorts of things. You'll see, something's gone very wrong with Mr. John, and he's tried liquor. He looked like a ghost, and in he went with his eyes straight before him, with never a look or a word for none of us: him that was always such a gentleman!"

I had never heard Byles make so long a speech. The crowd in the churchyard were talking in whispers and getting ready rice and slippers to throw at the bride and bridegroom. The ringers were ready with their hands on the ropes to ring out the merry peal as the bride and bridegroom should come out.

A murmur from the church announced them; out they came. Byles was right. John Charrington did not look himself. There was dust on his coat, his hair was dis-arranged. He seemed to have been in some row, for there was a black mark above his eyebrow. He was deathly pale. But his pallor was not greater than that of the bride, who might have been carved in ivory—dress, veil, orange blossoms, face and all.

As they passed out the ringers stooped—there were six of them—and then, on the ears expecting the gay wedding peal, came the slow tolling of the passing bell.

A thrill of horror at so foolish a jest from the ringers passed through us all. But the ringers themselves dropped the ropes and fled like rabbits out into the sunlight. The bride shuddered, and grey shadows came about her mouth, but the bridegroom led her on down the path where the people stood with the handfuls of rice; but the handfuls were never thrown, and the wedding bells never rang. In vain the ringers were urged to remedy their mistake: they protested with many whispered expletives that they would see themselves further first.

In a hush like the hush in the chamber of death the bridal pair passed into their carriage and its door slammed behind them.

Then the tongues were loosed. A babel of anger, wonder, conjecture from the guests and the spectators.

"If I'd seen his condition, sir," said old Forster to me as we drove off, "I would have stretched him on the floor of the church, sir, by heaven I would, before I'd have let him marry my daughter!"

Then he put his head out of the window.

"Drive like hell," he cried to the coachman; "don't spare the horses."

He was obeyed. We passed the bride's carriage. I forbore to look at it, and old Forster turned his head away and swore. We reached home before it.

We stood in the doorway, in the blazing afternoon sun, and in about half a minute we heard wheels crunching the gravel. When the carriage stopped in front of the steps old Forster and I ran down.

"Great heaven, the carriage is empty! And yet—"

I had the door open in a minute, and this is what I saw...

No sign of John Charrington; and of May, his wife, only a huddled heap of white satin lying half on the floor of the carriage and half on the seat.

"I drove straight here, sir," said the coachman, as the bride's father lifted her out; "and I'll swear no one got out of the carriage."

We carried her into the house in her bridal dress and drew back her veil. I saw her face. Shall I ever forget it? White, white and drawn with agony and horror, bearing such a look of terror as I have never seen since except in dreams. And her hair, her radiant blonde hair, I tell you it was white like snow.

As we stood, her father and I, half mad with the horror and mystery of it, a boy came up the avenue—a telegraph boy. They brought the orange envelope to me. I tore it open.

Mr. Charrington was thrown from the dogcart on his way to the station at half past one. Killed on the spot!

And he was married to May Forster in our parish church at half past three, in presence of half the parish.

"I shall be married, dead, or alive!"

What had passed in that carriage on the homeward drive? No one knows—no one will ever know. Oh, May! oh, my dear!

* * * *

Before a week was over they laid her beside her husband in our little churchyard on the thyme-covered hill—the churchyard where they had kept their love-trysts.

Thus was accomplished John Charrington's wedding.

THE MAN OF SCIENCE,
by Jerome K. Jerome

I met a man in the Strand one day that I knew very well, as I thought, though I had not seen him for years. We walked together to Charing Cross, and there we shook hands and parted. Next morning, I spoke of this meeting to a mutual friend, and then I learnt, for the first time, that the man had died six months before.

The natural inference was that I had mistaken one man for another, an error that, not having a good memory for faces, I frequently fall into. What was remarkable about the matter, however, was that throughout our walk I had conversed with the man under the impression that he was that other dead man, and, whether by coincidence or not, his replies had never once suggested to me my mistake.

As soon as I finished, Jephson, who had been listening very thoughtfully, asked me if I believed in spiritualism "to its fullest extent."

"That is rather a large question," I answered. "What do you mean by 'spiritualism to its fullest extent'?"

"Well, do you believe that the spirits of the dead have not only the power of revisiting this earth at their will, but that, when here, they have the power of action, or rather, of exciting to action? Let me put a definite case. A spiritualist friend of mine, a sensible and by no means imaginative man, once told me that a table, through the medium of which the spirit of a friend had been in the habit of communicating with him, came slowly across the room towards him, of its own accord, one night as he sat alone, and pinioned him against the wall. Now can any of you believe that, or can't you?"

"I could," Brown took it upon himself to reply; "but, before doing so, I should wish for an introduction to the friend who told you the story. Speaking generally," he continued, "it seems to me that the difference between what we call the natural and the supernatural is merely the difference between frequency and rarity of occurrence. Having regard to the phenomena we are compelled to admit, I think it illogical to disbelieve anything we are unable to disprove."

"For my part," remarked MacShaughnassy, "I can believe in the ability of our spirit friends to give the quaint entertainments credited to them much easier than I can in their desire to do so."

"You mean," added Jephson, "that you cannot understand why a spirit, not compelled as we are by the exigencies of society, should care to spend its evenings carrying on a laboured and childish conversation with a room full of abnormally uninteresting people."

"That is precisely what I cannot understand," MacShaughnassy agreed.

"Nor I, either," said Jephson. "But I was thinking of something very different altogether. Suppose a man died with the dearest wish of his heart unfulfilled, do you believe that his spirit might have power to return to earth and complete the interrupted work?"

"Well," answered MacShaughnassy, "if one admits the possibility of spirits retaining any interest in the affairs of this world at all, it is certainly more reasonable to imagine them engaged upon a task such as you suggest, than to believe that they occupy themselves with the performance of mere drawing-room tricks. But what are you leading up to?"

"Why, to this," replied Jephson, seating himself straddle-legged across his chair, and leaning his arms upon the back. "I was told a story this morning at the hospital by an old French doctor. The actual facts are few and simple; all that is known can be read in the Paris police records of sixty-two years ago.

"The most important part of the case, however, is the part that is not known, and that never will be known.

"The story begins with a great wrong done by one man unto another man. What the wrong was I do not know. I am inclined to think, however, it was connected with a woman. I think that, because he who had been wronged hated him who had wronged him with a hate such as does not often burn in a man's brain, unless it be fanned by the memory of a woman's breath.

"Still that is only conjecture, and the point is immaterial. The man who had done the wrong fled, and the other man followed him. It became a point-to-point race, the first man having the advantage of a day's start. The course was the whole world, and the stakes were the first man's life.

"Travellers were few and far between in those days, and this made the trail easy to follow. The first man, never knowing how far or how near the other was behind him, and hoping now and again that he might have baffled him, would rest for a while. The second man, knowing always just how far the first one was before him, never paused, and thus each day the man who was spurred by Hate drew nearer to the man who was spurred by Fear.

"At this town the answer to the never-varied question would be:—

"'At seven o'clock last evening, M'sieur.'

"'Seven—ah; eighteen hours. Give me something to eat, quick, while the horses are being put to.'

"At the next the calculation would be sixteen hours.

"Passing a lonely chalet, Monsieur puts his head out of the window:—

"'How long since a carriage passed this way, with a tall, fair man inside?'

"'Such a one passed early this morning, M'sieur.'

"'Thanks, drive on, a hundred francs apiece if you are through the pass before daybreak.'

"'And what for dead horses, M'sieur?'

"'Twice their value when living.'

"One day the man who was ridden by Fear looked up, and saw before him the open door of a cathedral, and, passing in, knelt down and prayed. He prayed long and fervently, for men, when they are in sore straits, clutch eagerly at the straws of faith. He prayed that he might be forgiven his sin, and, more important still, that he might be pardoned the consequences of his sin, and be delivered from his adversary; and a few chairs from him, facing him, knelt his enemy, praying also.

"But the second man's prayer, being a thanksgiving merely, was short, so that when the first man raised his eyes, he saw the face of his enemy gazing at him across the chair-tops, with a mocking smile upon it.

"He made no attempt to rise, but remained kneeling, fascinated by the look of joy that shone out of the other man's eyes. And the other man moved the high-backed chairs one by one, and came towards him softly.

"Then, just as the man who had been wronged stood beside the man who had wronged him, full of gladness that his opportunity had come, there burst from the cathedral tower a sudden clash of bells, and the man, whose opportunity had come, broke his heart and fell back dead, with that mocking smile still playing round his mouth.

"And so he lay there.

"Then the man who had done the wrong rose up and passed out, praising God.

"What became of the body of the other man is not known. It was the body of a stranger who had died suddenly in the cathedral. There was none to identify it, none to claim it.

"Years passed away, and the survivor in the tragedy became a worthy and useful citizen, and a noted man of science.

"In his laboratory were many objects necessary to him in his researches, and, prominent among them, stood in a certain corner a human skeleton. It was a very old and much-mended skeleton, and one day the long-expected end arrived, and it tumbled to pieces.

"Thus it became necessary to purchase another.

"The man of science visited a dealer he well knew—a little parchment-faced old man who kept a dingy shop, where nothing was ever sold, within the shadow of the towers of Notre Dame.

"The little parchment-faced old man had just the very thing that Monsieur wanted—a singularly fine and well-proportioned 'study.' It should be sent round and set up in Monsieur's laboratory that very afternoon.

"The dealer was as good as his word. When Monsieur entered his laboratory that evening, the thing was in its place.

"Monsieur seated himself in his high-backed chair, and tried to collect his thoughts. But Monsieur's thoughts were unruly, and inclined to wander, and to wander always in one direction.

"Monsieur opened a large volume and commenced to read. He read of a man who had wronged another and fled from him, the other man following. Finding himself reading this, he closed the book angrily, and went and stood by the window and looked out. He saw before him the sun-pierced nave of a great cathedral, and on the stones lay a dead man with a mocking smile upon his face.

"Cursing himself for a fool, he turned away with a laugh. But his laugh was short-lived, for it seemed to him that something else in the room was laughing also. Struck suddenly still, with his feet glued to the ground, he stood listening for a while: then sought with starting eyes the corner from where the sound had seemed to come. But the white thing standing there was only grinning.

"Monsieur wiped the damp sweat from his head and hands, and stole out.

"For a couple of days he did not enter the room again. On the third, telling himself that his fears were those of a hysterical girl, he opened the door and went in. To shame himself, he took his lamp in his hand, and crossing over to the far corner where the skeleton stood, examined it. A set of bones bought for three hundred francs. Was he a child, to be scared by such a bogey!

"He held his lamp up in front of the thing's grinning head. The flame of the lamp flickered as though a faint breath had passed over it.

"The man explained this to himself by saying that the walls of the house were old and cracked, and that the wind might creep in anywhere. He repeated this explanation to himself as he recrossed the room, walking backwards, with his eyes fixed on the thing. When he reached his desk, he sat down and gripped the arms of his chair till his fingers turned white.

"He tried to work, but the empty sockets in that grinning head seemed to be drawing him towards them. He rose and battled with his inclination to fly screaming from the room. Glancing fearfully about him, his eye fell upon a high screen, standing before the door. He dragged it forward, and placed it between himself and

194

the thing, so that he could not see it—nor it see him. Then he sat down again to his work. For a while he forced himself to look at the book in front of him, but at last, unable to control himself any longer, he suffered his eyes to follow their own bent.

"It may have been an hallucination. He may have accidentally placed the screen so as to favour such an illusion. But what he saw was a bony hand coming round the corner of the screen, and, with a cry, he fell to the floor in a swoon.

"The people of the house came running in, and lifting him up, carried him out, and laid him upon his bed. As soon as he recovered, his first question was, where had they found the thing—where was it when they entered the room? and when they told him they had seen it standing where it always stood, and had gone down into the room to look again, because of his frenzied entreaties, and returned trying to hide their smiles, he listened to their talk about overwork, and the necessity for change and rest, and said they might do with him as they would.

"So for many months the laboratory door remained locked. Then there came a chill autumn evening when the man of science opened it again, and closed it behind him.

"He lighted his lamp, and gathered his instruments and books around him, and sat down before them in his high-backed chair. And the old terror returned to him.

"But this time he meant to conquer himself. His nerves were stronger now, and his brain clearer; he would fight his unreasoning fear. He crossed to the door and locked himself in, and flung the key to the other end of the room, where it fell among jars and bottles with an echoing clatter.

"Later on, his old housekeeper, going her final round, tapped at his door and wished him good-night, as was her custom. She received no response, at first, and, growing nervous, tapped louder and called again; and at length an answering 'good-night' came back to her.

"She thought little about it at the time, but afterwards she remembered that the voice that had replied to her had been strangely grating and mechanical. Trying to describe it, she likened it to such a voice as she would imagine coming from a statue.

"Next morning his door remained still locked. It was no unusual thing for him to work all night and far into the next day, so no one thought to be surprised. When, however, evening came, and yet he did not appear, his servants gathered outside the room and whispered, remembering what had happened once before.

"They listened, but could hear no sound. They shook the door and called to him, then beat with their fists upon the wooden panels. But still no sound came from the room.

"Becoming alarmed, they decided to burst open the door, and, after many blows, it gave way, and they crowded in.

"He sat bolt upright in his high-backed chair. They thought at first he had died in his sleep. But when they drew nearer and the light fell upon him, they saw the livid marks of bony fingers round his throat; and in his eyes there was a terror such as is not often seen in human eyes."

Brown was the first to break the silence that followed. He asked me if I had any brandy on board. He said he felt he should like just a nip of brandy before going to bed. That is one of the chief charms of Jephson's stories: they always make you feel you want a little brandy.

WHAT DID MISS DARRINGTON SEE?
by Emma B. Cobb

It was not so very long ago, for it was only about a year before the outbreak of the great rebellion, that Colonel Sibthorpe, living at Catalpa Grove, County, Kentucky, wrote to Mr. Allen, a merchant in Boston, with whom he had large dealings, to procure for him a governess. The correspondent was requested to look out for a young person capable of "finishing" the education of the colonel's two motherless daughters, aged respectively eighteen and sixteen, and of preparing his younger son for admission to a Southern college.

Mr. Allen was at first not a little embarrassed by a commission so entirely out of the ordinary course of business; but as he had a strong desire to oblige his Kentucky friend and customer, he at once set about making inquiries for a suitable person to "fill the order." Whether his search was attended with much or little difficulty I am unable to say; I only know that it resulted in the engagement, at a liberal salary, of Miss Elizabeth Darrington, from whom I have derived the chief incidents of the story I am about to relate, and who has reluctantly consented to my making them public.

Perhaps you have seen Miss Darrington? If so, I dare be sworn that you remember her more vividly than many a handsomer woman. At the time I speak of she was about twenty-four, a small figure, slight now, but promising fullness as time should go on; a face neither beautiful nor plain in feature, but showing intellect and esprit, and a manner unmistakably that of a gentlewoman. (It is a word little used now, but it expresses what I mean far more accurately than the flip pant term "lady.") Sprung from one of the oldest and best families in Massachusetts—one which had produced governors and legislators in the early colonial time, and in nearly every generation since some man of shining mark—she had not only inherited a fair share of the family talent, but she had breathed an atmosphere of intellect and culture from her infancy. She had also been early forced by circumstances into a position of self-reliance, and had learned to think and act independently. The result was a character not so easily summed up as that of a woman of the model sort, made up after the ideal of newspaper homilists, and the reverend gentlemen who lecture on the "Woman Question." Such as these would have found something of a paganism in the very virtues of Miss Darrington, without, perhaps, perceiving that there was a touch of nobility even in her faults. Proud, certainly—every thing about her, from the curve of her well-cut lip to the high-arched instep of a rather small foot, attested to that fact. Cold? I am not so sure. Her best friends said so; and at least the glance of her eye was cool and steady. Yet she had a keen physical organization, and enjoyed life with a zest unknown to duller and narrower natures. In short, she was one of those women, peculiarly the product of our later civilization, in whom the brain is uppermost, feeling in abeyance, and gifted with a power of self-rule which, if they do suffer, enables them to hide it as skillfully as a Mohican. She liked men, but they seldom got farther with her than the point of good-comradeship. Very young men, by the way, were inclined to fight a little shy of her; but she liked shrewd elderly ones, and these were always her admirers. Her manner, too, was not the modest violet manner of the model woman; there was just a touch of conscious power in it—a fine, well-bred self-assertion, which stood her in good stead in her peculiar position at Catalpa Grove, and enabled her to keep the young ladies of the house very much in order. In those days Northern governesses of the meek sort used often to fare a little dismally among those high-spirited and not over-cultivated Southern girls. But one glance into the level gray eyes of Miss Darrington would have convinced a duller than the Sibthorpes that this was a woman on whom it would be dangerous to play off any airs of superiority. They had a wholesome fear of her at the end of the first hour, but they cordially liked her by the end of the first week, and their respect and liking never diminished while she remained with them. The truth is, real New England "blue blood" is the very bluest in America, and the pride it engenders is more than a match for the haughtiest "F. F. V."—a fact which our Southern friends did not know so well before the war as they do now, for the reason that in their isolated plantation life they were seldom brought in contact with the real thing. They had their estimate of the Northern spirit from second and third rate specimens. The Sibthorpes were fine girls, however, and when they found out the stuff the governess had in her they were ready enough to make Catalpa Grove a pleasant abode for her, and soon its gayeties were incomplete without her.

The grove was in a populous county, and within easy visiting distance of the city of L—. There was always open house, and a very delightful house at that. The colonel was a good specimen of the Kentucky gentleman, frank, hearty, hospitable, and well-bred, until you touched his prejudices. He greatly admired Miss Darrington, and, in deed, showed some disposition to give his feelings practical expression, but was skillfully checked by the lady before he had committed himself. It did not in the least suit her book to be made love to by her host. She had undertaken a profitable year's task, and she wanted the salary. She did not choose either to resign the chance of earning it or to be made uncomfortable by the presence in the house of a rejected suitor.

You think I am describing a hard and selfish woman. What do you think she was down there governessing for, that finely trained, thorough-bred creature, among those free-and-easy, not over intellectual Kentuckians? She was the eldest of four children. Her father was dead, and her mother a delicate, fine lady, as lovely and as helpless as a baby or a flower. Elizabeth was the support of the family. She kept the children at school, and wrote every week to her mother a long letter, full of fun and nonsense and merry rattle, to make that dear woman believe she had not a care in the world. But, trust me, she had plenty.

Miss Darrington had been about six months at the grove when, one morning in March, the household was thrown into a little cheerful commotion by a letter from Tom Sibthorpe, the colonel's eldest son, announcing his return home. He wrote to say that he should bring with him a friend, a young Cuban, with whom he had been traveling, and whom—for I am compelled to give him a fictitious name—I shall call Raphael Aldama. The expected advent of this stranger caused not a little excitement to the. young ladies of the grove. He was of Spanish birth, but his family had lived for years in Havana, and he had formerly been at school with Tom Sibthorpe in New Orleans. The girls had never seen him; but they told Miss Darrington the most remarkable stories about him, of his wonderful personal beauty, his astonishing strength, his terrible temper and reckless daring, his duels and scrapes. He was very rich, very haughty, very magnificent. They were wild to see him, but rather inclined to be afraid of him. He was said to be as irresistible with women as he was dangerous with men. Miss Darrington did not find their picture of

197

the expected guest particularly attractive. She laughed to herself, mentally decided that the romantic Cuban was probably a very ordinary young savage, and thought no more about him.

The travelers reached Catalpa Grove on the day expected. It was in the afternoon that they arrived; and his imperial highness, Signor Raphael, was pleased to retire immediately to bed, where he spent the night and the whole of the next day. All day long the two Sibthorpe girls were in a little fever of excitement, and were not above showing it. Alice could not practice her music lesson, and Rosalie had more trouble than usual with French verbs. They laid out their prettiest toilets for the evening, and teased Tom Sibthorpe with all sorts of questions about his friend. Miss Darrington listened, a little ennuyée, checked a satirical smile, and yawned behind her fan. When they had fluttered away she arrayed herself in the plain white dress which was her ordinary evening wear, with no ornament, except some scarlet blossoms of the Japan quince in her dark braids, and went down to play gallops and waltzes for the others to dance.

The evening was well-nigh spent, her fingers were getting tired, and she was playing half mechanically, her thoughts carried far away, when Alice Sibthorpe came toward her, leaning on the arm of a gentleman, and begged to present the Signor Aldama, who desired the pleasure of her acquaintance. She looked up, indifferently, and met the glance of an eye before whose fiery and intolerable splendor her own for an instant fell—for an instant only. She was quite too practiced a woman of the world to lose her self-possession, though for a moment compelled to acknowledge the force of a magnetism more powerful than her own. A voice peculiarly soft and melodious addressed her, and the sweet, measured tones in which she replied betrayed no disturbance. Alice took her place at the piano, and she moved to a sofa, the stranger placing himself at her side; and she found herself studying curiously the face before her.

It was a very handsome face. She acknowledged that instantly. A white forehead, smooth as a boy's, over which the black hair clustered in heavy rings; an arched nose, the wide delicate nostril of which had a quiver of pride in it, like what one sees in fiery young horses; lips full yet firm, a strange sweetness in their smile, yet a fierceness in their passionate curve which suggested possibilities of cruelty. The eye was large and looked like black velvet, with the flash of a diamond in its centre. With all this a figure strong yet slender, a springing, cat-like tread, and a manner full of lazy grace, yet marred by something of haughty indifference.

Miss Darrington looked now steadily into the eyes whose bold, strong glance had at first beaten down her own, and recognized the nature of the soul that looked out from them. "It is a case for Van Amburgh," she said to herself, "or Girard, the lion-tamer. What jungle can have reared a wild animal like this?" But the low musical voice in which he addressed her did not accord with his harsh impression, and his manner at the moment was almost reverent in its gentle respect.

From that evening an intimacy singularly close and confidential existed between these two. I say existed, for it was a thing which had no growth; it seemed to spring up, "full-statured, in an hour." But whether it were of the nature of love or friendship the lookers-on were puzzled to decide. But, at least, he seemed never willingly absent from her company, and she had an evident pleasure in having him near her. Yet she certainly made no effort to attract him. So much was admitted, even by the two Sibthorpe girls, who, having, perhaps, anticipated an admirer in their brother's friend may have felt a twinge of resentment at seeing him immediately carried off by the governess. But they were not ill natured, and they had no lack of admirers; so they soon accepted the situation, wondering a little, too, for it was not vanity in them to think that, in point of beauty as well as youth, they had the advantage. But Raphael had known plenty of beautiful women—had enjoyed to the full the incense of their admiration—while a woman with brains was a new revelation to him. The spell of intellect and culture he found irresistible. This was the more strange as he was the last man whom a superficial judgment would have supposed likely to be attracted by such qualities. He had very little culture himself, little education, indeed, in the ordinary sense of the word. But he had seen a great deal of life in his five-and-twenty years—a life of vivid impressions and keen emotions. He had always been his own master, knowing from boyhood no law but his own will. The result was a character fixed in its mould, yet giving the impression of immaturity. Though really older than Miss Darrington, he seemed to her like a grown-up child. His nature showed a tinge of barbarism, a certain antique simplicity, which seemed to belong to a past age. She could not fail to see that intellectually she was vastly his superior; and it is good evidence of the natural nobility of the man's nature that he, too, recognized that fact without resenting it. He had worshiped passionately at many a lovely shrine, but never quite free from the haughty feeling that his homage honored her on whom it lighted. Now, for the first time in his life, his boldness had become timidity, his audacity respect. The story of "Undine" may repeat itself in more forms than one. The soul in this half-savage breast sprang into conscious life with the first pure, unselfish love which had ever dwelt there. Unselfish, for he knew from the very first that it was hopeless. She was honest with him all through. She let him see that truly as she liked him, frankly as she admired him, she had only friendship to give him. Not that she told him so in words—a woman is a blunderer to whom such words are necessary—but he did not fail to perceive the truth.

Yet it must be confessed that she found in his companionship a wonderful charm, the secret of which she could never fully analyze. It might lie partly in his remarkable beauty—always a spell to any woman—or the intense personal magnetism by which he affected all who came near him. It might be the very contrast between her own complex but balanced nature and this romantic and ardent, though untutored soul. Then, too, he adored her, and what woman ever lived who did not love to be worshiped? His honest affection must have been inexpressibly soothing to her often-wearied spirit. I think she might even have loved him but for the recollection of—but that is her secret, and has nothing to do with my story.

So, though on the frankest terms of intimacy, they never talked of love. Without surrounding herself with any apparent defenses, she compelled him to a complete reserve in that direction. A coquette might have refused to listen to him; she assumed that he had nothing to say, and so persistently ignored the possibility of anything else that he could not escape the position she assigned him.

Of course it was not to be expected that this sudden and close intimacy could escape comment in the little circle at the Grove. But after the first dash of surprise they treated the matter with indifference, good naturedly, willing that the parties should please themselves. Only Tom Sibthorpe, gifted with a somewhat more acute observation than the rest, watched the pair with a puzzled interest.

"By Jove!" he said to his sister Alice, "I did not think the woman had lived who could so tame the tiger in Raphael Aldama. Can you tell me the secret of her power7 It is not coquetry; she never throws out a lure; yet the very soul of the man is on its knees before her. It can not be beauty; she is not so pretty as you, or Rose; though in the real air de grande dame she beats you both out of the field—that little thing, not over five feet high! I don't know but it is in her pride, after all. For the first time in his life Raphael has found some one prouder than he is. Do you believe she will marry him?"

199

"I should think so, certainly," replied Alice, rather surprised at the doubt.

"Possibly you are right. Women should know women. But I am not sure that she is one to say, 'all for love, and a world well lost.'"

"How can you be so censorious, Tom?" cried Alice, indignantly. "Miss Darrington is no more cold-hearted than you are. Besides, if it is a question of worldly advantage, she has every thing to gain from such a marriage."

"You think so, my dear, but she knows better. To her the losses might outweigh the gains."

"What would she lose?"

"The whole world in which she has hitherto lived and moved and had her being. Don't you see how opposite they are in character, in education, in ideas of life? She has been reared in the stimulating mental atmosphere of the North, and is, to say truth, a very fine specimen of its culture; has grown up in sympathy with the living forces of thought which move the modern world. He is like the child of some past civilization, who does not even known himself out of harmony with this thinking nineteenth century. There can be no spiritual kinship between the two. If she were to marry him she would lose the freedom she prizes beyond every thing, and gain, not a mate, but merely an adorer. And such an adorer! A woman might as well trust herself to a typhoon."

"Don't you think his love for her would last?"

"How can I tell? He has loved a hundred times before; though, to speak the truth, I never saw him in such earnest as now. But if he did not weary, she would. His passion is too exigeante; it would bore her in a little while."

"You seem to think she does not care for him."

"Nay; that is where I am wholly at sea. She is not one to wear her heart on her sleeve for such daws as we to peck at. But, after all, what does it matter? These things are always unequal. Il y a toujours l'un qui baise, et l'autre qui tend le joue."

"You are a horrid old cynic, Tom."

"Yes, dear; and a stupid one at that; so let us talk of something else."

So the warm spring days flew swiftly by, and the old house rang with the gayety of that careless Southern life; and these two floated on with the stream, enjoying the present, but knowing well that their plea sure could not last. At least she knew this. She understood that there could be no permanent tie between them. They had drifted together from opposite poles; they would soon drift apart again, and that would be the end. But it was not easy to keep him to this view.

"Why talk of the future at all?" he said, impatiently. "Let me at least dream that I have you forever. These hours are so sweet—I sip them slowly, like drops of some precious wine. I even fancy sometimes that the days go lingeringly, as if the very moments felt the joy they hold, and were loath to depart from us. We are but children playing in the sun; let us play that we are lovers—and love, you know, is eternal."

"Oh, but that is too idle."

"Yes; I will have it so," he said, evidently feeling that he was securing an advantage. "You insist that this companionship of ours is not any part of our real lives. It is a little dream we are dreaming together—a brief drama which we enact. In such a fictitious world it is no matter what roles we take for our own. I choose the part of your lover. You can listen to my vows, for it is only play, you know."

She laughed, but made no reply. She was unwilling, by objecting, to seem to attach any importance to this new freak. He never relinquished the ground her silence conceded; yet he seemed always to feel that this advantage was a stolen one, and was careful not to press it too far. Though after that he would often hold toward her the language of a lover, he was strangely gentle for one so naturally fierce and wild, and he played with this whim in a half sad, half tender way, which some times moved her more than she chose to show.

Raphael was passionately fond of music, and sang well in a wild, lawless way of his own, though in that, as in every thing else, quite guiltless of scientific method. He often chose to be present when Miss

Darrington was giving her morning lesson to the young ladies; and, as what he chose to do it w as rather difficult to prevent, both teacher and pupils soon learned to go on without paying any attention to him.

One memorable morning in May the two girls had finished their lesson and left the room. Raphael, who had been lying on a sofa by the window, with a newspaper over his face, as if asleep, flung it away as they closed the door.

"Now that those chatterers are gone, sing to me, Isabel," he said. It was one of his caprices to substitute for her stately English name of Elizabeth, whose conso-nants plagued his southern tongue, the softer Spanish form which is its equivalent.

"What will you have?" she asked, reseating herself. "Are you in a sober mood, or will something gay and sparkling suit you better?"

"Any thing you like will please me."

"That is a very flattering frame of mind in which to find one's audience. As a re-ward you shall hear this choice little bit from Tennyson's 'Maud,' which has just been set to music."

"Very well; I have not an idea who Tennyson is, and never heard of his 'Maud;' but if you like it I shall. I only want to hear your voice."

"What pretty things you say this morning! But I assure you that my grim tones do no justice to it. You should hear Alice."

"Alice screams like a macaw."

"That is not quite complimentary to my best pupil. But now, barbarian, be silent, and listen."

The song was the one, so familiar now, beginning, "There has fallen a splendid tear." She sang it in a way of her own, rolling out the words at the top, or rather bottom, of her voice, trying to imitate the deep, passionate tones of Maud's lover, as he stands, half stifled with impatience, listening in the hush of the summer night for the footfall that he loves:

> *"There has fallen a splendid tear*
> *From the passion-flower at the gate.*
> *She is coming, my dove, my dear;*
> *She is coming, my life, my fate.*
> *The red rose cries, 'She is near, she is near;'*
> *And the white rose weeps, 'She is late;'*
> *The larkspur listens, 'I hear, I hear;'*
> *And the lily whispers, 'I wait.'*
>
> *"She is coming, my own, my sweet;*
> *Were it ever so airy a tread,*
> *My heart would hear her and beat,*
> *Were it earth in an earthy bed;*
> *My dust would hear her and beat,*
> *Had I lain for a century dead;*
> *Would start and tremble under her feet,*
> *And blossom in purple and red."*

During the singing of the first stanza Raphael kept his position on the sofa, but the second had not proceeded far when, with a smothered exclamation, he started upright, and sat leaning eagerly forward, listening with a flushed and working face. At the close he sprang to his feet, and came toward her, his eyes burning like coals of fire.

"Jesu Maria! Why do you sing like that to me?"

The passion in his tones made her tremble, but she answered as calmly as possible: "I had no special reason. I thought the song a pretty piece of hyperbole, which would please you."

"It is not hyperbole; it is truth," he said, softly, a sudden paleness replacing the flush on his face. He stood close behind her, and leaned over to look at the sheet from which she had been singing. His fingers rested for a moment with a light touch upon her hair—a touch inexpressibly soft and caressing—as he repeated:

> "'My dust would hear her and beat, Had I lain for a century dead; Would start
> and tremble under her feet, And blossom in purple and red.'

"Why, yes," he went on, dreamily, "surely the earth does not furnish a grave so deep that the sound of her little foot above it would not send a thrill through his heart."

"Raphael, I think you rave."

"Indeed no," he said, smiling softly. "Can not you see that if I were really your lover, as we only play I am, neither death nor the grave could divide me from you? In life, distance might divide us. Your own coldness, the cruel conveniences of the world in which you live, might build themselves like a wall between us; but were this soul unchained by death I should be free to seek you, and the universe of God is not wide enough to divide me from her I love. Not highest heaven nor deepest hell could keep me from my darling."

"You would not appear to her in the fashion of the spectre bride groom, in the ballad of 'Leonora' we read the other day? Few ladies would like that."

She spoke lightly, for the scene was becoming too painful, and she felt that she must end it at any cost. But her effort failed. He only smiled—a grave, patient smile, strangely unlike himself, she thought—as he answered:

"No, surely. Do you think I would frighten her, or harm one hair of her little head? Not to terrify, but to bless, would I seek her. And she would know my soul at last, and read all its love for her—a love she was too blind to believe in here."

Tears sprang to her steadfast eyes. "Dear Raphael," she said, "I will not wrong you by jesting any more. I do know your generous regard for me, and I am grateful for it. But if I were to listen to you it would be the bane of both. We are not suited to each other. We belong to two different worlds. The air of yours would scorch and blast me, as mine would chill and destroy you."

"You do not care for me, then?"

"Indeed I do care. I was cold and lonely here, away from all I love; you came, and I was warmed with the sun of the tropics. It is you who give the charm to these sweet spring days which are passing so swiftly. But when they are gone that will be the end. You will leave us, and though you will think of me kindly for a while, the world of excitement and adventure will quickly renew its charm for you, and you will thank me then that I have left you unfettered."

"And you?" he asked, in a tone of some bitterness. "You will forget me, doubtless?"

"I shall never forget you," she answered, sadly. "I shall remember you always as the kindest, the most generous of friends. My life is one of labor and care; and this brief holiday we have spent together has the charm which only rare pleasures have.

To you it is like the rest of your life, and so its memory will fade the sooner."

"So you doubt alike my truth and constancy?"

"Doubt your truth? Ah, no. But for constancy—what is it? We are none of us constant—God be thanked, who gives us the power to change. How could we live if we had not that—if every sorrow held its keenness forever?"

"Do I cause you sorrow, Isabel?"

"Only when I see you unhappy. Did you not say that we were children playing in the sun? Then what have we to do with care? Let us play the play out merrily, for the end of it is near."

She staid for no reply, but smiling on him kindly, though with swimming eyes, she rose and left the room.

* * * *

A week later Raphael went. Imperative business compelled Tom Sibthorpe's departure, and his friend had no pretext for lingering longer. In the interval he bore himself toward Miss Darrington with a fair degree of the coolness she had been teaching him, but whether from pride or acquired indifference she could not tell. The day before his departure he ordered his horse immediately after breakfast, and rode to L—. She noticed, as he passed the window, that he had exchanged the white linen suit which, in common with other gentlemen at that season, he wore constantly, for a complete black dress.

He was gone nearly all day, only making his appearance after dinner was over, and the whole family assembled in the drawing-room. He had resumed his usual garb, and seemed in very gay spirits. Several guests were present, and he made himself brilliantly agreeable to them, flirted with Rose Sibthorpe, and paid any number of compliments to Alice on her singing. Miss Darrington played superbly, but he did not approach her. When she had finished, however, and walked away from the others into the shelter of a window, he soon followed.

"Have you heard," he said, "that I go tomorrow?"

"So Tom has been telling me."

"You speak very quietly. Do you understand that we part finally—that we shall never meet again?"

"Yes, I know."

The words were almost inaudible, for pain choked her voice. He went on:

"Well, then, since it is so—since we shall never be any thing to each other any more, will you not give me something which shall at times remind me of you? Otherwise I might forget you, you know."

"What shall it be?" she asked, faintly. The smile on his lips was almost more than she could bear.

"Any thing which you have worn, so it will seem a part of you."

"Wear this, then," drawing from her finger a little plain gold ring.

There was a flash like triumph in his eyes as he received it, and touched it to his lips before placing it upon his own finger.

"Now," he said, still speaking in the same slow tone, as if he were controlling it by an effort—"now, will you look at what I have here?"

He took a small parcel from the breast of his coat and placed it in her hand. She removed the wrapper, and there appeared a common jewel-case of purple morocco, which, on being opened, revealed, reposing on its velvet bed, a trinket of singular and beautiful workman ship. It was a large drop, or globe, of exquisitely cut crystal, enclosed in a fine net-work of gold.

"Do you like it?" he asked, as she did not speak.

"Who would not? It looks like a soap-bubble tangled in a golden nest, or a great dewdrop bound round with threads of Titania's hair. Surely you did not find such a rare and curious thing at L—?"

"No; I carried it there to-day. For what purpose I am not sure that I dare to tell you. It is an heir-loom in our family, and has come down to me through many generations. There is a tradition among us that it is a talisman, and brings good fortune to her who wears it. Will you wear it in memory of the last Aldama?"

Miss Darrington hesitated. "Ought you to part with a thing of such peculiar value?"

He answered with a strange smile: "I do not part with it. I only make of it a link between myself and you. While you wear it you can not wholly forget me. If you wish to do so, reject it."

She answered by fastening it to her watch-chain. Again that triumphant flash broke from his eyes. Some one approached the window. Their tete-a-tete must come to an end. He leaned toward her and whispered hastily: "Some day, when you look at it, you will learn how high my presumption has soared. But the link between us is riveted now. You can never undo it." The next moment he had moved away, and was laughing gaily with a group of ladies.

That night, in her own room, as Miss Darrington was laying aside her watch, she once more examined curiously the crystal drop. As she turned it over and over her fingers must have touched a small spring concealed in the gold net-work, for the globe parted in the middle, and the sides falling open, revealed a small but perfect photograph likeness of Raphael himself. This, then, was the errand which had taken him to L— that day; this was the piece of presumption which he had hesitated to confess to her. He had probably believed that she would not discover it till after he was gone. Should she tell him that she had done so, and reject a gift to which he evidently attached a half-superstitious importance? On consideration she decided against this course. It would bring about an exciting and perhaps stormy scene, and could do no good. They were not likely ever to meet again, so no embarrassment could ensue from her acceptance of his gift, and she need never wear it unless she chose.

The two travelers were to leave early next morning, as they had a ride of some miles to reach the nearest railway station. The heat was excessive, and Miss Darrington, who had not been well for some days, found herself languid and suffering; but she went down as usual. Alice Sibthorpe was in the room with her when Raphael came to say good by. He spoke his farewells lightly and gaily to both ladies, and left the room. Alice followed to say another parting word to her brother, and to watch with the rest the bustle of departure. Miss Darrington remained alone, and yielding to the languor of indisposition and the oppressive heat she sank down upon a lounge. A sadness deeper than she was prepared to feel, and which she chose to attribute mainly to physical depression, sent the slow tears stealing through her closed eye lashes.

So sunk was she in the listlessness of her sorrowful mood that she did not heed the opening of the door, or perceive that she was not alone until, looking up, she saw Raphael again beside her. His face was pale, his lips trembled, his eyes flashed darkly through the tears that filled them. He bent over her; she extended her hand. He caught and pressed it in his own so fiercely as almost to draw from her a cry of pain. He seemed making an effort to speak, but his voice died away in his throat.

There was a sound of footsteps approaching the door. He heard it and started. Then suddenly dropping on his knees beside her couch, and bending down to her feet, he kissed them passionately, again and again, and rising, darted from the room. She heard him spring down the staircase, and the next moment the clatter of his horse's hoofs dashing away, and the voice of Tom Sibthorpe swearing at him to stop.

Miss Darrington was both shocked and pained by an incident which revealed a feeling on the part of her friend so much deeper than she had thought possible. But she consoled herself with the reflection that with him all emotions, though keen, were transient. Some other woman, she believed, would soon ensnare his fickle fancy, and efface from his mind all memories of pain. "I shall regret him longer than he will me," she said, and turned to work as the best cure for sorrowful thoughts.

* * * *

The autumn of the year 1868 found Miss Darrington living in Boston. A busy woman now, for life with her had been steadily gathering new interests and occupations. Some youthful dreams, indeed, had faded out of sight, some triumphs anticipated once had been wholly missed; yet in the career she had marked out for herself a fair measure of success had rewarded her efforts, and won her the recognition so dear to us all. Without being a famous woman, she had secured a position which enabled her to make her social world what she would. She was happy and cheerful, for with her no sense was dulled, no power of enjoyment diminished; only the uneasy restlessness of youth had passed, and given place to the secure repose of one who has found her place and learned to fill it.

With a life thus pleasantly full, it was not surprising that the episode of her Kentucky sojourn gradually faded from her thoughts. As for her Cuban friend, it was seldom now that the idea of him returned to her. Beautiful as he had been to her, the passing tendresse she had felt for him had taken no hold upon her life. She had never woven his image with a single dream of the future; and the feeling with which she remembered him, though grateful and even tender, had no longing in it. The little globe of crystal still hung at her watch-chain, recalling, when it met her eye, a pleasant memory of those spring days they had spent together; but for that reminder she might perhaps not have thought of him at all. She had never seen him, and all that she knew of him could be briefly told. On the outbreak of the war he had entered the Confederate army, held the rank of colonel, and fought with reckless bravery. But becoming offended at some real or fancied slight put upon him by his commanding officer, he resigned his commission; and the next thing known of him he was enlisted on the Union side. Probably he was actuated each time more by a love of adventure than by any special sympathy with the cause either of Union or rebellion. Severely wounded in the third year of the war, he again withdrew from the service, and returned to Cuba. At Havana he had a quarrel—it was only about a dog—with an Englishman in the street; and the result was a duel, in which the Englishman was killed. To avoid the consequences of this affair he went to Mexico; and in that ever-seething caldron of revolution and tumult he was finally lost to view.

One evening late in September—it was the twenty-ninth, as she had reason afterward to note—Miss Darrington sat alone in the little room which served her as a study. It was a narrow but lofty apartment, its single high-arched window looked westward over the green trees of a square, with a glimpse of the Charles Riving shining beyond. A library table, a single tall book-case, a lounge, a bust or two, some flowers in the window—these were nearly all the objects noticeable in the room.

Miss Darrington, who had been unusually busy all day, laid down her pen, and, leaning wearily back in her arm-chair, turned her eyes on the glowing evening sky. It had been a day of unusual beauty, very warm for the season; and the sun was setting in a sky soft, brilliant, and clear. A flood of yellow light streamed on the quiet river and brightened the distant view. The spires and leafy domes of Cambridge swam in a golden haze. The softened radiance filled the little room, and, falling about the lady herself, seemed to wrap her in an atmosphere of reverie. She was dreamily conscious of the beauty of the parting day; but she was not thinking of that, or, indeed, of any thing definite. She was, in fact, physically and mentally tired; and it was perhaps owing to this that a kind of depression stole over her—not really a sense of pain or sorrow, only a heavy languor of spirit, a feeling more tinged with the hue of sadness than was habitual with her. A long time elapsed. The sunlight slowly withdrew; the splendor of the sky passed into the paleness of evening, and a few of the larger stars began to show them selves; but still she remained motionless, and half unconscious of place or time.

"Isabel!"

The name was uttered almost at her elbow in a low, clear voice, whose accents were unmistakable, even if she had not on the instant remembered who alone in all the world had ever called her by that name. She turned eagerly to welcome the unexpected guest. "Raphael!" she exclaimed, in accents of undisguised pleasure.

He was standing just within the room. The door, a heavy one, was closed; and she wondered in a flash of thought how it could have opened to admit him unheard by her. She half rose to meet him; but a strange thrill shot through her, and an irresistible force bound her to her seat. She looked at him fixedly. There was still enough of brightness in the fading twilight for her to recognize unmistakably his form and features. But his face was very pale, and there was a look upon it unlike any thing she had ever seen there. So sad, yet so still—so full of some strange calm—it filled her with awe. She noticed that he wore a dress half military in its character, with some tarnished gold embroidery upon the breast, and a large cloak, thrown back and falling from his shoulders as he stood, his hat in his hand, in an attitude of careless grace she well remembered. He was so near she could almost have touched him with her hand. But yet he never spoke; only his lips parted with a tender smile, and his eyes dwelt on her with a glance so intense, so full of fathomless love and sorrow, it was more than her heart could bear.

She tried to speak; but though her lips shaped his name, her voice died away in a husky whisper. Suddenly over the pale sad face broke a look of rapturous joy—a smile like the sunshine of heaven; and in that instant the figure vanished—was gone utterly in a breath; and the lady felt that she was alone.

Miss Darrington is not a nervous woman, but it was some minutes before she could summon sufficient calmness to act, or even to think. Then she rang her bell, and a servant came to the door. "Come in," she said, in answer to his respectful tap. But when he attempted to obey her the door was found locked on the inside. She remembered that she had herself turned the key some hours before to secure herself from interruption. Moreover, the man, on being questioned, declared with evident truth that no visitor had passed in or out of the house since noon. It was by a strong effort of will that she now drove back the superstitious feelings that assaulted her, and forced a smile at her own absurdity. Of course the thing was an illusion, a trick of the imagination played on by nerves overworn with work. It was odd, though, that imagination should have raised up so vividly the image of one who certainly had not recently been in her thoughts. Then, too, her memory could hardly have supplied some details of this vision; they were unfamiliar. Where could she have got the picture of her friend in that garb? The wide gray cloak, the gold-laced military dress—these were very unlike the negligent white linen suit in which she remembered him. Only on one occasion had she seen him dressed otherwise, and that was the day when he rode to L, to sit for the photograph which still hung at her side. On that day he had put on a black evening dress. Then the voice which had uttered her name—a name which only he had ever applied to her. How could imagination have raised that sound in her ear with such suddenness as to give her a shock of surprise?

It was odd, certainly; but she did not choose to indulge herself in morbid fancies upon the subject. Convinced that a low physical condition was really responsible for the illusion of which she had been the victim, she resolutely put the whole thing out of her mind, and set herself to get back the healthy tone to which nature entitled her. She left off writing, rode and walked frequently, and went much into society. But she was not able to dissipate the impression made upon her mind by what she had seen. Whenever she thought of it it was with a renewal of the same strange thrill which she had contended with at the time. She could not help recalling certain words which Raphael had once spoken to her, how he had vowed to seek her through the universe when death should have left him free to do so. Could such things be? And had death really freed that fiery and generous spirit? If so, where and when had he passed away? In a country so full of political and social turmoil as Mexico it was easy to imagine all possible contingencies, especially with a man of his temper. She found herself frequently turning to the columns of "Mexican correspondence" in the newspapers, for the chance of lighting upon his name; yet she knew well how easy it would be, in the chaos of that country, for a single stranger to vanish out of life and leave no trace. And then she told herself again that this was all nonsense and nerves; that her old friend was probably alive and well somewhere, and that he had forgotten her as completely as if she had never crossed his path. So, by degrees, the intensity of her first impression wore off, and her mind was regaining its accustomed poise, when a new incident occurred.

Tom Sibthorpe, at the close of the war, had settled himself to the practice of law in New York. He and Miss Darrington often met, and a warm friendship had grown up between them, kept alive by a frequent correspondence, not sentimental, but much like that which two clever men are apt to enjoy. One day early in December the lady received a letter from her friend, in which, after discussing in a lively manner one or two items of personal gossip, a new book, and the last bon-mot, the writer said:

"Have you heard that it is all over with our poor friend Aldama? He was one of the few victims of the almost bloodless revolution with which sleepy old Spain has just been astonishing the world. I was not unprepared to hear of him as involved in that affair, for I knew that the dream of a free and regenerated Spain had taken strong hold upon him. You remember that, notwithstanding his long residence in Cuba, he was always intensely a Spaniard in feeling. Seven or eight months ago he went to London, and fell in with Prim and his conclave of schemers. Of course they made much of him, for he was just the man for their purposes. His reckless courage, his familiarity with every species of dangerous adventure, his indifference to the ordinary objects of ambition, which took him out of the list of rivals, and the immense wealth at his command, would make him invaluable to them. He entered heart and soul into their schemes; but he seems to have been haunted by a presentiment that his life would be the cost. Some time in the summer he wrote me a long letter, in which, though it had occasional flashes of his old self, it was plain to see that he was oppressed by some strong foreboding. His life, he said, had never been of any use to himself or any one. He had wasted it all in the pursuit of a pleasure he had never found, chasing a phantom of happiness which had forever fled before him. It might partly redeem the worthlessness of such a life if he could strike one blow for Spain and liberty. If his country was to be free, some of her sons must bleed for her, and he could at least die as well as a better man. Then suddenly changing both his tone and topic, he referred to our school-days together, recalling certain wild frolics we two had shared, in a gay and witty way that made me laugh then, but which now I can only think upon with tears. That was the last I heard from him until a few days ago, when a letter from my sister Alice, who, as you know, is married to Mr. Manners, an Englishman living in Madrid, gave me the whole sad story.

"It was in the month of August that Raphael, choosing, as usual, the post of greatest danger, went from Paris to Madrid, to communicate with the heads of the conspiracy there. The southern provinces were already alive with insurrection, but none of his friends in the city thought of connecting him with the movement. Only George Manners, a young relative of my brother-in-law, became, to some extent, his confidant, and was deeply infected with his enthusiasm. The thing must have been well managed, for the extent and power of the uprising would seem to have been quite unrecognized. But events, as you know, moved very fast. The absence of the Queen from her capital furnished the insurgents with just the opportunity they required, and immediately the revolt became a revolution. Raphael, who must have held in his hands some important threads of the affair, remained in the city until the resignations of the Queen's ministry; but on the 20th of September he left Madrid to put himself in communication with Serrano, who was marching to give battle to the royalist forces. George Manners went with him, telling Alice that there was going to be a row, and he wanted to see it. A fortnight later George came back alone. The account he gives is not very clear as to details, but the main facts are plain enough.

"They succeeded in joining Serrano's forces a day or two before the engagement, which occurred on the 28th of September, not very far from Cordova; my recollection of the place, as named in the newspaper reports, is a little at fault. Raphael had a command, and in the action became separated from his friend. When the fight was over, the Queen's troops defeated and scattered, Manners tried in vain to find him. The young man had himself been taken prisoner, and only released when his captors found him a hinderance to flight, so his knowledge of the incidents of the fight was a good deal confused. After a two days' search, however, he learned that a wounded officer had been carried by some of his men into the hut of a peasant, the locality of which was pointed out to him, and had since died there. He hastened to the place, and in the still, cold form that lay there alone on a rude bench, covered with a rough cavalry cloak, he recognized his friend and ours."

Miss Darrington paused in her reading, and her breath came short and quick. The 28th of September! And he had lived for some hours after—how long she would never know. But she recalled with a shock that made every nerve quiver that it was on the evening of the 29th of September that she had seemed to see him in her own room!

It was some time before she could command herself sufficiently to go on with the letter.

"Poor Raphael," the writer continued; "there were splendid possibilities in him, if a bad education had not spoiled their promise. I hardly knew until he was gone how dear he had been to me. We were almost like brothers; and yet I know that he never fully revealed himself to me, and never would. After that visit to Catalpa Grove he was more than ever reserved. He was greatly changed, too; his boyish high spirits had vanished, and he seemed colder, graver, older by many years. I could not fail to see that his nature had been stirred to its profoundest deeps by some experience—whether of joy or pain I never knew. The key to his secret was not in my hands. Dear friend, I believe that if any one possessed such a key it was yourself. You knew him but a little while, but you read him far better than I. No need to tell you how rich in high impulses, in noble aspirations, was that generous, ungoverned soul. But the world was out of joint for him always. Only once did any hope to set it right seem offered him, and he missed that. If he had not—But forgive me. I am speculating upon contingencies which, per haps, were never possible."

Miss Darrington read no farther. The letter dropped from her hands, and her face was buried in them, while hot tears forced themselves through her fingers—tears of remorseful tenderness, as she thought how little she had prized, how little deserved, that strong, true, generous love which had held her to the last in such tender re-membrance; which had made its way across the ocean, across the wider, deeper gulf that divides us from the unseen world, to give to her the greeting of lips that were sealed, the last loving look of eyes that were forever closed to all on earth be-side!

She believed that. If you doubt it—if you think it can not be—will you tell me what it was that Miss Darrington saw?

A GHOST STORY,
by Mark Twain

I took a large room, far up Broadway, in a huge old building whose upper stories had been wholly unoccupied for years until I came. The place had long been given up to dust and cobwebs, to solitude and silence. I seemed groping among the tombs and invading the privacy of the dead, that first night I climbed up to my quarters. For the first time in my life a superstitious dread came over me; and as I turned a dark angle of the stairway and an invisible cobweb swung its slazy woof in my face and clung there, I shuddered as one who had encountered a phantom.

I was glad enough when I reached my room and locked out the mold and the darkness. A cheery fire was burning in the grate, and I sat down before it with a comforting sense of relief. For two hours I sat there, thinking of bygone times; recalling old scenes, and summoning half-forgotten faces out of the mists of the past; listening, in fancy, to voices that long ago grew silent for all time, and to once familiar songs that nobody sings now. And as my reverie softened down to a sadder and sadder pathos, the shrieking of the winds outside softened to a wail, the angry beating of the rain against the panes diminished to a tranquil patter, and one by one the noises in the street subsided, until the hurrying footsteps of the last belated straggler died away in the distance and left no sound behind.

The fire had burned low. A sense of loneliness crept over me. I arose and undressed, moving on tiptoe about the room, doing stealthily what I had to do, as if I were environed by sleeping enemies whose slumbers it would be fatal to break. I covered up in bed, and lay listening to the rain and wind and the faint creaking of distant shutters, till they lulled me to sleep.

I slept profoundly, but how long I do not know. All at once I found myself awake, and filled with a shuddering expectancy. All was still. All but my own heart —I could hear it beat. Presently the bedclothes began to slip away slowly toward the foot of the bed, as if some one were pulling them! I could not stir; I could not speak. Still the blankets slipped deliberately away, till my breast was uncovered. Then with a great effort I seized them and drew them over my head. I waited, listened, waited. Once more that steady pull began, and once more I lay torpid a century of dragging seconds till my breast was naked again. At last I roused my energies and snatched the covers back to their place and held them with a strong grip. I waited. By and by I felt a faint tug, and took a fresh grip. The tug strengthened to a steady strain—it grew stronger and stronger. My hold parted, and for the third time the blankets slid away. I groaned. An answering groan came from the foot of the bed! Beaded drops of sweat stood upon my forehead. I was more dead than alive. Presently I heard a heavy footstep in my room—the step of an elephant, it seemed to me—it was not like anything human. But it was moving from me—there was relief in that. I heard it approach the door—pass out without moving bolt or lock— and wander away among the dismal corridors, straining the floors and joists till they creaked again as it passed—and then silence reigned once more.

When my excitement had calmed, I said to myself, "This is a dream—simply a hideous dream." And so I lay thinking it over until I convinced myself that it was a dream, and then a comforting laugh relaxed my lips and I was happy again. I got up and struck a light; and when I found that the locks and bolts were just as I had left them, another soothing laugh welled in my heart and rippled from my lips. I took my pipe and lit it, and was just sitting down before the fire, when—down went the pipe out of my nerveless fingers, the blood forsook my cheeks, and my placid breathing was cut short with a gasp! In the ashes on the hearth, side by side with my own bare footprint, was another, so vast that in comparison mine was but an infant's! Then I had had a visitor, and the elephant tread was explained.

I put out the light and returned to bed, palsied with fear. I lay a long time, peering into the darkness, and listening.—Then I heard a grating noise overhead, like the dragging of a heavy body across the floor; then the throwing down of the body, and the shaking of my windows in response to the concussion. In distant parts of the building I heard the muffled slamming of doors. I heard, at intervals, stealthy footsteps creeping in and out among the corridors, and up and down the stairs. Sometimes these noises approached my door, hesitated, and went away again. I heard the clanking of chains faintly, in remote passages, and listened while the clanking grew nearer—while it wearily climbed the stairways, marking each move by the loose surplus of chain that fell with an accented rattle upon each succeeding step as the goblin that bore it advanced. I heard muttered sentences; half-uttered screams that seemed smothered violently; and the swish of invisible garments, the rush of invisible wings. Then I became conscious that my chamber was invaded— that I was not alone. I heard sighs and breathings about my bed, and mysterious whisperings. Three little spheres of soft phosphorescent light appeared on the ceiling directly over my head, clung and glowed there a moment, and then dropped— two of them upon my face and one upon the pillow. They, spattered, liquidly, and felt warm. Intuition told me they had—turned to gouts of blood as they fell—I needed no light to satisfy myself of that. Then I saw pallid faces, dimly luminous, and white uplifted hands, floating bodiless in the air—floating a moment and then disappearing. The whispering ceased, and the voices and the sounds, anal a solemn stillness followed. I waited and listened. I felt that I must have light or die. I was weak with fear. I slowly raised myself toward a sitting posture, and my face came in contact with a clammy hand! All strength went from me apparently, and I fell back like a stricken invalid. Then I heard the rustle of a garment it seemed to pass to the door and go out.

When everything was still once more, I crept out of bed, sick and feeble, and lit the gas with a hand that trembled as if it were aged with a hundred years. The light brought some little cheer to my spirits. I sat down and fell into a dreamy contemplation of that great footprint in the ashes. By and by its outlines began to waver and grow dim. I glanced up and the broad gas-flame was slowly wilting away. In the same moment I heard that elephantine tread again. I noted its approach, nearer and nearer, along the musty halls, and dimmer and dimmer the light waned. The tread reached my very door and paused—the light had dwindled to a sickly blue, and all things about me lay in a spectral twilight. The door did not open, and yet I felt a faint gust of air fan my cheek, and presently was conscious of a huge, cloudy presence before me. I watched it with fascinated eyes. A pale glow stole over the Thing; gradually its cloudy folds took shape—an arm appeared, then legs, then a body, and last a great sad face looked out of the vapor. Stripped of its filmy housings, naked, muscular and comely, the majestic Cardiff Giant loomed above me!

All my misery vanished—for a child might know that no harm could come with that benignant countenance. My cheerful spirits returned at once, and in sympathy with them the gas flamed up brightly again. Never a lonely outcast was so glad to welcome company as I was to greet the friendly giant. I said:

"Why, is it nobody but you? Do you know, I have been scared to death for the last two or three hours? I am most honestly glad to see you. I wish I had a chair— Here, here, don't try to sit down in that thing—"

But it was too late. He was in it before I could stop him and down he went—I never saw a chair shivered so in my life.

"Stop, stop, you'll ruin ev—"

Too late again. There was another crash, and another chair was resolved into its original elements.

"Confound it, haven't you got any judgment at' all? Do you want to ruin all the furniture on the place? Here, here, you petrified fool—"

But it was no use. Before I could arrest him he had sat down on the bed, and it was a melancholy ruin.

"Now what sort of a way is that to do? First you come lumbering about the place bringing a legion of vagabond goblins along with you to worry me to death, and then when I overlook an indelicacy of costume which would not be tolerated any-where by cultivated people except in a respectable theater, and not even there if the nudity were of your sex, you repay me by wrecking all the furniture you can find to sit down on. And why will you? You damage yourself as much as you do me. You have broken off the end of your spinal column, and littered up the floor with chips of your hams till the place looks like a marble yard. You ought to be ashamed of yourself—you are big enough to know better."

"Well, I will not break any more furniture. But what am I to do? I have not had a chance to sit down for a century." And the tears came into his eyes.

"Poor devil," I said, "I should not have been so harsh with you. And you are an orphan, too, no doubt. But sit down on the floor here—nothing else can stand your weight—and besides, we cannot be sociable with you away up there above me; I want you down where I can perch on this high counting-house stool and gossip with you face to face."

So he sat down on the floor, and lit a pipe which I gave him, threw one of my red blankets over his shoulders, inverted my sitz-bath on his head, helmet fashion, and made himself picturesque and comfortable. Then he crossed his ankles, while I renewed the fire, and exposed the flat, honeycombed bottoms of his prodigious feet to the grateful warmth.

"What is the matter with the bottom of your feet and the back of your legs, that they are gouged up so?"

"Infernal chilblains—I caught them clear up to the back of my head, roosting out there under Newell's farm. But I love the place; I love it as one loves his old home. There is no peace for me like the peace I feel when I am there."

We talked along for half an hour, and then I noticed that he looked tired, and spoke of it.

"Tired?" he said. "Well, I should think so. And now I will tell you all about it, since you have treated me so well. I am the spirit of the Petrified Man that lies across the street there in the museum. I am the ghost of the Cardiff Giant. I can have no rest, no peace, till they have given that poor body burial again. Now what was the most natural thing for me to do, to make men satisfy this wish? Terrify them into it! haunt the place where the body lay! So I haunted the museum night after night. I even got other spirits to help me. But it did no good, for nobody ever came to the museum at midnight. Then it occurred to me to come over the way and haunt this place a little. I felt that if I ever got a hearing I must succeed, for I had the most efficient company that perdition could furnish. Night after night we have shivered around through these mildewed halls, dragging chains, groaning, whisper-ing, tramping up and down stairs, till, to tell you the truth, I am almost worn out. But when I saw a light in your room tonight I roused my energies again and went at it with a deal of the old freshness. But I am tired out—entirely fagged out. Give me, I beseech you, give me some hope!" I lit off my perch in a burst of excitement, and exclaimed:

"This transcends everything! everything that ever did occur! Why you poor blundering old fossil, you have had all your trouble for nothing—you have been haunting a plaster cast of yourself—the real Cardiff Giant is in Albany!—[A fact. The original fraud was ingeniously and fraudfully duplicated, and exhibited in New York as the 'only genuine' Cardiff Giant (to the unspeakable disgust of the owners of the real colossus) at the very same time that the latter was drawing crowds at a museum is Albany,]—Confound it, don't you know your own remains?"

I never saw such an eloquent look of shame, of pitiable humiliation, overspread a countenance before.

The Petrified Man rose slowly to his feet, and said:

"Honestly, is that true?"

"As true as I am sitting here."

He took the pipe from his mouth and laid it on the mantel, then stood irresolute a moment (unconsciously, from old habit, thrusting his hands where his pantaloons pockets should have been, and meditatively dropping his chin on his breast); and fi-nally said:

"Well—I never felt so absurd before. The Petrified Man has sold everybody else, and now the mean fraud has ended by selling its own ghost! My son, if there is any charity left in your heart for a poor friendless phantom like me, don't let this get out. Think how you would feel if you had made such an ass of yourself."

I heard his stately tramp die away, step by step down the stairs and out into the deserted street, and felt sorry that he was gone, poor fellow—and sorrier still that he had carried off my red blanket and my bathtub.

THE SOUL OF ROSE DÉDÉ,
by M.E.M. Davis

The child pushed his way though the tall weeds, which were dripping with the midsummer-eve midnight dew-melt. He was so little that the rough leaves met above his head. He wore a trailing white gown whose loose folds tripped him, so that he stumbled and fell over a sunken mound. But he laughed as he scrambled to his feet—a cooing baby laugh, taken up by the inward-blowing Gulf-wind, and carried away to the soughing pines that made a black line against the dim sky.

His progress was slow, for he stopped—his forehead gravely puckered, his finger in his mouth—to listen to the clear whistle of a mocking-bird in the live-oak above his head; he watched the heavy flight of a white night-moth from one jimsonweed trumpet to another; he strayed aside to pick a bit of shining punk from the sloughing bark of a rotten log; he held this in his closed palm as he came at last into the open space where the others were.

"Holà, 'Tit-Pierre!" said André, who was half reclining on a mildewed marble slab, with his long black cloak floating loosely from his shoulders, and his hands clasped about his knees. "Holà! Must thou needs be ever a-searching! Have I not told thee, little Hard-Head, that she hath long forgotten thee?"

His voice was mocking, but his dark eyes were quizzically kind.

The child's under lip quivered, and he turned slowly about. But Père Lebas, sitting just across the narrow footway, laid a caressing hand on his curly head. "Nay, go thy way, 'Tit Pierre," he said, gently; "André does but tease. A mother hath never yet forgot her child."

"Do you indeed think he will find her?" asked André, arching his black brows incredulously.

"He will not find her," returned the priest. "Margot Caillion was in a far country when I saw her last, and even then her grandchildren were playing about her knees. But it harms not the child to seek her."

They spoke a soft provincial French, and the familiar *thou* betokened an unwonted intimacy between the hollow-cheeked old priest and his companion, whose forehead wore the frankness of early youth.

"I would the child could talk!" cried the young man, gayly. "Then might he tell us somewhat of the women that ever come and go in yonder great house."

The priest shuddered, crossing himself, and drew his cowl over his face.

'Tit-Pierre, his gown gathered in his arm, had gone on his way. Nathan Pilger, hunched up on a low, irregular hummock against the picket-fence, made a speaking-trumpet of his two horny hands, and pretended to hail him as he passed. 'Tit-Pierre nodded brightly at the old man, and waved his own chubby fist.

The gate sagged a little on its hinges, so that he had some difficulty in moving it. But he squeezed through a narrow opening, and passed between the prim flower beds to the house.

It was a lofty mansion, with vast wings on either side, and wide galleries, which were upheld by fluted columns. It faced the bay, and a covered arcade ran from the entrance across the lawn to a gay little wooden kiosk, which hung on the bluff over the water's edge. A flight of stone steps led up to the house. 'Tit-Pierre climbed these laboriously. The great carved doors were closed, but a blind of one of the long French windows in the west wing stood slightly ajar. 'Tit-Pierre pushed this open. The bedchamber into which he peered was large and luxuriously furnished. A lamp with a crimson shade burned on its claw-footed gilt pedestal in a corner; the low light diffused a rosy radiance about the room. The filmy curtains at the windows waved to and fro softly in the June night wind. The huge old-fashioned, four-posted bed, overhung by a baldachin of carved wood with satin linings, occupied a deep alcove. A woman was sleeping there beneath, the lace netting. The snow-white bedlinen followed the contours of her rounded limbs, giving her the look of a recumbent marble statue. Her black hair, loosed from its heavy coil, spread over the pillow. One exquisite bare arm lay across her forehead, partly concealing her face. Her measured breathing rose and fell rhythmically on the air. A robe of pale silk that hung across a chair, dainty lace-edged garments tossed carelessly on an antique lounge—these seemed instinct still with the nameless, subtle grace of her who had but now put them off.

On a table by the window, upon whose threshold the child stood atiptoe, was set a large crystal bowl filled with water-lilies. Their white petals were folded; the round, red-lined green leaves glistened in the lamp light. One long bud, rolled tightly in its green and brown sheath, hung over the fluted edge of the bowl, sway-ing gently on its flexible stem. 'Tit-Pierre gazed at it intently, frowning a little, then put out a small forefinger and touched it. A quick thrill ran along the stem; the bud moved lightly from side to side and burst suddenly into bloom; the slim white petals quivered; a tremulous, sighing, whispering sound issued from the heart of gold. The child listened, holding the fragrant disk to his pink ear, and laughed softly.

He moved about the room, examining with infantile curiosity the costly objects scattered upon small tables and ranged upon the low, many-shelved mantel.

Presently he pushed a chair against the foot of the bed, climbed upon it, lifted the netting, and crept cautiously to the sleeper's side. He sat for a moment regard-ing her. Her lips were parted in a half-smile; the long lashes which swept her cheeks were wet, as if a happy tear had just trembled there. 'Tit-Pierre laid his hand on her smooth wrist, and touched timidly the snowy globes that gleamed beneath the openwork of her night-dress. She threw up her arm, turning her face full upon him, unclosed her large, luminous eyes, smiled, and slept again.

With a sigh, which seemed rather of resignation than of disappointment, the child crept away and clambered again to the floor.

.... Outside the fog was thickening. The dark waters of the bay lapped the foot of the low bluff; their soft, monotonous moan was rising by imperceptible degrees to a higher key. The scrubby cedars, leaning at all angles over the water, were shaken at intervals by heavy puffs of wind, which drove the mist in white, ragged masses across the shelled road, over the weedy neutral ground, and out into the tops of the sombre pines. The red lights in a row of sloops at anchor over against Cat Is-land had dwindled to faintly glimmering sparks. The watery flash of the revolving light in the light-house off the point of the island showed a black wedge-shaped cloud stretching up the seaward sky.

Nathan Pilger screwed up his eye and watched the cloud critically. André fol-lowed the direction of his gaze with idle interest, then turned to look again at the woman who sat on a grassy barrow a few paces beyond Père Lebas.

"She has never been here before," he said to himself, his heart stirring curiously. "I would I could see her face!"

215

Her back was towards the little group; her elbow was on her knee, her chin in her hand. Her figure was slight and girlish; her white gown gleamed ghost-like in the wan light.

"Naw, I bain't complainin', nor nothin'," said the old sailor, dropping the cloud, as it were, and taking up a broken thread of talk; "hows'ever, it's tarnation wearyin' a-settin' here so studdy year in an' year out. Leas'ways," he added, shifting his seat to another part of the low mound, "fer an old sailor sech as I be."

"If one could but quit his place and move about, like 'Tit-Pierre yonder," said André, musingly, "it would not be so bad. For myself, I would not want——"

"The child is free to come and go because his soul is white. There is no stain upon 'Tit-Pierre. The child hath not sinned." It was the priest who spoke. His voice was harsh and forbidding. His deep-set eyes were fixed upon the tall spire of Our Lady of the Gulf, dimly outlined against the sky beyond an intervening reach of clustering roofs and shaded gardens.

André stared at him wonderingly, and glanced half furtively at the stranger, as if in her presence, perchance, might be found an explanation of the speaker's un-wonted bitterness of tone. She had not moved. "I would I could see her face!" he muttered, under his breath. "For myself," he went on, lifting his voice, "I am sure I would not want to wander far. I fain would walk once more on the road along the curve of the bay; or under the pines, where little white patches of moonlight fall be-tween the straight, tall tree trunks. And I would go sometimes, if I might, and kneel before the altar of Our Lady of the Gulf."

Nathan Pilger grunted contemptuously. "What a lan'lubber ye be, Andry!" he said, his strong nasal English contrasting oddly with the smooth foreign speech of the others. "What a lan'lubber ye be! Ye bain't no sailor, like your father afore ye. Tony Dewdonny hed as good a pair o' sealegs as ever I see. Lord! if there wa'n't no *diffick*ulties in the way, Nathan Pilger 'ud ship fer some port a leetle more furrin than the shadder of Our Lady yunder! Many's the deck I've walked," he continued, his husky voice growing more and more animated, "an' many's the vige I've made to outlandish places. Why, you'd oughter see Arkangel, Andry. Here's the north coast o' Rooshy"—he leaned over and traced with his forefinger the rude outlines of a map on the ground; the wind lifted his long, gray locks and tossed them over his wrinkled forehead; "here's the White Sea; and here, off the mouth of the Dewiny River, is Arkangel. The Rooshan men in that there town, Andry, wears pet-ticoats like women; whilse down here, in the South Pacific, at Taheety, the folks don't wear no clo'es at all to speak of! You'd oughter see Taheety, Andry. An' here, off Guinea——"

"All those places are fine, no doubt," interrupted his listener, "Arkangel and Taheetee and Guinee"—his tongue tripped a little over the unfamiliar names—"but, for myself, I do not care to see them. I find it well on the bay shore here, where I can see the sloops come sailing in through the pass, with the sun on their white sails. And the little boats that rock on the water! Do you remember, Silvain," he cried, turning to the priest, "how we used to steal away before sunrise in my fa-ther's little fishing-boat, when we were boys, and come back at night with our backs blistered by the sun and our arms aching, hein? That was before you went away to France to study for the priesthood. Ah, but those were good times!" He threw back his head and laughed joyously. His dark hair, wet with the mist, lay in loose rings on his forehead; his fine young face, beardless but manly, seemed al-most lustrous in the pale darkness. "Do you remember, Silvain? Right where the big house stands, there was Jacques Caillion's steep-roofed cottage, with the garden in front full of pinks and mignonette and sweet herbs; and the vine-hung porch where 'Tit-Pierre used to play, and where Margot Caillion used to stand shading her eyes with her arm, and looking out for her man to come home from sea."

"Jack Caillion," said Nathan Pilger, "was washed overboard from the *Suzanne* in a storm off Hatteras in '11—him and Dunc Cook and Ba'tist' Roux."

"The old church of Our Lady of the Gulf," the young man continued, "was just a stone's-throw this side of where the new one was built; back a little is our cottage, and your father's, Silvain; and in the hollow beyond Justin Roux has his blacksmith's forge."

He paused, his voice dying away almost to a whisper. The waves were beating more noisily against the bluff, filling the silence with a sort of hoarse plaint; the fog—gray, soft, impenetrable—rested on them like a cloud. The moisture fell in an audible drip-drop from the leaves and the long, pendent moss of the live-oaks. A mare, with her colt beside her, came trotting around the bend of the road. She approached within a few feet of the girl, reared violently, snorting, and dashed away, followed by the whinnying colt. The clatter of their feet echoed on the muffled air. The girl, in her white dress, sat rigidly motionless, with her face turned seaward.

André lifted his head and went on, dreamily: "I mind me, most of all, of one day when all the girls and boys of the village walked over to Bayou Galère to gather water-lilies. Margot Caillion, with 'Tit-Pierre in her hand, came along to mind the girls. You had but just come back from France in your priest's frock, Silvain. You were in the church door when we passed, with your book in your hand." A smothered groan escaped the priest, and he threw up his arm as if to ward off a blow. "And you were there when we came back at sunset. The smell of the pines that day was like balm. The lilies were white on the dark breast of the winding bayou. Rose Dédé's arms were heaped so full of lilies that you could only see her laughing black eyes above them. But Lorance would only take a few buds. She said it was a kind of sin to take them away from the water where they grew. Lorance was ever——"

The girl had dropped her hands in her lap, and was listening. At the sound of her own name she turned her face towards the speaker.

"*Lorance!*" gasped André. "Is it truly you, Lorance?"

"Yes, it is I, André Dieudonné," she replied, quietly. Her pale girlish face, with its delicate outlines, was crowned with an aureole of bright hair, which hung in two thick braids to her waist; her soft brown eyes were a little sunken, as if she had wept overmuch. But her voice was strangely cold and passionless.

"But ... when did you ... come, Lorance?" André demanded, breathlessly.

"I came," she said, in the same calm, measured tone, "but a little after you, André Dieudonné. First 'Tit-Pierre, then you, and then myself."

"Why, then——" he began. He rose abruptly, gathering his mantle about him, and leaned over the marble slab where he had been sitting. "'*Sacred to the memory of André Antoine Marie Dieudonné,*'" he read, slowly, slipping his finger along the mouldy French lettering, "'*who died at this place August 20th, 1809. In the 22d year of his age.*' Eighty years and more ago I came!" he cried. "And you have been here all these years, Lorance, and I have not known! Why, then, did you never come up?"

She did not answer at once. "I was tired," she said, presently, "and I rested well down there in the cool, dark silence. And I was not lonely ... at first, for I heard Margot Caillion passing about, putting flowers above 'Tit-Pierre and you and me. My mother and yours often came and wept with her for us all—and my father, and your little brothers. The sound of their weeping comforted me. Then ... after a while ... no one seemed to remember us any more."

"Margot Caillion," said Nathan Pilger, "went back, when her man was drownded, to the place in France where she was born. The others be all layin' in the old church-yard yander on the hill ... all but Silvann Leebaw an' me."

She looked at the old man and smiled gravely. "A long time passed," she went on, slowly. "I could sometimes hear you speak to 'Tit-Pierre, André Dieudonné; ... and at last some men came and dug quite near me; and as they pushed their spades through the moist turf they talked about the good Père Lebas; and then I knew that Silvain was coming." The priest's head fell upon his breast; he covered his face with his hands and rocked to and fro on his low seat. "Not long after, Nathan Pilger came. Down there in my narrow chamber I have heard above me, year after year, the murmur of your voices on St. John's eve, and ever the feet of 'Tit-Pierre, as he goes back and forth seeking his mother. But I cared not to leave my place. For why should I wish to look upon your face, André Dieudonné, and mark there the memory of your love for Rose Dédé?"

Her voice shook with a sudden passion as she uttered the last words. The hands lying in her lap were twisted together convulsively; a flush leaped into her pale cheeks.

"Rose Dédé!" echoed André, amazedly. "Nay, Lorance, but I never loved Rose Dédé! If she perchance cared for me——"

"Silence, fool!" cried the priest, sternly. He had thrown back his cowl; his eyes glowed like coals in his white face; he lifted his hand menacingly. "Thou wert ever a vain puppet, André Dieudonné. It was not for such as thou that Rose Dédé sinned away her soul! Was it *thou* she came at midnight to meet in the lone shadows of these very live-oaks? Hast *thou* ever worn the garments of a priest? ... They shunned Rose Dédé in the village ... but the priest said mass at the altar of Our Lady of the Gulf ... and the wail of the babe was sharp in the hut under the pines ... and it ceased to breathe ... and the mother turned her face to the wall and died ... and my heart was cold in my breast as I looked on the dead faces of the mother and the child.... They lie under the pine-trees by Bayou Galère. But the priest lived to old age; ... and when he died, he durst not sleep in consecrated ground, but fain would lie in the shadows of the live-oaks, where the dark eyes of Rose Dédé looked love into his."

His wild talk fell upon unheeding ears. 'Tit-Pierre had come out of the house. He was nestling against Nathan Pilger's knee. He held a lily-bud in one hand, and with the other he caressed the sailor's weather-beaten cheek.

"'Tit-Pierre," whispered the old man, "that is Lorance Baudrot. Do you remember her, 'Tit-Pierre?" The child smiled intelligently. "Lorance was but a slip of a girl when I come down here from Cape Cod—cabin-boy aboard the *Mary Ann*. She was the pretties' lass on all the bay shore. An' I—I loved her, 'Tit-Pierre. But I wa'n't no match agin Andry Dewdonny; an' I know'd it from the fust. Andry was the likelies' lad hereabout, an' the harnsomes'. I see that Lorance loved him. An' when the yaller fever took him, I see her a-droopin' an' a-droopin' tell she died, an' she never even know'd I loved her. Her an' Andry was laid here young, 'Tit-Pierre, 'longside o' you. I lived ter be pretty tol'able old; but when I hed made my last vige, an' was about fetchin' my las' breath, I give orders ter be laid in this here old buryin'-groun' some'er's clost ter the grave o' Lorance Baudrot."

His voice was overborne by André's exultant tones. "Lorance!" he cried, "did you indeed love me?—*me!*"

Her dark eyes met his frankly, and she smiled.

"Ah, if I had only known!" he sighed—"if had only known, Lorance, I would surely have lived! We would have walked one morning to Our Lady of the Gulf, with all the village-folk about us, and Silvain—the good Père Lebas—would have joined our hands.... My father would have given us a little plot of ground; ... you would have planted flowers about the door of our cottage; ... our children would have played in the sand under the bluff...."

A sudden gust of wind blew the fog aside, and a zigzag of flame tore the wedge-shaped cloud in two. A greenish light played for an instant over the weed-grown spot. The mocking-bird, long silent in the heart of the live-oak, began to sing.

"All these years you have been near me," he murmured, reproachfully, "and I did not know." Then, as if struck by a breathless thought, he stretched out his arms imploringly. "I love you, Lorance," he said. "I have always loved you. Will you not be my wife now? Silvain will say the words, and 'Tit-Pierre, who can go back and forth, will put this ring, which was my mother's, upon your finger, and he will bring me a curl of your soft hair to twist about mine. I cannot come to you, Lorance; I cannot even touch your hand. But when I go down into my dark place I can be content dreaming of you. And on the blessed St. John's eves I will know you are mine, as you sit there in your white gown."

As he ceased speaking, Père Lebas, with his head upon his breast, began murmuring, as if mechanically, the words which preface the holy sacrament of marriage. His voice faltered, he raised his head, and a cry of wonder burst from his lips. For André had moved away from the mouldy gravestone and stood just in front of him. Lorance, as if upborne on invisible wings, was floating lightly across the intervening space. Her shroud enveloped her like a cloud, her arms were extended, her lips were parted in a rapt smile. Nathan Pilger, with 'Tit-Pierre in his arms, had limped forward. He halted beside André, and as the young man folded the girl to his breast, the child reached over and laid an open lily on her down-drooped head.

The priest stared wildly at them, and struggled to rise, but could not. As he sank panting back upon the crumbling tomb, his anguish overcame him. "My God!" he groaned hoarsely, "I, only I, cannot move from my place. *The soul of Rose Dédé hangs like a millstone about my neck!*"

Even as he spoke, the cloud broke with a roar. The storm—black, heavy, thunderous—came rushing across the bay. It blotted out, in a lightning's flash, the mansion which stands on the site of Jacques Caillion's hut, and the weed-grown, ancient, forgotten graveyard in its shadow.

... And a bell in the steeple of Our Lady of the Gulf rang out the hour.

THE HOUSE OF THE NIGHTMARE,
by Edward Lucas White

I first caught sight of the house from the brow of the mountain as I cleared the woods and looked across the broad valley several hundred feet below me, to the low sun sinking toward the far blue hills. From that momentary viewpoint I had an exaggerated sense of looking almost vertically down. I seemed to be hanging over the checkerboard of roads and fields, dotted with farm buildings, and felt the familiar deception that I could almost throw a stone upon the house. I barely glimpsed its slate roof.

What caught my eyes was the bit of road in front of it, between the mass of dark-green shade trees about the house and the orchard opposite. Perfectly straight it was, bordered by an even row of trees, through which I made out a cinder side path and a low stone wall.

Conspicuous on the orchard side between two of the flanking trees was a white object, which I took to be a tall stone, a vertical splinter of one of the tilted limestone reefs with which the fields of the region are scarred.

The road itself I saw plain as a boxwood ruler on a green baize table. It gave me a pleasurable anticipation of a chance for a burst of speed. I had been painfully traversing closely forested, semi-mountainous hills. Not a farmhouse had I passed, only wretched cabins by the road, more than twenty miles of which I had found very bad and hindering. Now, when I was not many miles from my expected stopping-place, I looked forward to better going, and to that straight, level bit in particular.

As I sped cautiously down the sharp beginning of the long descent, the trees engulfed me again, and I lost sight of the valley. I dipped into a hollow, rose on the crest of the next hill, and again saw the house, nearer, and not so far below.

The tall stone caught my eye with a shock of surprise. Had I not thought it was opposite the house next the orchard? Clearly it was on the left-hand side of the road toward the house. My self-questioning lasted only the moment as I passed the crest. Then the outlook was cut off again; but I found myself gazing ahead, watching for the next chance at the same view.

At the end of the second hill I only saw the bit of road obliquely and could not be sure, but, as at first, the tall stone seemed on the right of the road.

At the top of the third and last hill I looked down the stretch of road under the overarching trees, almost as one would look through a tube. There was a line of whiteness which I took for the tall stone. It was on the right.

I dipped into the last hollow. As I mounted the farther slope, I kept my eyes on the top of the road ahead of me. When my line of sight surmounted the rise I marked the tall stone on my right hand among the serried maples. I leaned over, first on one side, then on the other, to inspect my tires, then I threw the lever.

As I flew forward, I looked ahead. There was the tall stone—on the left of the road! I was really scared and almost dazed. I meant to stop dead, take a good look at the stone, and make up my mind beyond peradventure whether it was on the right or the left—if not, indeed, in the middle of the road.

In my bewilderment, I put on the highest speed. The machine leaped forward; everything I touched went wrong; I steered wildly, slewed to the left, and crashed into a big maple.

* * * *

When I came to my senses, I was flat on my back in the dry ditch. The last rays of the sun sent shafts of golden green light through the maple boughs overhead. My first thought was an odd mixture of appreciation of the beauties of nature and disapproval of my own conduct in touring without a companion—a fact I had regretted more than once. Then my mind cleared, and I sat up. I felt myself from the head down. I was not bleeding; no bones were broken; and, while much shaken, I had suffered no serious bruises.

Then I saw the boy. He was standing at the edge of the cinder-path, near the ditch. He was stocky and solidly built; barefoot, with his trousers rolled up to his knees; wore a sort of butternut shirt, open at the throat; and was coatless and hat-less. He was tow-headed, with a shock of tousled hair; was much freckled, and had a hideous harelip. He shifted from one foot to the other, twiddled his toes, and said nothing whatever, though he stared at me intently.

I scrambled to my feet and proceeded to survey the wreck. It seemed distress-ingly complete. It had not blown up, nor even caught fire; but otherwise the ruin appeared hopelessly thorough. Everything I examined seemed worse smashed than the rest. My two hampers alone, by one of those cynical jokes of chance, had es-caped—both had pitched clear of the wreckage and were unhurt, not even a bottle broken.

During my investigations, the boy's faded eyes followed me continuously, but he uttered no word. When I had convinced myself of my helplessness I straightened up and addressed him:

"How far is it to a blacksmith shop?"

"Eight mile," he answered. He had a distressing case of cleft palate and was scarcely intelligible.

"Can you drive me there?" I inquired.

"Nary team on the place," he replied; "nary horse, nary cow."

"How far to the next house?" I continued.

"Six mile," he responded.

I glanced at the sky. The sun had set already. I looked at my watch: it was going seven thirty-six.

"May I sleep in your house tonight?" I asked.

"You can come in, if you want to," he said, "and sleep if you can. House all messy; ma's been dead three year, and dad's away. Nothin' to eat but buckwheat flour and rusty bacon."

"I've plenty to eat," I answered, picking up a hamper. "Just take that hamper, will you?"

"You can come in if you're a mind to," he said, "but you got to carry your own stuff." He did not speak gruffly or rudely, but appeared mildly stating an inoffen-sive fact.

"All right," I said, picking up the other hamper; "lead the way."

The yard in front of the house was dark under a dozen or more immense ailan-thus trees. Below them, many smaller trees had grown up, and beneath these a dank underwood of tall, rank suckers out of the deep, shaggy, matted grass. What had once been, apparently, a carriage-drive left a narrow, curved track, disused and grass-grown, leading to the house. Even here were some shoots of the ailanthus, and the air was unpleasant with the vile smell of the roots and suckers and the insistent odor of their flowers.

The house was of gray stone, with green shutters faded almost as gray as the stone. Along its front was a veranda, not much raised from the ground, and with no balustrade or railing. On it were several hickory splint rockers. There were eight shuttered windows toward the porch, and midway of them a wide door, with small violet panes on either side of it and a fanlight above.

"Open the door," I said to the boy.

"Open it yourself," he replied, not unpleasantly nor disagreeably, but in such a tone that one could not but take the suggestion as a matter of course.

I put down the two hampers and tried the door. It was latched, but not locked, and opened with a rusty grind of its hinges, on which it sagged crazily, scraping the floor as it turned. The passage smelt moldy and damp. There were several doors on either side; the boy pointed to the first on the right.

"You can have that room," he said.

I opened the door. What with the dusk, the interlacing trees outside, the piazza roof, and the closed shutters, I could make out little.

"Better get a lamp," I said to the boy.

"Nary lamp," he declared cheerfully. "Nary candle. Mostly I get abed before dark."

I returned to the remains of my conveyance. All four of my lamps were merely scrap metal and splintered glass. My lantern was mashed flat. I always, however, carried candles in my valise. This I found split and crushed, but still holding together. I carried it to the porch, opened it, and took out three candles.

Entering the room, where I found the boy standing just where I had left him, I lit the candle. The walls were whitewashed, the floor bare. There was a mildewed, chilly smell, but the bed looked freshly made up and clean, although it felt clammy.

With a few drops of its own grease I stuck the candle on the corner of a mean, rickety little bureau. There was nothing else in the room save two rush-bottomed chairs and a small table. I went out on the porch, brought in my valise, and put it on the bed. I raised the sash of each window and pushed open the shutters. Then I asked the boy, who had not moved or spoken, to show me the way to the kitchen. He led me straight through the hall to the back of the house. The kitchen was large and had no furniture save some pine chairs, a pine bench, and a pine table.

I stuck two candles on opposite corners of the table. There was no stove or range in the kitchen, only a big hearth, the ashes in which smelt and looked a month old. The wood in the wood-shed was dry enough, but even it had a cellary, stale smell. The ax and hatchet were both rusty and dull, but usable, and I quickly made a big fire. To my amazement, for the mid-June evening was hot and still, the boy, a wry smile on his ugly face, almost leaned over the flame, hands and arms spread out, and fairly roasted himself.

"Are you cold?" I inquired.

"I'm allus cold," he replied, hugging the fire closer than ever, till I thought he must scorch.

I left him toasting himself while I went in search of water. I discovered the pump, which was in working order and not dry on the valves; but I had a furious struggle to fill the two leaky pails I had found. When I had put water to boil I fetched my hampers from the porch.

I brushed the table and set out my meal—cold fowl, cold ham, white and brown bread, olives, jam, and cake. When the can of soup was hot and the coffee made I drew up two chairs to the table and invited the boy to join me.

"I ain't hungry," he said; "I've had supper."

He was a new sort of boy to me; all the boys I knew were hearty eaters and always ready. I had felt hungry myself, but somehow when I came to eat I had little appetite and hardly relished the food. I soon made an end of my meal, covered the fire, blew out the candles, and returned to the porch, where I dropped into one of the hickory rockers to smoke. The boy followed me silently and seated himself on the porch floor, leaning against a pillar, his feet on the grass outside.

"What do you do," I asked, "when your father is away?"

"Just loaf 'round," he said. "Just fool 'round."

"How far off are your nearest neighbors?" I asked.

"Don't no neighbors never come here," he stated. "Say they're afeared of the ghosts."

I was not at all startled; the place had all those aspects which lead to a house being called haunted. I was struck by his odd matter-of-fact way of speaking—it was as if he had said they were afraid of a cross dog.

"Do you ever see any ghosts around here?" I continued.

"Never see 'em," he answered, as if I had mentioned tramps or partridges. "Never hear 'em. Sort o' feel 'em 'round sometimes."

"Are you afraid of them?" I asked.

"Nope," he declared. "I ain't skeered o' ghosts; I'm skeered o' nightmares. Ever have nightmares?"

"Very seldom," I replied.

"I do," he returned. "Allus have the same nightmare—big sow, big as a steer, trying to eat me up. Wake up so skeered I could run to never. Nowheres to run to. Go to sleep, and have it again. Wake up worse skeered than ever. Dad says it's buckwheat cakes in summer."

"You must have teased a sow some time," I said.

"Yep," he answered. "Teased a big sow wunst, holding up one of her pigs by the hind leg. Teased her too long. Fell in the pen and got bit up some. Wisht I hadn't 'a' teased her. Have that nightmare three times a week, sometimes. Worse'n being burnt out. Worse'n ghosts. Say, I sorter feel ghosts around now."

He was not trying to frighten me. He was as simply stating an opinion as if he had spoken of bats or mosquitoes.

I made no reply, and found myself listening involuntarily. My pipe went out. I did not really want another, but felt disinclined for bed as yet, and was comfortable where I was, while the smell of the ailanthus blossoms was very disagreeable. I filled my pipe again, lit it, and then, as I puffed, somehow dozed off for a moment.

I awoke with a sensation of some light fabric trailed across my face. The boy's position was unchanged.

"Did you do that?" I asked sharply.

"Ain't done nary thing," he rejoined. "What was it?"

"It was like a piece of mosquito-netting brushed over my face."

"That ain't netting," he asserted; "that's a veil. That's one of the ghosts. Some blow on you; some touch you with their long, cold fingers. That one with the veil she drags acrost your face—well, mostly I think it's ma."

He spoke with the unassailable conviction of the child in "We Are Seven." I found no words to reply, and rose to go to bed.

"Good night," I said.

"Good night," he echoed. "I'll set out here a spell yet."

I lit a match, found the candle I had stuck on the corner of the shabby little bureau, and undressed. The bed had a comfortable husk mattress, and I was soon asleep.

I had the sensation of having slept some time when I had a nightmare—the very nightmare the boy had described. A huge sow, big as a dray horse, was reared up on her forelegs over the foot-board of the bed, trying to scramble over to me. She grunted and puffed, and I felt I was the food she craved. I knew in the dream that it was only a dream and strove to wake up.

Then the gigantic dream-beast floundered over the footboard, fell across my shins, and I awoke.

I was in darkness as absolute as if I were sealed in a jet vault, yet the shudder of the nightmare instantly subsided, my nerves quieted; I realized where I was and felt not the least panic. I turned over and was asleep again almost at once. Then I had a real nightmare, not recognizable as a dream, but appallingly real—an unutterable agony of reasonless horror.

There was a Thing in the room; not a sow, nor any other namable creature, but a *Thing*. It was as big as an elephant, filled the room to the ceiling, was shaped like a wild boar seated on its haunches, with its forelegs braced stiffly in front of it. It had a hot, slobbering red mouth, full of big tusks, and its jaws worked hungrily. It shuffled and hunched itself forward, inch by inch, till its vast forelegs straddled the bed.

The bed crushed up like wet blotting-paper, and I felt the weight of the Thing on my feet, on my legs, on my body, on my chest. It was hungry, and I was what it was hungry for, and it meant to begin on my face. Its dripping mouth was nearer and nearer.

Then the dream-helplessness that made me unable to call or move suddenly gave way, and I yelled and awoke. This time my terror was positive and not to be shaken off.

* * * *

It was near dawn: I could descry dimly the cracked, dirty window-panes. I got up, lit the stump of my candle and two fresh ones, dressed hastily, strapped my ruined valise, and put it on the porch against the wall near the door. Then I called the boy. I realized quite suddenly that I had not told him my name or asked his.

I shouted "Hello!" a few times, but won no answer. I had had enough of that house. I was still permeated with the panic of the nightmare. I desisted from shouting, made no search, but with two candles went out to the kitchen. I took a swallow of cold coffee and munched a biscuit as I hustled my belongings into my hampers. Then, leaving a silver dollar on the table, I carried the hampers out on the porch and dumped them by my valise.

It was now light enough to see to walk, and I went out to the road. Already the night-dew had rusted much of the wreck, making it look more hopeless than before. It was, however, entirely undisturbed. There was not so much as a wheel-track or a hoofprint on the road. The tall, white stone, uncertainty about which had caused my disaster, stood like a sentinel opposite where I had upset.

I set out to find that blacksmith shop. Before I had gone far the sun rose clear from the horizon, and almost at once scorching. As I footed it along I grew very much heated, and it seemed more like ten miles than six before I reached the first house. It was a new frame house, neatly painted and close to the road, with a whitewashed fence along its garden front.

I was about to open the gate when a big black dog with a curly tail bounded out of the bushes. He did not bark, but stood inside the gate wagging his tail and regarding me with a friendly eye; yet I hesitated with my hand on the latch, and considered. The dog might not be as friendly as he looked, and the sight of him made me realize that except for the boy I had seen no creature about the house where I had spent the night; no dog or cat; not even a toad or bird. While I was ruminating upon this a man came from behind the house.

"Will your dog bite?" I asked.

"Naw," he answered; "he don't bite. Come in."

I told him I had had an accident to my automobile, and asked if he could drive me to the blacksmith shop and back to my wreckage.

"Cert," he said. "Happy to help you. I'll hitch up foreshortly. Where'd you smash?"

"In front of the gray house about six miles back," I answered.

"That big stone-built house?" he queried.

"The same," I assented.

"Did you go a-past here?" he inquired astonished. "I didn't hear ye."

"No," I said; "I came from the other direction."

"Why," he meditated, "you must 'a' smashed 'bout sunup. Did you come over them mountains in the dark?"

"No," I replied; "I came over them yesterday evening. I smashed up about sunset."

"Sundown!" he exclaimed. "Where in thunder've ye been all night?"

"I slept in the house where I broke down."

"In that there big stone-built house in the trees?" he demanded.

"Yes," I agreed.

"Why," he quavered excitedly, "that there house is haunted! They say if you have to drive past it after dark, you can't tell which side of the road the big white stone is on."

"I couldn't tell even before sunset," I said.

"There!" he exclaimed. "Look at that, now! And you slep' in that house! Did you sleep, honest?"

"I slept pretty well," I said. "Except for a nightmare, I slept all night."

"Well," he commented, "I wouldn't go in that there house for a farm, nor sleep in it for my salvation. And you slep'! How in thunder did you get in?"

"The boy took me in," I said.

"What sort of a boy?" he queried, his eyes fixed on me with a queer, countrified look of absorbed interest.

"A thick-set, freckle-faced boy with a harelip," I said.

"Talk like his mouth was full of mush?" he demanded.

"Yes," I said; "bad case of cleft palate."

"Well!" he exclaimed. "I never did believe in ghosts, and I never did half believe that house was haunted, but I know it now. And you slep'!"

"I didn't see any ghosts," I retorted irritably.

"You seen a ghost for sure," he rejoined solemnly. "That there harelip boy's been dead six months."

REALITY OR DELUSION?
by Mrs Henry Wood

This is a ghost story. Every word of it is true. And I don't mind confessing that for ages afterwards some of us did not care to pass the spot alone at night. Some people do not care to pass it yet.

It was autumn, and we were at Crabb Cot. Lena had been ailing; and in October Mrs. Todhetley proposed to the Squire that they should remove with her there, to see if the change would do her good.

We Worcestershire people call North Crabb a village; but one might count the houses in it, little and great, and not find four-and-twenty. South Crabb, half a mile off, is ever so much larger; but the church and school are at North Crabb.

John Ferrar had been employed by Squire Todhetley as a sort of overlooker on the estate, or working bailiff. He had died the previous winter; leaving nothing behind him except some debts; for he was not provident; and his handsome son Daniel. Daniel Ferrar, who was rather superior as far as education went, disliked work: he would make a show of helping his father, but it came to little. Old Ferrar had not put him to any particular trade or occupation, and Daniel, who was as proud as Lucifer, would not turn to it himself. He liked to be a gentleman. All he did now was to work in his garden, and feed his fowls, ducks, rabbits, and pigeons, of which he kept a great quantity, selling them to the houses around and sending them to market.

But, as every one said, poultry would not maintain him. Mrs. Lease, in the pretty cottage hard by Ferrar's, grew tired of saying it. This Mrs. Lease and her daughter, Maria, must not be confounded with Lease the pointsman: they were in a better condition of life, and not related to him. Daniel Ferrar used to run in and out of their house at will when a boy, and he was now engaged to be married to Maria. She would have a little money, and the Leases were respected in North Crabb. People began to whisper a query as to how Ferrar got his corn for the poultry: he was not known to buy much: and he would have to go out of his house at Christmas, for its owner, Mr. Coney, had given him notice. Mrs. Lease, anxious about Maria's prospects, asked Daniel what he intended to do then, and he answered, "Make his fortune: he should begin to do it as soon as he could turn himself round." But the time was going on, and the turning round seemed to be as far off as ever.

After Midsummer, a niece of the schoolmistress's, Miss Timmens, had come to the school to stay: her name was Harriet Roe. The father, Humphrey Roe, was half-brother to Miss Timmens. He had married a Frenchwoman, and lived more in France than in England until his death. The girl had been christened Henriette; but North Crabb, not understanding much French, converted it into Harriet. She was a showy, free-mannered, good-looking girl, and made speedy acquaintance with Daniel Ferrar; or he with her. They improved upon it so rapidly that Maria Lease grew jealous, and North Crabb began to say he cared for Harriet more than for Maria. When Tod and I got home the latter end of October, to spend the Squire's birthday, things were in this state. James Hill, the bailiff who had been taken on by the Squire in John Ferrar's place (but a far inferior man to Ferrar; not much better,

226

in fact, than a common workman, and of whose doings you will hear soon in regard to his little step-son, David Garth) gave us an account of matters in general. Daniel Ferrar had been drinking lately, Hill added, and his head was not strong enough to stand it; and he was also beginning to look as if he had some care upon him.

"A nice lot, he, for them two women to be fighting for," cried Hill, who was no friend to Ferrar. "There'll be mischief between 'em if they don't draw in a bit. Maria Lease is next door to mad over it, I know; and t'other, finding herself the best liked, crows over her. It's something like the Bible story of Leah and Rachel, young gents, Dan Ferrar likes the one, and he's bound by promise to the t'other. As to the French jade," concluded Hill, giving his head a toss, "she'd make a show of liking any man that followed her, she would; a dozen of 'em on a string."

It was all very well for surly Hill to call Daniel Ferrar a "nice lot," but he was the best-looking fellow in the church on Sunday morning well-dressed too. But his colour seemed brighter; and his hands shook as they were raised, often, to push back his hair, that the sun shone upon through the south-window, turning it to gold. He scarcely looked up, not even at Harriet Roe, with her dark eyes roving every-where, and her streaming pink ribbons. Maria Lease was pale, quiet, and nice, as usual; she had no beauty, but her face was sensible, and her deep grey eyes had a strange and curious earnestness. The new parson preached, a young man just appointed to the parish of Crabb. He went in for great observances of Saints' days, and told his congregation that he should expect to see them at church on the morrow, which would be the Feast of All Saints.

Daniel Ferrar walked home with Mrs. Lease and Maria after service, and was invited to dinner. I ran across to shake hands with the old dame, who had once nursed me through an illness, and promised to look in and see her later. We were going back to school on the morrow. As I turned away, Harriet Roe passed, her pink ribbons and her cheap gay silk dress gleaming in the sunlight. She stared at me, and I stared back again. And now, the explanation of matters being over, the real story begins. But I shall have to tell some of it as it was told by others.

The tea-things waited on Mrs. Lease's table in the afternoon; waited for Daniel Ferrar. He had left them shortly before to go and attend to his poultry. Nothing had been said about his coming back for tea: that he would do so had been looked upon as a matter of course. But he did not make his appearance, and the tea was taken without him. At half-past five the church-bell rang out for evening service, and Maria put her things on. Mrs. Lease did not go out at night.

"You are starting early, Maria. You'll be in church before other people."

"That won't matter, mother."

A jealous suspicion lay on Maria—that the secret of Daniel Ferrar's absence was his having fallen in with Harriet Roe: perhaps he had gone of his own accord to seek her. She walked slowly along. The gloom of dusk, and a deep dusk, had stolen over the evening, but the moon would be up later. As Maria passed the school-house, she halted to glance in at the little sitting-room window: the shutters were not closed yet, and the room was lighted by the blazing fire. Harriet was not there. She only saw Miss Timmens, the mistress, who was putting on her bonnet before a hand-glass propped upright on the mantelpiece. Without warning, Miss Timmens turned and threw open the window. It was only for the purpose of pulling-to the shutters, but Maria thought she must have been observed, and spoke.

"Good evening, Miss Timmens."

"Who is it?" cried out Miss Timmens, in answer, peering into the dusk. "Oh, it's you, Maria Lease! Have you seen anything of Harriet? She went off somewhere this afternoon, and never came in to tea."

227

"I have not seen her."

"She's gone to the Batleys', I'll be bound. She knows I don't like her to be with the Batley girls: they make her ten times flightier than she would otherwise be."

Miss Timmens drew in her shutters with a jerk, without which they would not close, and Maria Lease turned away.

"Not at the Batleys', not at the Batleys', but with him," she cried, in bitter rebellion, as she turned away from the church. From the church, not to it. Was Maria to blame for wishing to see whether she was right or not?—for walking about a little in the thought of meeting them? At any rate it is what she did. And had her reward; such as it was.

As she was passing the top of the withy walk, their voices reached her ear. People often walked there, and it was one of the ways to South Crabb. Maria drew back amidst the trees, and they came on: Harriet Roe and Daniel Ferrar, walking arm-in-arm.

"I think I had better take it off," Harriet was saying. "No need to invoke a storm upon my head. And that would come in a shower of hail from stiff old Aunt Timmens."

The answer seemed one of quick accent, but Ferrar spoke low. Maria Lease had hard work to control herself: anger, passion, jealousy, all blazed up. With her arms stretched out to a friendly tree on either side,—with her heart beating,—with her pulses coursing on to fever-heat, she watched them across the bit of common to the road. Harriet went one way then; he another, in the direction of Mrs. Lease's cottage. No doubt to fetch her Maria—to church, with a plausible excuse of having been detained. Until now she had had no proof of his falseness; had never perfectly believed in it.

She took her arms from the trees and went forward, a sharp faint cry of despair breaking forth on the night air. Maria Lease was one of those silent-natured girls who can never speak of a wrong like this. She had to bury it within her; down, down, out of sight and show; and she went into church with her usual quiet step. Harriet Roe with Miss Timmens came next, quite demure, as if she had been singing some of the infant scholars to sleep at their own homes. Daniel Ferrar did not go to church at all: he stayed, as was found afterwards, with Mrs. Lease.

Maria might as well have been at home as at church: better perhaps that she had been. Not a syllable of the service did she hear: her brain was a sea of confusion; the tumult within it rising higher and higher. She did not hear even the text, "Peace, be still," or the sermon; both so singularly appropriate. The passions in men's minds, the preacher said, raged and foamed just like the angry waves of the sea in a storm, until Jesus came to still them.

I ran after Maria when church was over, and went in to pay the promised visit to old Mother Lease. Daniel Ferrar was sitting in the parlour. He got up and offered Maria a chair at the fire, but she turned her back and stood at the table under the window, taking off her gloves. An open Bible was before Mrs. Lease: I wondered whether she had been reading aloud to Daniel.

"What was the text, child?" asked the old lady.

No answer.

"Do you hear, Maria! What was the text?"

Maria turned at that, as if suddenly awakened. Her face was white; her eyes had in them an uncertain terror.

"The text?" she stammered. "I—I forget it, mother. It was from Genesis, I think."

"Was it, Master Johnny?"

"It was from the fourth chapter of St. Mark, 'Peace, be still.'"

Mrs. Lease stared at me. "Why, that is the very chapter I've been reading. Well now, that's curious. But there's never a better in the Bible, and never a better text was taken from it than those three words. I have been telling Daniel here, Master Johnny, that when once that peace, Christ's peace, is got into the heart, storms can't hurt us much. And you are going away again tomorrow, sir?" she added, after a pause. "It's a short stay?"

I was not going away on the morrow. Tod and I, taking the Squire in a genial moment after dinner, had pressed to be let stay until Tuesday, Tod using the argument, and laughing while he did it, that it must be wrong to travel on All Saints' Day, when the parson had specially enjoined us to be at church. The Squire told us we were a couple of encroaching rascals, and if he did let us stay it should be upon condition that we did go to church. This I said to them.

"He may send you all the same, sir, when the morning comes," remarked Daniel Ferrar.

"Knowing Mr. Todhetley as you do Ferrar, you may remember that he never breaks his promises."

Daniel laughed. "He grumbles over them, though, Master Johnny."

"Well, he may grumble tomorrow about our staying, say it is wasting time that ought to be spent in study, but he will not send us back until Tuesday."

Until Tuesday! If I could have foreseen then what would have happened before Tuesday! If all of us could have foreseen! Seen the few hours between now and then depicted, as in a mirror, event by event! Would it have saved the calamity, the dreadful sin that could never be redeemed? Why, yes; surely it would. Daniel Ferrar turned and looked at Maria.

"Why don't you come to the fire?"

"I am very well here, thank you."

She had sat down where she was, her bonnet touching the curtain. Mrs. Lease, not noticing that anything was wrong, had begun talking about Lena, whose illness was turning to low fever, when the house door opened and Harriet Roe came in.

"What a lovely night it is!" she said, taking of own accord the chair I had not cared to take, for I kept saying I must go. "Maria, what went with you after church? I hunted for you everywhere."

Maria gave no answer. She looked black and angry, and her bosom heaved as if a storm were brewing. Harriet Roe slightly laughed.

"Do you intend to take holiday tomorrow, Mrs. Lease?"

"Me take holiday! what is there in tomorrow to take holiday for?" returned Mrs. Lease.

"I shall," continued Harriet, not answering the question: "I have been used to it in France. All Saints' Day is a grand holiday there; we go to church in our best clothes, and pay visits afterwards. Following it, like a dark shadow, comes the gloomy Jour des Morts."

"The what?" cried Mrs. Lease, bending her ear.

"The day of the dead. All Souls' Day. But you English don't go to the cemeteries to pray."

Mrs. Lease put on her spectacles, which lay upon the open pages of the Bible, and stared at Harriet. Perhaps she thought they might help her to understand. The girl laughed.

"On All Souls' Day, whether it be wet or dry, the French cemeteries are full of kneeling women draped in black; all praying for the repose of their dead relatives, after the manner of the Roman Catholics."

Daniel Ferrar, who had not spoken a word since she came in, but sat with his face to the fire, turned and looked at her. Upon which she tossed back her head and her pink ribbons, and smiled till all her teeth were seen. Good teeth they were. As to reverence in her tone, there was none.

"I have seen them kneeling when the slosh and wet have been ankle-deep. Did you ever see a ghost?" added she, with energy. "The French believe that the spirits of the dead come abroad on the night of All Saints' Day. You'd scarcely get a French woman to go out of her house after dark. It is their chief superstition."

"What is the superstition?" questioned Mrs. Lease.

"Why, that," said Harriet. "They believe that the dead are allowed to revisit the world after dark on the Eve of All Souls; that they hover in the air, waiting to appear to any of their living relatives, who may venture out, lest they should forget to pray on the morrow for the rest of their souls."

"Well, I never!" cried Mrs. Lease, staring excessively. "Did you ever hear the like of that, sir?" turning to me.

"Yes; I have heard of it."

Harriet Roe looked up at me; I was standing at the corner of the mantelpiece. She laughed a free laugh.

"I say, wouldn't it be fun to go out tomorrow night, and meet the ghosts? Only, perhaps they don't visit this country, as it is not under Rome."

"Now just you behave yourself before your betters, Harriet Roe," put in Mrs. Lease, sharply. "That gentleman is young Mr. Ludlow of Crabb Cot."

"And very happy I am to make young Mr. Ludlow's acquaintance," returned easy Harriet, flinging back her mantle from her shoulders. "How hot your parlour is, Mrs. Lease."

The hook of the cloak had caught in a thin chain of twisted gold that she wore round her neck, displaying it to view. She hurriedly folded her cloak together, as if wishing to conceal the chain. But Mrs. Lease's spectacles had seen it.

"What's that you've got on, Harriet? A gold chain?"

A moment's pause, and then Harriet Roe flung back her mantle again, defiance upon her face, and touched the chain with her hand.

"That's what it is, Mrs. Lease: a gold chain. And a very pretty one, too."

"Was it your mother's?"

"It was never anybody's but mine. I had it made a present to me this afternoon; for a keepsake."

Happening to look at Maria, I was startled at her face, it was so white and dark: white with emotion, dark with an angry despair that I for one did not comprehend. Harriet Roe, throwing at her a look of saucy triumph, went out with as little ceremony as she had come in, just calling back a general good night; and we heard her footsteps outside getting gradually fainter in the distance. Daniel Ferrar rose.

"I'll take my departure too, I think. You are very unsociable tonight, Maria."

"Perhaps I am. Perhaps I have cause to be."

She flung his hand back when he held it out; and in another moment, as if a thought struck her, ran after him into the passage to speak. I, standing near the door in the small room, caught the words.

"I must have an explanation with you, Daniel Ferrar. Now. Tonight. We cannot go on thus for a single hour longer."

"Not tonight, Maria; I have no time to spare. And I don't know what you mean."

"You do know. Listen. I will not go to my rest, no, though it were for twenty nights to come, until we have had it out. I vow I will not. There. You are playing with me. Others have long said so, and I know it now."

He seemed to speak some quieting words to her, for the tone was low and sooth-ing; and then went out, closing the door behind him. Maria came back and stood with her face and its ghastliness turned from us. And still the old mother noticed nothing.

"Why don't you take your things off, Maria?" she asked.

"Presently," was the answer.

I said good night in my turn, and went away. Half-way home I met Tod with the two young Lexoms. The Lexoms made us go in and stay to supper, and it was ten o'clock before we left them.

"We shall catch it," said Tod, setting off at a run. They never let us stay out late on a Sunday evening, on account of the reading.

But, as it happened, we escaped scot-free this time, for the house was in a com-motion about Lena. She had been better in the afternoon, but at nine o'clock the fever returned worse than ever. Her little cheeks and lips were scarlet as she lay on the bed, her wide-open eyes were bright and glistening. The Squire had gone up to look at her, and was fuming and fretting in his usual fashion.

"The doctor has never sent the medicine," said patient Mrs. Todhetley, who must have been worn out with nursing. "She ought to take it; I am sure she ought."

"These boys are good to run over to Cole's for that," cried the Squire. "It won't hurt them; it's a fine night."

Of course we were good for it. And we got our caps again; being charged to en-join Mr. Cole to come over the first thing in the morning.

"Do you care much about my going with you, Johnny?" Tod asked as we were turning out at the door. "I am awfully tired."

"Not a bit. I'd as soon go alone as not. You'll see me back in half-an-hour."

I took the nearest way; flying across the fields at a canter, and startling the hares. Mr. Cole lived near South Crabb, and I don't believe more than ten minutes had gone by when I knocked at his door. But to get back as quickly was another thing. The doctor was not at home. He had been called out to a patient at eight o'clock, and had not yet returned.

I went in to wait: the servant said he might be expected to come in from minute to minute. It was of no use to go away without the medicine; and I sat down in the surgery in front of the shelves, and fell asleep counting the white jars and physic bottles. The doctor's entrance awoke me.

"I am sorry you should have had to come over and to wait," he said. "When my other patient, with whom I was detained a considerable time, was done with, I went on to Crabb Cot with the child's medicine, which I had in my pocket."

"They think her very ill tonight, sir."

"I left her better, and going quietly to sleep. She will soon be well again, I hope."

"Why! is that the time?" I exclaimed, happening to catch sight of the clock as I was crossing the hall. It was nearly twelve. Mr. Cole laughed, saying time passed quickly when folk were asleep.

I went back slowly. The sleep, or the canter before it, had made me feel as tired as Tod had said he was. It was a night to be abroad in and to enjoy; calm, warm, light. The moon, high in the sky, illumined every blade of grass; sparkled on the water of the little rivulet; brought out the moss on the grey walls of the old church; played on its round-faced clock, then striking twelve.

Twelve o'clock at night at North Crabb answers to about three in the morning in London, for country people are mostly in bed and asleep at ten. Therefore, when loud and angry voices struck up in dispute, just as the last stroke of the hour was dying away on the midnight air, I stood still and doubted my ears.

I was getting near home then. The sounds came from the back of a building standing alone in a solitary place on the left-hand side of the road. It belonged to the Squire, and was called the yellow barn, its walls being covered with a yellow wash; but it was in fact used as a storehouse for corn. I was passing in front of it when the voices rose upon the air. Round the building I ran, and saw—Maria Lease: and something else that I could not at first comprehend. In the pursuit of her vow, not to go to rest until she had "had it out" with Daniel Ferrar, Maria had been abroad searching for him. What ill fate brought her looking for him up near our barn?—perhaps because she had fruitlessly searched in every other spot.

At the back of this barn, up some steps, was an unused door. Unused partly because it was not required, the principal entrance being in front; partly because the key of it had been for a long time missing. Stealing out at this door, a bag of corn upon his shoulders, had come Daniel Ferrar in a smock-frock. Maria saw him, and stood back in the shade. She watched him lock the door and put the key in his pocket; she watched him give the heavy bag a jerk as he turned to come down the steps. Then she burst out. Her loud reproaches petrified him, and he stood there as one suddenly turned to stone. It was at that moment that I appeared.

I understood it all soon; it needed not Maria's words to enlighten me. Daniel Ferrar possessed the lost key and could come in and out at will in the midnight hours when the world was sleeping, and help himself to the corn. No wonder his poultry throve; no wonder there had been grumblings at Crabb Cot at the mysterious disappearance of the good grain.

Maria Lease was decidedly mad in those few first moments. Stealing is looked upon in an honest village as an awful thing; a disgrace, a crime; and there was the night's earlier misery besides. Daniel Ferrar was a thief! Daniel Ferrar was false to her! A storm of words and reproaches poured forth from her in confusion, none of it very distinct. "Living upon theft! Convicted felon! Transportation for life! Squire Todhetley's corn! Fattening poultry on stolen goods! Buying gold chains with the profits for that bold, flaunting French girl, Harriet Roe! Taking his stealthy walks with her!"

My going up to them stopped the charge. There was a pause; and then Maria, in her mad passion, denounced him to me, as representative (so she put it) of the Squire—the breaker-in upon our premises! the robber of our stored corn!

Daniel Ferrar came down the steps; he had remained there still as a statue, immovable; and turned his white face to me. Never a word in defence said he: the blow had crushed him; he was a proud man (if any one can understand that), and to be discovered in this ill-doing was worse than death to him.

"Don't think of me more hardly than you can help, Master Johnny," he said in a quiet tone. "I have been almost tired of my life this long while."

Putting down the bag of corn near the steps, he took the key from his pocket and handed it to me. The man's aspect had so changed; there was something so grievously subdued and sad about him altogether, that I felt as sorry for him as if he had not been guilty. Maria Lease went on in her fiery passion.

"You'll be more tired of it tomorrow when the police are taking you to Worcester gaol. Squire Todhetley will not spare you, though your father was his many-years bailiff. He could not, you know, if he wished; Master Ludlow has seen you in the act."

"Let me have the key again for a minute, sir," he said, as quietly as though he had not heard a word. And I gave it to him. I'm not sure but I should have given him my head had he asked for it.

He swung the bag on his shoulders, unlocked the granary door, and put the bag beside the other sacks. The bag was his own, as we found afterwards, but he left it there. Locking the door again, he gave me the key, and went away with a weary step.

"Good-bye, Master Johnny."

I answered back good night civilly, though he had been stealing. When he was out of sight, Maria Lease, her passion full upon her still, dashed off towards her mother's cottage, a strange cry of despair breaking from her lips.

"Where have you been lingering, Johnny?" roared the Squire, who was sitting up for me. "You have been throwing at the owls, sir, that's what you've been at; you have been scudding after the hares."

I said I had waited for Mr. Cole, and had come back slower than I went; but I said no more, and went up to my room at once. And the Squire went to his.

I know I am only a muff; people tell me so, often: but I can't help it; I did not make myself. I lay awake till nearly daylight, first wishing Daniel Ferrar could be screened, and then thinking it might perhaps be done. If he would only take the lesson to heart and go straight for the future, what a capital thing it would be. We had liked old Ferrar; he had done me and Tod many a good turn: and, for the matter of that, we liked Daniel. So I never said a word when morning came of the past night's work.

"Is Daniel at home?" I asked, going to Ferrar's the first thing before breakfast. I meant to tell him that if he would keep right, I would keep counsel.

"He went out at dawn, sir," answered the old woman who did for him, and sold his poultry at market. "He'll be in presently: he have had no breakfast yet."

"Then tell him when he comes, to wait in, and see me: tell him it's all right. Can you remember, Goody? 'It is all right.'"

"I'll remember, safe enough, Master Ludlow."

Tod and I, being on our honour, went to church, and found about ten people in the pews. Harriet Roe was one, with her pink ribbons, the twisted gold chain showing outside a short-cut velvet jacket.

"No, sir; he has not been home yet; I can't think where he can have got to," was the old Goody's reply when I went again to Ferrar's. And so I wrote a word in pencil, and told her to give it him when he came in, for I could not go dodging there every hour of the day.

After luncheon, strolling by the back of the barn: a certain reminiscence I suppose taking me there, for it was not a frequented spot: I saw Maria Lease coming along.

Well, it was a change! The passionate woman of the previous night had subsided into a poor, wild-looking, sorrow-stricken thing, ready to die of remorse. Excessive passion had wrought its usual consequences; a reaction: a reaction in favour of Daniel Ferrar. She came up to me, clasping her hands in agony—beseeching that I would spare him; that I would not tell of him; that I would give him a chance for the future: and her lips quivered and trembled, and there were dark circles round her hollow eyes.

I said that I had not told and did not intend to tell. Upon which she was going to fall down on her knees, but I rushed off.

"Do you know where he is?" I asked, when she came to her sober senses.

"Oh, I wish I did know! Master Johnny, he is just the man to go and do something desperate. He would never face shame; and I was a mad, hard-hearted, wicked girl to do what I did last night. He might run away to sea; he might go and enlist for a soldier."

"I dare say he is at home by this time. I have left a word for him there, and promised to go in and see him tonight. If he will undertake not to be up to wrong things again, no one shall ever know of this from me."

She went away easier, and I sauntered on towards South Crabb. Eager as Tod and I had been for the day's holiday, it did not seem to be turning out much of a boon. In going home again—there was nothing worth staying out for—I had come to the spot by the three-cornered grove where I saw Maria, when a galloping policeman overtook me. My heart stood still; for I thought he must have come after Daniel Ferrar.

"Can you tell me if I am near to Crabb Cot—Squire Todhetley's?" he asked, reining-in his horse.

"You will reach it in a minute or two. I live there. Squire Todhetley is not at home. What do you want with him?"

"It's only to give in an official paper, sir. I have to leave one personally upon all the county magistrates."

He rode on. When I got in I saw the folded paper upon the hall-table; the man and horse had already gone onwards. It was worse indoors than out; less to be done. Tod had disappeared after church; the Squire was abroad; Mrs. Todhetley sat upstairs with Lena: and I strolled out again. It was only three o'clock then.

An hour, or more, was got through somehow; meeting one, talking to another, throwing at the ducks and geese; anything. Mrs. Lease had her head, smothered in a yellow shawl, stretched out over the palings as I passed her cottage.

"Don't catch cold, mother."

"I am looking for Maria, sir. I can't think what has come to her today, Master Johnny," she added, dropping her voice to a confidential tone. "The girl seems demented: she has been going in and out ever since daylight like a dog in a fair."

"If I meet her I will send her home."

And in another minute I did meet her. For she was coming out of Daniel Ferrar's yard. I supposed he was at home again.

"No," she said looking more wild, worn, haggard than before; "that's what I have been to ask. I am just out of my senses, sir. He has gone for certain. Gone!"

I did not think it. He would not be likely to go away without clothes.

"Well, I know he is, Master Johnny; something tells me. I've been all about everywhere. There's a great dread upon me, sir; I never felt anything like it."

"Wait until night, Maria; I dare say he will go home then. Your mother is looking out for you; I said if I met you I'd send you in."

Mechanically she turned towards the cottage, and I went on. Presently, as I was sitting on a gate watching the sunset, Harriet Roe passed towards the withy walk, and gave me a nod in her free but good-natured way.

"Are you going there to look out for the ghosts this evening?" I asked: and I wished not long afterwards I had not said it. "It will soon be dark."

"So it will," she said, turning to the red sky in the west. "But I have no time to give to the ghosts tonight."

"Have you seen Ferrar today?" I cried, an idea occurring to me.

"No. And I can't think where he has got to; unless he is off to Worcester. He told me he should have to go there some day this week."

She evidently knew nothing about him, and went on her way with another free-and-easy nod. I sat on the gate till the sun had gone down, and then thought it was time to be getting homewards.

Close against the yellow barn, the scene of last night's trouble, whom should I come upon but Maria Lease. She was standing still, and turned quickly at the sound

234

of my footsteps. Her face was bright again, but had a puzzled look upon it.

"I have just seen him: he has not gone," she said in a happy whisper. "You were right, Master Johnny, and I was wrong."

"Where did you see him?"

"Here; not a minute ago. I saw him twice. He is angry, very, and will not let me speak to him; both times he got away before I could reach him. He is close by somewhere."

I looked round, naturally; but Ferrar was nowhere to be seen. There was nothing to conceal him except the barn, and that was locked up. The account she gave was this—and her face grew puzzled again as she related it.

Unable to rest indoors, she had wandered up here again, and saw Ferrar standing at the corner of the barn, looking very hard at her. She thought he was waiting for her to come up, but before she got close to him he had disappeared, and she did not see which way. She hastened past the front of the barn, ran round to the back, and there he was. He stood near the steps looking out for her; waiting for her, as it again seemed; and was gazing at her with the same fixed stare. But again she missed him before she could get quite up; and it was at that moment that I arrived on the scene.

I went all round the barn, but could see nothing of Ferrar. It was an extraordinary thing where he could have got to. Inside the barn he could not be: it was securely locked; and there was no appearance of him in the open country. It was, so to say, broad daylight yet, or at least not far short of it; the red light was still in the west. Beyond the field at the back of the barn, was a grove of trees in the form of a triangle; and this grove was flanked by Crabb Ravine, which ran right and left. Crabb Ravine had the reputation of being haunted; for a light was sometimes seen dodging about its deep descending banks at night that no one could account for. A lively spot altogether for those who liked gloom.

"Are you sure it was Ferrar, Maria?"

"Sure!" she returned in surprise. "You don't think I could mistake him Master Johnny, do you? He wore that ugly seal-skin winter-cap of his tied over his ears, and his thick grey coat. The coat was buttoned closely round him. I have not seen him wear either since last winter."

That Ferrar must have gone into hiding somewhere seemed quite evident; and yet there was nothing but the ground to receive him. Maria said she lost sight of him the last time in a moment; both times in fact; and it was absolutely impossible that he could have made off to the triangle or elsewhere, as she must have seen him cross the open land. For that matter I must have seen him also.

On the whole, not two minutes had elapsed since I came up, though it seems to have been longer in telling it: when, before we could look further, voices were heard approaching from the direction of Crabb Cot; and Maria, not caring to be seen, went away quickly. I was still puzzling about Ferrar's hiding-place, when they reached me—the Squire, Tod, and two or three men. Tod came slowly up, his face dark and grave.

"I say, Johnny, what a shocking thing this is!"

"What is a shocking thing?"

"You have not heard of it?—But I don't see how you could hear it."

I had heard nothing. I did not know what there was to hear. Tod told me in a whisper.

"Daniel Ferrar's dead, lad."

"What?"

"He has destroyed himself Not more than half-an-hour ago. Hung himself in the grove."

I turned sick, taking one thing with another, comparing this recollection with that; which I dare say you will think no one but a muff would do.

Ferrar was indeed dead. He had been hiding all day in the three-cornered grove: perhaps waiting for night to get away—perhaps only waiting for night to go home again. Who can tell? About half-past two, Luke Macintosh, a man who sometimes worked for us, sometimes for old Coney happening to go through the grove, saw him there, and talked with him. The same man, passing back a little before sunset, found him hanging from a tree, dead. Macintosh ran with the news to Crabb Cot, and they were now flocking to the scene. When facts came to be examined there appeared only too much reason to think that the unfortunate appearance of the galloping policeman had terrified Ferrar into the act; perhaps—we all hoped it!—had scared his senses quite away. Look at it as we would, it was very dreadful.

But what of the appearance Maria Lease saw? At that time, Ferrar had been dead at least half-an-hour. Was it reality or delusion? That is (as the Squire put it), did her eyes see a real, spectral Daniel Ferrar; or were they deceived by some imagination of the brain? Opinions were divided. Nothing can shake her own steadfast belief in its reality; to her it remains an awful certainty, true and sure as heaven.

If I say that I believe in it too, I shall be called a muff and a double muff. But there is no stumbling-block difficult to be got over. Ferrar, when found, was wearing the seal-skin cap tied over the ears and the thick grey coat buttoned up round him, just as Maria Lease had described to me; and he had never worn them since the previous winter, or taken them out of the chest where they were kept. The old woman at his home did not know he had done it then. When told that he had died in these things, she protested that they were in the chest, and ran up to look for them. But the things were gone.

FISHER'S GHOST,
by John Lang

In the colony of New South Wales, at a place called Penrith, distant from Sydney about thirty-seven miles, lived a farmer named Fisher. He had been, originally, transported, but had become free by servitude. Unceasing toil, and great steadiness of character, had acquired for him a considerable property, for a person in his station of life. His lands and stock were not worth less than four thousand pounds. He was unmarried and was about forty-five years old.

Suddenly Fisher disappeared; and one of his neighbours—a man named Smith—gave out that he had gone to England, but would return in two or three years. Smith produced a document, purporting to be executed by Fisher; and, according to this document, Fisher had appointed Smith to act as his agent during his absence. Fisher was a man of very singular habits and eccentric character and his silence about his departure, instead of creating surprise, was declared to be "exactly like him."

About six months after Fisher's disappearance, an old man called Ben Weir, who had a small farm near Penrith and who always drove his own cart to market, was returning from Sydney one night when he beheld, seated on a rail which bounded the road—Fisher. The night was very dark and the distance of the fence from the middle of the road was, at least, twelve yards. Weir, nevertheless, saw Fisher's figure seated on the rail. He pulled his old mare up, and called out, "Fisher, is that you?" No answer was returned; but there, still on the rail, sat the form of the man with whom he had been on the most intimate terms. Weir—who was not drunk, though he had taken several glasses of strong liquor on the road—jumped off his cart and approached the rail. To his surprise, the form vanished.

"Well," exclaimed old Weir, "this is very curious, anyhow;" and, breaking several branches of a sapling so as to mark the exact spot, he remounted his cart, put his old mare into a jog-trot and soon reached his home.

Ben was not likely to keep this vision a secret from his old woman. All that he had seen he faithfully related to her.

"Hold our nonsense, Ben!" was old Betty's reply. "You know you have been a drinking and disturbing of your imagination. Ain't Fisher agone to England? And if he had a come back, do you think we shouldn't a heard on it?"

"Ay, Betty!" said old Ben, "but he'd a cruel gash in his forehead and the blood was all fresh like. Faith, it makes me shudder to think on't. It were his ghost."

"How can you talk so foolish, Ben?" said the old woman. "You must be drunk sure-ly to get on about ghosteses."

"I tell thee I am not drunk," rejoined old Ben, angrily. "There's been foul play, Betty; I'm sure on't. There sat Fisher on the rail—not more than a matter of two mile from this. Egad, it were on his own fence that he sat. There he was, in his shirt-sleeves, with his arms a folded; just as he used to sit when he was a waiting for anybody coming up the road. Bless you, Betty, I seed 'im till I was as close as I am to thee; when, all on a sudden, he vanished, like smoke."

"Nonsense, Ben: don't talk of it," said old Betty, "or the neighbours will only laugh at you. Come to bed and you'll forget all about it before tomorrow morning."

Old Ben went to bed; but he did not next morning forget all about what he had seen on the previous night: on the contrary, he was more positive than before. However, at the earnest and often repeated request of the old woman, he promised not to mention having seen Fisher's ghost, for fear that it might expose him to ridicule.

On the following Thursday night, when old Ben was returning from market—again in his cart—he saw, seated upon the same rail, the identical apparition. He had purposely abstained from drinking that day and was in the full possession of all his senses. On this occasion old Ben was too much alarmed to stop. He urged the old mare on and got home as speedily as possible. As soon as he had unharnessed and fed the mare and taken his purchases out of the cart, he entered his cottage, lighted his pipe, sat over the fire with his better half and gave her an account of how he had disposed of his produce and what he had brought back from Sydney in return. After this he said to her, "Well, Betty, I'm not drunk tonight, anyhow, am I?"

"No," said Betty. "You are quite sober, sensible like, tonight, Ben; and therefore you have come home without any ghost in your head. Ghosts! Don't believe there is such things."

"Well, you are satisfied I am not drunk; but perfectly sober," said the old man.

"Yes, Ben," said Betty.

"Well, then," said Ben, "I tell thee what, Betty. I saw Fisher tonight agin!"

"Stuff!" cried old Betty.

"You may say stuff," said the old farmer; "but I tell you what—I saw him as plainly as I did last Thursday night. Smith is a bad 'un! Do you think Fisher would ever have left this country without coming to bid you and me goodbye?"

"It's all fancy!" said old Betty. "Now drink your grog and smoke your pipe and think no more about the ghost. I won't hear on't."

"I'm as fond of my grog and my pipe as most men," said old Ben; "but I'm not going to drink anything tonight. It may be all fancy, as you call it, but I am now going to tell Mr Grafton all I saw, and what I think;" and with these words he got up and left the house.

* * * *

Mr Grafton was a gentleman who lived about a mile from old Weir's farm. He had been formerly a lieutenant in the navy, but was now on half-pay and was a settler in the new colony; he was, moreover, in the commission of the peace.

When old Ben arrived at Mr Grafton's house, Mr Grafton was about to retire to bed; but he requested old Ben might be shown in. He desired the farmer to take a seat by the fire and then enquired what was the latest news in Sydney.

"The news in Sydney, sir, is very small," said old Ben; "wheat is falling, but maize still keeps its price—seven and sixpence a bushel: but I want to tell you, sir, something that will astonish you."

"What is it, Ben?" asked Mr Grafton.

"Why, sir," resumed old Ben, "you know I am not a weak-minded man, nor a fool, exactly; for I was born and bred in Yorkshire."

"No, Ben, I don't believe you to be weak-minded, nor do I think you a fool," said Mr Grafton; "but what can you have to say that you come at this late hour and that you require such a preface?"

"That I have seen the ghost of Fisher, sir," said the old man; and he detailed the particulars of which the reader is already in possession.

Mr Grafton was at first disposed to think with old Betty, that Ben had seen Fisher's Ghost through an extra glass or two of rum on the first night; and that on the second night, when perfectly sober, he was unable to divest himself of the idea

238

previously entertained. But after a little consideration the words "How very singular!" involuntarily escaped him.

"Go home, Ben," said Mr Grafton, "and let me see you tomorrow at sunrise. We will go together to the place where you say you saw the ghost."

Mr Grafton used to encourage the aboriginal natives of New South Wales (that race which has been very aptly described "the last link in the human chain") to remain about his premises. At the head of a little tribe then encamped on Mr Grafton's estate, was a sharp young man named Johnny Crook. The peculiar faculty of the aboriginal natives of New South Wales, of tracking the human foot not only over grass but over the hardest rock; and of tracking the whereabouts of runaways by signs imperceptible to civilised eyes, is well known; and this man, Johnny Crook, was famous for his skill in this particular art of tracking. He had recently been instrumental in the apprehension of several desperate bushrangers whom he had tracked over twenty-seven miles of rocky country and fields, which they had crossed bare-footed, in the hope of checking the black fellow in the progress of his keen pursuit with the horse police.

When old Ben Weir made his appearance in the morning at Mr Grafton's house, the black chief, Johnny Crook, was summoned to attend. He came and brought with him several of his subjects. The party set out, old Weir showing the way. The leaves on the branches of the saplings which he had broken on the first night of seeing the ghost were withered and sufficiently pointed out the exact rail on which the phantom was represented to have sat. There were stains upon the rail. Johnny Crook, who had then no idea of what he was required for, pronounced these stains to be "White man's blood;" and, after searching about for some time, he pointed to a spot whereon he said a human body had been laid.

In New South Wales long droughts are not very uncommon; and not a single shower of rain had fallen for seven months previously—not sufficient even to lay the dust upon the roads.

In consequence of the time that had elapsed, Crook had no small difficulty to contend with; but in about two hours he succeeded in tracking the footsteps of one man to the unfrequented side of a pond at some distance. He gave it as his opinion that another man had been dragged thither. The savage walked round and round the pond, eagerly examining its borders and the sedges and weeds springing up around it. At first he seemed baffled. No clue had been washed ashore to show that anything unusual had been sunk in the pond; but, having finished this examination, he laid himself down on his face and looked keenly along the surface of the smooth and stagnant water. Presently he jumped up, uttered a cry peculiar to the natives when gratified by finding some long-sought object, clapped his hands and, pointing to the middle of the pond to where the decomposition of some sunken substance had produced a slimy coating streaked with prismatic colours, he exclaimed, "White man's fat!" The pond was immediately searched; and, below the spot indicated, the remains of a body were discovered. A large stone and a rotted silk handkerchief were found near the body; these had been used to sink it.

That it was the body of Fisher there could be no question. It might have been identified by the teeth; but on the waistcoat there were some large brass buttons which were immediately recognised, both by Mr Grafton and by old Ben Weir, as Fisher's property. He had worn those buttons on his waistcoat for several years.

Leaving the body by the side of the pond and old Ben and the blacks to guard it, Mr Grafton cantered up to Fisher's house. Smith was not only in possession of all the missing man's property, but had removed to Fisher's house. It was about a mile and a half distant. He enquired for Mr Smith. Mr Smith, who was at breakfast, came out and invited Mr Grafton to alight; Mr Grafton accepted the invitation and after a few desultory observations said, "Mr Smith, I am anxious to purchase a piece of land on the other side of the road, belonging to this estate, and I would give a fair price for it. Have you the power to sell?"

"Oh yes, sir," replied Smith. "The power which I hold from Fisher is a general power;" and he forthwith produced a document purporting to be signed by Fisher, but which was not witnessed.

"If you are not very busy, I should like to show you the piece of land I allude to," said Mr Grafton.

"Oh certainly, sir. I am quite at your service," said Smith; and he then ordered his horse to be saddled.

It was necessary to pass the pond where the remains of Fisher's body were then exposed. When they came near to the spot, Mr Grafton, looking Smith full in the face, said, "Mr Smith, I wish to show you something. Look here!" He pointed to the decomposed body and narrowly watching Mr Smith's countenance, remarked: "These are the remains of Fisher. How do you account for their being found in this pond?"

Smith, with the greatest coolness, got off his horse, minutely examined the remains and then admitted that there was no doubt they were Fisher's. He confessed himself at a loss to account for their discovery, unless it could be (he said) that somebody had waylaid him on the road when he left his home for Sydney; had murdered him for the gold and banknotes which he had about his person and had then thrown him into the pond. "My hands, thank heaven!" he concluded, "are clean. If my old friend could come to life again, he would tell you that I had no hand in his horrible murder."

Mr Grafton knew not what to think. He was not a believer in ghosts. Could it be possible, he began to ask himself, that old Weir had committed this crime and— finding it weigh heavily on his conscience and fearing that he might be detected— had trumped up the story about the ghost—had pretended that he was led to the spot by supernatural agency—and thus by bringing the murder voluntarily to light, hoped to stifle all suspicion? But then, he considered Weir's excellent character, his kind disposition and good-nature. These at once put to flight his suspicion of Weir; but still he was by no means satisfied of Smith's guilt, much as appearances were against him.

Fisher's servants were examined and stated that their master had often talked of going to England on a visit to his friends and of leaving Mr Smith to manage his farm; and that though they were surprised when Mr Smith came and said he had "gone at last," they did not think it at all unlikely that he had done so. An inquest was held and a verdict of wilful murder found against Thomas Smith. He was thereupon transmitted to Sydney for trial, at the ensuing sessions, in the supreme court. The case naturally excited great interest in the colony; and public opinion respecting Smith's guilt was evenly balanced.

The day of trial came; and the court was crowded almost to suffocation. The Attorney-General very truly remarked that there were circumstances connected with the case which were without any precedent in the annals of jurisprudence. The only witnesses were old Weir and Mr Grafton. Smith, who defended himself with great composure and ability, cross-examined them at considerable length and with consummate skill. The prosecution having closed, Smith addressed the jury (which consisted of military officers) in his defence. He admitted that the circumstances were strong against him; but he most ingeniously proceeded to explain them. The power of attorney, which he produced, he contended had been regularly granted by

Fisher and he called several witnesses who swore that they believed the signature to be that of the deceased. He, further, produced a will, which had been drawn up by Fisher's attorney, and by that will Fisher had appointed Smith his sole executor, in the event of his death. He declined, he said, to throw any suspicion on Weir; but he would appeal to the common sense of the jury whether the ghost story was entitled to any credit; and, if it were not, to ask themselves why it had been invented? He alluded to the fact—which in cross-examination Mr Grafton swore to—that when the remains were first shown to him, he did not conduct himself as a guilty man would have been likely to do, although he was horror-stricken on beholding the hideous spectacle. He concluded by invoking the Almighty to bear witness that he was innocent of the diabolical crime for which he had been arranged. The judge (the late Sir Francis Forbes) recapitulated the evidence. It was not an easy matter to deal with that part of it which had reference to the apparition: and if the charge of the judge had any leaning one way or the other, it was decidedly in favour of an acquittal. The jury retired; but, after deliberating for seven hours, they returned to the court, with a verdict of guilty.

The judge then sentenced the prisoner to be hanged on the following Monday. It was on a Thursday night that he was convicted. On the Sunday, Smith expressed a wish to see a clergyman. His wish was instantly attended to, when he confessed that he, and he alone, committed the murder; and that it was upon the very rail where Weir swore that he had seen Fisher's ghost sitting, that he had knocked out Fisher's brains with a tomahawk. The power of attorney he likewise confessed was a forgery, but declared that the will was genuine.

This is very extraordinary, but is, nevertheless, true in substance, if not in every particular. Most persons who have visited Sydney for any length of time will no doubt have had it narrated to them.

THROUGH THE IVORY GATE,
by Mary Raymond Shipman Andrews

Breeze filtered through shuffling leafage, the June morning sunlight came in at the open window by the boy's bed, under the green shades, across the shadowy, white room, and danced a noiseless dance of youth and freshness and springtime against the wall opposite. The boy's head stirred on his pillow. He spoke a quick word from out of his dream. "The key?" he said inquiringly, and the sound of his own voice awoke him. Dark, drowsy eyes opened, and he stared half-seeing, at the picture that hung facing him. Was it the play of mischievous sunlight, was it the dream that still held his brain? He knew the picture line by line, and there was no such figure in it. It was a large photograph of Fairfield, the southern home of his mother's people, and the boy remembered it always hanging there, opposite his bed, the first sight to meet his eyes every morning since his babyhood. So he was certain there was no figure in it, more than all one so remarkable as this strapping little chap in his queer clothes, his dress of conspicuous plaid with large black velvet squares sewed on it, who stood now in front of the old manor house. Could it be only a dream? Could it be that a little ghost, wandering childlike in dim, heavenly fields, had joined the gay troop of his boyish visions and slipped in with them through the ivory gate of pleasant dreams? The boy put his fists to his eyes and rubbed them and looked again. The little fellow was still there, standing with sturdy legs wide apart as if owning the scene; he laughed as he held toward the boy a key —a small key tied with a scarlet ribbon. There was no doubt in the boy's mind that the key was for him, and out of the dim world of sleep he stretched his young arm for it; to reach it he sat up in bed. Then he was awake and knew himself alone in the peace of his own little room, and laughed shamefacedly at the reality of the vision which had followed him from dreamland into the very boundaries of consciousness, which held him even now with gentle tenacity, which drew him back through the day, from his studies, from his play, into the strong current of its fascination.

The first time Philip Beckwith had this dream, he was only twelve years old, and, withheld by the deep reserve of childhood, he told not even his mother about it, though he lived in its atmosphere all day and remembered it vividly days longer. A year after it came again; and again it was a June morning, and as his eyes opened the little boy came once more out of the picture toward him, laughing and holding out the key on its scarlet string. The dream was a pleasant one, and Philip welcomed it eagerly from his sleep as a friend. There seemed something sweet and familiar in the child's presence beyond the one memory of him, as again the boy, with eyes half-open to everyday life, saw him standing, small but masterful, in the garden of that old house where the Fairfields had lived for more than a century. Half-consciously he tried to prolong the vision, tried not to wake entirely for fear of losing it; but the picture faded surely from the curtain of his mind as the tangible world painted there its heavier outlines. It was as if a happy little spirit had tried to follow him, for love of him, from a country Iying close, yet separated; it was as if the common childhood of the two made it almost possible for them to meet; as if a

242

message that might not be spoken, were yet almost delivered.

The third time the dream came it was a December morning of the year when Philip was fifteen, and falling snow made wavering light and shadow on the wall where hung the picture. This time, with eyes wide open, yet with the possession of the dream strongly on him, he lay subconsciously alert and gazed, as in the odd unmistakable dress that Philip knew now in detail, the bright-faced child swung toward him, always from the garden of that old place, always trying with loving, merry efforts to reach Philip from out of it—always holding to him the red ribboned key. Like a wary hunter the big boy lay—knowing it unreal, yet living it keenly—and watched his chance. As the little figure glided close to him, he put out his hand suddenly, swiftly for the key—he was awake. As always, the dream was gone; the little ghost was baffled again; the two worlds might not meet.

That day Mrs. Beckwith, puffing in order an old mahogany secretary, showed him a drawer full of photographs, daguerreotypes. The boy and his gay young mother were the best of friends, for, only nineteen when he was born, she had never let the distance widen between them; had held the freshness of her youth sacred against the time when he should share it. Year by year, living in his enthusiasms, drawing him to hers, she had grown young in his childhood, which year by year came closer to her maturity. Until now there was between the tall, athletic lad and the still young and attractive woman, an equal friendship, a common youth, which gave charm and elasticity to the natural tie between them. Yet even to this comrade-mother the boy had not told his dream, for the difficulty of putting into words the atmosphere, the compelling power of it. So that when she opened one of the old-fashioned black cases which held the early sun-pictures, and showed him the portrait within, he startled her by a sudden exclamation. From the frame of red velvet and tarnished gilt there laughed up at him the little boy of his dream. There was no mistaking him, and if there were doubt about the face, there was the peculiar dress —the black and white plaid with large squares of black velvet sewed here and there as decoration. Philip stared in astonishment at the sturdy figure; the childish face with its wide forehead and level, strong brows; its dark eyes straight-gazing and smiling.

"Mother—who is he? Who is he?" he demanded.

"Why, my lamb, don't you know? It's your little uncle Philip—my brother, for whom you were named—Philip Fairfield the sixth. There was always a Philip Fairfield at Fairfield since 1790. This one was the last, poor baby! And he died when he was five. Unless you go back there some day—that's my hope, but it's not likely to come true. You are a Yankee, except for the big half of you that's me. That's southern, every inch." She laughed and kissed his fresh cheek impulsively. "But what made you so excited over this picture, Phil?"

Philip gazed down, serious, a little embarrassed, at the open case in his hand. "Mother," he said after a moment, "you'll laugh at me, but I've seen this chap in a dream three times now."

"Oh!" She did laugh at him. "Oh, Philip! What have you been eating for dinner, I'd like to know? I can't have you seeing visions of your ancestors at fifteen—it's unhealthy."

The boy, reddening, insisted. "But, Mother, really, don't you think it was queer? I saw him as plainly as I do now—and I've never seen this picture before."

"Oh, yes, you have—you must have seen it," his mother threw back lightly. "You've forgotten, but the image of it was tucked away in some dark corner of your mind, and when you were asleep it stole out and played tricks on you. That's the way forgotten ideas do: they get even with you in dreams for having forgotten them."

"Mother, only listen—" But Mrs. Beckwith, her eyes lighting with a swift turn of thought, interrupted him—laid her finger on his lips.

"No—you listen, boy dear—quick, before I forget it! I've never told you about this, and it's very interesting."

And the youngster, used to these willful ways-of his sistermother, laughed and put his fair head against her shoulder and listened.

"It's quite a romance," she began, "only there isn't any end to it; it's all unfinished and disappointing. It's about this little Philip here, whose name you have—my brother. He died when he was five, as I said, but even then he had a bit of dramatic history in his life. He was born just before wartime in 1859, and he was a beautiful and wonderful baby; I can remember all about it, for I was six years older. He was incarnate sunshine, the happiest child that ever lived, but far too quick and clever for his years. The servants used to ask him, 'Who is you, Marse Philip, sah?' to hear him answer, before he could speak it plainly, 'I'm Philip Fairfield of Fairfield'; he seemed to realize that, and his responsibility to them and to the place, as soon as he could breathe. He wouldn't have a darky scolded in his presence, and every morning my father put him in front of him in the saddle, and they rode together about the plantation. My father adored him, and little Philip's sunshiny way of taking possession of the slaves and the property pleased him more deeply, I think, than anything in his life. But the war came before this time, when the child was about a year old, and my father went off, of course, as every southern man went who could walk, and for a year we did not see him. Then he was badly wounded at the battle of Malvern Hill; and came home to get well. However, it was more serious than he knew, and he did not get well. Twice he went off again to join our army, and each time he was sent back within a month, too ill to be of any use. He chafed constantly, of course, because he must stay at home and farm, when his whole soul ached to be fighting for his flag; but finally in December 1863, he thought he was well enough at last for service. He was to join General John Morgan, who had just made his wonderful escape from prison at Columbus, and it was planned that my mother should take lithe Philip and me to England to live there till the war was over and we could all be together at Fairfield again. With that in view my father drew all of his ready money—it was ten thousand dollars in gold—from the banks in Lexington, for my mother's use in the years they might be separated. When suddenly, the day before he was to have gone, the old wound broke out again, and he was helplessly ill in bed at the hour when he should have been on his horse riding toward Tennessee. We were fifteen miles out from Lexington, yet it might be rumored that father had drawn a large sum of money, and, of course, he was well known as a Southern officer. Because of the Northern soldiers, who held the city, he feared very much to have the money in the house, yet he hoped still to join Morgan a lithe later, and then it would be needed as he had planned. Christmas morning my father was so much better that my mother went to church, taking me, and leaving lithe Philip, then four years old, to amuse him. What happened that morning was the point of all this rambling; so now listen hard, my precious thing."

The boy, sitting erect now, caught his mother's hand silently, and his eyes stared into hers as he drank in every word:

"Mammy, who was, of course, little Philip's nurse, told my mother afterward that she was sent away before my father and the boy went into the garden, but she saw them go and saw that my father had a tin box—a box about twelve inches long, which seemed very heavy—in his arms, and on his finger swung a long red ribbon with a little key strung on it. Mother knew it as the key of the box, and she had tied

244

the ribbon on it herself.

"It was a bright, crisp Christmas day, pleasant in the garden—the box hedges were green and fragrant, aromatic in the sunshine. You don't even know the smell of box in sunshine, you poor child! But I remember that day, for I was ten years old, a right big girl, and it was a beautiful morning for an invalid to take the air. Mammy said she was proud to see how her 'handsome boy' kept step with his father, and she watched the two until they got away down by the rose garden, and then she couldn't see little Philip behind the three-foot hedge, so she turned away. But somewhere in that big garden, or under the trees beside it, my father buried the box that held the money—ten thousand dollars. It shows how he trusted that baby, that he took him with him, and you'll see how his trust was only too well justified. For that evening, Christmas night, very suddenly my father died—before he had time to tell my mother where he had hidden the box. He tried; when consciousness came a few minutes before the end he gasped out, 'I buried the money'—and then he choked. Once again he whispered just two words: 'Philip knows.' And my mother said, 'Yes, dearest—Philip and I will find it—don't worry, dearest,' and that quieted him. She told me about it so many times.

"After the funeral she took little Philip and explained to him as well as she could that he must tell Mother where he and Father had put the box, and—this is the point of it all, Philip—he wouldn't tell. She went over and over it all, again and again, but it was no use. He had given his word to my father never to tell, and he was too much of a baby to understand how death had dissolved that promise. My mother tried every way, of course, explanations and reasoning first, then pleading, and finally severity; she even punished the poor lithe martyr, for it was awfully important to us all. But the four-year-old baby was absolutely incorruptible. He cried bitterly and sobbed out:

"'Farver said I mustn't never tell anybody—never! Farver said Philip Fairfield of Fairfield mustn't never bweak his words,' and that was all.

"Nothing could induce him to give the least hint. Of course there was great search for it, but it was well hidden and it was never found. Finally, Mother took her obdurate son and me and came to New York with us, and we lived on the little income which she had of her own. Her hope was that as soon as Philip was old enough she could make him understand, and go back with him and get that large sum lying underground—lying there yet, perhaps. But in less than a year the little boy was dead and the secret was gone with him."

Philip Beckwith's eyes were intense and wide. The Fairfield eyes, brown and brilliant, their young fire was concentrated on his mother's face.

"Do you mean that money is buried down there, yet, mother?" he asked solemnly.

Mrs. Beckwith caught at the big fellow's sleeve with slim fingers. "Don't go today, Phil—wait till after lunch, anyway!"

"Please don't make fun, Mother—I want to know about it. Think of it lying there in the ground!"

"Greedy boy! We don't need money now, Phil. And the old place will be yours when I am dead——" The lad's arm went about his mother's shoulders. "Oh, but I'm not going to die for ages! Not till I'm a toothless old person with side curls, hobbling along on a stick. Like this!"—she sprang to her feet and the boy laughed a great peal at the haglike effect as his young mother threw herself into the part. She dropped on the divan again at his side.

"What I meant to tell you was that your father thinks it very unlikely that the money is there yet, and almost impossible that we could find it in any case. But some day when the place is yours you can have it put through a sieve if you choose. I wish I could think you would ever live there, Phil; but I can't imagine any chance by which you should. I should hate to have you sell it—it has belonged to a Philip Fairfield so many years."

A week later the boy left his childhood by the side of his mother's grave. His history for the next seven years may go in a few lines. School days, vacations, the four years at college, outwardly the commonplace of an even and prosperous development, inwardly the infinite variety of experience by which each soul is a person; the result of the two so wholesome a product of young manhood that no one realized under the frank and open manner a deep reticence, an intensity, a sensitiveness to impressions, a tendency toward mysticism which made the fiber of his being as delicate as it was strong.

Suddenly, in a turn of the wheel, all the externals of his life changed. His rich father died penniless and he found himself on his own hands, and within a month the boy who had owned five polo ponies was a hard-working reporter on a great daily. The same quick-wittedness and energy which had made him a good polo player made him a good reporter. Promotion came fast and, as those who are busiest have the most time to spare, he fell to writing stories. When the editor of a large magazine took one, Philip first lost respect for that dignified person, then felt ashamed to have imposed on him, then rejoiced utterly over the check. After that editors fell into the habit; the people he ran against knew about his books; the checks grew better reading all the time; a point came where it was more profitable to stay at home and imagine events than to go out and report them. He had been too busy as the days marched to generalize; but suddenly he knew that he was a successful writer, that if he kept his head and worked, a future was before him. So he soberly put his own English by the side of that of a master or two from his bookshelves, to keep his perspective clear, and then he worked harder. And it came to be five years after his father's death.

At the end of those years three things happened at once. The young man suddenly was very tired and knew that he needed the vacation he had gone without; a check came in large enough to make a vacation easy; and he had his old dream. His fagged brain had found it but another worry to decide where he should go to rest, but the dream settled the vexed question offhand—he would go to Kentucky. The very thought of it brought rest to him, for like a memory of childhood, like a bit of his own soul, he knew the country—the "God's Country" of its people—which he had never seen. He caught his breath as he thought of warm, sweet air that held no hurry or nerve strain; of lingering sunny days whose hours are longer than in other places; of the soft speech, the serene and kindly ways of the people; of the royal welcome waiting for him as for everyone, heartfelt and heart-warming; he knew it all from a daughter of Kentucky—his mother. It was May now, and he remembered she had told him that the land was filled with roses at the end of May—he would go then. He owned the old place, Fairfield, and he had never seen it. Perhaps it had fallen to pieces; perhaps his mother had painted it in colors too bright; but it was his, the bit of the earth that belonged to him. The Anglo-Saxon joy of landowning stirred for the first time within him—he would go to his own place. Buoyant with the new thought, he sat down and wrote a letter. A cousin of the family, of a younger branch, a certain John Fairfield, lived yet upon the land. Not in the great house, for that had been closed many years, but in a small house almost as old, called Westerly. Philip had corresponded with him once or twice about affairs of the estate, and each letter of the older man's had brought a simple and urgent invitation to come South and visit him. So, pleased as a child with the plan, he wrote that he was coming on a certain Thursday, late in May. The letter sent, he went about in a dream of the South, and when its answer, delighted and hospitable, came simultaneously with one of those bleak and windy turns of weather which make New York, even in May, a marvelously fitting place to leave, he could not wait. Almost a week ahead of his time he packed his bag and took the Southwestern Limited, and on a bright Sunday morning he awoke in the old Phoenix Hotel in Lexington. He had arrived too late the night before to make the fifteen miles to Fairfield, but he had looked over the horses in the livery stable and chosen the one he wanted, for he meant to go on horseback, as a southern gentleman should, to his domain. That he meant to go alone, that no one, not even John Fairfield, knew of his coming, was not the least of his satisfactions, for the sight of the place of his forefathers, so long neglected, was becoming suddenly a sacred thing to him. The old house and its young owner should meet each other like sweethearts, with no eyes to watch their greeting, their slow and sweet acquainting; with no living voices to drown the sound of the ghostly voices that must greet his homecoming from those walls—voices of his people who had lived there, voices gone long since into eternal silence.

A little crowd of loungers stared with frank admiration at the young fellow who came out smiling from the door of the Phoenix Hotel, big and handsome in his riding clothes, his eyes taking in the details of girths and bits and straps with the keenness of a horseman.

Philip laughed as he swung into the saddle and looked down at the friendly faces, most of them black faces, below. "Goodbye," he said. "Wish me good luck, won't you?" and a willing chorus of "Good luck, boss," came flying after him as the horse's hoofs clattered down the street.

Through the bright drowsiness of the little city he rode in the early Sunday morning, and his heart sang for joy to feel himself again across a horse, and for the love of the place that warmed him already. The sun shone hotly, but he liked it; he felt his whole being slipping into place, fitting to its environment; surely, in spite of birth and breeding, he was southern born and bred, for this felt like home more than any home he had known!

As he drew away from the city, every little while, through stately woodlands, a dignified sturdy mansion peeped down its long vista of trees at the passing cavalier, and, enchanted with its beautiful setting, with its air of proud unconsciousness, he hoped each time that Fairfield would look like that. If he might live here—and go to New York, to be sure, two or three times a year to keep the edge of his brain sharpened—but if he might live his life as these people lived, in this unhurried atmosphere, in this perfect climate, with the best things in his reach for everyday use; with horses and dogs, with out-of-doors and a great, lovely country to breathe in; with—he smiled vaguely—with sometime perhaps a wife who loved it as he did— he would ask from earth no better life than that. He could write, he felt certain, better and larger things in such surroundings.

But he pulled himself up sharply as he thought how idle a daydream it was. As a fact, he was a struggling young author, he had come South for two weeks' vacation, and on the first morning he was planning to live here—he must be lightheaded. With a touch of his heel and a word and a quick pull on the curb, his good horse broke into a canter, and then, under the loosened rein, into a rousing gallop, and Philip went dashing down the country road, past the soft, rolling landscape, and under cool caves of foliage, vivid with emerald greens of May, thoughts and dreams all dissolved in exhilaration of the glorious movement, the nearest thing to flying that the wingless animal, man, may achieve.

247

He opened his coat as the blood rushed faster through him, and a paper fluttered from his pocket. He caught it, and as he pulled the horse to a trot, he saw that it was his cousin's letter. So, walking now along the brown shadows and golden sunlight of the long white pike, he fell to wondering about the family he was going to visit. He opened the folded letter and read:

"My dear Cousin," it said—the kinship was the first thought in John Fairfield's mind—"I received your welcome letter on the 14th. I am delighted that you are coming at last to Kentucky, and I consider that it is high time you paid Fairfield, which has been the cradle of your stock for many generations, the compliment of looking at it. We closed our house in Lexington three weeks ago, and are settled out here now for the summer, and find it lovelier than ever. My family consists only of myself and Shelby, my one child, who is now twenty-two years of age. We are both ready to give you an old-time Kentucky welcome, and Westerly is ready to receive you at any moment you wish to come."

The rest was merely arrangements for meeting the traveler, all of which were done away with by his earlier arrival.

"A prim old party, with an exalted idea of the family," commented Philip mentally. "Well-to-do, apparently, or he wouldn't be having a winter house in the city. I wonder what the boy Shelby is like. At twenty-two he should be doing something more profitable than spending an entire summer out here, I should say."

The questions faded into the general content of his mind at the glimpse of another stately old pillared homestead, white and deep down its avenue of locusts. At length he stopped his horse to wait for a ragged Negro trudging cheerfully down the road.

"Do you know a place around here called Fairfield?" he asked.

"Yessah. I does that, sah. It's that ar' place right hyeh, sah, by yo' hoss. That ar's Fahfiel'. Shall I open the gate fo' you, boss?" and Philip turned to see a hinge-less ruin of boards held together by the persuasion of rusty wire.

"The home of my fathers looks down in the mouth," he reflected aloud.

The old Negro's eyes, gleaming from under shaggy sheds of eyebrows, watched him, and he caught the words.

"Is you a Fahfiel', boss?" he asked eagerly. "Is you my young marse?" He jumped at the conclusion promptly. "You favors de fam'ly mightily, sah. I heerd you was comin'"; the rag of a hat went off and he bowed low. "Hit's cert'nly good news fo' Fahfiel', Marse Philip, hit's mighty good news fo' us niggers, sah. I'se bt-longed to the Fahfiel' fam'ly a hundred years, Marse—me and my folks, and I wishes yo' a welcome home, sah—welcome home, Marse Philip."

Philip bent with a quick movement from his horse and gripped the twisted old black hand, speechless. This humble welcome on the highway caught at his heart deep down, and the appeal of the colored people to southerners, who know them, the thrilling appeal of a gentle, loyal race, doomed to live forever behind a veil and hopeless without bitterness, stirred for the first time his manhood. It touched him to be taken for granted as the child of his people; it pleased him that he should be "Marse Philip" as a matter of course, because there had always been a Marse Philip at the place. It was bred deeper in the bone of him than he knew, to understand the soul of the black man; the stuff he was made of had been southern two hundred years.

The old man went off down the white limestone road singing to himself, and Philip rode slowly under the locusts and beeches up the long drive, grass-grown and lost in places, that wound through the woodland three-quarters of a mile to his house. And as he moved through the park, through sunlight and shadow of these

248

great trees that were his, he felt like a knight of King Arthur, like some young knight long exiled, at last coming to his own. He longed with an unreasonable seizure of desire to come here to live, to take care of it, beautify it, fill it with life and prosperity as it had once been filled, surround it with cheerful faces of colored people whom he might make happy and comfortable. If only he had money to pay off the mortgage, to put the place once in order, it would be the ideal setting for the life that seemed marked out for him—the life of a writer.

The horse turned a corner and broke into a canter up the slope, and as the shoulder of the hill fell away there stood before him the picture of his childhood come to life, smiling drowsily in the morning sunlight with shuttered windows that were its sleeping eyes—the great white house of Fairfield. Its high pillars reached to the roof; its big wings stretched away at either side; the flicker of the shadow of the leaves played over it tenderly and hid broken bits of woodwork, patches of paint cracked away, windowpanes gone here and there. It stood as if too proud to apologize or to look sad for such small matters, as serene, as stately as in its prime. And its master, looking at it for the first time, loved it.

He rode around to the side and tied his mount to an old horse-rack, and then walked up the wide front steps as if each lift were an event. He turned the handle of the big door without much hope that it would yield, but it opened willingly, and he stood inside. A broom lay in a corner, windows were open—his cousin had been making ready for him. There was the huge mahogany sofa, horsehair-covered, in the window under the stairs, where his mother had read Ivanhoe and The Talisman. Philip stepped softly across the wide hall and laid his head where must have rested the brown hair of the little girl who had come to be, first all of his life, and then its dearest memory. Half an hour he spent in the old house, and its walls echoed to his footsteps as if in ready homage, and each empty room whose door he opened met him with a sweet half-familiarity. The whole place was filled with the presence of the child who had loved it and left it, and for whom this tall man, her child, longed now as if for a little sister who should be here, and whom he missed. With her memory came the thought of the five-year-old uncle who had made history for the family so disastrously. He must see the garden where that other Philip had gone with his father to hide the money on the fated Christmas morning. He closed the house door behind him carefully, as if he would not disturb a little girl reading in the window, a little boy sleeping perhaps in the nursery above. Then he walked down the broad sweep of the driveway, the gravel crunching under the grass, and across what had been a bit of velvet lawn, and stood for a moment with his hand on a broken vase, weed-filled, which capped the stone post of a gateway.

All the garden was misty with memories. Where a tall golden flower nodded alone from out of the tangled thicket of an old flowerbed a bright-haired child might have laughed with just that air of starred, gay naughtiness, from the forbidden center of the blossoms. In the molded tan-bark of the path was a vague print, like the ghost of a footprint that had passed down the way a lifetime ago. The box, half-dead, half-sprouted into high unkept growth, still stood stiffly against the riotous overflow of weeds as if it yet held loyally to its business of guarding the borders. Philip shifted his gaze slowly, lingering over the dim contours, the shadowy shape of what the garden had been. Suddenly his eyes opened wide. How was this? There was a hedge as neat, as clipped, as any of Southampton in midseason, and over it a glory of roses, red and white and pink and yellow, waved gay banners to him in trim luxuriance. He swung toward them, and the breeze brought him for the first time in his life the fragrance of box in sunshine.

Three feet tall, shaven and thick and shining, the old hedge stood, and the garnered sweetness of a hundred years' slow growth breathed delicately from it toward the great-great-grandson of the man who planted it. A box hedge takes as long in the making as a gentleman, and when they are done the two are much of a sort. No plant in all the garden has so subtle an air of breeding, so gentle a reserve, yet so gracious a message of sweetness for all of the world who will stop to learn it. It keeps a firm dignity under the stress of tempest when lighter growths are tossed and torn; it shines bright through the snow; it has a well-bred willingness to be background, with the well-bred gift of presence, whether as background or foreground. The soul of the box tree is an aristocrat, and the sap that runs through it is the blue blood of vegetation.

Saluting him bravely in the hot sunshine with its myriad shining sword points, the old hedge sent out to Philip on the May breeze its ancient welcome of aromatic fragrance, and the tall roses crowded gaily to look over its edge at the new master. Slowly, a little dazed at this oasis of shining order in the neglected garden, he walked to the opening and stepped inside the hedge. The rose garden! The famous rose garden of Fairfield, and as his mother had described it, in full splendor of cared-for, orderly bloom. Across the paths he stepped swiftly till he stood amid the roses, giant bushes of Jacqueminot and Marechal Niel; of pink and white and red and yellow blooms in thick array. The glory of them intoxicated him. That he should own all of this beauty seemed too good to be true, and instantly he wanted to taste his ownership. The thought came to him that he would enter into his heritage with strong hands here in the rose garden; he caught a deep-red Jacqueminot almost roughly by its gorgeous head and broke off the stem. He would gather a bunch, a huge, unreasonable bunch of his own flowers. Hungrily he broke one after another; his shoulders bent over them, he was deep in the bushes.

"I reckon I shall have to ask you not to pick any more of those roses," a voice said.

Philip threw up his head as if he had been shot; he turned sharply with a great thrill, for he thought his mother spoke to him. Perhaps it was only the southern inflection so long unheard, perhaps the sunlight that shone in his eyes dazzled him, but, as he stared, the white figure before him seemed to him to look exactly as his mother had looked long ago. Stumbling over his words, he caught at the first that came.

"I—I think it's all right," he said.

The girl smiled frankly, yet with a dignity in her puzzled air. "I'm afraid I shall have to be right decided," she said. "These roses are private property and I mustn't let you have them."

"Oh!" Philip dropped the great bunch of gorgeous color guiltily by his side, but still held tightly the prickly mass of stems, knowing his right, yet half-wondering if he could have made a mistake. He stammered:

"I thought—to whom do they belong?"

"They belong to my cousin, Mr. Philip Fairfield Beckwith"—the sound of his own name was pleasant as the falling voice strayed through it. "He is coming home in a few days, so I want them to look their prettiest for him—for his first sight of them. I take care of this rose garden," she said, and laid a motherly hand on the nearest flower. Then she smiled. "It doesn't seem right hospitable to stop you, but if you will come over to Westerly, to our house, Father will be glad to see you, and I will certainly give you all the flowers you want." The sweet and masterful apparition looked with a gracious certainty of obedience straight into Philip's bewildered eyes.

"The boy Shelby!" Many a time in the months after, Philip Beckwith smiled to himself reminiscently, tenderly, as he thought of "the boy Shelby" whom he had read into John Fairfield's letter; "the boy Shelby" who was twenty-two years old and the only child; "the boy Shelby" whom he had blamed with such easy severity for idling at Fairfield; "the boy Shelby" who was no boy at all, but this white flower of girlhood, called—after the quaint and reasonable southern way—as a boy is called, by the surname of her mother's people.

Toward Westerly, out of the garden of the old time, out of the dimness of a forgotten past, the two took their radiant youth and the brightness of today. But a breeze blew across the tangle of weeds and flowers as they wandered away, and whispered a hope, perhaps a promise; for as it touched them each tall stalk nodded gaily and the box hedges rustled delicately an answering undertone. And just at the edge of the woodland, before they were out of sight, the girl turned and threw a kiss back to the roses and the box.

"I always do that," she said. "I love them so!"

Two weeks later a great train rolled into the Grand Central Station of New York at half-past six at night, and from it stepped a monstrosity—a young man without a heart. He had left all of it, more than he had thought he owned, in Kentucky. But he had brought back with him a store of memories which gave him more joy than ever the heart had done, to his best knowledge, in all the years. They were memories of long and sunshiny days; of afternoons spent in the saddle, rushing through grassy lanes where trumpet flowers flamed over gray farm fences, or trotting slowly down white roads; of whole mornings only an hour long, passed in the enchanted stillness of an old garden; of gay, desultory searches through its length and breadth, and in the park that held it, for buried treasure; of moonlit nights; of roses and June and Kentucky—and always, through all the memories, the presence that made them what they were, that of a girl he loved.

No word of love had been spoken, but the two weeks had made over his life; and he went back to his work with a definite object, a hope stronger than ambition, and, set to it as music to words, came insistently another hope, a dream that he did not let himself dwell on—a longing to make enough money to pay off the mortgage and put Fairfield in order, and live and work there all his life—with Shelby. That was where the thrill of the thought came in, but the place was very dear to him in itself.

The months went, and the point of living now was the mail from the South, and the feast days were the days that brought letters from Fairfield. He had promised to go back for a week at Christmas, and he worked and hoarded all the months between with a thought which he did not formulate, but which ruled his down-sitting and his up-rising, the thought that if he did well and his bank account grew enough to justify it he might, when he saw her at Christmas, tell her what he hoped; ask her —he finished the thought with a jump of his heart. He never worked harder or better, and each check that came in meant a step toward the promised land; and each seemed for the joy that was in it to quicken his pace, to lengthen his stride, to strengthen his touch. Early in November he found one night when he came to his rooms two letters waiting for him with the welcome Kentucky postmark. They were in John Fairfield's handwriting and in his daughter's, and "place aux dames" ruled rather than respect to age, for he opened Shelby's first. His eyes smiling, he read it.

"I am knitting you a diamond necklace for Christmas," she wrote. "Will you like that? Or be sure to write me if you'd rather have me hunt in the garden and dig you up a box of money. I'll tell you—there ought to be luck in the day, for it was hidden on Christmas and it should be found on Christmas; so on Christmas morning we'll have another look, and if you find it I'll catch you 'Christmas gif' as the darkies do, and you'll have to give it to me, and if I find it I'll give it to you; so that's fair, isn't it? Anyway—" and Philip's eyes jumped from line to line, devouring the clear, running writing. "So bring a little present with you, please—just a tiny something for me," she ended, "for I'm certainly going to catch you 'Christmas gif'."

Philip folded the letter back into its envelope and put it in his pocket, and his heart felt warmer for the scrap of paper over it. Then he cut John Fairfield's open dreamily, his mind still on the words he had read, on the threat—"I'm going to catch you 'Christmas gif'." What was there good enough to give her? Himself, he thought humbly, very far from good enough for the girl, the lily of the world. With a sigh that was not sad he dismissed the question and began to read the other letter. He stood reading it by the fading light from the window, his hat thrown by him on a chair, his overcoat still on, and, as he read, the smile died from his face. With drawn brows he read on to the end, and then the letter dropped from his fingers to the floor and he did not notice; his eyes stared widely at the high building across the street, the endless rows of windows, the lights flashing into them here and there. But he saw none of it. He saw a stretch of quiet woodland, an old house with great white pillars, a silent, neglected garden, with box hedges sweet and ragged, all waiting for him to come and take care of them—the honor of his fathers, the home he had meant, had expected—he knew it now—would be some day his own, the home he had lost! John Fairfield's letter was to tell him that the mortgage on the place, running now so many years, was suddenly to be foreclosed; that, property not being worth much in the neighborhood, no one would take it up; that on January 2nd Fairfield, the house and land, were to be sold at auction. It was a hard blow to Philip Beckwith, With his hands in his overcoat pockets he began to walk up and down the room, trying to plan, to see if by any chance he might save this place he loved. It would mean eight thousand dollars to pay the mortgage. One or two thousand more would put the estate in order, but that might wait if he could only tide over this danger, save the house and land. An hour he walked so, forgetting dinner, forgetting the heavy coat which he still wore, and then he gave it up. With all he had saved—and it was a fair and promising beginning—he could not much more than half-pay the mortgage, and there was no way, which he would consider, by which he could get the money. Fairfield would have to go, and he set his teeth and clenched his fists as he thought how much he wanted to keep it. A year ago it had meant nothing to him, a year from now if things went his way he could have paid the mortgage. That it should happen just this year—just now! He could not go down at Christmas; it would break his heart to see the place again as his own when it was just slipping from his grasp. He would wait until it was all over, and go, perhaps, in the spring. The great hope of his life was still his own, but Fairfield had been the setting of that hope; he must readjust his world before he saw Shelby again. So he wrote them that he would not come at present, and then tried to dull the ache of his loss with hard work.

But three days before Christmas, out of the unknown forces beyond his reasoning swept a wave of desire to go South, which took him off his feet. Trained to trust his brain and deny his impulse as he was, yet there was a vein of sentiment, almost of superstition, in him which the thought of the old place pricked sharply to life. This longing was something beyond him—he must go—and he had thrown his decisions to the winds and was feverish until he could get away.

As before, he rode out from the Phoenix Hotel, and at ten o'clock in the morning he turned into Fairfield. It was a still, bright Christmas morning, crisp and cool, and the air like wine. The house stood bravely in the sunlight, but the branches above it were bare and no softening leafage hid the marks of time; it looked old and sad and deserted today, and its master gazed at it with a pang in his heart. It was his, and he could not save it. He turned away and walked slowly to the garden, and stood a moment as he had stood last May, with his hand on the stone gateway. It was very silent and lonely here, in the hush of winter; nothing stirred; even the shadows of the interlaced branches above lay almost motionless across the walks.

Something moved to his left, down the pathway—he turned to look. Had his heart stopped, that he felt this strange, cold feeling in his breast? Were his eyes—could he be seeing? Was this insanity? Fifty feet down the path, half in the weaving shadows, half in clear sunlight, stood the little boy of his lifelong vision, in the dress with the black velvet squares, his little uncle, dead forty years ago. As he gazed, his breath stopping, the child smiled and held up to him, as of old, a key on a scarlet string, and turned and flitted as if a flower had taken wing, away between the box hedges. Philip, his feet moving as if without his will, followed him. Again the baby face turned its smiling dark eyes toward him, and Philip knew that the child was calling him, though there was no sound; and again without volition of his own his feet took him where it led. He felt his breath coming difficulty, and suddenly a gasp shook him—there was no footprint on the unfrozen earth where the vision had passed. Yet there before him, moving through the deep sunlit silence of the garden, was the familiar, sturdy little form in its Old-World dress. Philip's eyes were open; he was awake, walking; he saw it. Across the neglected tangle it glided, and into the trim order of Shelby's rose garden; in the opening between the box walls it wheeled again, and the sun shone clear on the bronze hair and fresh face, and the scarlet string flashed and the key glinted at the end of it. Philip's fascinated eyes saw all of that. Then the apparition slipped into the shadow of the beech trees and Philip quickened his step breathlessly, for it seemed that life and death hung on the sight. In and out through the trees it moved; once more the face turned toward him; he caught the quick brightness of a smile. The little chap had disappeared behind the broad tree trunk, and Philip, catching his breath, hurried to see him appear again. He was gone. The little spirit that had strayed from over the border of a world—who can say how far, how near?—unafraid in this earth-corner once its home, had slipped away into eternity through the white gate of ghosts and dreams.

Philip's heart was pumping painfully as he came, dazed and staring, to the place where the apparition had vanished. It was a giant-beech tree, all of two hundred and fifty years old, and around its base ran a broken wooden bench, where pretty girls of Fairfield had listened to their sweethearts, where children destined to be generals and judges had played with their black mammies, where gray-haired judges and generals had come back to think over the fights that were fought out. There were letters carved into the strong bark, the branches swung down whisperingly, the green tent of the forest seemed filled with the memory of those who had camped there and gone on. Philip's feet stumbled over the roots as he circled the veteran; he peered this way and that, but the woodland was hushed and empty; the birds whistled above, the grasses rustled below, unconscious, casual, as if they knew nothing of a child-soul that had wandered back on Christmas day with a Christmas message, perhaps, of goodwill to its own.

As he stood on the farther side of the tree where the little ghost had faded from him, at his feet lay, open and conspicuous, a fresh, deep hole. He looked down absent-mindedly. Some animal—a dog, a rabbit—had scratched far into the earth. A bar of sunlight struck a golden arm through the branches above, and as he gazed at the upturned, brown dirt the rays that were its fingers reached into the hollow and touched a square corner, a rusty edge of tin. In a second the young fellow was down on his knees digging as if for his life, and in less than dive minutes he had loosened the earth which had guarded it so many years, and staggering with it to his feet had lifted to the bench a heavy tin box. In its lock was the key, and dangling from it a long bit of no-colored silk, that yet, as he untwisted it, showed a scarlet thread in the crease. He opened the box with the little key; it turned scrapingly, and the ribbon crumbled in his fingers, its long duty done. Then, as he tilted the heavy weight, the double eagles, packed closely, slipped against each other with a soft clink of sliding metal. The young man stared at the mass of gold pieces as if he could not trust his eyesight; he half thought even then that he dreamed it. With a quick memory of the mortgage he began to count. It was all there—ten thousand dollars in gold! He lifted his head and gazed at the quiet woodland, the open shadowwork of the bare branches, the fields beyond lying in the calm sunlit rest of a southern winter. Then he put his hand deep into the gold pieces, and drew a long breath. It was impossible to believe, but it was true. The lost treasure was found. It meant to him Shelby and home; as he realized what it meant, his heart felt as if it would break with the joy of it. He would give her this for his Christmas gift, this legacy of his people and hers, and then he would give her himself It was all easy now—life seemed not to hold a difficulty. And the two would keep tenderly, always, the thought of a child who had loved his home and his people and who had tried so hard, so long, to bring them together. He knew the dream-child would not visit him again—the little ghost was laid that had followed him all his life. From over the border whence it had come with so many loving efforts it would never come again. Slowly, with the heavy weight in his arms, with the eyes of a man who had seen a solemn thing, he walked back to the garden sleeping in the sunshine, and the box hedges met him with a wave of fragrance, the sweetness of a century ago; and as he passed through their shining door, looking beyond, he saw Shelby. The girl's figure stood by the stone column of the garden entrance. The light shone on her bare head, and she had stopped, surprised, as she saw him. Philip lifted his hat high, and his pace quickened with his heartthrob as he looked at her and thought of the little ghostly hands that had brought theirs together; and as he looked the smile that meant his welcome and his happiness broke over her face, and with the sound of her voice all the shades of this world and the next dissolved in light.

"'Christmas gif',' Marse Philip!" called Shelby.

THE COLD EMBRACE,
by Mary Elizabeth Braddon

He was an artist—such things as happened to him happen sometimes to artists.

He was a German—such things as happened to him happen sometimes to Germans.

He was young, handsome, studious, enthusiastic, metaphysical, reckless, unbelieving, heartless.

And being young, handsome and eloquent, he was beloved.

He was an orphan, under the guardianship of his dead father's brother, his uncle Wilhelm, in whose house he had been brought up from a little child; and she who loved him was his cousin—his cousin Gertrude, whom he swore he loved in return.

Did he love her? Yes, when he first swore it. It soon wore out, this passionate love; how threadbare and wretched a sentiment it became at last in the selfish heart of the student! But in its golden dawn, when he was only nineteen and had just returned from his apprenticeship to a great painter at Antwerp, and they wandered together in the most romantic outskirts of the city at rosy sunset, by holy moonlight, or bright and joyous morning, how beautiful a dream!

* * * *

They keep it a secret from Wilhelm, as he has the father's ambition of a wealthy suitor for his only child—a cold and dreary vision beside the lover's dream.

So they are betrothed; and standing side by side when the dying sun and the pale rising moon divide the heavens, he puts the betrothal ring upon her finger, the white and tapering finger whose slender shape he knows so well. This ring is a peculiar one, a massive golden serpent, its tail in its mouth, the symbol of eternity; it had been his mother's, and he would know it amongst a thousand. If he were to become blind tomorrow, he could select it from amongst a thousand by the touch alone.

He places it on her finger, and they swear to be true to each other for ever and ever—through trouble and danger—sorrow and change—in wealth or poverty. Her father must needs be won to consent to their union by and by, for they were now betrothed, and death alone could part them.

But the young student, the scoffer at revelation, yet the enthusiastic adorer of the mystical, asks:

"Can death part us? I would return to you from the grave, Gertrude. My soul would come back to be near my love. And you—you, if you died before me—the cold earth would not hold you from me; if you loved me, you would return, and again these fair arms would be clasped round my neck as they are now."

But she told him, with a holier light in her deep-blue eyes than had ever shone in his—she told him that the dead who die at peace with God are happy in heaven and cannot return to the troubled earth; and that it is only the suicide—the lost wretch on whom sorrowful angels shut the door of Paradise—whose unholy spirit haunts the footsteps of the living.

* * * *

The first year of their betrothal is passed, and she is alone, for he has gone to Italy, on a commission for some rich man, to copy Raphaels, Titians, Guidos, in a gallery at Florence. He has gone to win fame, perhaps; but it is not the less bitter—he is gone!

Of course her father misses his young nephew, who has been as a son to him; and he thinks his daughter's sadness no more than a cousin should feel for a cousin's absence.

In the meantime, the weeks and months pass. The lover writes—often at first, then seldom—at last, not at all.

How many excuses she invents for him! How many times she goes to the distant little post-office, to which he is to address his letters! How many times she hopes, only to be disappointed! How many times she despairs, only to hope again!

But real despair comes at last, and will not be put off any more. The rich suitor appears on the scene, and her father is determined. She is to marry at once. The wedding-day is fixed—the fifteenth of June.

The date seems to burn into her brain.

The date, written in fire, dances for ever before her eyes.

The date, shrieked by the Furies, sounds continually in her ears.

But there is time yet—it is the middle of May—there is time for a letter to reach him at Florence; there is time for him to come to Brunswick, to take her away and marry her, in spite of her father—in spite of the whole world.

But the days and the weeks fly by, and he does not write—he does not come. This is indeed despair which usurps her heart and will not be put away.

It is the fourteenth of June. For the last time she goes to the little post-office; for the last time she asked the old question, and they give her for the last time the dreary answer, "No; no letter."

For the last time—for tomorrow is the day appointed for the bridal. Her father will hear no entreaties; her rich suitor will not listen to her prayers. They will not be put off a day—an hour; tonight alone is hers—this night, which she may employ as she will.

She takes another path than that which leads home; she hurries through some by-streets of the city, out on to a lonely bridge, where he and she had stood so often in the sunset, watching the rose-coloured light glow, fade, and die upon the river.

* * * *

He returns from Florence. He had received her letter. That letter, blotted with tears, entreating, despairing—he had received it, but he loved her no longer. A young Florentine, who has sat to him for a model, had bewitched his fancy—that fancy which with him stood in place of a heart—and Gertrude had been half-forgotten. If she had a rich suitor, good; let her marry him; better for her, better far for himself. He had no wish to fetter himself with a wife. Had he not his art always?—his eternal bride, his unchanging mistress.

Thus he thought it wiser to delay his journey to Brunswick, so that he should arrive when the wedding was over—arrive in time to salute the bride.

And the vows—the mystical fancies—the belief in his return, even after death, to the embrace of his beloved? O, gone out of his life; melted away for ever, those foolish dreams of his boyhood.

So on the fifteenth of June he enters Brunswick, by that very bridge on which she stood, the stars looking down on her, the night before. He strolls across the bridge and down by the water's edge, a great rough dog at his heels, and the smoke from his short meerschaum-pipe curling in blue wreaths fantastically in the pure morning air. He has his sketch-book under his arm, and attracted now and then by some object that catches his artist's eye, stops to draw: a few weeds and pebbles on the river's brink—a crag on the opposite shore—a group of pollard willows in the distance. When he has done, he admires his drawing, shuts his sketch-book, empties the ashes from his pipe, refills from his tobacco-pouch, sings the refrain of a gay drinking-song, calls to his dog, smokes again, and walks on. Suddenly he opens his sketch-book again; this time that which attracts him is a group of figures: but what is it?

It is not a funeral, for there are no mourners.

It is not a funeral, but a corpse lying on a rude bier, covered with an old sail, carried between two bearers.

It is not a funeral, for the bearers are fishermen—fishermen in their everyday garb.

About a hundred yards from him they rest their burden on a bank—one stands at the head of the bier, the other throws himself down at the foot of it.

And thus they form the perfect group; he walks back two or three paces, selects his point of sight, and begins to sketch a hurried outline. He has finished it before they move; he hears their voices, though he cannot hear their words, and wonders what they can be talking of. Presently he walks on and joins them.

"You have a corpse there, my friends?" he says.

"Yes; a corpse washed ashore an hour ago."

"Drowned?"

"Yes, drowned. A young girl, very handsome."

"Suicides are always handsome," says the painter; and then he stands for a little while idly smoking and meditating, looking at the sharp outline of the corpse and the stiff folds of the rough canvas covering.

Life is such a golden holiday for him—young, ambitious, clever—that it seems as though sorrow and death could have no part in his destiny.

At last he says that, as this poor suicide is so handsome, he should like to make a sketch of her.

He gives the fishermen some money, and they offer to remove the sailcloth that covers her features.

No; he will do it himself. He lifts the rough, coarse, wet canvas from her face. What face?

The face that shone on the dreams of his foolish boyhood; the face which once was the light of his uncle's home. His cousin Gertrude—his betrothed!

He sees, as in one glance, while he draws one breath, the rigid features—the marble arms—the hands crossed on the cold bosom; and, on the third finger of the left hand, the ring which had been his mother's—the golden serpent; the ring which, if he were to become blind, he could select from a thousand others by the touch alone.

But he is a genius and a metaphysician—grief, true grief, is not for such as he. His first thought is flight—flight anywhere out of that accursed city—anywhere far from the brink of that hideous river—anywhere away from remorse—anywhere to forget.

* * * *

He is miles on the road that leads away from Brunswick before he knows that he has walked a step.

It is only when his dog lies down panting at his feet that he feels how exhausted he is himself, and sits down upon a bank to rest. How the landscape spins round and round before his dazzled eyes, while his morning's sketch of the two fishermen and the canvas-covered bier glares redly at him out of the twilight.

257

At last, after sitting a long time by the roadside, idly playing with his dog, idly smoking, idly lounging, looking as any idle, light-hearted travelling student might look, yet all the while acting over that morning's scene in his burning brain a hundred times a minute; at last he grows a little more composed, and tries presently to think of himself as he is, apart from his cousin's suicide. Apart from that, he was no worse off than he was yesterday. His genius was not gone; the money he had earned at Florence still lined his pocket-book; he was his own master, free to go whither he would.

And while he sits on the roadside, trying to separate himself from the scene of that morning—trying to put away the image of the corpse covered with the damp canvas sail—trying to think of what he should do next, where he should go, to be farthest away from Brunswick and remorse, the old diligence coming rumbling and jingling along. He remembers it; it goes from Brunswick to Aix-la-Chapelle.

He whistles to the dog, shouts to the postilion to stop, and springs into the coupé.

During the whole evening, through the long night, though he does not once close his eyes, he never speaks a word; but when morning dawns, and the other passengers awake and begin to talk to each other, he joins in the conversation. He tells them that he is an artist, that he is going to Cologne and to Antwerp to copy Rubenses, and the great picture by Quentin Matsys, in the museum. He remembered afterwards that he talked and laughed boisterously, and that when he was talking and laughing loudest, a passenger, older and graver than the rest, opened the window near him, and told him to put his head out. He remembered the fresh air blowing in his face, the singing of the birds in his ears, and the flat fields and roadside reeling before his eyes. He remembered this, and then falling in a lifeless heap on the floor of the diligence.

It is a fever that keeps him for six long weeks on a bed at a hotel in Aix-la-Chapelle.

He gets well, and, accompanied by his dog, starts on foot for Cologne. By this time he is his former self once more. Again the blue smoke from his short meerschaum curls upwards in the morning air—again he sings some old university drinking song—again stops here and there, meditating and sketching.

He is happy, and has forgotten his cousin—and so on to Cologne.

It is by the great cathedral he is standing, with his dog at his side. It is night, the bells have just chimed the hour, and the clocks are striking eleven; the moonlight shines full upon the magnificent pile, over which the artist's eye wanders, absorbed in the beauty of form.

He is not thinking of his drowned cousin, for he has forgotten her and is happy.

Suddenly someone, something from behind him, puts two cold arms round his neck, and clasps its hands on his breast.

And yet there is no one behind him, for on the flags bathed in the broad moonlight there are only two shadows, his own and his dog's. He turns quickly round—there is no one—nothing to be seen in the broad square but himself and his dog; and though he feels, he cannot see the cold arms clasped round his neck.

It is not ghostly, this embrace, for it is palpable to the touch—it cannot be real, for it is invisible.

He tries to throw off the cold caress. He clasps the hands in his own to tear them asunder, and to cast them off his neck. He can feel the long delicate fingers cold and wet beneath his touch, and on the third finger of the left hand he can feel the ring which was his mother's—the golden serpent—the ring which he has always said he would know among a thousand by the touch alone. He knows it now!

His dead cousin's cold arms are round his neck—his dead cousin's wet hands are clasped upon his breast. He asks himself if he is mad. "Up, Leo!" he shouts. "Up, up, boy!" and the Newfoundland leaps to his shoulders—the dog's paws are on the dead hands, and the animal utters a terrific howl, and springs away from his master.

The student stands in the moonlight, the dead arms around his neck, and the dog at a little distance moaning piteously.

Presently a watchman, alarmed by the howling of the dog, comes into the square to see what is wrong.

In a breath the cold arms are gone.

He takes the watchman home to the hotel with him and gives him money; in his gratitude he could have given the man half his little fortune.

Will it ever come to him again, this embrace of the dead?

He tries never to be alone; he makes a hundred acquaintances, and shares the chamber of another student. He starts up if he is left by himself in the public room of the inn where he is staying, and runs into the street. People notice his strange actions, and begin to think that he is mad.

But, in spite of all, he is alone once more; for one night the public room being empty for a moment, when on some idle pretense he strolls into the street, the street is empty too, and for the second time he feels the cold arms round his neck, and for the second time, when he calls his dog, the animal shrinks away from him with a piteous howl.

After this he leaves Cologne, still travelling on foot—of necessity now, for his money is getting low. He joins travelling hawkers, he walks side by side with labourers, he talks to every foot-passenger he falls in with, and tries from morning till night to get company on the road.

At night he sleeps by the fire in the kitchen of the inn at which he stops; but do what he will, he is often alone, and it is now a common thing for him to feel the cold arms around his neck.

Many months have passed since his cousin's death—autumn, winter, early spring. His money is nearly gone, his health is utterly broken, he is the shadow of his former self, and he is getting near to Paris. He will reach that city at the time of the Carnival. To this he looks forward. In Paris, in Carnival time, he need never, surely, be alone, never feel that deadly caress; he may even recover his lost gaiety, his lost health, once more resume his profession, once more earn fame and money by his art.

How hard he tries to get over the distance that divides him from Paris, while day by day he grows weaker, and his step slower and more heavy!

But there is an end at last; the long dreary roads are passed. This is Paris, which he enters for the first time—Paris, of which he has dreamed so much—Paris, whose million voices are to exorcise his phantom.

To him tonight Paris seems one vast chaos of lights, music, and confusion—lights which dance before his eyes and will not be still—music that rings in his ears and deafens him—confusion which makes his head whirl round and round.

But, in spite of all, he finds the opera-house, where there is a masked ball. He has enough money left to buy a ticket of admission and to hire a domino to throw over his shabby dress. It seems only a moment after his entering the gates of Paris that he is in the very midst of all the wild gaiety of the opera-house ball.

No more darkness, no more loneliness, but a mad crowd, shouting and dancing, and a lovely Débardeuse hanging on his arm.

The boisterous gaiety he feels surely is his old light-heartedness come back. He hears the people round him talking of the outrageous conduct of some drunken student, and it is to him they point when they say this—to him, who has not moistened his lips since yesterday at noon, for even now he will not drink; though his lips are parched, and his throat burning, he cannot drink. His voice is thick and hoarse, and his utterance indistinct; but still this must be his old light-heartedness come back that makes him so wildly gay.

The little Débardeuse is wearied out—her arm rests on his shoulder heavier than lead—the other dancers one by one drop off.

The lights in the chandeliers one by one die out.

The decorations look pale and shadowy in that dim light which is neither night nor day.

A faint glimmer from the dying lamps, a pale streak of cold grey light from the new-born day, creeping in through half-opened shutters.

And by this light the bright-eyed Débardeuse fades sadly. He looks her in the face. How the brightness of her eyes dies out! Again he looks her in the face. How white that face has grown! Again—and now it is the shadow of a face alone that looks in his.

Again—and they are gone—the bright eyes, the face, the shadow of the face. He is alone; alone in that vast saloon.

Alone, and, in the terrible silence, he hears the echoes of his own footsteps in that dismal dance which has no music.

No music but the beating within his breast. Then the cold arms are round his neck—they whirl him round, they will not be flung off, or cast away; he can no more escape from their icy grasp than he can escape from death. He looks behind him—there is nothing but himself in the great empty salle; but he can feel—cold, deathlike, but O, how palpable!—the long slender fingers, and the ring which was his mother's.

He tries to shout, but he has no power in his burning throat. The silence of the place is only broken by the echoes of his own footsteps in the dance from which he cannot extricate himself. Who says he has no partner? The cold hands are clasped on his breast, and now he does not shun their caress. No! One more polka, if he drops down dead.

The lights are all out, and, half an hour after, the gendarmes come in with a lantern to see that the house is empty; they are followed by a great dog that they have found seated howling on the steps of the theatre. Near the principal entrance, they stumble over—

The body of a student, who has died from want of food, exhaustion, and the breaking of a blood-vessel.